G

A NOVEL

If the ultimate immorality of man rules supreme, David Graceson will be dead before the week is over. As an outspoken and cynical New Yorker, his error was lashing out vehemently, at the government's corruption and its unaccountable and scandalous behavior.

Set in New York after a devastating earthquake. David is thrown into a world where the walls have ears and where angels fear to tread.

No one would have guessed that the ex-president of the United States was a psychopath. James Elliot Thorne was incensed with Graceson's tone, volume and subject matter. In the midst of a re-election attempt, Graceson's revelations were enough to quell any political resurrection. And even though Thorne was advised to 'let sleeping dogs lie', he took Graceson as a serious threat to his campaign and set out exterminate him with vengeance.

Caught in the vortex of terror with him is Elly O'Connor, a childhood friend and computer genius with the State Department. Together they are engulfed in a whirlwind of intrigue and suspense that involves ruthless assassinations, blackmail, treason and psychotic self-delusions. All of which point a path to the highest office in the land.

Also drawn into the web of deceit and paranoia is, hard as nails, FBI agent Frank Mackinnley. The veteran finds himself dealing with a level of cloak and dagger so sordid in its implication that he has to find new ways just to survive. His experience in the world of high stakes double cross is most valuable now, but is it enough?

The three race against seemingly sure failure, confronting the most powerful organization in the world, while coming face to face with the most ominous force challenging the human spirit. Hell, and its usher… the president.

GOLIATH

VAN PORNARAS

WE PUBLISH BOOKS

UNITED STATES OF AMERICA

The people, facts and events of this story are pure fiction. Any similarity between them, and persons living or dead, are purely coincidental. The story is the fabrication of the mind of the author and in no way, either implied or referred, represents any historical or factual happenings. Van Pornaras

We Publish Books
P.O. Box 1814
Rancho Mirage, CA 92270

www.WePublishBooks.com
E-mail: Van@wepublishbooks.com

Library of Congress Cataloging in Publication Data:

Pornaras, Van
GOLIATH
Printed in the United States

GOLIATH/ by Van Pornaras
1. FICTION 2. SUSPENSE FIC030000

ISBN 1-929841-06-X

First Printing, 2004

We Publish Books

Dedication

For the three angels that share my life.
The one I married,
and the other two that arrived early.

CONTENTS

-1-

The headlines screamed with blatant audacity of the crime wave that engulfed the city and of the escalating temperature that rode shotgun with it. Six hundred murders, and it was only half way through the year; ninety nine degrees at eight o'clock in the morning and Mother Nature promised to cremate the city by noon. Tempers were legendary in Manhattan, short enough to begin with but the mugginess cut fuses to a quarter of regular lengths. There was less tolerance on the streets; more fights and the crime seemed to increase exponentially as the day wore on.

The traffic gasped along 42nd. Nobody moved, even with the persuasion of horns. Random gunfire was audible yet the sirens of salvation were never heard. People didn't scream or run. They just looked to the north, beyond the traffic jam and kept up their conversations without missing a syllable.

Vampire-like junkies had become more brazen in the heat and crawled from their usual darkness to find a breeze to cool their frenzied minds. They smoked and snorted there in the light of day, unashamed or afraid of the heat. They cursed and spit on passers by, and condemned them for their conformity. The crowd would cower and walk as far away from them and pray their positive saliva did not strike them.

The police were there. You could see them parked, watching the cataclysm. Yet the unlawful were many and better equipped, nor were they restricted by the code of the police force. Cops fought crime only when they knew they could live to tell about it. It was not due to their own weakness or cowardice; it was a reality that cops got killed in New York when there was not sufficient backup. So most just watched from the relative security of their vehicles as the criminals became more outlandish in the practice of their trade.

Stinking vagrants were extraordinarily fragrant for that time of year. They were congregating in a sparse group and working the afternoon lunch crowd for handouts. They were a mainstay in the city, always there, never to leave, like roaches they would endure anything that the elements threw at them and they could never be eliminated. Everyday, any hour you would side step at least one of them to get to where you wanted to go.

Some of them were castaways from institutions while others had abandoned society and ranted their solutions as if the writings of Socrates were left to them in his will. He was one of them. A learned man. One who seemed to have been cast out of the socially acceptable because of his MENSA status. He spoke eloquently enough when you could hear him, when he was not mumbling in the midst of an Aqua Velva high.

He stood on the steps of the library everyday at the same time. Surprisingly for a derelict, he was extremely punctual. He would start his ranting just before quitting time and by five he was painting syllabic masterpieces. The words flowed from him like a never-ending ribbon of silk. At times his voice would explode into tumultuous rage and the crowd that gathered would jump in surprise. His words had power and softness. They had texture and form. Many would gather to hear him speak and on occasion, a hundred people would not be an extraordinary gathering. The cops knew him. He was OK and never bothered anyone for money. They let him talk and gather the crowds and they would listen to him. He was a breath of fresh air in a choking city. He spoke mostly of truths, about the bible but not in a bible- thumping, slam-it-down-your-throat-'till-you-buy-it attitude. He informed you, like buying a car from a friend, he would tell you the good the bad and the ugly about the book. Where it made sense, where it didn't, why it didn't, why it should.

Today though, the content of his monologue was vengefully heated. His talk was one of the final truths of John and he was angry today, the cops were worried. Very few people gathered to listen for he emitted a sense of real apprehension.

"There is evil here!!" He screamed passionately.

His voice made the passers by jump in their step. "Deep within your souls you carry it like a fetus. Do you feel it? It will grow. And grow, and take your soul unless you cut it from your womb and free yourself. There is no one here who does not harbor within them this seed of discontent. It feeds on the flesh of mankind and turns the heart into a caustic pool of poison. Many a man has drowned in this pool; evil has placed its foot upon their heads and accelerated the submergence. The catastrophes have started. You see them glorified on your televisions, on your networks and in your theatres. In your minds you exalt them. Why? They show that there is no kindness or respect left in the world. All of you hate someone. This is cold reality. Most of you have dragged someone down to some level of degradation, instead of loving thine enemies, like the Lord tells us to. We have been given the opportunities, yet you all feel the need to ignore the warnings sent to us and you carry on our way to moral destitution."

He stopped and looked at the crowd who had gathered. He eyed them and knew that most of them had been affected by the evil that he spoke of. Some were beaten or raped or abused, others were felons running from the law. They were all in some form of captivity in the hands of moral decay. He was saddened at the sight of them.

"Tomorrow is fast approaching. With every minute that passes we stray further and further from salvation and closer and closer to the blackness of heartless evil. You all see fit to gamble, to take the chance, I tell you that you are all fools and will lose. You bank on the notion that the Lord is as real as Peter Pan and that the Book is but a best seller from olden days. That there is no truth in the writings of John or Daniel or Mathew. You bet on the idea that The Day will not come, that we all will live forever. I do not think so." His voice quieted and he was hushed by the sorrow that he envisioned.

"This is a bad bet." He shook his head ever so slightly. "The day will come, I assure you, just like it did with Noah. The rains will fall and you will all drown in the debauchery of your pleasures. Lucifer has enticed your spirits with hedonistic lures and some of you actually invite him to stay in your souls. He has made you complacent in your beliefs and you laugh at the words of the prophets. Laugh now, my sorry friends, for the end will find you scratching on the ark of salvation and your cries will be unheeded...ignored as you turn a deaf ear the words of our Master now."

He hung his head and took in the silence of the crowd that remained. They would not listen even though they stood and endured his eulogy to mankind. They would walk away and again cheat on their families, steal from their neighbors and kill to get the Devil's candy, drugs. They were all beyond salvation. God would help those who help themselves, but these creatures were isolated from the notion of redemption.

He wept for them. As his tears fell, shots were fired from behind him. They caused him to spasm and wince in agony. His eyes widened and he wrenched his head backwards to see the one that had defied the Lord's first commandment.

The shooter was young. He could not have been more than twenty. Dressed in the style of the day, a rebel, a maverick, a punk. The gun he wielded was large and very expensive-looking and the wounded speaker wondered where one could possibly attain such a piece of artillery at such an age.

"Go to hell old man!! You should keep your mouth shut 'cause you might piss someone off!" The young man laughed demonically as he turned and scurried into the afternoon crowd.

The police ran after him as the old man fell to the ground. The wound burned with the sin of indifference. The blood poured from his shoulder and the crowd dispersed lest the gunman return.

There he lay on the steps of the library and awaited someone, anyone to attend to his situation. One cop returned and propped him up.

"You'll be alright, Fred, it's just a flesh wound. You'll be preachin' same time tomorrow."

"You are a good man." He looked at the face officer. Although he hurt, his eyes were forgiving and sincere. "He has a place reserved for you. For all the evil that there is in the world, there is also kindness. He knows who you are."

The crowd slowly reassembled around the old man. This time to see if the wound was fatal.

Behind them the opulent doors of the library on 42nd street opened stubbornly, inch by inch, finally they swung open as a young man in his early thirties came stumbling through the doors with his arms loaded down with books. He was slender, with the form of a long distance runner. David Graceson, a handsome man, though not a lady-killer, strode past the growing crowd on the steps.

"Son!! Heed the written word." Fred beseeched him.

"Yeah, old man, the written word." David brushed him off. "I work in the city library. I have to 'heed the written word'". He mumbled as he made his way toward the street.

As he approached the trafficked-swamped street, he kept his eye on the derelict in the officer's arms. He had been shot. "What a crazy city. Who the hell shoots a bum?" he posed to himself, as he wrenched his neck further to see what was happening on the steps. As he set one foot onto the street, a yellow cab came screeching to a halt inches away from him. It scared the hell out of David and his books flew out of his arms like freedom-bound pigeons. The cabby leaned on the horn, stuck his head out the window and let out a stream of obscenities that would embarrass a marine.

"Get off my case!" David retaliated, as he went to pick up his books.

The cabby, still on the horn, inched forward towards David.

David stood up defiantly and stared at the windshield of the cab.

"You want to run me down? Just try it. Come on! Try it, jerk!" It had been a bad day. It started bad and had been going downhill ever since, and with this incident; it showed no signs of letting up. The cabby silenced himself and the vehicle and allowed the pedestrian to gather his booty. With everything in order, David leered at the cabby and cautiously crossed the next two lanes, but not before the hack let loose with another string of profanities and a solo-fingered salute.

"Yeah, yeah, you're an English major." David shook his head and moved towards the parking lot where he parted with 20 bucks for parking. He shook his head, "Criminals!" He set the books on the roof of his car and reached for the keys. He was just about to unlock the door when he noticed the driver's side window was a shattered spray all over the drivers seat.

"Damn!!" He cursed aloud. "What is this? I need this?!! Christ!!" He threw his hands up in complete surrender. "I just can't believe this is happening." He looked to the heavens. "Is this ever going to end?"

He cleared the seat of fragments and took inventory. The stereo was gone, not surprisingly. His Serengeti's were gone, all his tapes and his copy of Tolstoy's War and Peace. He shook his head. Educated thieves he thought. He loaded up the back seat and headed west to his riverside apartment, wondering how far he would get before some one t-boned him in an intersection.

He arrived at his apartment without incident and made his way in. His building must have been at least three hundred years old. Probably the plumbing and the heating were that old, the rest of the building must have been built around it. The elevator mostly worked, thank Christ for that. It was a crapshoot whether he would have to climb the fifteen flights every day, or pray for a quick drop should the elevator not function at a hundred percent.

His apartment was a caldron. Always. It seemed to be hotter than in the bowels of Satan himself. Except in the winter when he would freeze his butt off and clamor on the radiator for some salvation. He needed a better place to live but what for? He seldom had visitors. He just read a lot, philosophized, debated with Bill Buckley, and beat more than ninety-eight percent of the contestants on Jeopardy. God help them if it was American politics or history. He was batting 1000 for the past 8 years. He was unstoppable.

There in the silence he surrendered his weight to an old armchair he bought at a garage sale out in the country for ten bucks, and he read the number one best seller of all times, The Bible. He was never one to go to church, weddings and baptisms, the occasional funeral, nor was he a bible thumper. In fact, he had never even picked up the Bible until last Thursday when there was a whole column entitled "The Bible" on Jeopardy. He had never read the Good Book, so he figured it a good opportunity to pick one up and enrich his soul, not to mention his photographic memory and his Jeopardy ammunition. He started on Thursday night and today; Tuesday he entered the final chapter of Revelations.

The book itself was a fascinating read, but not much humor in it though. It read like Kafka on his birthday, Albee at Christmas. Something about it though captured him and possessed him to continue. He knew how it ended, the Judas did it, but that's not why he read. The reason why quickly became secondary in Genesis and by the time he read John he was completely awe-struck at the number one best seller the world over. And now in the midst of Revelations he was paralyzed with fear.

He had read horror novels, good ones, but this fear was too real. The prophecies foretold for the entire world to believe, scared him. There was reason to fear the images that were borne into the mind. The terror that the seers foretold were overwhelmingly frightening and made him want to have spent all his Sundays of all his years of all his lives in church. Fridays and Saturdays wouldn't have been a bad idea either.

The night was one of those that seemed to inspire jubilation. It had for as long as he could remember. And this night, tonight, was not going to be any different than the ones of years past. It was the first day of summer vacation. You would think that for a librarian it would be the start of hell season, but for David and his select friends, it was one damn good reason to celebrate, and they took full advantage of it.

The boys all headed out to the Cerebral Vacation, their favorite sanity picnic spot and watering hole. There they would congregate at least twice a month to shoot the breeze, rack up some cherry ball, and argue over world politics, taxes, history and dream about some of the easier women in the club.

David was drinking his first day of summer vacation drink, Jack Daniels and Blue. He preferred the Canadian beers, they had substance and they packed a kick. Along with the Daniel's, he was sure to be a blur by 1:00. But what the hell, it was summer.

The conversation gained the momentum of a hurricane as they roughed up more topics this night than any other. The volume of their debates seemed to be fuelled by their incessant alcoholic consumption and raged higher to combat the blaring jukebox.

"The taxes are revolting and a revolt is in order!!"

David spoke up in a voice just a mite too loud, "The only problem with the good old U.S. of A. is that it's too bloody big to throw a successful coup!!" He was like a locomotive picking up speed, as the drone in the bar seemed to die down. Many people stared at the table of pseudo intellectuals and tried desperately to hear what the left-winger had to say. David was in the drivers seat hitting runaway speeds. With a brain full of Jack and angered at the system, nothing was sacred.

"What are those weasel politicians up to? What have they been into for God's sake? Scandals? Conspiracies? Tell me about the Iran hostage crisis? Crisis? What Crisis?" He rolled his eyes. "Iraq was probably in somebody's day book, and way back, Cuba and the Missile Crisis, Bay of Pigs, Vietnam, how about Kennedy's Dallas Street redecorating party? Believe me when I tell you, somebody's really messing with us!!"

The talk turned and swerved, backed up, turned around and ended up in David's face. They were staring at him now and waiting. What the hell were they looking at?

"What!!?"

"You want to elaborate on that, Pal?" David's best friend, Evan asked.

Elaborate? On what? David's head wobbled like the head of a toy dog in the back of an Italian Impala. What the hell did he say? He fought hard with Jack for possession of his senses. Somewhere back in the folds of his brain he pulled out the root of his rage. "The white house if packed full of liars. The politicians win their votes by trying to convince you that each of their lies aren't as bad as the next guys. You cast your vote and hope that there is some shred of honor in the electoral system. But in the end, you get it in the end; screwed up the ass because the man is in power now and he can do what ever the hell he pleases. My vote is my half of the politicians contract. He presents me with an offer. I accept it by paying him with my vote. If he reneges on his end of the deal then I think that I have the right to charge him." David sat back in his chair pleased with his response. His smugness was short lived as he bolted up to ad to his statement. "And further more, I truly believe I have the right to sue the bastards for breach of contract and misrepresentation and a few other things that I can't think of right now. What do ya'all think of that?!"

Just as his friends were about to jump on him a hand tapped David on the shoulder. Whoever it was, couldn't have chosen a more suitable time for interruption. David wobbled his head back towards the adjoining booth.

"Yeah?" David slurred his greeting and tried hard to focus.

"You have some interesting notions that I couldn't help but overhear. I'm Edward Freeman. I'm a political columnist with the Times. I wonder if I could have a word with you?"

David was too numb to move. He just shifted his position and peered around the back of his seat. "Shoot."

"David? That's your name isn't it?"

"Yeah. That's me. Graceson."

"Well David your idea of bringing litigation against the ex president is so outrageous that it may actually be a very feasible and lucrative endeavor. I've never even heard of the notion but I am more than certain that the action could be filed. I wonder if at some point in the next week we could get together and elaborate on this issue. Personally I think it would make a great story, and if you do want to bring it out as a class action suit, the Times would be a great platform to attract a huge number of people, not to mention you could probably get free legal counsel. If not from the Times then from some other firm that may catch the story. Is that alright with you?"

David tried to look at the reporter and figure out which one of the three he should zero in on. After shaking his head, he realized there was only one. "You want to do a story on my theories? Sure. How about

Monday? You'll find me in the Public Library, make it about two in the afternoon."

"Two o'clock Monday is good. It will give me some time to look into all your allegations and I can get a sound base from there. I like the idea David and I think this thing can really fly. I'll see you then. Thanks." He offered his hand and David accepted.

"Monday. Two. Done. Call first, will ya." He shifted his weight and was back at the table with his friends. "You see boys. You all think I'm nuts but the Times wants to talk to me about all my theories. They have to hold some kind water, don't you think?"

They all looked at each other and then back to David just as his head dropped to the table like an anvil and he was out like a light.

He thanked God in all his infinite brilliance that He put the first day of summer on a Saturday. Only 'he', who created alcohol, could give him mercy on this the morning of the mother of all hangovers. His head was a kaleidoscope of pain. His tongue was Velcro and somehow fur had been affixed to it. He tried, but failed, to retrace the path to this point in time and space. To hell with it he thought, if it was important, it would come back to him. If it wasn't then it could go to hell. He spent most of the day asleep on the couch with the drapes drawn tight trying hard to forget how horrible he felt.

When the phone rang it clamored and resounded louder and louder until the only manner to silence the beast was to appease its hunger for a response. He fumbled his way to it and answered it in the midst of a Lynchburg-induced fog. The voice was faint, yet assertive, driven by purpose, direct.

"Shut your mouth, Graceson, or we'll shut it for you. There will be no story."

That was all the voice said. He held the receiver for a confused moment and stared at it curiously before dropping it into the cradle.

"What the hell?"

The office building on 53rd was a monument to the corporate attitude. It is crisp, clean and razor sharp. Edges cut, steel, no stone. No carpet, marble. Only oak was present where wood was needed, but it was seldom used. The whole building was cold and efficient and moved with the fluidity of time, one movement bleeding into the next. The security was tight everywhere and even tighter on the sixth floor, which was occupied by eight desks, a bank of computers that could rival MIT, a wall of monitors and a large conference table encompassed by thirty chairs. All the window blinds were drawn and it was cold on this floor, almost too cold. Here they would meet when emergencies dictated and this was bordering on DEFCON 3.

All the upper echelon was present, except four of the honor guard and two from intelligence, this meeting did not warrant their attention at this point in the plan. There was an air of concern nonetheless. They would be there half the night planning their strategy for the next forty eight hours then leave with their orders and return in three days to report.

It was a fairly simple plan, but one that was to be handled delicately and covertly.

The next few days were ones filled with anxiety. David went about his business in his normal mode but still Sunday's abrupt telephone threat kept playing havoc with his nerves. It must have been Evan, even though he denied it on Monday, he was sure it was that little runt.

Evan and David were friends since childhood. They lived two doors away from each other, went through all grade levels together, went to university together and graduated the same year from different courses. They were more than friends. If David cut, Evan would bleed, blood brothers so to speak. Still Evan possessed the most bizarre sense of humor; so much so that David could never tell at times whether the tale was real or his chain was being yanked. Sunday's call must have come from Evan, regardless of the denial.

The phone rang. He picked it up. It was Evan was asking to meet him at Straps for lunch. David accepted as long as his 'Shut your mouth' denying friend picked up the tab. Evan accepted. "It's important." He added. David hung up the phone and was just about to leave when the newspaper caught his attention. The picture of the man was vaguely familiar. He was a journalist with the Times and he was found with his throat slit in classic Columbian necktie fashion the story read. David read the story faster and the name Edward Freeman jarred his memory. Jesus, he mumbled to himself. He had an appointment with the man today. He looked at his watch, one thirty. No wonder he hadn't called. The thought sent a chill through David and he wondered what could the man have been working on that would cause him such a grotesque demise. He shook with the thought and went about his plans.

They met at Straps just after one. David was already inside when Evan joined him at a booth by the front window. Straps was a joint, a real joint, not one of these nouveau-trendy roadhouses that franchised corporate yuppies dreamed up. A true bluesy, smoke hanging four feet from the ceiling at noon, place. The decor was early scuz, but it was impeccably clean, David always wondered how that was accomplished. Evan ordered a Bud, David a Blue, "No Blue? Miller then."

Evan turned his smile to the waitress to one of almost discontent when he drilled David.

"Would you mind telling me what the hell Saturday night was all about?" asked Evan.

David was silent, like a child who had wet his pants on the way home from school and tried to feign innocence.

"Man you were some kind of pissed off about something and I'm hoping to God your brain was drowned by the booze to make you talk like you did. You were god damned rabid. I've known you for far to long to think that nothing was wrong with you so speak to me man, speak!" Evan had moved up and over top of the table and was demanding a response.

David turned his gaze away, stared out the window and searched the busy Manhattan Street for his answer.

"Evan, doesn't it ever get to you? It gets to me!" He continued surveying the street. "Sure I drank a lot, so what! I got drunk and I guess I let the world know how I felt." He reared his attention back to Evan. "I was angry bud, fed up and sick of the way we're being smacked around by the bureaucrats. I'm angry and ...and...maybe I'm just scared."

"Of what?" egged Evan.

"Haven't you noticed pal? Ever recall so many natural disasters as we have had in the last year? Listen man, I studied history for years and never has the world seen this wrath before. I just finished reading the Bible man; it's all in there. I don't mean to sound like a wus but Armageddon scares the hell out of me"

"What?!! That holy-roller horseshit? Man, are you kidding me. You're an intellectual, act like one and tell me what the hell that book is. It's a chronicle; a damned diary passed down from uncle Jesuit to cousin Reuben down the line 'til Max at the corner deli finally put his two cents in it to make it complete. It's all written by shepherds to keep the lamb in line."

"Evan, pal, bubby, I know what you're saying, but something inside me is telling me otherwise. I just finished reading Revelations and it's heavy. Evan, this is proclaimed as the final chapter of man. This chapter is so frightening with its predictions that if tomorrow is foreseen with the accuracy of the past forty years; we're in for some really big trouble. Forget Nostradamus. He just read the book and put some names to it. Floods, earthquakes, fires, hurricanes, tornadoes, famine, disease, war...atrocities, man! The signs of the times. It's all there and it's all happening. Do you realize according to the scriptures Lucifer is here with us right now!! He's here now man! He could be that yahoo over there at the bar, he could be the Chinese guy at the fruit market, hell it could even be some hooker out on 42nd street. He could have been here for years and causing nightmares like Hitler or Stalin. He could have started polio or TB. He could have even blown up the space shuttle Challenger!! Evan, listen to me man, I'm not losing my mind. It may seem that way, but I've got all my gray matter intact."

Evan stared at him for the longest time. He slowly gazed around the room, trying to still the waters of turmoil that his best friend had swirled in his head. He was scared, for David not for any thing else. He turned and looked at his best friend

"You don't need to talk to me man, you need to see a shrink, or see a priest at least, maybe one of them will set your head on straight and let you know that you're sinking into some sort of paranoid delusion that's going to find you on the ledge of a 42nd story window, ready to do a perfect swan dive. Please man, if for no one else do it for me. Please."

The NY library was sparsely occupied during the summer months. Never overflowing with students as throughout the school year, yet there were enough patrons to dictate a staff load of fifteen. Even with that amount, you would think that someone could be found to assist in the hunt for that ever-elusive book. It was too bad it was David's day off, she thought.

Elly was not new to this library, nor to any library on the eastern seaboard. She had seen a lot of them even with her nose buried deep into reference material. They all seemed to be pretty much the same and she swore that the same miserable old bitch with the snotty attitude and the outdated hairstyle was cloned and worked in all of them. She would sooner suffer the anguish of the book expedition and exploration than to stir the beast in the size 15 polka dot dress.

After twenty minutes of digging into the confidential files of the library's computers, Elly concluded that the book had been either stolen, misfiled or eaten, and that the computers in the state library needed an anti-hacking program.

She was damn good with a computer. She knew everything about them and was more at ease with them than with most people. People were quite rude. Computers were sneaky. She liked sneaky, she was as sneaky as they got and most people she knew were fully aware of it as one of her finest attributes. It was not a flaw but more a gift. Working in the State Department as one of the country's foremost computer analysts, her ability to manipulate others for her needs without letting them realize it, definitely aided certain situations.

Elly was a petite woman, 25 years old, with a shape that could stop the Concorde in mid flight. She was stunning; with eyes that could suck your soul into a hormonal abyss, and enough well placed curves to baffle any Formula 1 driver. She was captivating, and with brains worthy of MENSA induction, she was dangerous. She was not threatening at all, very demure as a matter of fact, but with a subtle hint of schoolgirl charm.

She had been with the State Department for three years now and since her start there, she had escalated to top ranking official in no time. She knew more than her own job well, she knew everybody else's job even better than they did and for that reason she was in demand from the moment she would walk into the office. At 6:45 and she would claw her way out of the office at 5:00, fighting tooth and nail to escape. She loved it though, and would not trade it for anything.

Jefferson R. Fleming was her immediate superior in the D.C. branch where she worked. He was a nervous sort who never had time for anything but work. He never married, never cared to date, just worked and went home putting in time until his retirement six months away. He was obsessive, neurotic and smelled of body odor even first thing in the morning, but he was a good man with a caring heart and that was all that mattered to her. Elly liked him because he was intelligent and could give her the mental jousting that she needed to stay sharp. He played a multitude of psychological games, and he kept score on a board in his office. He won most of the battles but Elly learned more each game. She would beat him soon she thought, and smiled at the notion of a rematch once she got back to DC.

She was out of the office now for a well-deserved vacation. Three weeks away from the office, of sleeping in, of wearing Nike's and Levis. Three glorious weeks without phones or keyboards, or pineapples that couldn't do their own jobs themselves. She was free and was going to enjoy it to the hilt.

She came back home for two weeks to see her parents, Evan and hopefully David. It had been far too long since she and David had spoken alone. There was always someone around during Christmas or Thanksgiving that would prevent them from getting reacquainted during the short time she was up to visit. So now, with two weeks free in her day planner (which she left at home), she would make time to meet with the man she had known all her life. The man she dreamed of as her husband in grade school and fantasized about as a hormonally imbalanced teenager. This would be a high priority meeting, once she finished with her last bit of research in the library.

In the riverside apartment, just breathing was enough exertion to soak oneself with sweat. The windows were open as far as they would go and then pushed further to see if they could surpass their limit. The front door of the apartment was open as well, trying to coax some semblance of a draft. It helped, but at the cost of having total strangers walk by and gaze into his apartment. David didn't care; they could come in and take whatever they wanted as long as they left the T.V. and his ten-dollar armchair.

He was sitting on the window ledge, feet dangling over the edge, a Blue in hand. Tangerine Dream ebbed in the background, Underwater Sunlight, or Thief. Whichever it was, it lulled him. He didn't hear the footsteps come into his apartment, and wouldn't have if the music didn't break for the next song. He turned around quickly and almost lost his balance on the ledge. He only saw the back of a large man with a baseball cap, white t-shirt, and faded denim as he walked out of the apartment. David yelled at him, but the man kept on walking.

He ran to the door of his apartment and called to the man again. "Hey!! What the hell...?"

"Hey, bub, I'm sorry" The intruder stopped in the hallway.

David caught up to him but kept his distance. The man was huge, 280 pounds easy. A chest and arms that could be rented for advertising space, David looked at the face of the behemoth expecting to see a number on his forehead, a mailing address perhaps.

The man spoke apologetically and with a heavy Jersey accent

"Yo, I'm so sorry pal. I did'na know you live 'ere. I was lookin' for Andrews, he use ta live in dat apawtment an I was lookin' fo' 'im. You been 'ere long? Jackson use ta live dare at leas' tree years ago, dats da las time I seen 'im 'ere."

David's nerves settled ever so slightly. Jackson Andrews used to live in his apartment prior to him. He periodically got mail addressed to him, even though he moved out about two and a half years ago. David was still tense, but not enough so that he would physically address this landmark. He eased up just enough to tell the intruder that Andrews had moved to Connecticut and that he had the address should he want it. The walking condo appreciated the offer and followed David back into his apartment. There, David gave him Andrews' Connecticut address and a couple of pieces of mail. One had just arrived that morning for a one Jackson D. Andrews from Time Life publishers and another letter, a fairly colorful envelope from The Organization for the Care and Resurrection of Africa, OCRA. That was almost funny; David thought when he first noticed it three weeks ago. David asked if he was heading out to Andrews now. If so, then perhaps could he drop off the letters?

The man said he was going out to visit his friend and it would not be a problem. He took the letters, apologized for all the trouble and left.

David still felt on edge, but once across the threshold, he closed the door and looked about his apartment. The heat engulfed him and he was uncomfortably comfortable once more.

The lamp above the bed started first, swaying in tiny circles. Being asleep he would not have noticed, but it started to rattle once the circles grew larger. He opened his eyes just in time to see it come crashing down towards his bed. He had just that much time to move and he moved faster than Mexican food the day after. He didn't have time to investigate. His thigh was wet with his fear as the first real tremor hit his apartment building.

The force was incredible. Everything was blasted out of position and propelled a good ten feet from origin. The foundation was rocked and the plaster was falling in chunks the size of Honda's from the ceiling.

It was Saturday morning, around eleven and the quake was a wake up call to New York. He didn't look outside. The devastation would be inconceivable. The day was well under way, and from under the desk in his bedroom he saw massive pieces of concrete fall from above his bedroom window.

Two minutes in total, Jennings would tell them later, two minutes that lasted an hour, two minutes of unadulterated terror.

The screams from the apartment upstairs came careening through the hole in the ceiling and they chilled his soul. God have mercy, he prayed. Evan heard another scream; this one frightened him even more for it emanated from his own apartment, from his own lungs.

Two minutes, one hundred twenty seconds later and one hundred eighty six people were dead, a thousand or so injured and countless missing. It was Mother Nature's mathematics.

It wasn't until 12:15 when the air raid sirens and emergency broadcast system finally stopped their incessant screaming. The Big Apple fell from the tree and landed out of Eden with the force of an atomic blast. Six point five on the shaker scale.

The damage was far more intense on the Island Sound than elsewhere but how the bridges were spared only God could tell. Even the Atheists thanked Him for that one.

Evan was paralyzed with fear. His butt and legs were numb. The last aftershock rippled through at a subtle four point seven at about one and he was still in the same spot that the lamp chased him to. He hadn't moved for almost two hours. Where would he go anyway? The twenty-story complex was literally dancing, doing some possessed hula-hula thing for too damn long for him to even think about moving. He only thought of his family, his little sister, David's rambling about Revelations and of his own mortality. Two god damn hours thinking of ones own mortality is just two hours far too many.

The three hundred year old building was built with three hundred year old pride and patience and was one of the very few buildings that had slight damage. David watched CNN for most of the morning scouring the footage for anything that slightly resembled Evan's apartment building and hoped to God that he didn't see his best friend being covered with a sheet, or dragged from the rubble. Then after an hour he was there, for a fleeting moment, he saw Evan, clad only in a blanket, walking across the screen. Alive. David was ecstatic.

There was no way to get a hold of Evan, but more so sooner than later he would show up at the three hundred year old building and could make it home for as long as he wanted. In the meantime David made his way out of the apartment. He ventured down to the corner market to pick up some steaks, vegetables and fruit. Every news box he passed he saw the picture of Edward Freeman. Something about it bothered him but he couldn't understand why. Maybe because he had just met the man. He seemed nice enough so why would anyone want to kill him in mob-like style. He continued to think about it as he made his way to the liquor store to pick up beer and a forty of Jack Daniels, they would both need something to remove the edge.

It was a beautiful day. The sun was brilliant and warm and the sky was a shade of blue that Kodak dreamed of capturing and putting on an advertisement. Mother Nature was apologizing for her tantrum.

The sun beat on David's face as he walked towards his home, when the cheap paper bag the Chinese grocer gave him, ripped at the base and all the fruits spilled to the street. He bent to pick up his escaping bounty and cursed his misfortune. Man, how far can a damn orange roll? He thought to himself. It rolled far enough, almost fifteen feet due east and smack next to a wino sprawled by a garbage can. It was a race now. Could David get to the orange before the bum spotted it? It would be close. Five more feet and... He looked asleep but it was camouflage to prevent from being hassled, David assumed.

The wino, insulated from the heat with a layer of filth, reached down to his knee and grasped the orange with a gentle grip. He held the fruit for a moment before actually looking at it, as if to guess what the treasure was that befell him. A Cheshire smile graced his face as he beheld the round orange miracle. Still smiling, he turned to David and bowed his head in gratitude. Then he reached into his pocket and pulled out a folded, colorful piece of paper. Oh great, Canadian money, David cringed, but it was not. The bum unfolded the paper and tried to smooth it out. He handed it to David like a Rolls Royce owner handing over a twenty to the valet.

"Thank-you, kind sir. May God bless you and yours and keep you safe in this, the final hour." He tendered.

David shook his head and wondered if that's where he would end up if he did not heed Evan's advice on the ridiculous notion of Armageddon.

"You're welcome, Pops. Enjoy and...uh...God bless you, too." David turned, crumpled up the wino's tip, took three steps and looked at the paper before tossing it. He froze. The color was vaguely familiar. He un-crumpled the bum's payment as quickly as possible. His heart stopped dead, and then started up like an AK 47 in the heat of action. The final fold revealed the return address of the Organization for the Care and Resurrection of Africa, OCRA. Addressed: Jackson D. Andrews.

The quake caught Elly coming out of the library, twenty feet from her Nissan Pathfinder. In the open parking lot there was no threat of danger except for attempting an exit. She was afraid for her brother though. Evan was the only one on the Island Sound that she knew, and she pleaded with all her soul that he was in the city at the time. Preferably at David's. Even at Macy's or somewhere. Anywhere away from his apartment. She sat in her truck and cried. After her initial shaking stopped she tried her brother by phone. There was no signal. Ma Bell was obviously offended by Mother Nature's rudeness. Her crying intensified when the recording came on for the third time. 'Your call cannot be completed as....'

The parking lot was jammed but emptying slowly, so she stayed where she was. The windows of her Pathfinder were tinted so she jumped in the back seat and tried to relax, knowing that no one could see her there alone. She sat with her knees drawn up to her chest for an agonizing hour before she picked up the phone and called the only other person she could think of.

The connection took longer than normal to connect, but it finally did and it rang and rang like it did the last five times she called. This time just as she was about to hang up the other end engaged.

"Yeah?" was the aggravated greeting, anxious and nervous.

"David?" she inquired reluctantly.

"Wrong num..." click...dial tone.

Elly hung up her phone and stared at it for a long moment. She worked with numbers and keypads all day and was a walking Nynex. She couldn't have dialed the wrong number. Then again she was shaky and may have mistakenly hit the six when she meant to hit the five. Either way, she'd wait another ten minutes before trying him again.

There in the controlled chaos of the mid-city parking lot, she was anxious. She reached for her briefcase and dragged out her lap top and modem and hooked them up to her cellular phone. She had to do something. If she couldn't get answers from anyone that she knew, she would hunt for them herself. Was Evan alive? Check the hospitals for any new admissions. Back doors would be the only way to get into those confidential files and they would be a cakewalk. She was busy in her computer state toying with the hospitals computer links, and all the rest of her emotions would have to wait.

He ran from the elevator towards his apartment. Just steps from the door he saw the photograph on the ground. In his haste he mistook it for litter but as his stride took him over it, his sight caught it. He stopped dead in his tracks and looked back quickly. Panic enveloped him as he bent over to pick it up. The man was beaten horribly and his face showed the most signs. If not for his tongue hanging from the wound in his throat, David never would have made the connection. It was Freeman the journalist. He stared at the photo as he walked trance-like to his apartment.

His door always gave him a hard time, but now he had no patience for it. He unlocked it and pushed on it, it would not give. He kicked it hard and it flew open smashing a hole into the wall where the doorknob connected. He slammed it shut, triple bolted it and threw the groceries, less one orange, onto the kitchen table. "What's going on?" He yelled at the photograph.

He had a death grip on Andrews letter from OCRA. He stared at it and the picture with the conviction of a renowned psychic. What was this letter doing in the hands of the wino? Was it thrown in the garbage? Was Andrew's 'friend' too lazy to carry the letters to Connecticut? Who was the behemoth anyway? There were far too many questions and not enough answers. David thought of the behemoth, but could not remember one feature on him except his massive arms and expansive chest. Who the hell was he? He had made it all the way into his apartment before David realized he was there. Was he looking for something?

Did he take anything? David scoured his apartment for any indication that anything was missing. He counted everything, even cutlery. Everything seemed to be present and accounted for. His pictures were all there. What little jewelry he owned was still there. Cash, stereo, wallet everything was where it should be. The only thing stolen was his peace of mind. He sat deep in his armchair and stared at the photograph.

As if Andrews' letter was not enough to send him into convulsions the picture threw him into another realm of fear. How did it land in front of his apartment? Was there a cop who lived on his floor and he dropped it? He knew nobody on his floor and he blamed himself now for not being more sociable. It was a coincidence. It had to be. There was no way that he, and Freeman's death were connected. He tried hard to convince himself that it was only a fluke in the cosmos that brought that photo into his apartment, let alone his life. But that, and the letter? What were the odds on that type of coincidence? Phenomenal, astronomical.

He stared at the two articles for an incredibly long period of time. There were no answers.

It was quiet in the apartment and the usual hell hot heat engulfed him. It made him lazy, and just as mental exhaustion was about to consume him, the phone screamed for attention. It made him jump clear out of the chair. David ran to get it, it would be Evan he was sure. He got to the phone and was about to pick it up when he noticed it. It was subtle, unworthy of note on any day when he felt more secure. Even now it could be his consummate paranoia over exaggerating the slightest little thing. It was there by the table leg, a footprint in the pile of the rug.

He used to draw pictures on the carpet after his mother vacuumed. That was fun but this sent a chill throughout his soul and shrank his skin two sizes too small. The phone was still ringing. The footprint was smaller than David's, and was the only one in the area. The ringing was ceaseless and after the twentieth scream he snatched the phone abruptly. "What!!?"

he snapped.

"David?" a soft voice crackled over the receiver. It had been crying and still trembling. It was a familiar voice and one that he needed now.

"Elly? Oh God, is that you? It's good to hear from you! Are you all right? Are you with Evan? Is he alright?" David suddenly realized he was rambling and stopped to give Elly a chance to respond.

"Yes, I'm alright. No I'm not with Evan, so I don't know if he's OK, but I'm trying to find out on line where the hell he is. I've got nothing on him so far."

David explained that he saw her brother on CNN, that he was walking and unhurt. He went further to explain that undoubtedly Evan would end up at his apartment and that she should make her way over and they could wait together. Elly promised she would be there as soon as traffic would allow.

David hung up the phone and stared at the footprint in the pile. What the hell was happening to him, and to his life? He was a stable man just forty-eight hours ago and now the fiber of his existence was unraveling a string at a time. He studied the print and quickly wiped it with his foot as if to erase it from existence.

"I can't deal with this too. It had to have been there before. It had to be and I just didn't notice it."

Mackinnley was a dick. Figuratively, literally and occupationally. He headed up intelligence in the D.C office for the bureau and had only to answer to the director. He didn't have to answer to the one who ran the country, he was a criminal anyway you looked at it. They all were who sat in the big chair but he couldn't touch them. This one that came in last go round seemed fine enough but he had learned not to say anything until at least the third year, then he would pass judgment. The new boy had a head start; the outgoing president was a nightmare. Every one felt it and most were afraid. James Elliot Thorne, born June 6, '33, in Death Valley on the night of the most violent storm in the country's history. Thorne carried that violent nature with him like a birthright. Mackinnley thought of how he could have hidden that rage for an entire campaign, without letting it slip once. Thorne was a master charmer, eloquent and auspicious. Everyone thanked God when the Democrat beat him out and sent him running. The country rejoiced and Mackinnley finally relaxed the muscles in his back and neck for the first time in four years. Still, the democrat was a potential royal pain.

Mackinnley was a big man, not obese, solid and thick as an old oak. He was tall, 6'6", 290 lbs, front line form, he smoked half a pack of Camel filtered a day, a whole pack and then some if the case was getting hot or if he was drinking, which was anytime after noon, except Sundays.

His office was large enough to comfortably accommodate fifteen seated. The large desk he sat at looked small in comparison to his frame. He sat on the corner of it and spoke on the phone in "hmms" and "ums". Mackinnley was practiced in reading faces and phones cheated him out of truth. He dropped the phone in the cradle and stared out the window, lit up a smoke and drew it in deep. His brother had died in the New York earthquake. Mackinnley called the man upstairs, told him he was off to New York to make the necessary arrangements and that he would be back in a week. He buzzed his secretary, and she was in his office before he let go of the call button.

"Write!" he barked.

She jumped in her seat.

"I'm going to New York, I need plane tickets, anyone but American. Hotel, downtown. Car, preferably a Cadillac with air and move on it! I want to be out of here by four. Go, go, move!!"

His command sent her scrambling for the sanctuary of her desk; she grabbed the Rolodex with one hand, the phone with the other and was moving.

Mackinnley cleared up some things in his office, set the alarms, locked the doors, instructed her to have the necessary papers sent to his apartment and left the building.

In his apartment he watched CNN and saw footage of New York. He thought of his brother, and then all the work he would have when he got back. He watched the broadcast for ten minutes then packed.

The papers arrived by departmental driver. Mackinnley was ready. He drafted the messenger instead of a cab. At 3:33 the plane took off from Dulles en route to LaGuardia.

The knock on the door was so faint that it almost went unnoticed. David approached the door cautiously not knowing whom to expect. Elly, Evan, the behemoth, or someone with smaller shoes than his own. The knocking continued, this time with more volume and urgency. David was consumed with anxiety. He grabbed the handle of the door and opened it ever so slightly, enough to get a peek through the crack. In his other hand a pipe wrench large enough to knock out a Kodiak was at the ready. He saw her on the other side of the door and couldn't open it fast enough. God she was beautiful. Even more so then he last remembered her, and that was only six months ago at Christmas. She flung her arms around him and almost crushed his ribs. Tears streamed all over her face, her nose was red and she'd obviously been in this condition for a while. He dropped the wrench and cradled her in his arms. He ushered her into his apartment, closed the door, triple bolted it and brought her to the couch. She had not said a word since her arrival, only sobbed like a little girl. David held her close and tried to reassure her that everything was going to be all right and that Evan would be there shortly and that he would be fine. Her tears seemed to subside and she pulled away from him, just enough to be able to focus on his face.

"Oh David, I'm so glad you're here! I'd be a total mess if you weren't. You haven't heard from him have you? I hope he's OK. You said you saw him on TV. Are you sure it was him and he was all right?"

"Yes Elly, I saw him. I'm certain it was he, and he's fine. It will just take some time for him to get here. Where do you think he can go? Your parents' place? No way! It would take him days to get out there. He's coming here. I know it and he should be here in about an hour, hour and a half at the most. Do you hear me, angel?" He used to call her that when she was twelve and it stuck with him. Just that word alone took most of the fear away. She was safe, David too and shortly Evan would be at the door and they would all be together once more.

"Like a drink in the mean time?"

"I'd love several, thanks. Got something serious?" Elly chided.

"Jack Daniels," he replied with a raised eyebrow. "Care for a belt?"

"Hit me. On ice please."

They didn't talk. They sat on the couch, she nestled in his arms as they both stared out the window at the afternoon sun skirting off the buildings. The apartment was quiet.

They waited. For Evan. For peace of mind. For the right moment to move. It was just three years ago that they had moved closer to becoming lovers. They were friends for almost forever, growing closer to the consuming fire that blazed in each of their hearts. They longed for the moment. You could sense it when they were close even if you didn't know them; people knew that they were destined for one another. Their smiles, and closeness, how they touched each other's arms when they spoke. The look of yearning and hunger in their eyes when the other spoke, it was inevitable that the stars would align and they would hold onto each other and never let go. Wrap themselves in the comfort of each other and become one in a knot of desire that they both dreamed of. For all of his life he had wanted her. Even when he teased her about being just a kid or worse yet 'a girrrrl', he wanted her. From the time she blossomed into the ripe young woman and before, he longed to kiss her but dreaded the ramifications should his friends find out. And now on the couch, in the glow of the sunset, he wanted to ignite the fires of desire, to feel her body rise as he kissed her mouth, to bring her body to the pinnacle of rapture, and to hear her scream out his name with complete release. He watched her and imagined her twisted in a knot of wicked abandon, entangled in his mind and body and in his soul forever.

But for now he could just watch her and imagine. There would be lots of time for that but he could not wait much longer.

-2-

The marble foyer echoed with the sound of a lone set of footsteps. The stride was long and confident and did not break rhythm once from the front door of the corporate offices, to the awaiting elevator. A key was placed in its lock and the highly glossed stainless steel doors glided swiftly shut. The whir of the elevator lasted seconds and then halted effortlessly. The doors peeled open to reveal the sixth floor offices. The black marble floors were gleaming. The lights were always left on. There was not a switch on the entire floor. The computer banks blinked and whizzed magnetic tape almost perpetually. The room was empty, less the lone man with the long stride. He sat in the chair at the head of the huge conference table and unloaded his briefcase. Two files were withdrawn, one at least three inches thick and another which was only half an inch. He studied the second file. He flipped it open and picked up the eight by ten glossies. They were Black and white. He hated black and white. He was from the Deep South and that phrase seemed ungodly, black and white together. He was not too fond of color for the same reason but he needed the pictures. He couldn't get drawings.

The first was a group of young men at a bar. He recognized the bar. It was the Cerebral Vacation. A place the socialites, and CEO's, lawyers and corporate hot shots would cut loose on the weekends. It was notorious for its after hours entertainment. A nineties "speak-easy." Most of the general clientele knew nothing of the drugs, the gambling and the live sex shows that went on in the lavishly adorned secret basement. It was a private club, very private. 1.5 million to become a lifelong member and to obey the rules, on penalty of revoking ones long life privilege. Some were granted membership without fees because of their affiliations with certain organizations. They too were bound by the rules.

The picture was crisp and clear. Four casually dressed men, out on a Saturday night. The picture had captured the youngest looking of the four circled in red. Could he be the one? He thought to himself. The young man in the photo was also in the next nine. One picture concerned him. The young man was talking with another at the next booth. This could have been a very disastrous combination but Terrace had done a marvelous piece of work. He studied them all, every angle. The work was done well, and so it should have been. The 'Vacation' was outfitted with cameras and microphones at every table. The security of the high paying patrons was far too important. They paid for their protection. At any given time you could find twenty official delegates. They composed of three judges, and a prime minister. There was a president, perhaps a king. It included cartel members, both oil and drug. They were dressed in jeans and cowboy boots you couldn't tell a sheik from one the members of the band.

After reviewing the notes he thought of their analysis. The intelligence team came up empty, very rare for them. This was a leading indicator that the subject was clean. They found nothing, heard nothing, and for all they knew, there was nothing to report.

He closed the file and moved it to low scale priority.

Elly had fallen asleep. Her emotions had run a gamut and the Daniels pushed her over the edge. She needed the rest. In the orange light that was cast about the room, he watched her. He had watched her grow up when they all lived in the burbs. She was a cute little girl, very witty. Yet she clung to him like gum on the bottom of his shoe. It was annoying at times, most of the time, but still he and Evan were her guardians. No one was to hurt little Elly angel. They made sure of it.

At sixteen she was seeing a sleaze ball from the south side. It was a rebellious, attention-grabbing move. She got stung in the process when the guy roughed her up. That was the time when he and Evan spent two whole days hunting the son-of-a-bitch down, found him and beat the hell out of him so badly he was hospitalized for a month. She never knew about that, nor the prom when her date stood her up. She had waited for the guy she had pined over for months to ask her to go. He finally asked her, but he never showed to pick her up that night. Again he and Evan found him and acquainted the unfeeling bastard with pain and Mercy General's Trauma Center. He always loved her, but never told her. She was Mary to his George in the early years of 'It's a Wonderful Life'.

He watched her sleep, brushed her hair from her cheek, and was about to kiss his sleeping beauty when a thunderous pounding came crashing on the door. It scared the two of them half to death. David jumped and stared at the door, like a deer caught in headlights. The thunder emanated from the other side and Elly looked at him wondering why the hell he wouldn't open the door. She jumped up on the third pounding and went to answer it.

She unlocked the first latch and David tried to speak but couldn't.

The second and third dead-bolts where thrown open. She flung the door open. David would have passed out for lack of oxygen had it not been Evan standing there. David breathed, a sigh of relief.

Elly jumped onto her brother and smothered him with kisses and hugs. Evan was home, and everything was fine now.

After a lengthy shower Evan entered the living room. It was huge. The apartment itself was close to a thousand square feet. Two bedroom, large bathroom and rent controlled. You couldn't ask for anything better except for a little bit cooler.

"You got the heat on in here pal?"

David turned to Evan smiled "Yeah, we're freezing our butts off out here. Oh while you're up, could you close the window and throw another log on the fire? Thanks."

David was always a smart ass.

He joined his sister on the couch and smiled as he grabbed her hand.

"So little sis', what's the news from the nation's capital?

"Forget Washington. Are you OK?"

"I'm doing fine as I can be, all things considered. I've got no ID, no money. I'm persona non gratta." David returned with the beer and Evan related his adventures right from the lamp all the way to the apartment. "Strange thing though, these cops corralled me and asked me my name and then took me into the chopper. I got scared 'cause we just took off as soon as I got in and sat down. I thought I was bleeding to death or something 'cause these guys were moving. They dropped me off on the roof of some hospital and another bunch of guys, doctor types and orderlies were already there waiting. Anyway I cut loose while they were processing me for x-ray, I didn't need anything other than a drink, so here I am."

Mackinnley buried the last remaining member of his family. He stood alone now, knowing the family name would end with him. The thought somehow brought on an eerie feeling of isolation. The service was short, quaint and reserved. Few were present but no one spoke. The reverend's last prayers faded, Mackinnley said goodbye and was gone.

He got back to his hotel and called the office. Things had changed and he was to remain in New York. The Pope was to visit the earthquake stricken island and his orders were to stay there and the team would meet with him and arrange security for "God's right hand man".

Great, he thought. There was enough chaos happening not to have to bring some major security mission here to bless the afflicted. Security would be a joke. It was impossible and he told the man so. It came straight from the top and there was nothing either one of them could do about it.

"Just do it Mackinnley and don't give me a hard time about it."

He hung up the phone hard. "Damn!!" The last thing he needed was another headache. "What the hell does the Pope think he'll do here?"

Mackinnley was not religious and he actually hated organized religion. He believed there was a heaven but no hell, they were living in it, and now he had to protect some yahoo in a silly hat, who didn't speak any English as he gave God's wishes to the survivors and His blessings to the dead. It was all bullshit. He shook his head and stared out the window.

The Pope in New York, after an earthquake. Christ, it just smelled of trouble. He grabbed his jacket and went looking for a bar.

The New York streets were a swelling tide of people. They splashed him around the streets and took him where he didn't want to go. Anywhere they were going he didn't want to follow. He found refuge in a doorway where he saw a "Miller" neon sign.

He opened the door and was greeted by a shapely young hostess.

"Welcome to the Cerebral Vacation! Will you be joining us for lunch, sir?" She had a smile that could convert Liberace.

"Just the bar" he replied with his best etiquette. He was no Bond but he was still fairly attractive in a brutish sort of way. She smiled at him and directed him to the bar.

The barman spotted him. "Rusty-nail!" Mackinnley was impressed.

"And keep them coming" he added.

The bartender was a blur of efficiency Drambuie, Scotch, Chivas, "hmmm", ice, no cherry, excellent! He was a true artist, Mackinnley thought. The bartender knew people. No fruity cherry. He was a good judge of character as well. Mackinnley drank quietly, watched ESPN and slowly got drunk.

He had an uneasy feeling that he was trying to escape. He felt a twinge of anxiety, almost paranoia. He thought it was his brother watching him from above. He was almost right.

CLICK

The sun was up well before Elly or Evan awoke. Elly slept in David's room, Evan in the den on a pull out couch and David on the chesterfield in the living room. He couldn't sleep, at six AM he clicked on the TV and rifled through all the channels. Evangelists, evangelists, evangelists, Ninja Turtles, David and Goliath. He stopped there and watched for a moment. He used to hate the show as a kid, but remembered Goliath and his infamous call, "*Daaaaavieee, Daaaaaavieee.*" He kept his finger on the remote and kept changing stations. CNN, New York earthquake. It was old news, now there was talk of the Pope coming to New York. He hit the remote. Evangelists, evangelists, Turtles, nothing.

At 7:30 Elly sledged her way into the living room in an overly large t-shirt that said, '*IF YOU DREAM, DREAM BIG*'. David chuckled; she looked like Woodstock with her hair all over the place.

"Morning, angel."

"Mrng." she mumbled as she nuzzled up to him on the couch. Was she still sleeping? David wondered. He was starting to become quite uncomfortable, as she curled up closer to him. Parts of him where awake well before the rest of him and now with Elly nuzzled up to him it was becoming more of a strain to hold back his morning salute. How the hell was he going to make it to the john with Spike at full mast? He looked at Elly and tried not to think of her bare thigh and the warmth between them. He wanted to but this was neither the time nor the place with her brother within earshot, so instead he thought of fat ugly nuns. Big, fat, hairy, smelly nuns. It wasn't working, Roseanne in a bikini, Mama Cass in a g-string it was working, and he was cured. Elly wiggled and slowly awoke.

"Hi" she said cooed.

He mumbled something, trying to restrain the resurrection.

"Want some coffee?" She asked.

"Love some." He replied with polite constraint.

She was up but not before her t-shirt rode up her thigh and revealed her entire right leg and a tuft of blond.

"Oh God!!" He stretched to cover his apparent loss of composure. She turned to glance at him just as he was adjusting his equipment. She turned back towards the kitchen and smiled devilishly.

David made a mad dash to the bathroom to relieve his bladder. It would take too long to relieve the whole matter.

He left the john, donned a pair of jeans in his bedroom and met Elly back in the living room.

"Coffee's up. How do you take it? Still just black?"

"Yeah that's fine."

They drank in silence and David wished that she would put something else on. It was getting unbearable.

The sound of the toilet flushing announced Evan's imminent arrival. She tugged at her t-shirt and brought it down to a respectable level, just before her brother rounded the corner.

"Oh man," Evan bitched as he stretched and reached to re-align his spine, "I think I would have been more comfortable sleeping on the rubble in my own apartment."

"Why do you think I slept out here on this couch?" David snickered.

"Nice guy," Evan shot back. "You wait 'til an earthquake levels your joint. I'll make you sleep in the fridge you dick!!"

The conversation eased the tension. Elly got up and headed for the shower leaving the best of friends to discuss what they wished. They talked of the last 24 hours. It had been a different hell for both of them.

"You OK?" David asked, not wanting to appear rude by bringing up his own problems first.

"Yeah, I'll live. Major drag though. I don't have any idea what to do first. ID. I guess. Then down to the DMV, another picnic. I'm gonna spend the rest of my life in line-ups and up to my ass in forms. It's better if they think I'm dead and that way I owe no one anything."

"Evan" David interrupted unable to contain his concern. "I think I'm in some kind of trouble."

"What'd you do now?"

"I don't know if I've done anything. Weird stuff's going on around me."

"Maybe it's this new kick of yours pal, maybe it's the four horsemen. You talk so damn much man you could be in trouble for any number of things. You were mouthing off on Saturday, everything from the failure of democracy to the conspiracy of the few ruling the world. You were pretty damn vocal about too many touchy things, and at the Vacation of all places, David. Come on man you should know that a lot of bigwigs hang there. It's U.N. clientele."

David shook his head slowly. It just didn't make sense. "Ev, sure I may have been just a mite too loud for the upper crust there, but people express opinions like that all the time. It's not like the secret police are going to come and drag me out of my bed in the middle of the night, for Christ's sake", after saying this David thought of the curious telephone call and the visitation. Visitations?

"You think we don't have our own version of the secret police David? You know better than that, but if you have doubts, Elly's in the other room ask her. She's our own Washington source pal, She'll reassure you."

"You know...there have been some strange things happening lately."

"Strange? How strange?" Evan leaned forward.

"Just that phone call. The one I thought was you."

Evan looked at him with a skeptically raised eyebrow.

"Okay", David continued "and some strange visitor...maybe two. I'm not sure, but I think someone was in here. Nothings missing, but someone's been here.

"Sure Goldilocks. You believe in the gustapo now?"

"Knock it off man." After David explained about the big man, the letter from the wino, and the footprint in the rug. "Then I find a Polaroid of Freeman, that journalist from the Times. You know, the guy who wanted to do my story? I find it in the hall just steps from my door. Just lots of things like that. Little coincidences that are putting me on edge and I just can't shake this feeling that someone's...I don't know ...just there watching or messing with me."

Evan was silent for a moment assessing the information.

"If I were you, I would assume nothing. You would make yourself less crazy."

David was silent. He stared at the floor and fidgeted. Evan made more sense than ever and that scared him even more.

-3-

The road seemed to lead to nowhere. It was hell and the topography was indicative of the ride to the same. There were more curves and dips and potholes than anywhere in the entire state. It was like that for three miles. If any one continued on it after the first mile their kidneys would definitely explode. If they made their way clear and into the second mile, security would most definitely have their sights set on the head of the driver. The other posts would take the passengers and drop them cold. If they didn't have clearance they were to be eliminated. Period. There were to be positively no surprise visits. If anyone had eluded security, by some miracle, and successfully ventured into the third mile quadrant, he would eliminate the intruders as well as all of security himself. There was to be no second chance. There was one second chance given, once long time ago and it would never happen again. The intruders were disposed of, and connections in the highest and lowest of places enabled entire family histories to be erased from existence.

After the three-mile mark, the road became civil. A half-mile of cobblestone paved the drive to the main house and a quarter mile in. Two twenty-foot Grecian pillars standing like two monoliths graced either side of the road to a spectacular lodging. It was three stories high and adorned by eight more columns on its facade. The main structure spanned six hundred feet frontage and it was all white. It was an off white, not a crisp, clean, innocent white. It was an old almost haunting white. There were fewer windows than one would expect and those that were there had the blinds drawn. There was a great garden of red flowers that annexed the entire front of the house. The flowers varied in size and species but not in color. They where all deep red, almost oxblood.

The interior of the structure was extravagantly decorated with antiques that spanned all of time. There was a stone wheel in the center of the main foyer with not so much as a rug in the expansive entrance along with it. The rest of the rooms were elegantly adorned with discriminating taste. Clothing from the middle ages, hung delicately on walls. Armor and swords, paintings and sculptures of the worlds most acclaimed stood as sentries at each doorway. De Vinci's, Monet's, Rodin's, and Rembrandts were exquisitely displayed. The rooms were sparsely furnished, lest they took away from the works. Each room was enormous and echoed any sound. But no sound ever emerged.

He was draped in a shawl as he stared at slab of stone from the Mesozoic era in the library. It was the first piece the family had attained. He stared at it knowingly. The scene was a hunt. One hunter and twenty animals. Deer of some sort. One fallen and the hunter at the draw with his spear. The next would fall soon he thought. But it never happened. The hunter was stuck in time, forever holding his spear, never throwing, and waiting for the right moment.

James Elliot Thorne shared his museum with no one. His wife had died just after the '98 election and he was left alone to realize his destiny. He was yet a young man. At sixty-four, he still had what it took to seize the most powerful country in the world and lead it to a new tomorrow. He dreamed of the day in 2004, when the Democrat would cower and all those that chose him would be enlightened by his new found strength. He had plans and they would become reality, but now much work had to be done to ensure victory in the distant election. There was much politicking and fund raising, persuasion and enticement to be done to feed the flames of resurrection.

He stayed in the study for hours at a time and worked. He had lost the last election and he was not about to lose the next one. But to appease the people and make them believe was going to be a difficult task. He truly hated them, but power was the trophy he sought. And he would regain his rightful place in history. He swore it on his family name. It was his sole destiny and he was the sole ruler of it. One, then three more gunshots in rapid sequence went off in the second mile quadrant. He twisted his ear to listen for any more. There were none. One minute later the phone rang and he answered it on hands free.

"Who?" was all he said.

"Four youths, sir. A one Paul White, male..."

"I don't give a shit what they are, I want to know *WHO* they are!!" Thorne bellowed as he interrupted the other voice.

"The computers have nothing on them sir. Youths, two sixteen, two seventeen. Two males, two females, the car's clean."

Thorne soaked up the news. He was emotionless.

"Dump them." He hung up and smiled.

There would be no forgiveness to trespassers. Ten people a month ventured near his oasis and all of them disappeared from the face of the earth. Mostly kids. Some driving, others walking. Either way, they would be extracted like weeds from his garden and thrown away.

Elly emerged from bedroom in a pair of well-worn Levi's, Nike's and a pale pink muscle shirt. She was bra-less and David tried hard not to notice, but did.

"I'm off to do some major shopping for my big brother!" She declared as if she had just won the lottery. "Same size as at Christmas Eve?"

"Elly, it's not necessary for you to...yeah...the same sizes thanks" He needed clothes; Elly had impeccable taste and loved to shop. Why deprive her?

She went over to the couch where her brother was seated, came up beside him and kissed him on the cheek.

"See you, love you." She sauntered over to David on the couch, leaned in front of him and kissed his forehead, allowing him full view of her charms. "See you, love you." She winked at him slyly and was out the door giggling like the little schoolgirl again.

David swore she'd kill him if she kept it up.

The boys sat around the apartment until boredom crept up on them and they headed out for a drink and a change of pace. They left Elly a note informing her of their relocation to a more lively place and that they would return in a while. David wrote on the bottom of the page; '*P.S. Thanks, I owe you*'. They left the note on the fridge and were out the door.

Twenty minutes later they were greeted by a shapely young hostess who cooed, "Hello gentlemen, lunch or the bar?"

David and Evan awaited a third option. It never came. They took the bar.

The 'Cerebral' didn't really get packed on Sunday's until about six, and now, at three, there was little action. Still, the bar had four or five perches free. One spot was open with three seats together. They made their way toward the barstools and sat down. Beside David was seated a man the size of Montana.

The barman ventured down their way. "Jack Daniels and a Blue chaser for you..." he pointed to David, "...and you look like a Bud man, right?" to Evan.

They looked at each other, then the barman.

"How the hell did you know that?"

"It's my job, David," answered the barman professionally. He prepared the drinks and presented them to the two dumbfounded patrons.

Evan was amazed. David was frightened. Could this be the guy with the smaller shoes that was in his apartment? He was about to lean over the bar to check, when the barman confessed his source.

"You gentlemen were here last Saturday. Party of four. You sat in the forth booth from the front. I remember you David because you were keeping the waitress hopping with your Jack and Blue all night. Plus your pals were pleading with you to keep your voice down. Unsuccessfully, I might add. That's how I got your name and order. I remembered. You're a hard person to forget."

David relaxed a bit. It sounded plausible. He shot back the Jack and sipped on the Blue.

Evan stared at David with concern. If the barman knew his name and could hear the discussion clear across the club on a busy Saturday night, then God only knew who else might have also taken note.

"So what are you going to do pal?"

David shrugged his shoulders and said nothing.

"Maybe you should call the police."

"Maybe, maybe not. They'll probably laugh at me, tell me to drink less coffee and watch fewer Hitchcock films!"

The large man's ears perked at the word police. Mackinnley was never one to pry into matters that he was not assigned to. He kept quiet, lost interest in the TV, and paid closer attention to the conversation beside him.

"I still can't get over this whole thing Evan. So, I shot my mouth off. What could I have said that has someone interested in me so much that they're in my apartment and calling me telling me to shut my mouth?" David's paranoia was contagious.

"Keep it down, man!" Evan whispered. They both scanned the Vacation and focused back on the subject matter.

"I remember going on about government spending and taxes. Hell everyone bitches about that. Iran, that was yesterday's news. Assassinations, they're even older news."

"You were on pretty heavy about conspiracies Dave. Maybe you hit a raw nerve."

"I know jack shit except for what I've read."

"Maybe what you've read into is what has got them pissed off."

"Right Evan. Maybe that shit about the anti-Christ is the cause. Maybe Satan himself was in the bar and trying to pick-up a few souls and I was blowing his cover." His sarcasm was heavy.

The barman changed the channels on the television, got to a commercial and was called away. When the programmed resumed, it was a documentary: "James Elliot Thorne: The Power Years". David looked up at the screen.

"There. There's the real anti-Christ."

"You said it pal." The voice was heavy and emanated authority. David turned and looked at the mammoth and was glad the huge man agreed. "Mackinnley, Frank Mackinnley," as he put forward a bear paw of a hand.

"David Graceson pleased to meet you. Evan, Frank Mackinnley."

David cordially introduced.

The TV rambled on about the life of the ex-president. Nothing that David didn't know. They spoke of Korea, how Thorne's jet was shot down over the Sea of Japan and how he was left to float for five days before he was spotted by a reconnaissance flight. He was the sole survivor. Apparently he was an integral player in the Vietnam "policing action" and how at forty years of age he became the youngest director of the CIA.

"I didn't know that about Korea!" exclaimed Evan.

"The bugger floated for days with nothing but water slapping him in the face. He must have sold his soul for someone to find him out there. What are the chances?" Mackinnley added.

"What about Vietnam?" Evan questioned. "What's this 'integral player' bit?"

David recited as if reading from an encyclopedia. "On December 12, 1960 an operative for the United States government in Vietnam was stationed on a frigate 60 miles east off the coast of Vietnam. The ship's captain was asleep at the time the frigate came under an 'alleged' attack from a Vietcong fishing boat. At four o'clock in the morning the special envoy called Washington and informed the president that the U.S.S. Columbia was fired upon and requested permission to return fire. Permission was granted and the United States of America was inducted into the Vietnam War." David continued, "Yet there was never any evidence of an attack on the frigate. Foreign affairs still has it pegged as a false call. Nothing would have happened if the truth was told by the operative, but the *Times* got a call shortly after four thirty in the morning, Washington time, from a 'reliable source'. They ran the frigate attack story and the nation was outraged by eight a.m. Government intervention was demanded by the public and the war papers were signed post-haste, pre-consultation. Thus by '63, 15,000 of our boys went straight to hell as American casualties escalated even more by the day."

Mackinnley was impressed.

Evan was intrigued. "Who was the operative?"

David looked at Evan and slowly turned to Mackinnley. He lifted his arm and pointed to the smiling face on the screen.

"James Elliot Thorne."

"Don't it figure." Mackinnley shook his head and all three sat in silence.

Evan started at David, "You read all this stuff in a book?"

"No, several books. I took versions from one book then from another and pieced it all together. It's all true. You can research it yourself. You wouldn't believe how much shit this man's involved with, boys. Take the Iran hostages, for example. There is talk that it was all staged for election purposes. How come the hostages were let loose just before the election? That contra crap. You tell me who was director of the CIA at the time? Thorne. Who was vice president when that officer got nailed for the contra scandal? Who led the allied forces to the Middle East? How come the fact that Storm war ended just after Thorne got kicked out of the White House? The way I figure it, Thorne and all his infinite power as president, manipulated the recent history of the United States one way or another and caused nothing but grief to us and the rest of the world.

There was a frenzied tone on the sixth floor. The sound had been piped in and the three intelligence men were nervous. One man came from the window where he stared at the Cerebral Vacation across the street. He walked back to the conference table. His stride was long and confident. Jason Charon was not impressed with the situation. He picked up the half-inch folder on the table and looked at it without opening it. He called off the initial surveillance. His name and history were on the line. Now time was a precious commodity. Before the news hit the end of the three-mile road, he and his team would have to quell this loudmouth. He should have let his man snap his neck in his own apartment or pushed him from the window ledge when he could have. That chance was gone but they were professionals paid to make more opportunities.

From their vantage point a single shot could take anyone out with no questions asked but it was specified that nothing of the sort would happen within a three-mile radius of the club. The lawbreaker laid down the law.

The pictures came through on the computer an hour and a half ago. There were twenty in all so far. One man sitting alone at the bar. A large man who drank rusty nails and didn't say much. Francis Mackinnley. Born March 25, 1948. D.C residence. The Federal Bureau of Investigation. Charon hated G-Men. The next was of a younger man An Evan O'Connor, born April 2, 1969. His residence in Long Island, a social worker. There was nothing on him. The third man he new too well. His name, David Graceson. This was indeed the one. Trouble with a big mouth. The worst kind of trouble, thought Charon. People can't help but listen to big mouths, no matter how irritating and uncouth they are. Now this one was spilling out just a bit too much information. Word of mouth had killed a lot of people. Graceson would be one of them.

Fifteen minutes later the elevator doors opened and the rest of the team had arrived. They sat at the conference table and awaited the plan. Charon headed up the team. He spoke in a low voice. One that resonated deep within his chest and seemed to irritate the ear once it hit.

"We have a problem. David Graceson, a librarian for the New York Library system has alluded to a series of accusations concerning the integrity of this institution and the man it represents. His tactics are deemed to be very annoying to the powers that be and he is to be eliminated. We have twenty-four hours. This assignment will be simple.

He is paranoid. That is his only clue. I suspect that even he does not know that he is a security leak. Plug him before he figures it out. He's an articulate and intellectual young man. Only time will help him. We will not allow him that privilege!" Charon's voice had increased in volume.

This was a priority assignment and was to be successful at any cost. This would take precedence over anything.

It could have happened any where at any time in New York, and it happened outside the Cerebral Vacation. The gunshots from the uzi spat forth death. They came from an old red Buick, by balaclava'd faces accompanied by screams in a foreign language.

The windows of the club were blown out and sprayed all over the interior. The people in the front booths were all hit at least eight times each. The hostess, two waiters and one man at the end of the bar had been taken out along with all the patrons in the front ten feet of the club.

David, Evan and Mackinnley hit the floor in unison as the barrage continued. David looked at Evan and poked him.

"You hit?"

Just a grunt would have been enough to let him know there was hope for his friend.

"Jesus Christ!! What the hell is going on?" Evan just gasped, and then "No, Dave, I think I'm OK. Shit!!!

"Frank! Frank!? You alright?" David looked at Mackinnley who had his gun drawn and at the ready for the assailants to come crashing through the doors. He had been there before and was trained for it.

David was afraid now. Truly afraid for his life. The uzi's were for him. He knew it. And now he had just spent the last two hours talking with a man that was going to kill him. This was certain. Mackinnley saw the fear in David. He felt it more so. He reached into his pocket and pulled out his ID.

"Mackinnley, FBI."

David almost shit his pants. "FBI? What the hell are you doing here?" David screamed at him in a whisper.

"I'm getting god damn drunk and listening to your enlightening biography of James Elliot Thorne!" Mackinnley hissed back.

From the floor no one could see the trio. The gunfire passed and all was quiet in the bar except for the jukebox pumping out Palisades Park.

The sirens screamed up the street as they headed for the Cerebral Vacation. Mackinnley knew there would be far too many questions and far too much of his time taken trying to accommodate some pencil dick from NYPD. "Come on." He tugged at David. The three got up as glass tinkled all over the place. They made their way to the back alley and were four blocks away before they stopped running.

They ended up in a deserted alley, far enough away to be able to stop and try and catch their breath.

"I'm so sorry guys. I didn't mean to get you involved. Evan I'm sorry! Oh Christ what about Elly! God I hope they didn't try the apartment first. Please let her be OK! Please God!!!" He dropped to his knees and tried valiantly to maintain composure.

"What the hell's with him?" Mackinnley prodded Evan.

Evan ignored Mackinnley for the moment and tried to reassure David that all would be all right. It was New York after all and drive by shootings were the norm and it was not his fault He helped David up, visibly shaken and trembling. Mackinnley led them out of the alley and down the street to a bar with Chinese writing on the outside.

They made their way down the stairs and in. The place was fairly dark. A stage in the center of the club had two beautiful oriental women dancing provocatively to the loud music and removing articles of clothing in a seductive display of tease to Aerosmith's 'Rag Doll'. The waitress approached their table at the back and took their orders.

"Three Budweisers!" yelled Mackinnley to get over the noise.

The three sat silently, the two in fear, Mackinnley empathetic to their first shooting and questioning David's plea of guilt.

David composed himself enough to tell Mackinnley of his situation. He told him everything and he rambled. Mackinnley hated rambling, but he put up with it. He wasn't able to come up with any answers. David seemed a bit more at ease by talking to a cop, but still extremely paranoid. Every movement in the club caught his eye and he questioned it. Mackinnley assured him that nobody had followed them and that no one in the club could hear them, let alone speak any English. He was safe for now. They watched the dancers for a few minutes before he again remembered Elly.

"I've got to make a call." David got up and headed for the phone. He stopped the waitress and gave her the universal thumb and pinkie to the ear sign. She pointed to the back hall and he was there.

The phone rang eternally. He let it ring for two more minutes and she finally answered it.

"Hello!" Her voice was hurried. She'd been running.

"Elly, are you alright?"

"Yeah, David. I heard the phone ringing from down the hall and I ran like hell to get it. Then the damn door gave me a hard time and with all these bags I've got, I'm lucky I didn't fall and bust my face."

David thanked all the powers of the universe that she was not hurt. "Listen Elly, listen carefully. Evan and I are OK and this is what I want you to do. You remember when you were ten?"

"David, are you high? What are you up to?"

"Elly I'm not screwing around. Remember when you were ten and you fell off your bike and broke your arm? Don't say where on the phone

Elly, please trust me. I want you to go there now. Bring a change of clothes for all of us and if you've got cash, bring it too. I've got a stash of bills in my black cowboy boots in the front hall. We'll meet you there in fifteen minutes. Get out of the apartment as quickly as you can and take the back stairs. OK Elly, do you remember where?"

"Yes David, I remember, but you're scaring me. What's going on?"

"I'll tell you everything once we meet but for now be careful and hurry. Bye."

"David!! She yelled.

He was just about to hang up when he heard her scream.

"Elly!! Elly!! Are you alright?"

There was silence on the other end of the line. David panicked.

"ELLY!!" he screamed.

"I'm here David...I love you."

She couldn't have said it any softer.

"I'll be there in fifteen minutes. Bye."

David held the phone long after she had hung up. And even as hell was swallowing him up in big painful bites, he felt damn good just now. He walked back to the table where Evan and Mackinnley were discussing something or another and stopped as soon as David had approached.

David dropped a ten on the table and tugged on Evan's shirt. "Listen Frank, uh...I...uh...we would like to thank you for your help, you were a great help. Sorry if I chewed your ear off but we've got to split. Trust me, it's been a blast. Pardon the pun."

"David. Let me help..."

"Thanks but no thanks Frank. Gotta go."

With that, David dragged his best friend towards the phone, down the back hall and into the alley. They headed south at a fast pace to where Elly broke her arm when she was ten.

All hell broke loose on the sixth floor. Charon was caught so off guard by the red Buick's attack, that his head was spinning.

"Who the hell were they?" He screamed at the boys from intelligence.

"How the hell should we know, Charon? It happened two minutes ago and you expect us to know already! Give your head a serious shake."

There was no love lost between any of them. They hated each other more than they hated the boss and even more than the average soul on the street. But they needed each other.

The uproar continued for approximately forty seconds before the film footage and sound was piped in and onto the large screen at the head of the conference table. The screen was split in four.

"Camera one covers the western approaching path along East 53rd. Camera two covers the eastern approach and camera three and four scan the front, one high, one low, both wide angle lenses." Ellis Scillo commentated. He was a specialist in security for the Cerebral Vacation and only the Cerebral Vacation. At this moment he was too frightened to look at any of them let alone talk to them. He continued his briefing. "Here on camera one we get the first visual, red '76 Buick Riviera, New York tags, stolen two days ago. Same MO reported in four other drive by's in the past eight months."

The information was pumping out of the computers and he was reading, translating and placing it in logical order as quickly as possible.

"All four other drive by's had same weapons, uzi's, four of them, covered faces, in out gone. Highly effective. Very messy. There were four of them in the car, all armed. They cruised up East 53rd and opened fire just before the club and kept on firing 'til just after. Here on camera three and four," he froze the image, "you see all four assailants firing. The bulletproof glass had no hope of sustaining that type of barrage. Camera two shows them fleeing at high speed rounding the corner, and gone."

They sat and took notes, as Scillo reviewed the footage over and over. On his sixth examination of the film he got his break. Camera one captured the Buick approaching. The two gunmen in the front had balaclavas on already. But one of them in the back was leaning towards the front, apparently talking with the driver. He did not have his balaclava on yet.

Scillo jumped up "I got one!!" he rejoiced.

The frame was frozen. Sitting at a keyboard, he zoomed the image, adjusted the pixel size and re-zoomed. He utilized the high-resolution image enhancement and filled the entire screen with the uncovered face of the rear seat gunman. There was no comment by intelligence, no of them recognized him.

This was not a problem. Scillo input the image into the main computer and in two minutes the computer regurgitated a rap sheet a mile long. Scillo read from the printout as the printer kept spewing out more and more information. They waited for him to speak. They could wait a little longer the bastards. He decided to share the information.

"Ahmad Mohammed Radjatsingham," he said tripping over each syllable. "Wanted in fourteen countries for various bombings, shootings and several hostage takings. He is suspected in a dozen or so terrorist attacks throughout the world and figures as prime suspect in the assassination of Israel's Prime Minister earlier this year. This guy is a gem. You think we can get him a job?"

The printer finally stopped after eight pages. Copies were made and distributed to intelligence only. The honor guard sat at the far end of the table and awaited instructions. The rap sheet was damn near useless. It would be impossible to find him and they knew it.

They had more problems and Scillo was getting more agitated. He parted the Venetians with his thumb and forefinger and scrutinized the police activity below. He monitored the audio feed via headphones and listened to the aftermath intently. It would be next to impossible for the police or anyone else to find the sub-basement in the Vacation. Still, it unnerved him. From what he could tell via audio feed, there were twenty dead. That alone would make the clientele uneasy and his boss furious.

He walked back to the monitor station and surveyed all camera angles. He concentrated on the front of the club. There at the front booth in the corner, lay King Kahid, his chest ripped apart and half exposed to the world. His head leaned back against the wall as a trickle of blood traced the ridge of his nose and dripped into the cavernous opening of his chest. Scillo wondered why they used color monitors; it was graphic enough in black and white.

The phone rang. *The* phone rang and demanded to be picked up. The shrill continued which was an eternal sin. Nobody dared answer it. If someone didn't answer it before the next ring, the wrath would increase exponentially. Charon grabbed it before the third clamor and brought it to his ear hesitantly. He was not afraid of anything but his taskmaster. He apprehensively addressed the phone.

"Yes, sir?"

The voice was heard twenty feet away by the others at the conference table. There was no need for the hands free mode; they all heard his venomous assault.

"You are far too presumptuous to think!" The authoritative voice bellowed. "If you endear the thought of existence, you will heed this advice. If Radjatsingham is not before me in four hours, you will understand the meaning of eternal suffering. DO YOU UNDERSTAND?"

"Yes sir, very clear sir." Charon was intimidated and visibly disturbed, which caused all the others to become nervous.

The voice persisted. "The man you seek can be found. Search Queens. He will be at, or in the vicinity of, Ali Baba's. You have four hours to bring him to me. There is far too much work to be done. I need Graceson and there is another matter to deal with soon after. You have no time, I have very little of it to spare. Do not disappoint me any more or your heart will be my lunch."

Charon hung up the phone gently. It was suitably black. A harbinger. He was fortunate his leader could not kill him over the phone.

He looked up at the faces around the conference table and barked at them, "Queens! Ali Baba's or in the area! He's around there and he's wanted alive. We have four hours, I want it done in two." It was not necessary to say, they already knew.

The whole room emptied except for Charon and Scillo. They stayed back and stared through the window at the cataclysm across the street. It was a mess in every sense and they had precious time to clean it up.

The afternoon was a whirlwind. The young man in the bar was quite shaken because he believed he had uncovered something that he was not aware of. He was an astute individual, with a perceptive mind, analytical without being preposterous and Mackinnley thought he'd make a great agent. Still the bar room discussion played on his mind. James Elliot Thorne had disappeared after the election just over two years ago and there was no trace of him at all. The government computers had nowhere to send his pension, no income was filed, no sightings, nothing. It seemed far to strange and now that David questioned the man's integrity and scruples, more questions arose in Mackinnley's mind.

The phone rang in his hotel room. He answered it simply "Hmm."

"Mackinnley, twenty men are awaiting your presence at the Hilton. Check out of where you are now and report there. We've got a suite in your name and a conference room which will be command central for operation 'Angelwing'."

How cute, Mackinnley mused. What was with all these code names that sounded as if the director's eight-year-old daughter thought them up.

"I'll be there in an hour." He hung up the phone and packed.

Mackinnley left immediately, flagged a cab down and got to the Hilton in no time.

There he checked in, dumped his bags in his room and headed to the conference room. It was a buzz with activity. Maps of Long Island and the route lined the walls. Twenty additional phone lines were brought in. Power cables fed computers with enough juice to light up a small country. There were rookies sidestepping each other, wrapped up in their respective duties. The entire east wall of the conference room was plastered with photographs of each square foot of the route the procession would take. There were enough holes to hide a tank let alone some deranged lunatic with a .33 and good sight. Mackinnley would have objected to the visit but no one would have listened. The team of photographers was there for two days already, snapping away pictures. Forty more agents were en route to survey the itinerary of the Pope's venue. The only saving grace would be that he would be in the 'Pope Mobile', the infamous bulletproof bubble buggy.

He oversaw the entire operation and made sure the details were all in order. They were and he was covered. He sat in a conference chair and stared out the window. Somewhere out there was a terrified young man running for his life not knowing what move to make next and hoping it would not be his last. He thought of David and wished he hadn't run off so fast without even taking so much as a phone number. He shook his head and hoped that neither David nor Evan would do something stupid and end up in the obits.

A rookie approached Mackinnley anxiously. "Sir, the director is on line one for you. He says it's quite urgent."

"Hmm" grunted Mackinnley as he punched line one.

"Mackinnley, I've got to take ten of your men for two days. I know this is unorthodox but a situation has presented itself there in New York and it demands our attention immediately."

"Hmm."

The director persisted, "An international figure, King Kahid, was just assassinated in a club called the Cerebral Vacation."

Mackinnley felt the chill run up his spine and across the top of his head.

"Send ten out there and they'll know what to do."

Mackinnley was perplexed. He was in the bar and did not recognize anyone that would remotely resemble some dignitary. No bodyguards. No limos. No official uniforms. He was a witness to an international crisis and he saw nothing. He would keep his mouth shut. He thought about David and felt pity for him. The uzi's sought and found King Kahid and they were not meant for David.

"Poor bastard."

-4-

Elly was just about to exit David's apartment when the voices outside drew near, at first loudly, then to a whisper as they approached the door. They stopped outside the apartment and waited. She remembered David's urgency and his warnings of being careful. Was his concern for the voices on the other side? Elly ducked quietly below the peephole. The drapes had been drawn for security earlier and no light passed beneath the door. Then the thunder came. The knock was too loud for Girl Scouts. She shook with every pounding of the door. The voices spoke, ominously, again with the pounding. She was almost in tears as she bit her lip and prayed that they would leave and not break the door down. The voices hushed, she heard a rustle of material and a slip of paper was pushed under the door just in front of her feet. The sounds of footsteps echoed down the hall and the thunder emanated from the next door. Elly finally breathed.

She looked down at the paper and twisted it around so she could read what scared the hell out of her. It was a newsletter from Saint Gabriel's church. It read: *'The New York earthquake was a sign of the imminent doom that the prophets foretold. Holy restitution is the only path to salvation come the great rapture. Seek the word of the Lord and ye shall be saved and brought to Him on gilded wings of angels, trumpeting your arrival to God's Kingdom.'* The address of the church was on the bottom of the leaflet along with a name, Reverend Archibald Deerfield.

Elly almost laughed out loud. The event that almost gave her a heart attack was an invitation to salvation. She folded the leaflet and stuffed it in her pocket. She opened the door only when she could no longer hear the footsteps or voices. She locked it, and made a mad dash for the back stairs and was out the back doors and ten blocks away before she stopped looking over her shoulder for someone on her trail.

She arrived at Riverside Park five minutes before the prescribed time and sat under a tree forty feet from the site, which caused her so much agony when she was ten. She scoped the area for anything suspicious and saw nothing out of the ordinary. She sat back and caught her breath, remembering that sunny summer day; fifteen years ago, when she tried to catch up to her 'boyfriend' David.

He and Evan tried to lose her on their bikes when a dog, a Pekinese or something, not even a real dog, crossed her path and she went over the handlebars, landed haphazardly and broke her arm. .

She chuckled to herself remembering how fast Evan and her 'lover boy' came back to save her. For all the pain she was in, she ignored it as her eyes soaked up her hero, David. As she remembered him then, he came around the bend in the path now, with Evan at his side. She would have run to them if not for the man coming up behind them. She wanted to scream at them but was not sure what to say.

He wore a heavy trench coat and dark glasses. He had both hands in his pockets and was moving quite swiftly along the path toward her men. He was ten feet behind them when she spotted two of New York's finest coming from the flanks. They tackled him, one went high, the other low and they tumbled revealing that the man had nothing on under his trench coat. David and Evan were startled by the commotion and ran.

"A damn flasher. Jesus". Elly was relieved. The coast was clear as she emerged from the shelter of the shade and ran towards David and Evan. She approached David with outstretched arms and kissed him. Evan stood back.

"What the hell is this?" He demanded in a false sense of dismay.

"Jesus Evan, he was closer. You want me to run around David to get to you to hug you instead first so you don't get upset? Give me a break! Here!" She jumped towards him and gave him a hug to rival boa constrictors. She plastered his face with kisses all over. "You happy now?" she asked him.

"Yeah, I guess so. But I now know why I never wanted a dog."

The afternoon was spent running the gamut of emotion. Elly's arrival eased some of the anxiety and they all sat in the shade of an oak.

"Everything go smooth?" Enquired David.

"A couple of bible thumpers scared the hell out of me at the apartment. They dropped this off for you." She handed him the leaflet.

David read it and on any other day he would have laughed at it. He did not laugh. His heart pounded almost too loud. Too much of this was popping up. There in the park he felt the surge of imminent peril. The air was heavy and it bore down on his lungs as he felt the summer heat become hell hot.

It was not his mind playing a game. It was not circumstantial evidence. Maybe, just maybe, all the signs laid down by the prophets in Revelations were indeed the gospel truth. The thought terrified him.

David was left alone with Reverend Archibald's invite to salvation.

He sat with his back against a wooden fence and viewed the park. The sun was still high enough over the horizon to allow for a few more hours of light and warmth. He focused on the leaflet and endured his quest for truth.

The moments hung on infinitely, and the shade of the oak they were beneath drew longer, until they were almost in the light of the late afternoon sun again. David was still distraught. He had stopped shaking an hour ago but his eyes skirted across the park constantly looking for anything that might resemble trouble. Elly had tried to calm him and restore his security but she gave up before she upset him further.

Not more than thirty feet away a destitute man dressed in shabby clothes began an incessant recantation of the wisdom of John. David vaguely remembered the man from somewhere, but could not place the face.

His words were jumbled and confused and he ranted on about the prophecies foretold. He was not a prophet, he told the few passers by, and he just spread the words of the prophets. He was a mere messenger, he admitted. David's vision was trapped by this wretched figure. He thought of Aqualung from Jethro Tull. The man was clad in rags whose original colors were indistinguishable. His hair was long and straggled and his beard was a pathetic knot of dreadlocks. He looked as though his entire life was spent cowering from drunken teenagers bent on punishing him for laughs. He was scarred and some wounds were still fresh. The blood stained shoulder zeroed in David's memory. He was the bum that was shot in front of the library.

He was a beaten man but the physical pain did not stop him from his mission. He was the messenger Fred. His voice was loud and full of purpose. His rambling turned into a descriptive unfolding of the testament. David recognized the words. They were definitely from the scriptures. Fred seemed to become focused on the matter at hand and continued his deliberation on The Word. David sat up straighter and listened intently to Fred's interpretation of the gospel. He quoted with the eloquence of a learned scholar. His words were a fountain of images that splashed the mind with vibrant colors. His speech had texture, rough as burlap and the next moment soft as satin. He was a true linguistic artist. David moved closer towards Fred. He was compelled to listen to this ragged man.

Fred raged: "He will come. Mark the words of John as he professes the arrival of the anti-Christ. Many words are written. Many of you may have read. But most of you laugh at the wisdom of the ages as it is told through His messengers."

The few in the crowd before Fred laughed aloud and waved him off, but Fred continued regardless. "There are many warnings that have been written, and you should know them. Beware he who will lead a great nation and appear dead only to return on the day before Judgment. He is Lucifer. He will have the mark of the beast, and his name will be of the wild. He will be with us on that Day of Judgment to claim the world and destroy all that is good. The Day draws near my friends, for the harbingers have arrived. There will be a great inequality, says the Bible, and so it is. Crimes that were only dreamed of five or ten years ago are reality today. Children killing parents, crimes towards children, atrocities in war, the drugs, the famine, the disease, the beatings...there is no brotherhood of man. Satan has awoken from his expulsion and his evil will run rampant lest we pray and subdue the forces that work to desecrate the work of the Lord. There is pestilence and destruction!"

"There is war with brother armed against brother. There are signs that the earth is changing, twisted in Satan's hands he shakes the foundation. Winds scream out the terror of his name with gale force. The oceans swell with the terror of Hell and flood the land of mortals. Lucifer will not rest. There have been landslides, volcanoes, hurricanes and floods. Here in New York a message that your lives will change for eternity was brought forth in the earthquake from the evil one. Disease and suffering, rivers of blood and the skies will become dark in the middle of the day. These prophecies told thousands of years ago, are all coming true today. If you open your eyes you will see the signs of the times, heed them and you will assent to the Lord on the Day of Rapture.

You may know Lucifer. He may know you. But if you know the Lord you shall be saved. Think of all that is said, and all that will be. Lucifer is the ultimate evil and he awaits the day when he will rule."

David shook uncontrollably as Fred finished his sermon. Tears streamed from his eyes as the Apocalypse was spelled out for him. The Anti-Christ's description reminded David of someone but he just could not place whom.

He scrambled back to Elly and Evan.

"We gotta go now." He was hurried.

"Where?" Evan asked.

"I don't know. We just gotta get the hell out of here."

-5-

The street of Queen's reeked of garbage. The heat seemed to ferment the stench and it pierced the nose and squinted the eyes. The spicy "aroma" of the Ali Baba club poured out of the back door adjacent to the kitchen and favorably complemented the foul street smell. Four of the sixth floor guards entered the rear door with confidence. They threw people aside and ploughed their way to the front of the club. Another group of five drove through the front door and in unison pulled out their weapons. Three un-holstered large imported handguns, the fourth a sawed off shotgun and the fifth brandished what appeared to be a razor-gun from under his dark trench coat. All eyes darted to the front of the club and then to the back when the original four guards wrestled passed the doors and entered the main room. The firepower of the nine could have taken all thirty or so patrons out in seconds. The clientele had all seen weapons, grew up with them, and most carried weapons on their person, but this presence was formidable.

They stared at the outlaws with their hands in plain view.

"Radjatsingham!" The largest gunman demanded.

A wiry man stood up from the back corner table. He was thin with a dark face, hollow but with very defined features. A large, fairly recent scar outlined his right cheekbone from ear to nose. His eyes were as black as night and his hair was thick and curly, but short. His slight frame wound between the tables as he made his way to the front doors. He said nothing. There was no need to, he knew who they were. He stepped closer to the largest of the men and with thumb and forefinger of each hand he opened his jacket to reveal two holsters both packed. Two guards made their way towards him and stripped him of his armament. They threw him against the wall and frisked him thoroughly. Other than a razor nothing else was found. They all exited the club and piled into the three black stretch limos that awaited them outside and sped off north, in the direction of Astoria.

The trip was spent in silence. Radjatsingham smoked some putrid smelling cigarette and enjoyed the ride. Even the three-mile stretch of bone jarring road did not phase him. He was used to it. It hadn't changed in the twenty years he had traveled it on his own.

The limos stopped in succession and the first one had the largest guard open the rear door. He hauled Radjatsingham out by his collar. Being a small man, 140 lbs., he moved quickly and dropped the guard with one roundhouse to the temple. The large man was out cold as the rest of the guards scrambled, with weapons drawn, to subdue the wiry one. They kept their distance but Radjatsingham ignored them. He made his way to the lavish doors and pushed them open.

He walked past the large stone wheel in the foyer and down the hall to the second door on the right. He walked in without so much as a sound. The library was a collectors dream. Hundreds of thousands of books lined the shelves. Some were old, very old, others quite new and without a creased spine. It was impressive. Behind the expansive desk, the back of a chestnut colored high back chair faced him.

The voice was direct and assertive driven by purpose, "You are an embarrassment to the profession."

"I did what I do." Radjatsingham conceded.

"The job was not done," The voice retaliated. "You destroyed my club, you eliminated a very important client, got the FBI involved and the target was not hit!!" The voice was over-bearing.

The self-righteous Radjatsingham lost his arrogant air in the commanding presence of James Elliot Thorne.

He had arisen from his chair and stared out the window. With his back to Radjatsingham he blasted him with a barrage of degrading and sometimes bigoted jargon, still without looking at him. Three minutes passed and JET turned his face away from his humbled guest.

"If I didn't need you for another job I would rip your heart out and piss in your chest. You caused me a great inconvenience, one I am sure you would more than gladly recompense." JET turned his head and burrowed his eyes into the soul of the terrorist. Radjatsingham tried to free his gaze from the hypnotic eyes but couldn't.

"Sit." commanded JET.

They sat for an hour and discussed the past, the present and the future plan. The mood lost its intensity and Radjatsingham slipped back into his imperious attitude.

The discussion ended and JET excused Radjatsingham to a guest room to retire for the evening. He picked up the phone and called his secretary. "Send an invitation for the gala to a Mr. David Graceson. Make it for two. Complimentary. His address is on file. Send it out immediately, I want it there in twenty minutes." He hung up the phone gingerly and contemplated the next evenings campaign dinner.

There would be at least a thousand supporters all more than eager to rub elbows with each of the other one thousand dollar-a-plate paying benefactors.

Graceson would be there.

He was sure of it.

The crowd was still growing outside the Cerebral Vacation as the morbid rubber-neckers distorted themselves to catch a glimpse of a splattered head or an exploded abdomen. The police had cordoned off the perimeter eighty feet from the face of the club yet the crowd was pressing it into sixty. Horses were brought out and the thought of fire hoses crossed the mind of a few officers, but with an aggravating bullhorn and some fed up cops, the crowd withdrew and allowed the area to be secured.

The three box shaped Ford Fairmont's lumbered through the crowd. They stopped just far enough to respect the crime scene, and from within emerged nine Federal Agents. They all wore the tell-tale Ray Ban aviators and cheap suits. None smiled, even the rookies looked robotic. They were efficient in their work. The most senior addressed the police officer in charge and seized command and jurisdiction. The nine, systematically gathered clues and evidence. The constant clicking of a camera was the backdrop for the detective ballet. Fifteen memory sticks were burned off within five minutes of their arrival. Bags were filled with any thing that had a remote chance of being physical evidence, distances were measured and bodies examined. The King lay in the corner booth and the blood had stopped pouring from him a half an hour ago. A swamp five feet in diameter had formed underneath him on the rug.

They systematically worked from the front window back. One covered the street scouring for any shred of evidence; a shell, a tire track.

More than two hours were spent dissecting and investigating the club. The leader of the team was a Hispanic, Enigo Gonsalvez. As he supervised the rest of the detectives, he sauntered around the place, noticing it's pretentious style, deciding it was not a place that he would frequent. He walked slowly about the club, towards the back. There was no one with him, or about him yet he felt crowded.

He ventured into the spotless kitchen surveying the surroundings. Out of instinct, bred from time spent in bars, both professionally and recreationally, he decided to check the johns. That's where the shit goes down, he thought to himself with a smile.

The staircase to the heads was extravagantly adorned. Engraved oak handrails and an oriental rug, probably worth a small fortune, covered the stairs. Crystal lamps illuminated the stairwell. Even the walls were covered with expensive fabric and paintings with lavish frames. Gonsalvez shook his head and wondered why any one would go to that much trouble to decorate a staircase.

He got to the bottom of the steps but was compelled to turn around and look up at the staircase again. There had to be something down here that would explain the lavish decor. It was a bar, he thought. Average nightclubs are not this luxuriant, nor do they have a king with no bodyguards around for that matter.

Gonsalvez stared at the floor. From the wear of the carpet, he determined that most people turned to the right after descending the stairs. He looked that way and saw a short hall way and an exit door. He turned behind him and saw both male and female washrooms.

This was odd. Most traffic in a club would tend to beat a path to the washrooms not an alarmed exit. He contorted his face with query, approached the door and peered at it. He looked up at the ceiling and then back at the stairs. He drew out a floor plan of the establishment in his mind and this exit did not fit into it. Geographically it would be difficult for it to be an authentic exit. He pushed at the bar handle and an alarm screamed but the door did not yield. He released the grip and the alarm silenced just as a distinguished man appeared at the foot of the steps. They were each surprised in encountering the other. The man was trembling ever so slightly, and Gonsalvez picked it up.

"You work here?" Gonsalvez prodded.

"I am the manager Sir. May I help you?"

"You let me ask the questions," snapped Gonsalvez. "This is a huge fire hazard, I'm sure your aware."

"This exit is no longer in order sir," the manager offered. "Since the fire of the establishment next door three years ago, that door has been welded shut. The hall that leads from there to the rear of the building was destroyed and thus not accessible in the event of evacuation."

Gonsalvez stared at the manager, then at the door. It was welded. The welds were visible and he was embarrassed that he did not notice them. He was about to accept the managers' excuse when he noticed the sweat on the managers' forehead form a drop and land on his lapel. Gonsalvez swung around and touched his hand to the door.

"Three years ago?" Gonsalvez had the Cheshire smile.

"Yes, sir, three years ago." The voice rattled.

The federale turned his head, and still smiling added, "Then why the alarm?"

The manager was lost for words and shook his head. There was slight panic in his eyes, and he loosened his collar. Gonsalvez was onto something. He called on two other detectives as the manager stayed frozen in his assigned place.

The three scrutinized the door. It had to open.

"Even if I have to blow the shit out of this thing with plastics, I'll get it open sir," the rookie promised.

"It'll open without plastics Wilson." Gonsalvez loved the spirit of the rookies. "Take some of that 'kick-ass' energy of yours and get a rescue unit over here with some tools and we'll crack this sucker open."

"What is it Gons?" said the other agent.

"Who the hell knows?"

-6-

The evening news was plastered with Cerebral Vacation coverage. Pictures of the exploded facade were strewn over every channel and reporters had a heyday with the prospects of more terrorist activity in the Big Apple.

King Kahid was dead; a very ostentatious and blatant assassination attempt was successful and took the life of a favorable dignitary. The reasons for his murder remained a mystery, with no group assuming responsibility. The FBI was on the scene, they kept repeating over and over again, as if that comment alone would revive the dead King.

The paranoid trio watched the news from in front of an electronics store. David stood in awe at the footage. He hung his head and almost cried. Why would he have thought the uzi's were for him? How could he have got wrapped up into such a tight paranoid net that distorted his vision of reality? He was ashamed and embarrassed and could not face his friends.

They stood in front of the window for ten minutes, watching all the angles, which that specific news team could expose. With each minute David shrunk more and more until he wished the earth would open up and swallow him whole.

"David? You alright?"

Elly was indeed an angel. Caring in spirit, comforting and selfless. He loved her and God, he was glad she was there now.

"I can't believe all this. I feel like such an idiot." He crouched on his haunches and buried his face in his hands.

Evan stood there and watched his friend fall apart. It was indeed sad, but there was nothing that he could say. He was angry with him. He just shook his head and tried not to spit on him. He turned and walked up the street without saying a word.

"David." Elly whispered, "David." Her voice became stern. "David, look at me." she cradled his face with her tiny hands. Her tone changed and she spoke gently now. "It's all over. Let's just go home and we'll have a few drinks and everything will be just fine. Come on."

Her voice was as soft as an angel's smile and it warmed his fragmented soul. She was right; it was all over, if it had indeed started at any point. He arose from the ground and together they walked, arms around each other until they caught up to Evan and all together, they made their way back to David's apartment.

It took them twenty minutes to reach the three hundred year old structure and with each step David assured himself that all of this was a self induced state of hysteria, brought on by a literal translation of Revelations. He would definitely be fine. He looked over at Elly and smiled his first smile since the shooting.

The door of David's apartment was intact further reassuring all of them. It was as stubborn as always and only gave in with a hefty kick. It flew open, crashed into the already holey wall and revealed a very elegantly addressed envelope on the floor before them. They all stared at the envelope.

"How do you rate a Sunday delivery?" Evan questioned cynically.

"It has no stamp Dick Tracy." David retorted as he bent to pick up the letter. It was weighted, only because of the gauge of the paper. It was addressed to 'Mr. David Graceson and Guest' with no return address on its face.

"Who's it from?"

"Evan, do I look like Kreskin?" David peeled the back of the envelope open and removed a distinguished invitation.

"Looks like someone wants me at a real fancy shmancy party."

"Who?" squealed Elly.

“David read aloud, *"Dear Mr. Graceson and Honored Guest. You are cordially invited to attend the grand opening of the James Elliot Thorne wing of the Metropolitan Museum of Art. To honor Mr. Thorne for his generous contribution to the museum. Monday, June 29th, Cocktails 6:00 PM, Dinner 7:30 PM. Formal attire. By invitation only."*

"Hmmph. Fancy that. David, I didn't know you were a socialite. And here all this time I thought you were just an average Joe."

"Give me a break Elly. I can't go to this thing. I'd love to go but I'm just not into it. Thorne's probably gearing up for the elections and it will be a political dog and pony show."

"Hey, I like dogs and ponies David, lets go." Evan was eager.

"What do you mean, 'lets go'? Maybe Elly would like to go. What do you say Miss Elly?" David bowed at the waist and arced his arm to his right side. "Would me lady join me at the gala event of the century?" He mocked the English gallantry.

"Well, sir..." Her English accent was dreadful, "...I'd love to but not this time, I'm not much on politicking. You two go. I know you'll both love it. You'll need tuxedos, you know, and they didn't give you too much time, either. You'll have to pick them up first thing in the morning."

This is exactly what David needed to pull him out of his state. He was a culturo-phile. He loved the arts and history and was intrigued at what Thorne and his money hungry ancestors had stolen from masses in history. It would be safe around the ex-president David thought. He was still a little edgy though.

With just one shot the entire structure could come down. There were a few surfaces to air missiles in the ammunition room on the sixth floor. Scillo was tempted to use one now to rid the headache that was coming to a boil across the street. He was scared, damn scared of the outcome. He wore a path in the marble floor from the window to the bank of monitors divulging the inner movements of the Vacation. He panned each monitor, especially the one showing a young Hispanic G-man in the basement. The computers had already spit out his bio and there was absolutely nothing incriminating or useful. Only living member of the Gonsalvez family, no wife, no kids nothing they could use. Scillo ran back to the window just as the emergency rescue team arrived.

"Shit!!" he yelped.

Just then the phone rang. He grabbed it, not realizing which phone it was. "Yeah! What?" he answered belligerently.

There was silence on the other end, which aggravated Scillo even more. The vulgarities were a microsecond away when he realized he was on *THE* phone. He swallowed hard to keep his lunch from spewing. His apology was stuck behind the tuna sandwich in his throat and did not make it out in time. The voice howled on the other end and Scillo was paralyzed with fear.

"This emergency is far too critical for me to kill you where you stand, but mark my words you will be dead before the week is over! You will complete this assignment and I will exterminate your pathetic soul myself. You miserable fuck, listen to me very carefully and perhaps I will spare your worthless existence. We cannot stop them from discovering the 'Club' but we can stop them from finding out who owns it. I want you to create a loop in the files. You have minutes, I assure you. You will create eight different companies and holding groups that will each be owned by each other. The first company owning the second who owns the third etc. until the eighth company will own the first. Do you understand me? It's like Eshers staircase you imbecile, no beginning no end. Do it now!!"

The phone had come down so hard on the other end that it sounded like gunfire. Scillo winced and dropped the phone every so softly in the cradle, as if the other end could still receive. He ran to the computer terminal and blazed his way through corporate initializations and start ups and within ten minutes eight different companies, all with history and all with monies in their respective accounts, were scattered all across the world with the soul purpose of hiding the origins of the "Club" across the street.

The phone rang the instant the final company was completed. He picked it up before the first ring ended and addressed it with precise manner and respect.

"Yes, sir." He suppressed the gag reflex.

"Well done."

"Thank-y---" *Click.*

Scillo didn't care whether the man hung up. He had his life. He walked over to the window, now curiously not in fear. The rescue team had just finished unloading the last of their own arsenal; steel saws, Jaws of Life and a variety of other power tools that would in no way find the link across four lanes of traffic.

The bureau commandeered several floors in four hotels in the downtown core. In total there were eighty-five agents assigned to 'Angelwing'. The National Guard was also tossing in a platoon of two hundred, as well as half the NYPD, to aid in the protection of the holy man. Mackinnley was impressed with the muscle that the government bestowed on him but still could not fathom how effective it would be. They had strategic plans for the entire route, starting from the pious man's hotel the next morning, to the airport the following night. There were thirty agents assigned to escort the Pope from the airport this evening and stand by his side until the morning shift relieved them. It looked good in theory, but Mackinnley's skin crawled with the notion of only 48 hours of planning going into this fiasco. If it succeeded, then he would be amazed and the boys in Washington would think nothing of it. The bastards. Who did they think they were fooling? It would be a panic from the moment the Pope landed until the moment he took off, and Mackinnley would sweat off ten pounds in the duration.

The conference room in the Hilton became a hive of activity. Too many phones rang, too many people asking too many damn questions and far too many rookies banging into each other. The fever was nowhere near breaking.

Another rookie approached Mackinnley, another damn question, he thought.

"Sir, Gonsalvez on line three. He says it's urgent."

Mackinnley liked Gonsalvez. They were partners for two years before Mackinnley got moved to his supervisory position. He was a good man and one of the best, yet he worked hard at being better. Mackinnley liked that. He punched the flashing light on the phone and snatched the receiver.

"Gons, What have you got?"

"I'm not quite sure but I think you should get down here. Things are starting to get very strange. This is no ordinary nightclub boss. I'll explain when you get here.

"I'll be there in as soon as I can."

Mackinnley grabbed his jacket and was out the door.

He arrived at the Vacation within fifteen minutes and the club was nowhere near how he had remembered it. He wondered whether the assailants had returned for more rounds of gunfire. The walls were either ripped down or in the process of being so. There was a chain saw of sorts starting up somewhere in the back of the club, and NYPD just stood back and was glad someone else was going to catch shit for this.

"Where's Gonsalvez!" Mackinnley bellowed to be heard over the racket that persisted in the club. Someone pointed.

At the bottom of the stairs Mackinnley scoped Gonsalvez. The chain saw stopped its screeching and Gonsalvez made his way to his superior. "That was damn fast boss, what'd you do, fly? This is the status. We arrived. What, three hours ago? And it was all routine. About forty-five minutes ago it goes completely haywire. Fletcher and Whiteside are gathering evidence up front, when Fletcher hits the bar. The bullets flew pretty heavy and kicked the shit out of the front end of the bar. That's where the bartender bought it. There must have been half an inch of booze on the floor from all the broken bottles. The back of the bar got destroyed and the mirror on the back wall gets smashed. And Fletcher finds a glint coming off the back wall. There's no mirror left to glint, so he looks closer and low and behold, he's staring into a lens. He pulls it out but no camera. All fiber optics. He looks further down the bar and every three feet another lens. They're positioned like that all the way around the club, both sides. That's not all. We start tearing the place apart and now we find microphones, everywhere Mac. Unidirectionals, multi-directionals, some very sophisticated equipment. Whoever wired this place knew exactly what they were doing.

"Where does it lead to?" Mackinnley probed.

"We haven't got that far yet, but we're working on it."

"What gives *here*, Gonsalvez?" asked Mackinnley peering over his colleagues shoulder. Gonsalvez winced and hoped that the rescue boys could save him now by discovering something beyond the exit door, they didn't. Gonsalvez was on his own.

"You forget how to get out of here Gons?" Mackinnley was not one for jokes and this comment was laced with cynicism.

The entire story was related to Mackinnley. He admired the intuitiveness of the young agent but still poked, "I'm sure you inquired with the staff how this door opens?"

"No one will say a word. They are all scared as hell. Something big ass is down here and they would rather remain loyal to the secret than to talk to us. That fuels my hunch. There's got to be something beyond that door that will help us with the Kings death."

Mackinnley asked the rescue team to take their machines and move back. He stepped up to the door and inspected it himself as he searched for any indication of how to open it. After two minutes he called the rescue boys over and told them to crack it.

The heavy-duty chain saw screamed to life and screeched through the door. The work was not easy because of the gauge of the steel. They cut a hole approximately one foot by one foot, enough to get a look as to what lay behind. The final cut was made and Mackinnley grabbed a flashlight from the belt of a rescue worker and stepped up to the hole. He peered into the aperture and called back to Gonsalvez.

"Gons. Do you remember one of your compadres, Geraldo?"

Gonsalvez was vexed. "Don't tell me it's a Capone's vault? Shit! Mac I could have sworn there was something there. God damn!"

The Hispanic temper came out in a fine display of fury. Gonsalvez picked up a sledgehammer that stood beside him and ploughed the wall to the left of the fire exit.

Mackinnley jumped back and howled at his colleague. "Hey Gons. Relax pal. It was a hunch and a damn good one. Sometimes you hit and sometimes you miss. That's what it's..." Mackinnley's pardon was interrupted, by what could only be described as a vision.

"Mac? You OK?"

Mackinnley smiled and offered Gonsalvez his restitution.

"Capone's vault, Gons." Mackinnley waved a finger at the cracked cinder block.

A soft glow emanated from the cavern created by Gonsalvez' rage as he caught a glimpse of the 'vault'. From his vantage point, all Mackinnley could scope was a swatch of rug and a table leg. He made his way up off the floor and instructed his colleague.

"It's all yours Gons. You started it you might as well finish it."

He stood back as Gonsalvez swung into the wall with the conviction of a grand-slam homer. The wall groaned with every pounding and Gonsalvez did not let up until he made enough room for a truck to pass through. When he stopped all that could be seen was the soft lights cutting ribbons through the dust. Even with the adrenalin pumping him, Gonsalvez did not move. Impatience and eagerness caused loss of life in his line of work. The concealment of this 'vault' would lend it to being booby-trapped. The men stood and gazed into the cavity. There were no laser security lights that cut through the dust but still they stood rooted.

The vault was opulently appointed. The floor was sunken thirty feet and above the hall hung a majestic crystal chandelier whose very size reflected decadence. The hole had welcomed them to a balcony of sorts high above the floor and from their vantage they gawked at the grandeur of the hall. It emanated wealth and prosperity. The furniture was elegant and auspicious, from another era, antique, luxurious. The paintings that adorned the walls were magnificent examples of renaissance splendor. Mackinnley stood before the opening in the wall.

"Oh my Christ!" was all he could utter. "Gons, what in God's name is this?"

Gonsalvez was as equally perplexed. "I haven't the damnedest idea but this is one hell of a place." He dragged his gaze away from the room reluctantly and turned to his superior. "You gonna go in?"

Mackinnley still dumbfounded by the discovery, shook his head very slowly. "No Gons, not yet." His words were dream like. "Get that manager over here on the double. We'll send him in there first to see if the coast is clear."

Within seconds the now not so distinguished gentleman stood before Mackinnley. He was minuscule before Mackinnley's massive frame and he still shook.

"Y-y-yes s-s-sir?" The voice of the manager cracked.

Mackinnley nodded his head towards the hole in the wall.

"Explain." His voice was deep and resonated with rule.

The shaking man turned his gaze to the hole in the wall and then back to Mackinnley. He was about to speak when his gaze shifted to the ceiling at the foot of the stairs. His words were lodged and would not be freed. He hung his head and was speechless.

"Talk to me!" roared Mackinnley in a tone that even made Gonsalvez hold back from pissing his pants. The manager crossed his hands before him and sobbed.

"What the hell is this? " He grabbed the manager by the back of his head and threw him into the gaping wound in the wall. The manager stumbled and landed on the railing guarding the balcony seats. Still he said nothing. Both Mackinnley and Gonsalvez now entered the great hall slowly, still awaiting a barrage of gunfire to wash all over them.

They excused the manager and went about the hall inspecting the entire square footage. From the main floor the perspective was overwhelming. The chandelier was massive and everything else was done up in such style as to remind one of Buckingham Palace.

There was a round stage at the far end of the hall that was floored with red satin. It spanned thirty feet in diameter. Plush couches surrounded the stage with tables before each of them. On either end of the palatial room, seventy-foot bars stood spotless awaiting patrons seeking refreshment. Mackinnley made his way towards the north end bar and noticed a menu. The board was thirty feet long and inscribed with intricate calligraphy. Written upon it was a list of entrées, drinks and something that raised Mackinnley's eyebrows. The list of more than twenty-five illicit drugs did not shock him half as much as the 'Sexual Smorgasbord' did. He stepped closer to see half of the Kama Sutra on the daily special.

No prices were indicated on either menus and Mackinnley wondered how much the 'Swiss Stewardess Slurp' would go for.

He ventured behind the bar as Gonsalvez explored on his own. The bar had the most expansive selection he had ever seen. The finest in drink graced this Mecca of libation. An enormous refrigerator with glass doors covered the back third of the bar. Mackinnley opened one unit and discovered what appeared to be twenty kilos of heroin, kilos of cocaine and assorted cannabis products. He shook his head and expected to see Rod Serling behind him. He turned away from the fridge and scanned the length of the bar. There was no sight of any cash register anywhere.

"Gons?! What the hell is this place?"

"Mac I don't have a God damned clue. But I'll tell you one thing. The people who frequent this establishment are definitely playing with fire. There is a program on that far wall with times and stars for certain sex shows. Live ones!

The fridge is full of dope." Mackinnley added. "There has to be at least fifteen million in shit in there. I can't believe it's all in the open like this. It's private for sure and we must be pissing off a hell of a lot of people by cracking this thing. Get on the horn and get me info on this joint. Who owns it, when it was purchased, anything that can help us. Call the Hilton and get Douglas down here with a CPU, modem and get me a cellular phone down here I've got some serious work to do." "Boss. I hate to cut you down, but what about the Pope. He comes in tomorrow morning."

"Shit!!" Mackinnley scrambled to uncover his watch. "Get me that phone and let me worry about that."

Mackinnley worried about that. He worried about this. He worried about the King's countrymen. Above all else, Mackinnley could not shake the cameras out of his mind. They were watching the whole thing. He knew it. They may be frightened, or maybe nervous but somewhere out there, someone was watching every move he made and he wondered just who it might be.

-7-

The private, wide-body airplane touched down on an empty runway at LaGuardia airport, as the turbines wailed. The craft approached the terminal and stopped almost a mile from any building. Thirty seconds later an envoy of official vehicles surrounded it and awaited the signal to move. Like pilot fish, they clung close to the plane, as it and its holy cargo were escorted to the hangar that awaited them. As they neared, the front line of cars sped up and reached the doors before the plane. Forty agents scrambled from their vehicles and, with guns cocked and at the ready, stood guard at all vantage points of entry. The massive doors drew open in perfect time, as the bird drew closer. The cockpit disappeared into the crack between the doors as the plane slowly moved into its bay. The wings just grazed the still opening doors. Once inside, the vessel was completely surrounded by the awaiting regiment of the National Guard.

There were stringent precautions being implemented for the new visitor, he was vulnerable here. In a city packed to the gills with enough lunatics per capita, nothing was sacred here, nothing.

Mackinnley's plans were running smoothly. In all there were one hundred agents and National Guards that covered security. They saw to it that the Pope touched down, disembarked, and got to his hotel safely escorted.

The stairs made contact with the jet and the latch was thrown. The door was pushed open and two rather large grizzly looking Pope cops stepped forward. Each one stood on either side of the door and awaited the next of the entourage. Another four gorillas exited the craft next along with two others armed with briefcases. The four were very heavily armed and moved far more cautiously than the first two. The four armed men split and two stayed at the top of the stairs as the second two advanced halfway down. The men with briefcases descended the stairs and stood by the awaiting limousine. Once all had cleared the doorway the original two covered it with their immense frames and stood there inflexible.

The men with briefcases scanned the awaiting limousine with a variety of electronic detection devices. They were a blur of activity as they covered the entire vehicle. When both were satisfied with their findings, they started the vehicle, spoke into their headsets and signaled clear.

There was some movement behind the human wall but it was indistinguishable. Then the original two moved slowly and with purpose. The Pope was in transit and they were his shields. With eyes alert they constantly scanned the perimeter for sudden movement, maintaining only ten inches between themselves and the pontiff. The one set of heavily armed guards followed behind the holy man, again only inches away. The other guards had made their way to the bottom of the stairs and waited.

There were no cordial greetings of any sort, no ground kissing. The rear door of the limo was opened and the Pope manipulated his robes and entered.

All was going as smooth as planned. His Grace could thank God for that, or Mackinnley.

Mackinnley got his phone. No sooner had he powered it up when it chirped to life.

"Yeah."

"Mackinnley? Are you out of your goddamned mind? I specifically told you to *send* ten men down there to take care of the situation, not for you to personally inspect the god damned place. Your responsibility is with 'Angelwing' and 'Angelwing' alone." The director was irate. Mackinnley was defiant.

"A situation has presented itself."

"I don't give a shit if Hoffa showed up there inside a piñata. You have a god damned responsibility and I'll be damned if you or anyone is going to defy my orders! How The hell you got a supervisory posting in the bureau with your damned insubordination Mackinnley, I'll never know! But listen damn close to me Mackinnley, you've got minutes to get back to your assignment or so help me I'll have your fat hairy ass in a maximum security prison with the words 'I hate niggers' tattooed to your forehead, so fucking fast you'd wish you had never been born. Do we understand each other?... Do you understand me *Francis*?"

Mackinnley was not impressed with the director's cheap shot. His given name was taboo and everybody knew that. He could have justified his presence there but he knew he was wrong for coming to the club.

"Yeah, yeah I understand...suuurrr." His insubordination was blatant.

"You damn well better. Now get back to the Hilton now!"

The director did not wait for an answer as he hung up.

Mackinnley almost hurled the phone across the room. He looked at Gonsalvez, who must have told someone what was happening and it got to the director.

Mackinnley said nothing of the matter to his colleague.

"Take over here and find me something. Gons make this thing real big." He winked at Gonsalvez and was up the stairs on his way out though the hole Gonsalvez made.

"Hey, Gons!" He called from the balcony steps. "Find the real door will ya?"

Gonsalvez mock saluted him and feigned a baseball swing.

Mackinnley cursed his way past all the work in the club and wished he could be there when the hammer came down. This smelled so juicy that he actually salivated. But lost his appetite once he approached the spot he was sitting at several hours ago.

He stopped where the stool he'd been on lay. At the time he did not have the opportunity to witness the actual destruction that had occurred. A fair number of rounds had found their way to within six feet of him and his drinking companions. Any closer and there would be a different six feet separating him from the action, any action.

He lit a smoke and looked at the bar. Straight in front of his perch he saw the glint of the camera eye. The lens, still intact in the wall, stared back at him with the leer of a Cyclops. Mackinnley stared back at it as he inhaled deeply from his smoke.

"I can't see you yet you bastard, but I'll find you. I swear to God I'll find you." He exhaled the smoke from the corner of his mouth and shook his head. He scrutinized the Cerebral for a while longer and then sauntered to the front door. In the far corner the carcass of the King was draped with a yellow cover. Mackinnley drew deeply from his filtered Camel and thought of the dignitary there in civilian clothes. It had been determined that four men at the next table were his entourage. Strange, he thought. He looked toward the back of the club and visualized the palatial hall. "That's where you should have been drinking, Kahid." He commented under his exhale. Mackinnley shot his gaze back to the cloaked King. He butted his smoke out on the floor and reflected on this thought.

If any one would be partying in the back room of this particular club then it would certainly be a king. The hall's obscure location dictated discretion and privacy for the most discriminating tastes. Maybe, Mackinnley thought, the hall was a club for the corrupt, rich and the inconspicuously famous.

Mackinnley amused himself with the thought of joining a club like that and laughed at the thought of fees. For a club that had no cash registers, 15 million in dope in the fridge and 'Swiss Stewardess Slurp' on the menu, registration must be at least ten lifetimes work. He walked out of the club shaking his head at the thought.

His Cadillac was parked within spitting distance of the club. He sank in the plush seat and fired up the vessel. He slowly pulled out into traffic and made his way towards the Hilton. He noticed the car behind him right away but gave it some more time before he acted. He turned right here and left there and after the fifth turn he realized it. The large sedan was trailing him. He took three more turns at random and it was still there, hot on his tail. From the last turn he made it out to be newer model Lincoln. Black. He was just about to floor it and lose the tail when he turned right and they turned left. Mackinnley was irked and as he studied the rear view he caught the Hilton out of the corner of his left eye. He cut the wheel hard and just caught the driveway in time to avoid wheel damage.

It was well past midnight when he stopped into the conference room. All seemed to be in order. The Pope had arrived intact and was delivered to his hotel. That's all Mackinnley wanted to know.

Positions were all posted for the next day's procession and an early morning meeting with NYPD and the National Guard was slated. There were a few minor details he worked on for an hour and made his way up to his suite just after one AM.

In his bed he thought of the club, of the cameras. Did they know who and what he was? Someone owned the place and they were sure as hell wealthy and powerful.

Then he thought of what he didn't want to think of. The black Lincoln. Was he being followed or was he suffering from David's contagious paranoia?

The night had swallowed him whole. The sleep had blown a breath of death into his veins and taken him away from all of life's infinite turmoil. As dreams of Swiss stewardesses undulated in his brain, the floor creaked. He shot up in bed and reached for his revolver. Its absence was nothing short of paralyzing.

He was entombed in the darkness of his room and was blinded with fear. In all his years with the bureau, Mackinnley had no reference to fall back on now. The floor did not creak enough in his room to reveal the location of his intruders. The assailants approach was detected too late.

The cold of the steel razor touched his throat just above his clavicles. Before is reflexes could kick in and react to the assault, his throat was slit with a slow deliberate stroke. The blade was so sharp; it made the incision almost painless. The right carotid was severed first and his brain immediately became light. His gurgling lungs coughed up his life's essence and his breath came short and in gasps.

By the time the razor ended its journey across his throat, Mackinnley fought for each second of consciousness. Just as his heart pounded out an ever-diminishing S.O.S., he scrambled to the floor and screamed with a voice that emanated as a hiss from the gaping wound in his throat. His tongue fell through the hole and he choked on it. He coughed hard and clawed his way to the door. As he reached up for the knob it disappeared into the darkness that surrounded him. He reached up and his hands came back empty.

His head wobbled and fell back and instead of hitting the floor, it hit his pillow.

His adrenalin jolted him out of the most realistic dream that he'd ever experienced. The sweat poured from him and he shook uncontrollably. The clock on the nightstand announced the third hour of the morning and Mackinnley was not about to close his eyes again for the rest of his life.

After a shower, that washed most of the nightmare away, Mackinnley headed out the door of his hotel room and ambled down the darkened streets. The night air was humid and clung to his skin like cellophane. He was still uncomfortable with the dream and now, standing on the corner two blocks from the Hilton, Mackinnley saw a vision of a black Lincoln as it rounded the corner. His senses were betraying his mind and he became angry with himself.

He stood on the corner and lit up a smoke. The night yielded no breeze, and the temperature was a balmy 85. There was little traffic on the street with him.

It was just after four in the morning, when the Times van dropped the newspaper off in the box. It weaved from one side of the street to the other and back again as it stopped to fill every box with the paper.

Mackinnley stepped back from the curb when the van approached the box he was standing beside. The brakes screeched and echoed down the desolate downtown streets. A young man jumped out of the back of the truck and moved quickly to fill the newspaper box, before the driver took off without him.

This day was guaranteed to be a day to remember. He hoped the Pope ordeal would pass without incident. What Gonsalvez would come up with today was anyone's guess. King Kahid's death would stir an awful lot of commotion, and would the black Lincoln visit him again?

The notions were relentless and he tried to shake them from his head. This time was his own. And he would enjoy it before the rigors of the working day would rob him.

The peace was short lived. Somewhere off in the distance the unmistakable sound of gunfire was heard. It occurred west of him at least half a mile off, but the sound of the shots echoed off the windows in every store around him. Mackinnley stared in the direction of the blasts but saw nothing. The towering buildings obstructed any possible view of the event. Seconds later the faint sounds of emergency vehicles were heard wailing towards the source of the thunder. They became inaudible as the seconds passed and whatever danger there was, it was far enough away from him. That was all he cared to think about it.

He lit another cigarette and parked himself on a storefront widow ledge and rested his elbows on his knees. His cigarette burned slowly in the muggy night air and he fought to keep it alight with deep inhales. He exhaled hard and tried to hit the newspaper box with the smoke. He watched the smoke just reach the box and hang there in space.

He saw a partial headline of the Times through the smoke, and it grabbed his attention. '*MAN SOUGHT IN KING'S ASSASI*' is all that he could make out. He got up from his position, stretched and cracked his joints while tossing his smoke off to the side. Loose change clinked in his pocket as he sifted for correct change. He hauled out only half the coins and hoped that he caught the right combination and not just damned pennies. He pumped in the coins and freed a paper from the box. He picked up the paper and what he read almost made him throw up. The entire headline exclaimed '*G MAN SOUGHT IN KING'S ASSASSINATION*'. He unfolded the paper, which revealed two pictures.

He vomited hard and fast. The King laid in the corner booth of the Vacation in one picture and beside it a picture of himself, on the floor of the Vacation with gun pointed to the front of the club and towards the King. The picture was crystal clear and although out of text, it was incriminating enough to make Mackinnley wonder if he had actually taken part in the execution.

He read the story fast. Blah, blah, King Kahid, Cerebral Vacation, assassination. He found the meat of the story and read with apostolic conviction. "It is suspected that a team of terrorists accompanied by an agent of the Federal Bureau of Investigation spearheaded the attack on the club Cerebral Vacation. King Kahid was killed from a gunfire barrage that also took the life of ten others. The prime suspect is believed to be an agent for the FBI, a one Francis Mackinnley."

The retch arose from the bottom of his pelvis and hurled his intestinal contents from both his mouth and nose. Twice again the spasms of regurgitation overtook him. He dropped to the ground just as the screams of sirens came shrilling around the corner. Three more cruisers approached the Hilton as he ducked into a nearby alleyway. He stayed there for five minutes longer until all personnel had entered the hotel. He looked up and down the street and then turned into the alley. Just before submerging himself in the darkness of the alley, he saw another vehicle approaching.

This one moved far slower and stopped almost a hundred feet from the hotel. Mackinnley fought back the impulse to heave as the black Lincoln slowly cruised by him in the darkness.

The two un-assuming friends walked along the crowded street of the downtown core. The tuxedo rental was up three more. The weatherman was right for once and the sun shone in a glorious display of brilliance. There was not a cloud in the sky to shield one, even temporarily, from the heat.

"It's too damn hot, man." Evan wiped his forehead as he griped.

"Even so, you can't complain about what it brings out." David nudged his friend and signaled him to look left.

"Nice. Very nice. Reminds me, you hungry?" The long tanned legs crossed the street towards them. They belonged to a most beautiful Scandinavian looking woman who was amply blessed.

"Damn, do I love the summer!" David professed.

"What's not to love?" Added Evan.

They entered the men's wear store and were fitted and furnished with their respective tuxedos. Fifty-five minutes later they hit the streets with garment bags in hand and ventured into a coffee shop for a cup of joe.

Ethel's was a quaint little dive. The decor was original fifties. The counter was the original malamite and the stools that imparted the clientele, were a gaudy lime green with some tartan that neither one could look at long enough to describe. They parked themselves at a booth and ordered two coffees and toast. The music was nostalgic. It sounded pre-Chuck Berry, but they enjoyed it.

"Pretty strange, you getting that invite to this thing David, wouldn't you say?"

David looked at his friend. "No. Not really. Evan, I've been a lifelong member of the New York Cultural Appreciation Committee for maybe fifteen years. Remember my parents thought it would enrich my mind, way back. Not a real classic present when you're eight. I can appreciate it now. It has its perks you know. I get to see any exhibits I want, before the public. I get in free and since we give book lists to the museum for background on displays, Donna Dimitriou, the curator, lets me in for private showings. David winked at his friend.

"In the museum? Get out of here. Where?" Evan was piqued.

"Where else but where you find the big bone." David laughed at his own joke. The more he thought about it the harder he laughed. "Evan, you're such a pigeon."

He chuckled some more and tried to drink his coffee. He just got the cup to his lips when he spotted the front page of the *Times* being read at the next table.

David almost dropped his cup in his lap. "Holy shit!!"

Evan saw the look of terror in his friend's eyes and spun his head around to see what alarmed him. "Oh my God!" he exclaimed.

"G-man sought in Kings assassination? Evan, That's Mackinnley!!"

"Shhhhhhh," Evan beseeched. "Keep it down."

"Quick, give me some change, I'll grab a paper." David reached out to Evan.

Evan scrounged his pockets and tossed David the allotted change.

Seconds later David ran through the door with the paper. He placed it sideways on the table so they both could read.

"It is Mackinnley! Hell that's me beside him. Well parts of me. See? I can't believe this. You believe this?"

"I don't know David. It could be true. If he was FBI, don't you think he would have stayed in the club after the shooting?"

"Gimme a break. You think he really dusted the King, or was even involved in it? You're not serious?" David implored.

"Things were too damn crazy in there for me to remember if he shot anyone, David. Still I can't figure out why he would leave. Look here. It says here that he returned to the club six hours later. Maybe he left something there that would incriminate him. I doubt that he knew he had been photographed, when he returned. If he was innocent, don't you think he would have told someone right away that he was there? David, I know this guy helped us out, or so we thought, but it just doesn't fit."

David's head swam. He could not believe that Mackinnley was guilty of anything other than probably drinking on the job. The 'hit and run' theory was one of some substance and validity and David hated it. But Evan had a feasible view. David's paranoia re-surfaced ever so slightly. The picture of Mackinnley was cropped in such a place that his own face was cut from the picture. Just three more inches to the left and he would have also been sought by the authorities.

Pictures don't lie, he kept telling himself, but he was there and if the picture in the paper had included him, then he would definitely be suspected of involvement. That was a lie.

"David." Evan nudged his friend's elbow. "Yo David!"

David was transfixed by his thoughts and had a hard time hearing his friend.

"Yeah, what?" He responded from within a haze.

"Look David, there's nothing we can do about this so don't worry about it, OK? Let's just get out of here and forget about him." Evan tossed a five on the table to cover the tab and they were out the door, with David still gawking at the photo, disbelieving the accompanying story.

The street greeted them with typical New York hospitality, rudeness. David, still with his face in the newspaper, side- stepped a mailbox but did not see the lamppost. He walked right into it. Evan was on his right, ogling some woman in a translucent sundress and did not forewarn David of either sight.

David's head rung with the impact, and it brought tears to his eyes. His brains spun and vision became blurred. Had it not been for the mailbox behind him he would have landed on his butt. His brains were a kaleidoscope of colors accompanied by a high-pitched dog whistle sound. He leaned against the mailbox and twisted his neck from side to side. It ached, as well, from the jarring. He stretched his neck back and rubbed it. While looking up, he saw a man leaning out a window. The figure was familiar. His mind raced from scenario to scenario to try and verify the identity of this man.

His hair was short and his face, in profile, was unremarkable .It was not until he leaned forward in the window that David recognized the man. He was massive, 280 maybe 300 pounds. Those arms that rested on the window ledge were the give away. It was the behemoth that had visited his apartment.

"You bastard." David mumbled under his breath, lest the mammoth had extraordinary hearing. "You're the one that started this incessant paranoia in me, you muscle-headed bastard."

Across the street at the Palace, a crowd gathered and police and soldiers maintained a perimeter for which the crowd to adhere. The situation was very official looking with limousines, and police cars and an abundance of police escort motorcycles. Just in front of the doors of the hotel, a vehicle that would be fitting in a cartoon was parked. It had a huge bubble on top of it.

David wrenched his sore neck to see what the commotion was all about. The crowd grew larger by the second and gridlocked the street with pedestrian traffic. It continued to swell as the anticipation of the event was almost peaking. His neck ached, and, he wanted to twist it, but feared he would miss the spectacle. So he suffered and stared towards the hotel entrance.

Five minutes passed and David could endure no more. Whatever the event, he would see it on CNN He twisted his neck finally and tipped his head back to ease the pain. There above him, in the window where the behemoth had stood, he saw the barrel of a rifle.

The cry was on his tongue to forewarn anyone, just as the crowd screamed with delight. The awaited personality exited the hotel.

"The Pope?" David screwed up his face with perplexity. "All these people out to see the Pope?"

The thought was so painful it overcame his physical ailment.

"The Pope! God!! No!!" David howled.

David's need to see, over-rode the pain in his neck, as he looked up in time to see the smoke come from the barrel of the rifle. His sight was redirected back to the pontiff, whose head had just snapped back in a violent jerking motion. The crowd shrieked in unison as the Pope dropped to the floor and the back of his scalp was propelled back into the lobby of the hotel.

No sooner did the gunshot go off; than did the rifle get hurled into the crowd from the behemoth's window. David watched the last half of the rifle's descent. It traveled a good thirty feet before it hit three people and then the ground. David looked up and the window was empty.

Upon hitting the ground, the rifle discharged another round creating pandemonium within the crowd. The authorities made a mad scramble for David's side of the street but with all hell breaking loose, it was almost impossible to get there. By the time the police made there way to the far side of the street, the assailant could have been in Rio, David thought, as he stayed frozen in his spot.

Two officers ran up to David and grabbed him. The shock over took him and he fought. His motions were too sudden and his head pounded intensely. He could no longer hear and he blacked out.

-8-

The night was spent in an abandoned building that had been condemned at least twenty-five years ago, yet was spared the indignity of demolition. There, Mackinnley tried to figure out his situation.

He knew that he had not fired any bullets. He had checked in the alley just to convince himself, the clip in the Berretta was full. He was being set up by whoever owned the bar and that infuriated him. He would not be able to investigate until the autopsy on the King proved that they were all uzi bullets that hit him. Even so, the photograph implicated him and because of his impudent attitude towards the NYPD pencil dicks, he was up to his ass in trouble. He knew he should have stayed in the bar after the shooting. He knew he should have told Gonsalvez, at least, that he was there when the bullets ripped apart the bar. He knew that there was no where to go now that his picture was splattered all over the front page of the *Times* and every syndicated press affiliate, not to mention every damn television news broadcast. He had made his own Most Wanted list.

He had tried to get hold of Gonsalvez, but he was not taking any calls in the middle of the night. The keys for the Caddy were on his dresser in the hotel. He couldn't rent another car; they would need a credit card and I.D. There was no hope of getting out of the city. Every avenue would be covered. He knew their game plan and checked his strategies and ran them parallel with the predictable ones of the bureaus. He was stuck, as a wanted man, in a city where he knew no one. There was only one prospect for him. The young man with the paranoid delusions, it was a hell of a choice but the only one he could even remotely consider.

It was nearing noon when he gambled a move out of the hovel. He was still presentable in his shirt and jacket and he was thankful that he had his Ray Bans for anonymity. The morning sun was blinding even with the glasses. He cowered is way to a phone booth.

"What the hell was his last name?" He mumbled to himself.

He rifled through the phone book, "Grays? Graydon? Shit!!"

He was furious. Why did he have do drink so much in the club, he cursed himself.

"Come on baby. Come to papa. Graystone?" His eyes perked.

"David Graystone. That's it!" As he whipped through the pages of the phone book he came upon Grayston. There was no D. Graystone.

"Damn!!"

He picked up the receiver and dialed information. The voice came across the line like it was interrupted from a washroom break.

"Information, yes?"

"Graystone David. He's on the east side by the river somewhere." Mackinnley could only remember bits and pieces from the conversation in the strip club.

"Just a minute please." The voice replied with forced politeness. "I have a listing for a D. Graystone in Harlem."

David was not from Harlem, Mackinnley was most certain.

"That's not it...," he growled. "Keep checking."

"I have only two other listings, a D. Grayston, in the Bronx, and a David Graceson with no address listed." She responded with that disdainful tone.

"I'll take them both." He grumbled rudely.

She gave him both numbers and he dialed them in turn. Neither line answered. He hung up the phone after the second call, so hard that it cracked the receiver.

"God damned kid!!"

He walked slowly and inconspicuously towards a coffee shop that looked uncrowded. He kept the glasses on, ordered a large coffee and two donuts and left to amble on towards the vicinity of the east side.

The heat was welcome in his house. The windows were painted shut and there was no air-conditioning. It was stifling in the study where Thorne spent most of his time. He was happy today and that was reason to worry. He seldom smiled when not on the campaign trail, and today he was elated. This worried Radjatsingham.

He had known Thorne for twenty years and worked solely for him for the past fifteen. In all that time he had only seen him smile thrice, In November '64 and when that other King was dethroned and on September 11 when six months of planning had paid off for him. Those times were cherished but not as much as this hour. Radjatsingham wished he had that last assignment. Instead the man with the smiling face saved him for another rinky-dink pop.

The room was too hot for Radjatsingham. He squirmed in the heat and fought for each breath. It came labored and heavy and induced a wheeze from his lungs.

Thorne wanted his guests uncomfortable and on edge. It gave him even more power over the meek that entered his haunt. All were weak. Radjatsingham was no different than the rest, he had no conscience and he had no direction. There was nothing in his heart, and he was easily swayed from the path. Thorne could spot them a mile away. The so-called rebels, the ones that stood for nothing and fell for anything. They had nothing without Thorne and anything was better than the nothing that engulfs the soul. Most of them were empty, of mind, of soul, of character. Thorne found them and they became the un-dead. He gave them purpose and relevance. In turn they did his work, no matter what the cost, for they were committed and commissioned and indebted for eternity. He was their savior and they worked without question.

Standing there, suffering in the contemptuous heat, the devout Radjatsingham waited with baited breath for Thorne to command the details of future events.

"The plan is simple. You will aim and fire and you will eliminate this man." Thorne tossed a photograph at Radjatsingham.

The wiry one twisted the picture upright and studied the face he had seen before.

"There will be a very fine line and an extremely close call. Your timing will be flawless and the precision you are praised for will be its most accurate. From the balcony in the main hall, you will do your work. The seating arrangements are such that your sight will be open. We have been through this enough times that it should be understood. Everything that you will need is already in place and awaiting your mastery. Failure is not an option. Understood?"

Radjatsingham nodded affirmation.

Thorne dismissed Radjatsingham. He ran from the den and out into the gardens where the ninety-eight degree afternoon sun cooled him. He could breathe again. Thorne watched him from the window and wondered how Radjatsingham would ever get used to hell.

The night would prevail. His nemesis would be abolished and the approach to a new day would be within grasping range.

He awoke to the wailing of the sirens. He was lying on his back in the back of a police cruiser and his head throbbed. He sat upright at the exact moment the vehicle came to a screeching halt. He did not hear the tires squeal but he felt the cage as it smashed into his forehead. The dog whistles sounded again in ears.

The policeman apologized profusely as he offered David a hand to get out of the car.

David's head reeled with confusion. He wondered if he was being arrested. He looked at his hands and saw no handcuffs binding his wrists. Was he arrested he thought to himself. He stared at the officer with childlike inquisitiveness.

"You'll be fine pal. Don't worry." The voice was consoling but offered no real answers.

"Am I arrested?" David inquired.

The youngest officer laughed aloud. "You want to confess something?"

His humor indicated something that did not involve pictures and prints. David looked up at the officer lending the helping hand and saw the Emergency sign of some hospital behind him. He immediately drew his hand to his head and could hear the dried blood flake off his forehead. He removed his hand and saw traces of fresh blood that covered it.

The emergency nurses were attentive and polite and David wondered where all the horror stories ever originated. They processed him and the proper medical attention was administered quickly and with care. Five stitches later, and some painkillers to boot, he was discharged. The injury did not necessitate admission or observation.

On his way out of the hospital, the youngest officer noticed him and ran to his side.

"David, is it? How you feelin'?"

"I'll live." David responded reluctantly. Friendly cops worried him.

"You remember anything from this afternoon in front of the Palace David?" The cop prodded.

The Pope. David had forgotten the event. His mind raced and with every lap his head hurt. He brought his hand up to his forehead and squinted his eyes. "Yeah, I think so." He whispered.

"Where I was standing, above me, there was this guy I had seen before. He was in the third, maybe forth floor window. I was rubbing my neck after I smacked that fucking post, and I stretched my neck and I saw this guy. Anyway, I looked across the street and saw the huge crowd. I stretched my neck again and there was a rifle barrel in the window where this guy had been. I looked at the Palace and the Pope stepped out. I thought the Pope? I looked up and there was smoke coming from the rifle and then the Pope went down."

The story was retold en route to the station. David had agreed to give a statement and look at some mug shots. In the station four other officers and two who were introduced as FBI questioned his statements. After fifteen minutes of questions, they stopped and spoke amongst themselves.

From behind all the ringing in his ears, David heard the federal agents talking.

"Do you think they could be connected?" posed one.

"Could be. Two huge hits in twenty four hours."

"We do have a connection," added the first.

"Get outta here. Don't tell me you think Mackinnley has something to do with the Pope?"

"Why not? He mapped out the whole schedule and security. Who else would know where and when the man would be most vulnerable? He was in the Cerebral Vacation when that shit went down. I tell you he's our link. Put an APB out on him and dedicate every agent in New York to this. Go!!"

The other agent left the room.

"Mr. Graceson, can you recall anything else?" pumped the federal agent.

David did know more. He knew that Mackinnley did not fire a round in the club. He knew that he wouldn't have been involved with the Pope's ordeal.

"No sir, not that I can think of now. Everything I can remember I've already told the other officers." David stirred in his seat and rubbed his neck.

"Alright Mr. Graceson, thank you very much for your help and should we be needing anything else we will get in touch with you."

"Anything I can do to help, sir." David offered and was out the door.

"Can we offer you a lift Mr. Graceson?"

"That would be great, thanks."

"What a crazy world." David muttered to himself as he entered the building. He thanked God the elevator was working today and it took him to his floor without event. In his apartment he read the note from Elly. She wondered where the hell he was. That Evan and she were out looking for him and that if he got home before either of them, then to sit down and don't move until they got back.

David felt bad that he had not called them but they would get over it he thought just as the phone rang.

"Elly?" David asked into the receiver.

"David Graceson?" The voice was deep yet hushed.

"Maybe." David replied cautiously.

"It's Frank." The voice still remained hushed.

"Mackinnley?? Is that you?" David was anxious.

"Yeah, it's me. Listen, I have to meet you now." Mackinnley lost the hush and spoke with more urgency.

"You're in deep shit, Frank. Where the hell are you?"

"West 72nd and Riverside. Is that close to you?"

"Close enough. There's a park about just behind you. I'll meet you by the fountain in five minutes." David felt the rush and his head swelled with the onset of the paranoia again.

"I appreciate this David. I'll see you in five."

David hung up the phone wrote a note to Elly, and was out the door.

In the nation's capital Harold D. Jacobs was taking the kicking of his life. In all his years as director of the Federal Bureau of Investigation, he had never received such a going over, as he was this day. The phone in his office had not stopped ringing from the moment the *Times* had come out, and just when the fervor seemed to ebb the Pope was assassinated in broad daylight.

Both New York incidents were attributed to the Bureau and the last call Jacobs took was half an hour of flack from the president.

From between calls he screamed at his secretary to call New York and get a hold of Gonsalvez. In twenty seconds his secretary got the lines connected.

"Gonsalvez? What the hell is going on up there?" He hollered into the phone.

"Sir...uh...Gonsalvez is not here sir." The rookie's voice cracked twice and was noticeably shaky in response.

"Where the fuck is he?" bellowed Jacobs.

"Sir...he...uh...he is on site at the Cerebral Vacation, sir."

He punched the hook on the phone and dialed the cellular that was originally delivered for Mackinnley. The phone only rang once before Gonsalvez had answered.

"Yeah, Gonsalvez."

"Jacobs here. What in the name of Christ is going on up there Gonsalvez? In twenty-four hours the Bureau has taken more shit than in the past three decades. Where's Mackinnley?" The director was livid but tried to maintain his perspective.

"Haven't got a clue, sir. He was here when you spoke to him last and I haven't seen him since."

"Find him! I want him before NYPD finds him. I want his butt ugly face in the Hilton by nightfall and if you have to, shoot the son of a bitch to keep him there. I'll be there in the morning. In the meantime, get yourself back to the Hilton and take over command immediately."

Jacobs was incensed. Mackinnley was a pain in the ass right from the beginning. He had always had a hard time with him. Since that bungled episode with the Santanista's, the heat was on and never let up. Mackinnley was an excellent agent but never failed to drag the bureau through any shit that occurred. His file was loaded with letters of reprimand concerning conduct unbecoming. Insubordination topped the list with eight letters alone. But he also had letters and praises from too many high-ranking officials to justify his ousting from the bureau.

Jacobs looked over Mackinnley's file. He was with the bureau for almost twenty years and had caused the bureau embarrassment in every one of those years. Too many times the special investigations team was sent to hound-dog him for suspected espionage and wrong doings but all had come up clean. Mackinnley knew how the bureau worked and could have got around them. Jacobs didn't like him and to see him pay for the Pope's assassination would be his crowning glory.

He snatched the phone from the cradle and plugged at the keypad. His secretary answered and he calmly asked her to get the number for Jefferson Fleming in the State Department.

Fifteen seconds later, and he was connected.

"Hello?" The voice seemed bothered by the interruption.

"Jeff, this is Harold Jacobs. How are you?" Jacobs simulated sincerity.

"Harold! How are you and what do you want you old trout?" The two began to speak without formalities.

"You may have heard about New York. We have a situation that is proving to be quite an embarrassment to us all here. I need your help on this. You think you can spare an hour this afternoon?"

"Three o'clock is clear with me. I'll see you here then."

"Three is fine. I'll see you then." Jacobs hung up the phone and wondered if that was a shot he just took from the tight ass.

"Old trout?" He shook his head and got himself organized for his afternoon meeting with the state department's Fleming.

-9-

The Cerebral Vacation was fast becoming a dismembered limb of the sixth floor. Scillo watched in horror both from the window and whatever screens were still transmitting from the within the club. He watched as the FBI was dissecting seventy million dollars worth of social club. He was hurt more than angry.

Behind him Charon sat at the conference table with the rest of intelligence. They prepared the security for the gala that evening. In all there would be enough firepower to take on a small army and win. Fifty-five men would encompass the museum and its main hall where dinner was to be served.

Charon was meticulous in detail and from the plans given to him by Thorne every conceivable facet was covered. There were metal detectors being erected at all entrances as they spoke and nothing would pass security.

Scillo whined from the monitor. Most of his lenses were discovered now. Even the ones in the women's washroom were uncovered. He winced with the pain of not being able to witness the activities there any more. He had attained so much pleasure from the female hygienic habits.

Charon looked at Scillo with a pathetic grin. "The washrooms?" He gave him disgusted look.

"Yes." Scillo groaned, mortified at the loss.

"You're a very sick man Scillo. You need help." Charon shook his head and returned to his security project. Scillo surveyed the scenes in the club. His sights were drawn to the bar where some agent had just dug deep into the wall.

"Shit!!" He jumped out of his chair with his eyes riveted on the screen.

"Now what?" Charon looked over. "Did they discover the men's washroom too, you sicko?"

Scillo looked over to Charon with the color draining from his face rapidly. In seconds Scillo was gray with fear.

"What?" Charon felt the consternation and was drawn to the monitors in haste.

"What the hell is that?" He pointed to a black box on screen four. It was no bigger than a cigar box and had four large cables entering it from the one side and one small cable exiting another, or vice versa Charon could not tell.

"Scillo what is that thing?" There was mounting concern in his voice and if Scillo was afraid of the finding, he felt that he soon would be as well. He grabbed Scillo by the scruff of the neck and shook him out of his hypnotic trance.

"Answer me you bastard!! What is that box?" Charon was tempted to shoot his associate but would never solve the riddle if he did.

Scillo looked at Charon with trepidation. Afraid to speak aloud lest Thorne had the sixth floor wired as well.

"That box connects all the fiber optic leads and converts them from a digital to an analogue signal. At which point it can be sent from the club over a phone line to this office. Here we have the analogue to digital converters, which allow us to view what is happening over there without being there. We were going to go with a satellite feed but the risk of being discovered was greater via that route than by phone lines." Scillo had terror written all over his face.

Charon was confused. Electronics were not his forte and the words that Scillo spoke meant nothing to him.

"What the hell are you saying? In English man, English!!"

"What I'm saying is, that box is connected to a number of phone lines. Those phone lines are connected to certain offices, which pick up the signal and change it into a picture. Understand so far?" He patronized Charon.

"They are also connected to a certain individual whom we all cherish and adore, who I believe, would not want the public to know that he owns that particular club. Still with me?"

He was trying Charon's patience. If not for the severity of the situation he would definitely have killed him.

"So you're saying that box links the club with this office and with Thorne?" Charon inquired and waited for a negative reply that he knew would never come. His head leaned toward Scillo and turned to catch the 'no' he waited so dearly to hear now.

"Yes." Scillo hung his head and waited for the bullet.

"Seventy million dollars goes into the construction of that club and you hook up surveillance through the fucking yellow pages. Are you out of your fucking mind? I can't fucking believe this!"

Charon was rabid. The powerful voice blasted the frail Scillo and the worst was yet to come.

The phone rang. Scillo stared at it as the second ring took an eternity. He inspected Charon's face for mercy. It was not there. The door was too far to make a run for it, and the window was too strong to give for an escape. The monitor revealed the black box being tampered with and the second ring still had not sounded. He placed his hand on the receiver and heaved it to his ear.

"Destroy the entire building now, club and all, I want it rubble within minutes."

The voice was calm and soothing. There was no need to panic, Scillo thought. He breathed again.

The voice continued, "Scillo?"

"Yes sir?" He humbly replied.

"You're a dead man. Give me Charon." Again the voice was calm.

Scillo handed the receiver to Charon who nodded, "Yes, sir," looked at Scillo, "Yes, sir." and hung up the phone.

"What did he say?" implored Scillo.

"He said that he'd see you later." With that Charon pulled out his revolver and shot Scillo twice in the face.

There were few people in the park that afternoon. It was large enough to take a walk in but not large enough to get tired doing it. Mackinnley sat in an isolated section of the park under a huge oak tree. The shade covered him from the sun and he sat close enough to the tree to look as though he were part of it. He was secure in this spot as he awaited David.

The five minutes that were anticipated turned into ten, then fifteen. An anxious feeling grew in the pit of Mackinnley's stomach, as there was a flicker of doubt whether David would turn him in to the authorities. The fifteen minutes turned to twenty and Mackinnley got scared and was about to flee when he noticed a young man wandering aimlessly. His sights were not fixed and he scoured the park for something or someone.

Mackinnley focused behind the young man, then around him. There seemed to be no shadow on him. Still, he let David walk by him and from the shadow he waited for anyone else that may be following him. Two minutes later Mackinnley emerged and made his way cautiously towards David. He approached the young man and did not speak until he was beside him.

"Don't look at me." Mackinnley instructed.

David fought the urge to turn his head.

Mackinnley spoke as he passed. "Meet me at the Blackmore Tavern." Without turning his head he followed the path around the bend.

David slowed down once Mackinnley passed him. His stride became far more leery and he just then realized the true severity of the situation. He figured that Mackinnley was being tailed or that he himself was. Although the sun shone upon him and the temperature exceeded the 95-degree mark, he shuddered with a chill that felt like death breathing down his neck.

His instincts took over and he wrenched his neck to look behind him. Everyone looked suspicious and he cursed Mackinnley for the feeling of paranoia that stirred in him again.

He walked toward the Blackmore but passed it. He did not look directly into it but just caught Mackinnley's gaze as he walked into the coffee shop next door. There, David ordered a coffee and grabbed a seat at the back and watched the front. His heart raced and his eyes hurt with the strain of concentration. He wondered if he was playing the game correctly.

After five minutes in the coffee shop he found the back door and slipped into the pungent alley. There he hoped the Blackmore's rear door would give and allow him entry into the smoke filled pub. It succumbed to a gentle tug and David slipped into the English inn. Taped pipe music was playing greeted him.

He found Mackinnley at a booth facing the front. He shuffled himself into the seat across from him and forced a smile.

"Hey Frank. How you doing?"

"David, What the hell happened to you?"

"This?" He crossed his eyes and tried to focus on his forehead. "I had a run in today. It's nothing. What the hell happened to you? Tell me Frank, so I know. Did you do it? Are you involved?" David was almost afraid to ask.

"No, David." Mackinnley responded flatly. "I'm the fall guy. This whole thing went down and I was in the wrong place at the wrong time."

"How the hell did they get you on film?"

"The whole god damned place is wired, David." Mackinnley exclaimed.

"Wired? You mean with microphones?"

"With microphones, cameras you name it, all kinds of surveillance. You can't fart in there without someone recording it. The place is monitored all the time."

David's apprehension engulfed him.

"Then my paranoia is well-founded."

"A paranoid," Mackinnley interjected. "Is one who is aware of all the facts?" He smirked.

"This is no joke," David snapped. Still maintaining his hushed tone. He raised his head and looked about the pub. He wondered if this place was safe. If any place was safe.

"Tell me about it. Your ass is not on the Most Wanted list. I'm a god damned fugitive. The way I see it, we've upset someone and they are out with a vengeance to seek retribution. Who or what, I don't have the vaguest idea, but they mean serious business."

David stared at Mackinnley. "I don't mean to rain on your parade Frank, but maybe it's just you." David's mind raced as he searched for any possibility that didn't include him in the whole scenario.

Mackinnley became silent. His history crept up on him. The years with the bureau had been rough and any number of individuals or organizations would love to see him rot in a federal penitentiary.

The words of Jacobs came resounding in his ears. Something about tattooing his forehead and throwing him in a federal pen. Mackinnley slumped in his seat and leaned back.

"Hey Frank, it's just a theory. It might be all bullshit. I don't know. I'm new at this detective crap."

"Out of the mouths of babes." muttered Mackinnley. "You've got a damn good point. There might be some validity to that thought. A lot of people don't like me, hard as that may seem, and one of them is playing for keeps. We've got to get..."

"Whoa! Frank. What's this 'we' crap? It's not me they're after and I'm sorry if I'm a party-pooper but I'm not any part of this 'we' thing."

Mackinnley came back with the Wisdom of Solomon. "David," He spoke sternly, "You are into this thing whether you like it or not. You were in the club when the King was shot. You left the scene with a prime suspect. You never reported it to the police. And I'll tell you another thing you little Twinkie, If 'they' choose, 'they' could have your picture out there on the front page incriminating your skinny little butt as well."

Mackinnley didn't have to yell. His eyes cut through David's soul and he felt the intensity of the large man’s anger.

David sat back in the bench, trying to move as far away from Mackinnley as he could. His escape was limited and he endured the reproach.

"I don't need this aggravation, Frank. I just got over an excessive dose of looking over my shoulder. I don't need any more. I can't help you. I'm sorry." He slowly got up from his seat.

Mackinnley grabbed him by the shirt and hauled him back down in his seat. "Listen to me you chicken shit. You will help me. What I'm asking is some damned compassion for your fellow man. You know damn well I didn't fire a single round in the club and that someone is letting all this shit fall on me. Well Davie, I'll tell you this. If you don't find some kindness in your soul, I'll call the authorities myself and confess that you were an accomplice to my adventure. You like that?"

"You wouldn't."

"Faster than that. If you don't have it in your heart, well David, I can't find it in mine. Your lily-white butt in prison would definitely be in demand. Think about it." Mackinnley let go of the shirt and sat back. All that could be said had been. All that he could do was wait for a response.

David looked at Mackinnley, and even though he hated him now, he knew that he was right. He could testify in a court of law that Mackinnley did not fire his gun and to abandon him would not be right. After all, he did help the two of them before.

"I'll help you the best I can Frank. What do you want?"

"I need a place to stay tonight, and no I won't bother you. Where is there a little motel around here?"

"About five miles from here there's a little place called the Knotty Wood Hotel. It's usually quiet."

"Fine, I'll check in there and I'll meet you there tomorrow at nine in the morning."

"You want me to go to the desk and ask for Frank Mackinnley's room? I don't think so." David was getting snotty.

"What's your mother's maiden name, smart-ass?" Mackinnley was getting riled.

"Gabriel." David confessed. "Why?"

"I'll check in under the name David Gabriel, that way you come and ask for me without any problems, OK?" Mackinnley spoke in a condescending tone.

David glared at him. "Yeah, yeah, I understand."

"Done then, I'll see you tomorrow at nine.

"It looks like I don't have a god damned choice."

"You don't. Be careful."

David left the pub by the back door and walked halfway down the alley. There he found another restaurant door open, he entered and then exited out the front door. He flashed a quick glance toward the Blackmore and then walked quickly back to his apartment.

The walk took no time, but it felt like he aged ten years in the process.

The traffic had started moving again outside the Vacation. All lanes were open except for the curb lane, which was still draped with police tape. There were very few people still left to gawk at the proceedings within the club, most of them had left when all the bodies had been taken out. Outside, three uniformed police officers kept a watchful eye out. All was quiet as the forty or so federal agents worked on dissecting the club for clues.

From around the corner, the smoky gray Fairmont cruised at the speed limit. As it approached the bullet-ridden facade of the Cerebral Vacation, it slowed down. As if loaded down with rubber-neckers, it almost stopped in front of the club.

The officer took note of the vehicle and suspected some other tight assed federal agents on their way to help in the investigation. He looked away and sought a smoke from one of his partners.

The Fairmont did not stop. It rolled in front of the club at a painfully slow speed. From the back seat, the anti aircraft rocket was hoisted and aimed at the building. The officer saw the weapon and his reaction time was quick enough to jump out of the line of fire as he watched the Fairmont squeal away.

The other two officers didn't have a prayer. The rocket came right for them and they dropped to the ground in hopes of avoiding being hit. It flew into the club and detonated more than two thirds of the way in. The explosion had set off a charge so immense, that the entire face of the club was launched off the building. Any windows that were left were blown out to rain down on the street.

The screams within the Vacation were short lived. The club belched out a series of explosions that shook the entire block. Both buildings on either side succumbed to the blast and surrendered their weight and structure to the detonation.

Within seconds, the three buildings collapsed into a heaping mountain of debris. There was nothing but dust and wind as the buildings sighed their last breath of life.

The buildings across the street were showered by debris from the blast. Even structures four blocks away rocked with the force.

It took fifteen minutes for the dust to clear enough for one to get a look at the ruins. The rescue teams had arrived and they stood about not knowing where to start.

Fire engines sirened their arrival in stereo with the police, but neither teams knew where to begin. To find any life in the mess that stood before them would be next to impossible.

-10-

The office was ill lit. It was fastidiously clean, yet had a dank, musty aroma emanating almost perpetually. Whether it came from the furniture or the carpet one could not tell. The air was stale and still as if nothing ever moved in the room to create chaos.

It was much smaller than the position would dictate, but Fleming called it home. In all the years he occupied the position, twenty-eight in total, he had never changed one bit of the decor. He had not so much as hung a picture on the drab, dingy beige walls.

His desk was meticulously organized with everything in geometric sync. Nothing was ever moved or worked on in anything other than ninety-degree angles. Even his paper clips were stored in a parallel order on a desk magnet. He went over everything at task five times before signing it, sending it or filing it.

Jefferson R. Fleming was far too nervous to give anyone reason to reprimand his work. He lived in fear of being fired, and losing his pension more so in the last three years. Thus, his days started at four thirty in the morning and ended near ten at night in order to complete the day's work.

He always worked with the door locked and the phone off the hook. Interruptions unnerved him and nothing would be allowed to come between him and his assigned tasks.

He looked up from his desk at the clock on the wall. It was five minutes to three. He finished his work, checked it for the fifth time and filed it, as he usually did, on the right corner of his desk.

At precisely three, he unlocked the office door and swung it open. Jacobs should have been outside waiting, but he wasn't. Fleming should have guessed it but hoped that after all the years of knowing him, Jacobs would, for once be on time.

As if the wish was heard and granted, Jacobs rounded the corner casually. He chatted up Fleming's new secretary, a cute little redhead. He spotted Fleming and revealed his watch.

"How do you like that Jeff? Three o'clock on the button."

"You got lucky Jake. Come in." Fleming invited the director into his office.

"What's on your mind?" He enquired.

"Right to business, good, I have no time for idle chit-chat. We have a major situation happening in New York."

"I heard all about it. Should have been giving out popcorn with that show Mr. Director." Fleming was not without humor; it was just his timing that was ailing.

"There's no time to get cute Jeff. I just got my face chewed off by the righteous boy upstairs and I don't need any more right now. What I need are some damn answers. Someone owned the Cerebral Vacation, the club that got destroyed. I want to know who that someone is. I want it all confidential, a personal favor. No one can know what for, I just want it."

"One of your boys was in on it, as far as I gather. Find him and he might know." Fleming remained haughty.

"We can't find him. Damn it, Jeff! The place got blown off the face of the earth half an hour ago, along with forty of my men and god knows how many civilians. I got a report of at least fifteen million in drugs alone were stored there and just as they were about to give me some important information on something, the phone goes dead in my hands. I hear later that a damn rocket got fired into the club. Damn drugs and rockets and dead diplomats and an agent in the thick of things, Jeff I'm begging for some help. Get one of your computer hot shots on this and dig damn deep to find me something that I can use. I believe that I can nail Mackinnley, but I want the people behind the club even more." Jacobs was frantic and there was desperation that echoed in his voice.

"This comes dangerously close to our jurisdiction Jake. But I'll help you because I'm curious of your curiosity. I'll get someone on it soon. She's on vacation now up in New York co-incidentally, and will be back next week. Can you wait that long? If you can't, I can't help you, she didn't leave a number."

"Shit Jeff, can't you work on it?" Jacobs was getting angry.

"Jake, I'm the boss. I don't do work. I've got other people here, but it'll take them just as long as if you waited for Elly." Fleming offered Jacobs the choice, efficiency and speed or hit and run with the rest of his crew.

"What does she look like? I'll put out an all points out on her." Jacobs was obsessed.

"Jake! She's on her vacation." Fleming shook his head and chuckled at Jacobs' compulsion.

Jacobs realized his thought was a stupid one as soon as he said it. There was nothing to do but wait for this Elly girl to return and get things started.

The door was not locked in his apartment. It was not even closed completely. He stood before it and wondered whether to run and never come back or go in and see whatever hell had wrought upon his home. He placed his fingertips on the door and pushed it open cautiously. The interior was still intact and music played softly from his bedroom. Nobody was visible and that made his heart race even more. His lungs ceased, and his blood ran cold through his veins. Frozen in his spot expecting the worst, he was caught off guard by the footsteps behind him.

The poke in the ribs was more frightening than painful. He jumped out of his skin and tried to maintain both bladder and sphincter control. Elly laughed hard at the vision of David jolting in the hall as if he had stuck his finger in a light socket.

"Jesus Christ, Elly! You scared the shit out of me!"

"Me scare you? Listen to me you selfish egocentric jerk! Where the hell have you been? We've both been worried sick about you. We had no clue on where to look for you and you didn't call. Damn it David you can't do that to me." Her anger turned soft and the tears started to roll from her eyes. "We didn't know if you got mugged or what. What if you were in the hospital or something?" She sniffled to stymie her tears.

"I *was* in the hospital Elly." David played it to the max.

"Oh God are you alright? What happened to you?" She inspected his forehead and her tears flowed.

He could have told her the truth but it had no substance, "I had a run in with a POSTman. I'm OK, some stitches that's all. Where's Evan?" David brushed past the issue fast enough to evade any more embarrassing answers.

"He's inside doing guy things. I just stepped out to drop the garbage down the chute, you know, girl things." She shoved David into the apartment and closed the door behind them.

"Evan!! David's home!!" Elly screamed down the hall to her brother.

From around the corner of the bathroom, Evan popped out his head, "Hey bud how you doin'? Elly got worried about you. I told her you were a big boy and that you would be fine. You fine?"

"Fine."

"See, Elly? I told you he was fine." Evan popped his head back into the bathroom and continued his shaving. "David, its four thirty now, I'll be done in here in about half an hour then you can get yourself ready. Sound alright with you?"

"Fine with me Evan. Take your time."

The door of the bathroom closed and David made his way to the couch and flopped on his back. Elly came up to him and sat on the floor in front of him.

"Did you hear about the Pope?" She asked him.

"Yeah, I was there. It was horrible. I don't want to talk about it again." David pleaded.

"Again?"

"I told the police I saw who did it but I can't remember the guy's face. Sorry Elly, but we'll talk about it later." He was tired of the whole thing already.

"Did you hear about the Cerebral Vacation?" She saw his eyes flutter.

"The King is dead." David surrendered.

"Someone blew the hell out of it with a rocket. Some surface to air missile or something. They used them in the Gulf War."

David bolted upright. "Blew it up? Who?"

"They don't know for sure but reports say that a car with Government plates passed by and fired one rocket and then took off. They suspect that agent Mackinnley." Elly was so nonchalant about the whole affair.

David stared towards the television. "What time did this happen?"

"About one-thirty, maybe two."

It was impossible for Mackinnley to be there. He was with him at that time. David grew more uneasy. This was getting far too large and complicated for him to remotely comprehend. The thought of skipping town for a while crossed his mind and then he remembered Mackinnley's threat. He believed Mackinnley would. He was stuck until tomorrow.

"David, is everything alright?" She stared at him lovingly.

Even with his mind racing, he noticed her eyes. They pulled him closer until he was drawn to her.

His lips touched hers in a soft and tender kiss. His hand came over and cradled her face as hers came up to embrace him. His fears and worries evaporated, leaving him free to surrender his accumulated desires. He had wanted to kiss her for the longest time, and now it seemed worth the wait. She pulled him closer and he rolled off the couch and onto the floor beside her. They both giggled with the excitement of high school kids. He pushed the coffee table away to make room for them on the floor. A pillow was salvaged from the couch and he placed it behind her head. The music from the bedroom played an old song 'Special Angel' and he brought it to her attention. She smiled and he kissed those smiling lips with intensity. It gained momentum with the building of passion and she wrapped her arms around him and drew him closer. Her fingers dug deep into his shoulders as their mouths sought each other's with the hunger of new love. He was above her and she wrapped her legs around him like a boa and squeezed him into her. She felt the certainty of his desire as it strained against the confines of his jeans. She liked the feel and ground her hips into his pressing pelvis. She pushed him away long enough to look into his eyes.

"I've always loved you, David. Always." Her voice was soft as spring rain.

"I love you, Angel." He replied sincerely.

With the words still hanging in the air, he grabbed Elly and carried her to his room, ignoring the fact that her brother, his best friend, was in the shower and would be out in fifteen minutes. It did not matter to him nor to Elly who had already peeled off her jeans and her T-shirt. The woman before him mesmerized David. She lay there, sprawled out like a kitten in his bed. In her bra and panties she could have set him off like canon just by lying there, but she writhed about just to tease him additionally.

David had enough of the tease. She had tormented his mind and his body far too long for any normal man to endure. He removed his jeans and his erection protruded far enough to make his purpose well known. She gaped at the wrapped present that she dreamt of for so long. He stepped closer to her and she reached for the thin material that separated her from his pleasures. Her fingers reached past the band and inched their way toward the hardness that she longed for.

"You got any dry towels out there David? David? Elly?"

"NOOOOO" David screamed at the intrusion on his mission.

"You've got no dry towels?" Evan's voice came through clearer now that the water stopped. "David, you've got to have more than two damn towels in this place. I'll get them myself."

Both David and Elly locked sights then rolled onto the floor to avoid being spotted by big brother.

The door of the bathroom opened and Evan tiptoed to the closet that held the extra towels. He grabbed two then headed back to the bathroom. He closed the door but not completely.

Elly giggled hysterically.

The moment was lost but Elly reached for her man and kissed him sweetly. Her giggles continued as she kissed him. He almost cried.

"David." She cooed. "We'll have to pick this up later." She reached for her jeans and slipped into them covering the terrain he longed to explore. Her T-shirt was on and she was armored once again. David sat there on the floor staring at his lap until the blood got back to his brain and he got dressed and met Elly in the living room.

Evan emerged from the bathroom with the high priced towel wrapped around his waist. "Hey David, who got you these towels, these are nice."

He looked at Evan with great disdain, "Your parents did." David moped.

Elly began to laugh. "Doesn't it just figure my mother would be involved in this?"

David could not contain the need to laugh at the irony.

"Is that really funny?" Evan was oblivious to the inside joke.

"Get dressed pal. We don't want to be late." David urged his friend.

Evan left the two alone again. Once out of the room David chased Elly around the couch and caught her by the armchair. He took both her arms and held them behind her back. He kissed her hard and her tongue darted into his mouth with soul-searching purpose. He pulled away but not before he dipped his head down to her left breast and lightly bit the nipple through her T-shirt.

"You little bugger!" She squealed as she went to hit him, but his game plan was drawn. He flew toward the bathroom with Elly hot on his heels. He got there three strides in front of her, locked himself in and started to get ready.

By five-thirty the two cavaliers were ready for the gala in their tuxedos, which suited and fit them both quite favorably. They looked good but not gay.

Elly complimented them as she walked around them. "Very nice." She grabbed a cheek of David's buns. "Very, very nice."

"Thanks sis. Look, we've got to go. What are you going to do tonight?" Evan inquired with his big brother tone.

"I'm heading up to Carol's place. You remember Carol don't you?" She stared at David and gave him a stern look. "You went out with her, last year was it David?" She was catty.

"Yeah...uh...a couple of times. It was...uh...interesting. You going to be there all night?" David tried to dodge the claws.

"Yes." Her pitch was cool. "She's invited me to a party she's throwing. Should be nice. Why?"

"If this thing's a drag maybe we'll join you." David tried for recompense.

Her eyes perked and the claws retracted. "You'll come in your tux's?" She purred.

"That all depends on who's there." Evan grinned.

"You're a pig." She feigned disgust. "You've got the number don't you David?
Call when you leave the gala."

She kissed them both. "Have fun boys." She closed the door behind them and headed off to the bedroom and disrobed to her undies. She lay there for an hour as she dreamt of the moment that almost was.

The conference room in the Hilton was still. Most of the remaining agents were dismissed for the day and Gonsalvez sat by the window alone. He stared out towards the Cerebral Vacation and mourned the loss of the agents who were killed. They were good men and did not deserve to die so horribly. He was fortunate for the new orders that came to him just fifteen minutes before the blast. It gave him ample time to get out of the club before it was wiped off the face of the earth. He thought over the sequence of events. A king gunned down. A major world leader assassinated as the Bureau watched. And now the murderous blast that killed so many colleagues, and friends. One person was connected to all these events. But Mackinnley? They were his friends too, in the Vacation. Mackinnley? "God help us all if that's true," thought Gonsalvez.

The plans for the Pope's visit were strewn across the room. They were useless. The evidence from the Cerebral Vacation investigation did not even make it out of the club before it was destroyed. A rocket for Gods sake. He shook his head and remembered when gun control used to be a problem let alone anti aircraft artillery. The city was coming apart and he and the bureau did not even have the slightest idea where to begin. Mackinnley was the only clue and he was one of their own. Gonsalvez stepped away from the window and planted himself in front of a computer screen.

He did not know where to look first. He started with the registration of the Cerebral Vacation. The link was slow to the Bureau's computers and he wondered when they would get state of the art computers, it was only the nations security, he thought. The link was made and he punched in the information requests. After ten minutes of digging he was back where he started, no further. The club was owned by a number of companies, which owned each other. There were companies spanning the globe that had their respective fingers in the club's operation. All the records were in order and presented themselves with legitimacy but still with all the owners there was no real father of this club on record.

There was definitely the smell of scandal but as to who was involved, no evidence could be found, or if it was found it had promptly been blown to hell. The hall in the basement of the club proclaimed a very expensive clientele. The drugs alone would have the DEA and themselves working for months to trace. He sat in front of the computer and watched the cursor blink at him. He eyed it for five more minutes before he turned off the unit and closed shop for the night.

He got to his room just as the phone rang.

"Gonsalvez here."

"Gons. Listen carefully; I did not have anything to do with the King's death, the Pope or with the blast. Understood?" Mackinnley's voice was deliberate and driven. The sound of traffic could be heard behind the voice and was difficult to place.

"Mackinnley, if you've got nothing to worry about come in and we'll talk about it."

"Gons, give me a break. I know how the game is played. For Christ's sake I taught you, so don't give me this 'it'll be alright' shit. They'll nail me to the cross for this. Especially since I never told anyone I was there in the first place. It was wrong but I just thought it was a drive by and nothing to worry about. I was wrong."

"Mac, listen to me. If you say you had nothing to do with it I believe you. Come in and I'll see to it that you are treated fairly."

"Sorry Gons. I can't do that. Jacobs wants my sorry ass and this is just the perfect opportunity to screw it. I need some information Gons. I'm calling in favors now, pal. This is the rainy day I've been saving for and I know you'll help me. You know damn well I didn't kill all those men. I'm going to do some snooping myself to help prove it. I'll be in touch."

The phone went dead and Gonsalvez was left just as stranded as with the computers.

"Son-of-a-bitch Mackinnley" Gonsalvez smiled, "always stirring up shit."

The Metropolitan Museum was lighted like a beacon in the night. It called for attention with the strength of twenty searchlights as they lit up the night sky. A stream of limousines, paraded to the front doors where their wealthy passengers disembarked and were ushered along the carpeted runway into the building by white-gloved men.

The night was for the well to do, the exorbitantly wealthy. The percentages of guests were old money Republicans that wished to see the return of their leader. Three years of the bleeding heart liberal were three years too many and they wished they could vote next week to oust him. The atmosphere was stuffy with the musty smell of old money, of old order.

The two friends milled about, completely lost in the crowd of wealth. David glanced about and recognized ten different men who were billionaires. He bet that not one of the hundreds of people present could tell a Van Gogh from a Monet. They knew nothing of culture unless it was in the form of yogurt. They were pretentious and belligerent and he hated them. Not because they had money, because they kept money, not saved it, hoarded it. While people on the street died each moment of exposure or hunger, they would throw away eight hundred dollar caviar because no one liked the Beluga this year, or the stocks went up so they would splurge on emeralds from Columbia. David wondered why he showed up. He smelt poor. They could tell. He knew they stared at him in his rented tuxedo, and wondered how he got in. God, how he hated the rich.

"Let's go, the doors are opening." Evan was eager to shmooze with the likes of the Jamisons and Forbes, or anyone of the many who carried heavy clout about them like cologne. This was a dream for him. He was like a child at Christmas, in front of the department store window. His eyes were aglow with wonderment as a trillion dollars worth of guests were all around him in the great hall.

The crowd shuffled into the next room where the James Elliot

Thorne wing was now taking its first honored guests. They passed through a series of metal detectors and entered the hall.

It was truly magnificent. The works were displayed graciously and were of indisputable elegance. There were paintings from artists he had known of but works he had never seen before. David recognized the stroke of Van Gogh on a painting entitled Elephants and Roses. Monet's Summer Dreams in Blue. They were exquisite. They were marred, though. Not the works but the hall. Heavily armed guards stood as sentry every twenty feet around the walls. They took from the paintings, as does a shark from swimming. Thus enjoyment of the works was limited to simple wading, when a long swim out would have been better.

There were sculptures and busts, more paintings and one work that encompassed a large portion of the west wall. It was heralded as one of the most controversial in the collection. The painting was from a sixteenth century artist, a fairly obscure Italian painter by the name of Antonio Scolaricci. The painting was of two men and a woman. In the foreground, pages of a book were strewn across the floor, torn from it recently as pages still drifted from the ceiling. In the hand of one man, a page from the book. He laughed as he pointed to the other man who was beside the bound and blindfolded woman. The woman was bound to a cross. She wept and her mouth was agape with sorrow. Her clothes, whatever shreds she still had upon her, were fairly new and stylish for the times. Her chest was exposed and was stained with blood that oozed from her blindfold. The man beside her was naked, his body covered with earth and mud. His eyes were covered with a mask yet his face remained visible. He laughed hard and his back arched. His right hand was bloodied to the elbow and he held a knife. The woman's belly had been cut lengthwise from below cleavage to above pubis and bled violently. His left hand was withdrawing the woman's womb that contained a life. It was not a child but an animal of sorts, curled in fetal position and covered with thick long hair. The title was 'The Second Genesis'. David almost threw up when he saw it. It was a hideous display of a vile act. Whatever the message the artist was trying to convey was lost in the vulgarity of visual medium.

There was so much texture to the painting that David could smell the blood. He wanted to turn away but was compelled to look at it some more. The more he looked at it, the more obscene it became. He walked away still hearing the screams of the raped birth. His stomach flipped and he choked down whatever was coming up.

He needed a drink. He ordered a Jack Daniels on ice and sipped it slowly. Just then the events of the evening began.

The feedback squelched as the master of ceremonies took command of the microphone. "Honored friends, welcome. We are most delighted to see you all here tonight to celebrate with us the opening of the James Elliot Thorne Wing here at the Metropolitan. Without further adieu let me introduce to you, our most honored guest, Mr. James Elliot Thorne!"

The crowd welcomed Thorne with great enthusiasm. They cheered until the man at the podium started to speak. His voice commanded silence and his presence dictated respect. His words were simple.

"I would first of all like to graciously extend my immense gratitude to all of you, my honored friends and supporters. Without your generous support and goodwill my candidacy would be non-existent. My purpose is to lead this country and its populace to a better realm to where our forefathers anticipated we would be. The world is a cavern, this country its treasure. Buried deep in the ground are the riches and rewards that will be discovered once I am placed in my rightful seat. Come with me, to a place we were told of when we were children. A place where our furthest reaching desires can be reality and all that was foretold will unfold in a bounty of splendor. There is nothing to fear. The future is but our destiny unfulfilled. Next year at this time, the reins of this extraordinary country will be surrendered to our victory. And then we will display the rule that was decreed."

The audience seemed mesmerized by the vision he instilled with his oration. They applauded him and his promise. The thunder of ovation resounded in the great hall and was only ceased when Thorne's voice quelled them.

"My friends, let us enjoy the dinner you so amiably paid such an exorbitant price for." Thorne chuckled with his finest campaign face.

David was not impressed. Somehow the pre-dinner speech was marred with certain undertones that did not sit well with him. He studied the man of the hour. His face was formed into a social smile, and was blatantly pretentious. What would a man with all these priceless pieces of art need with a fund raising dinner? His thought was at its peak when he locked eyes with Thorne.

Although the man smiled, Thorne instilled fear in David, an overwhelming fear that engulfed him. The great hall became too small and the air felt thin. Thorne stared at him and the smile changed to a knowing grin. It was unnerving and David wormed in his chair. Thorne approached the table with his gaze still locked on. He knew something, David thought. He felt his mind being racked and exposed and he hated the feeling. He cursed Thorne for this desecration of privacy and the paranoia he induced.

Thorne drew closer to the table and Evan was ecstatic. "David, maybe I can get a picture with him." The last place David wanted Thorne was at their table, conversing, exchanging thoughts and plastic sentiments. David wanted to run but his legs would not respond. It was too late. Thorne had encroached upon the table and started chatting with the billionaire Rosenstien. He did not look at the man when he spoke. He looked at David for the longest time. The press begged for a photograph.

The man from the *Times* positioned the two men, Thorne and Rosenstien, for a picture that would no doubt grace the front page of tomorrow's paper. They stood and faced the camera in diplomatic handshake position, just to the left of Evan and David.

"Here's my chance." Evan whispered to his friend. "It'll be an opportunity of a lifetime, front page of the *Times*?" Evan manipulated himself so that he could stand up just when the picture was to be snapped.

"Smile." Commanded the photographer.

Evan stood just a split second before the camera flash exploded simultaneously with the gunshot.

The crowd erupted into a panicked chorus of screams as Evan's body was catapulted back five feet. The bullet had caught him in the chest and splattered his heart onto the next table. David was crippled with shock. His eyes sprang open in horror. David's vision scanned the room for the gunman. Jesus Christ! Twice! In one day? He thought in a panicked state. From where he sat, it could have been any one of the armed guards that stood sentry. His best friend lay on the floor five feet away from him. He stared at him and was about to drop to him but the vision that caught his eye was just as frightening. In the corner of the great hall stood a massive man dressed in the same clothes as the rest of the guards. He was armed and at the ready as he ran towards Thorne.

This was too much for one man to handle, David conceded. Too much death and this one was too close to home. Then he saw it. The huge security guard was covering Thorne's slight frame. At first he didn't recognize him, but then David realized that the man in uniform, protecting Thorne's life, was the same man who had been in his apartment and the same man whom he had seen in the window with the rifle just before the Pope had been shot. Jesus. Thorne?

David looked to the floor."I'm so sorry Evan." He was about to scramble for the door when artillery was fired. He had suspected that one would hit him and he ducked to the floor. The gunshots continued, but towards the balcony. The bullets ricocheted off the ceiling and walls and perforated the entire balcony. Two hands raised in the sign of surrender from the cover of the perch. As the wiry looking East Indian man stood up, his body was inundated with machine gun fire. It writhed with ballistic bliss and was launched to the back of the loft.

David watched in horror, from the relative safety of the floor at the display of warfare in the lyceum. Most of the guests were stampeding in chaotic fashion to the exits. Others groveled under tables and prayed that Heaven would spare them.

David had to get out. He looked back at his friend's body and then started his escape. He kept his head down and crawled along the floor towards the exit. The rug was splattered with blood and spilled drinks as people had tipped over tables in an attempt to shield themselves. David quickened his way over a path of purses and ashtrays and high-heeled shoes abandoned in the flight. He had no time to weep or tend to his friend. He was in fear for his life. The behemoth was there. He must have known he saw him in front of the Palace. It was definitely a set-up.

He shed his tie on the run and kept on going until his legs could not take him another step. He had weaved through Central Park, through back streets and alleyways; he threaded a path away from the museum and backtracked just in case they might be following him. He had long since escaped the pandemonium in the museum, and was now at least four miles from the place where his best friend's body lay in a bloody puddle. He racked his brain and could think of nothing but the hole in Evan's thorax and the hole in his own heart. He leaned with his back against a wall and slid down to the ground and cried. After a moment he thought of Elly and knew that he should be the one to tell her of her brother.

He scrambled into his pocket for change and ran to a phone. Carol's number was retrieved from his memory with substantial difficulty and he dialed wrong twice before the phone was connected with the correct party.

"Hello?" The voice was slurred.

"Let me speak to Elly O'Connor." His tone was hurried and rude.

"Who?"

David could understand why drunks got rolled.

"Get me Carol, it's her fuckin' house!!"

"OK man, you don't havfa get hostile." The phone was dropped on the floor and hung there for two minutes. The party clamored in the distance as laughter was heard over and over again.

"Helloooo!"

"Carol, it's David, I have to talk to Elly now!" He was demanding and had forgotten any semblance of manners.

"Davie!!" She was drunk and excited to hear from her old lover. "What do you want with her Davie, I'm the one you want?"

"Your right Carol it is you I want. Let me talk to Elly so I can tell her it's all over, OK?"

"Sure Davie. Are you coming over soon?"

"Yeah. I'll be there in ten. Let me talk to Elly." David swore he would never drink again. God, how he hated drunks.

"See you soon Daviee, baby bear." She dropped the phone and her rendition of '*My Boyfriend's Back*' could be heard in the distance.

Moments later the phone was connected with Elly. "What the hell is going on? You and Carol are getting back together?" Elly was serious.

"Elly I love you and only you and right now there is nobody else in my life, I swear to you. Listen I can't come to the party."

"But David you said you would." She whined like a little girl.

"I know, but you have to listen to me. Leave the party now and meet me at Straps. You know that blues joint on 42nd? I'll be there in a few minutes."

"You'll be there? Where's Evan." There was more curiosity in her voice than concern.

"Uh...he's still at the museum. He'll be there for quite a while." He could not lie, but he could doctor the truth for now.

"He's a die hard Republican." She chortled.

"Leave now." David was demanding.

"I'm on my way out." She said in a rush.

David hung up the phone and thought of the past twenty-four hours. There was far too much death that surrounded him. The King, the Pope, the attempt on Thorne and the abrupt end of his best friends life. All of them pivoted around him.

His head spun with turmoil and now he wondered if he had anything to do with all of it. The death. He stood in the shadows and awaited Elly. The traffic was very light for that time of night and few cars passed by him. He gazed out from his sanctuary onto the street and saw a car moving slowly down the street as if its occupants were lost.

"The museum is that way," he said under his breath as the black Lincoln cruised by his shadow.

No sooner did the street clear, than Elly's Pathfinder rounded the corner. He jumped in and kissed her."Let's go." He barked.

"Back to your apartment?" She smiled devilishly.

"Uh...no. Just drive a bit." He was occupied with thought.

David had little time to calculate his approach. He needed Elly with him, to know she was safe. Then they would find some place to go. She looked at him and sensed his unease. "I love you David." She reached for his hand and pulled over to the side of the dim lit street.

She eyed him with concern and squeezed his hand gently. "Is something wrong, David?"

He looked at her as tears pooled up in his eyes but did not fall. "Elly." He swallowed hard. "Elly Evan is dead." The word hung in the air between them.

"Dead? What do you mean dead?" She started to shake with confusion and the tears started.

"He was shot in the museum. I don't know what happened, it was crazy in there."

"No you've got to be mistaken. He can't be dead. He's my big brother, he's not dead. He's not dead. He can't be. David please tell me he's not dead. Oh God!!" She was hysterical. The truck was too small for him to console her. She hammered on the steering wheel and David reached for her.

"Elly, I'm truly sorry, angel." He held her close in a supportive embrace.

Her tears flowed and she mumbled incoherently. David wanted to cry, but one of them had to be strong at this point. He held her for a long while until she stopped her hysterics.

"Why didn't you stay there?" She pressed him for response. "You're his best friend. Why did you leave him in the museum?"

David felt guilty enough without someone else pointing it out. "I think they were aiming for me. Evan stood up to get into a picture and that's when the bullet caught him in the chest." He realized he should not have got so graphic and regretted that it spurred her to tears again.

"Who David? Who's trying to kill you now?" She cursed him through her tears. "We spent yesterday running from the boogie man cause you were scared as hell about something, and now my brother is dead and you run out on him because someone is trying to kill YOU. Do you need help David? Tell me if you do please. This is far too crazy for me." Her rage was all consuming. She glared at him with spite and disgust.

He was ashamed but certain that someone was after him. He was not committable.

"Elly." He offered his excuse. "The guy I saw kill the Pope, he was there. In the museum. He was one of the security guards. He was covering Thorne when the initial gunfire went off. That's why I thought they were after me. I saw him downtown and maybe he wanted me dead so I couldn't testify."

"Are you sure it was the same guy?"

"The same guy that wandered into my apartment the other day too. It was him. I'm positive. I couldn't stay with Evan. Elly you know I would do anything for him, but it would do us no good if we were both dead on the floor in the museum now, would it?"

She was hypnotized by the theory and felt better that David had not deserted her brother. Still his paranoid state was getting to be stale. This was a new twist that sounded believable.

"So now what do we do?"

David thought. "Let me drive and I'll think of something."

They switched seats and David drove in silence.

They passed the Blackmore Tavern and David thought of that afternoon. His head perked up and he hit the gas.

"Where are you going? Are we not going back to your apartment? David?"

"We can't. They know where I live. I've got a friend we're going to see."

They drove in silence until they approached the lack luster sign of the Knotty Wood Motel.

-11-

The press had a field day in the Metropolitan. There were enough bullet holes to fill four pages of newsprint. Two dead bodies and an ex-president in a room full of billionaires. What a story. The young man was an innocent bystander. The man in the balcony was one of the most wanted men in the world, Ahmad Mohammed Radjatsingham

Thorne was not in a social mood. He looked at the body of the young man on the floor and shook his head in disgust. He turned his gaze to the balcony and shook his head again. He said nothing but the look on his face indicated frustration. Thorne was becoming more enraged by the moment, at incompetence more so than anything else. His stage was set with all the press at his feet and he erupted into a political speech.

"This is absolutely revolting. This fine country of ours is going to hell. In this city alone the moral fiber is disintegrating at an alarming rate. Two prominent individuals and an innocent young man have died in the past twenty four hours, not to mention the countless other fine members of our law enforcement agencies who have perished in the line of duty." His voice escalated in volume and tenacity. "This is the fault of our present government. Never in my years as president has this type of violence occurred. My foremost mission is to clean up this country and bring back the respect to humanity that is so dreadfully needed. Guns kill people. The simplicity of this statement should be understood by all. Tonight a terrorist tried to end my life. For whom he was employed I do not even dare to speculate, but by the grace of divine powers I was spared. This is an omen. My work is not done yet and it is I who will battle these forces that choose to violate the doctrines of our society. My condolences are extended to this young man's family and to the countrymen of King Kahid. To all of you who are suffering the loss of the divine pontiff, I too am emotional at this time. Understand this one promise. Next year may be too late to correct the damage that the present administration has afflicted on this country. My solemn oath is to remedy the situations that cause people malaise. You have my word on this."

The cameras snapped photographs while busy journalists recorded Thorne's sermon from the mount. He was in his glory and reveled in the adoration of the press. They were putty in the right hands and he molded them into pillars, which he stood upon, hovering above them and the rest of the world.

Sidestepping the body of the young man, Thorne exited the Metropolitan, and his entourage drove off in the darkness without the aid of their headlights.

Back in the museum the police finished photographing the young man's body. They traced his silhouette with the notorious dead chalk, then wrapped and carried him off.

His wallet identified him as Evan O'Connor, age 35. Residence, Long Island. The police marked down the particulars and then went about the search for next of kin.

The lobby of the Knotty Wood Motel was a closet sized cesspool. It was cluttered with litter and stunk of stale cigar. The decor was early Hiroshima. Even the rats had more dignity than to present their selves here. How could anyone check in here was Elly's thought, as she crossed the threshold into the office?

The man behind the desk was perfect. For those people who wanted to maintain anonymity for their afternoon rendezvous, this was the man they would hope to see. He was a short man. Wide as he was tall, with a few strands of hair ineptly covering his freckled head. He had to be almost legally blind with the thick glasses he wore. He fumbled his way to the desk after Elly tapped the bell for the eighth time. He must have been deaf as well. He bent down almost to the level of the desk and floundered his hands about to find the registry.

"How many?" He inquired without even looking up.

"I'm looking for a David Gabriel, please." She was sultry.

"Gabriel, Gabriel. Let's see." He pressed his face almost flush with the book and went over two pages of names. As if the place rocked with guests. "Gabriel, here we are. Room 8, just at the end that way." He pointed to the south end of the motel. “Are you staying the night? 'Cause if you are that's an extra twenty bucks!" He lifted his gaze and looked towards a lamp on the other side of the room, thinking it was she.

"No I'm not staying."

Her voice startled him and he reeled his head towards her correct location.

"Room 8 then. I'll be checking to make sure your not there in the morning. Here me?"

"Yes sir. You old fart." She mumbled on her way out.

"Thank-you, you too," he congenial replied.

She jumped into the Pathfinder and headed to the end unit. They parked the truck in front of Room 8 and knocked lightly on the floor.

"Frank." David whispered.

There was no sound inside.

He knocked again, this time with purpose. "Frank, it's David, David Graceson. Open the door."

The chain within the room rattled and the door parted ever so slightly.

"David?"

"Yeah, Frank it's me."

The door opened and the two rushed in as if the whole of the world was after them.

"What the hell is going on David, and who is this?" Mackinnley drank up Elly. The smile on his face pushed aside his apprehension, once she completely entered the light.

"Frank, this is Elly O'Connor. Evan's sister, my girl-friend." He looked at her face and he noticed the first sign of joy since they met that evening.

"I'm pleased to meet you Miss Elly, but this is not the best time for cordial introductions." Mackinnley was gruff, but not rude.

"Frank, listen, Evan is dead. He was shot tonight at the Met during the opening of the Thorne wing. I think that they were after me and Evan got in the way. I couldn't go back to my apartment so I thought that maybe you could help. You know that 'we' thing." David smirked.

Mackinnley was getting tired of the paranoid's delusions; he shook his head with disgust. "David, some guy got killed in Miami today, you think that bullet was meant for you as well?" May I remind you that yesterday you thought that the uzi's were for you? Now you tell me that this bullet had your name on it. Are you completely out of your mind?" Mackinnley was serious. His eyes drilled David and he became overbearing.

"No! I'm not crazy!! Mackinnley, don't pull rank on me or play goddamned psychologist here. If we've got this damn '*we*' thing happening, '*we*' better start treating each other with a lot more respect. I may not know a hell of a lot about detective shit, but I do know my life. This kind of stuff does not happen in my life. People don't get killed around me every day. They may in your life but I'm an ordinary guy and this is not ordinary stuff." David was tired of being pushed around by everybody, of being scared and of being thought of as asylum potential.

"I'm sorry David." Offered Mackinnley. "But I'll tell you one thing though. You're going to need that fire inside, my friend, keep it. Now tell me about what happened tonight." Mackinnley lost his harshness and slowly took on the air of a big brother. He listened intently as David detailed the entire nights itinerary.

"You say you'd seen this huge guy before?"

"Yeah. Twice. Once in my apartment, the guy just waltzed right in and then out, he said he was looking for the guy that lived there before me, which was probably bullshit. He was probably scoping my place for something. The second time I saw him he was pulling the trigger on the Pope. The guy is everywhere. Then he's in uniform at the gala. Whether he's museum security or Thorne's personal bodyguard I..."

"Wait!" Mackinnley interrupted. "You've been to the museum before. The security doesn't carry the armor that you described. We have to find out if Thorne hired security or if it's his own. If we can tie a link from condo man to Thorne we can really bring the house down. But we have a major problem here. I can't go out in the street looking for answers and we don't have any tools. Christ, even a computer would be a god send now." Mackinnley was both elated and frustrated.

"There are computers in the library and Elly here is a genius with them. Did I tell you she's with the state department?"

"The state department!!" Mackinnley jumped up with excitement. "The fuckin' state department. That's just incredible." He ran and hugged Elly. "Thank-you God, oh thank-you, thank-you!"

The man was overcome with joy and he danced with Elly on the floor to silent music.

"The state department, oh yeah, the state department oh yeah. I used to hate the state, but I love it today, the state department oh yeah." Mackinnley sang his merry little song like a possessed leprechaun.

"Frank. Hey Frank! Have you lost your mind?"

"David the state department has more information on anyone in the world than either the CIA or the FBI." He spoke in lilts as he kept up his little jig. "The only thing better than Elly working in the state department, is if she worked in the computer department of it." He stopped his jig and looked at Elly through squinted eyes.

Her smile grew. "Mr. Frank? I do."

"No. You're teasing me. She's teasing me isn't she David?" He frantically inspected David's face for reassurance that she was teasing him.

"Frank, she's the foremost specialist with computers in the state department. She's the one pal. The big Kahuna."

"Thank you Lord!!" He reached his arms up to heaven as if to hug the Lord himself. "Oh yes!! Yes, yes, yes, yes, yes!!" The jig started up again. "Oh how I love the state department.

David looked at Elly. Mackinnley's exuberance was in sharp contrast to her sadness. She smiled for Mackinnley and David, but behind the smile were tears of sorrow. The past two days had taken their toll and her usual bright eyes now had deep bruises of exhaustion under them. The loss of Evan hadn't been allowed to sink in. She and he both had not even had time to mourn their loss. But he knew that she was fiery and

Mackinnley was right, she was a huge asset.

Mackinnley stopped his display of exhilaration and sat in the corner chair. His heart bled for Elly. He hated to see little girls being sad and now there was nothing he could do to help her. He wanted to say something, to console her, to reassure her, but he remained silent and watched her as his toughness melted away.

It was almost two hours later when Elly finally fell asleep from exhaustion. David undressed her and put her under the sheet. Mackinnley waited out side the motel room and David joined him shortly.

"Well Frank. What does the '*we*' team do now?"

He looked at David and slapped his knee. "David my friend, there is a light at the end of the tunnel. First we have to get Elly to those computers in the library. As far as I am aware, there is a computer link to Washington called ATC or something like that, which can access government files. Not the big ones, but if Elly is one of the best I'm sure that she can hook up with her own computers and get some information on line. We have to find out who owns the Cerebral Vacation. It seems to me, and this is just a hunch, that all this started from there. Your adventure and mine. It's the common denominator. The place was wired to the tits and something either you or I said got to the wrong ears. They have tried several times to silence us but to no avail. The rest has been a game with them. What the Pope has to do with it, again I have no clue at this point in time, but you saw the guy and reported it to the police.

"Another theory is that they may be tied in with the authorities. Big money usually is. You can't run a club like the Cerebral Vacation and not attract some suspicion. If you subscribe to that view, then my friend you are screwed even more. The bad guys are after you and the police as well. The way I see it, they know you were around when the Pope was assassinated and you were there when the attempt on Thorne came down. Before you interrupt, let me continue. I know the attempt was not on Thorne, but the press will see it that way, you can bet on it. Now, I'm a detective with NYPD and your name and face keep popping up in two major crimes, what am I going to think?

"I think that in a city as big as New York, what the hell is this librarian from the east side doing in both places if he's not involved? If my suspicions are correct, tomorrow's paper will have that picture of Thorne that billionaire guy and Evan with a bullet hole in him, on the front page along with a picture from the Cerebral Vacation with me, and you. Mark my words David these people are playing real hardball. They don't want either of us to show our faces in this country for the next ten years!"

"So the only way we can get any information is through Elly and her connections with the DC databanks? Frank this is insane. We can't hole up in this shit-shack forever."

"No we won't. We will fight back and we will win. It doesn't always, but this time good will prevail over bad. '*We*' are three now David. Me with good ol' FBI logistics. Elly with her computers and you with your library card. Hell we can take on the world."

"Frank I'm sure you've lost your god damned mind."

"Help me find it sir." Mackinnley chided. "What section, in the library do I find *minds*?"

"In your case it would be under fairy tales."

Mackinnley laughed.

David stared at the Pathfinder's tires and wondered how tomorrow's front page was going to alter his life.

-12-

In the haunt at the end of the three-mile road, Thorne relished the weather. The temperature was a stifling one hundred and three degrees in his abode and he sat in his leather chair in shirt and jacket. He wrote in his journal.

This night was not a complete failure. The wiry man was gone and so was any link between history and him. Fifteen years of terrorist activity were untraceable to the origins of his office. They were good years. He thought of the bombings in embassies across the world. And moreover, the assassinations of prominent world leaders and hostage takings. 9/11 was his favorite. For the first time, and not to be the last, he was ruler of the world. It was all too easy to fool them all and manipulate so many. Oil games were so much fun.

The Colombians provided an outlet. The Cartel made his life so interesting. All that hide and seek, and Radjatsingham worked so hard at organizing the whole distribution of over four hundred thousand kilos of cocaine. Radjatsingham was a good man in his books. His errors were costly, in terms of time more than anything else. Plans were sidetracked because of error. The attempt on the president was a case in point. His chest was targeted and hit but prick refused to die. The aide got brain damage but he was not the one to hit. Like tonight. The wrong man was taken out but hopefully all would fit into place shortly.

There would be much work to do to rid the ointment of this minuscule fly. Thorne sat and stared at the picture from the Vacation. The three sat at the bar and stared at the television. They were three blind mice he thought to himself. In his maze, he would change the walls and never let them find the cheese. They would run in circles, dizzying themselves, becoming less confident as the moments passed. They would smell the prize, but lose themselves further and further until starvation and surrender were inevitable. Thorne smirked at the thought.

Not since South Africa did he have so much fun tormenting the human spirit. He funded the governments for their beliefs, his beliefs. They were pathetic symbols of power until he entered the scope. His expressions changed their world and still today this conflict envelopes their existence. Oh, what a game. What money can buy is true entertainment. To watch the human spirit as it fights the invincible. It will succumb to the slightest pressure and beg for salvation from any one. He was salvation. He was the bank and he funded anything that caused turmoil and suffering. The news was cartoons for him. He laughed at the homeless, he put them there and their plight was a joke. They could never go back he made sure of it. He kept them weak and hopeless.

The world had never known illness like his manufactured strains of virus. Too many people, with far too many healthy attitudes. Cancer needed a new twist, and in the late sixties his associates in the research department in Atlanta released a neuro-targeted strain into the water supply in Los Angeles. It's effects were too slow for the suffer seekers. He had them work on another form of spirit breaker.

Millions upon millions were spent on the research of Black Apple. He would cast man out of the garden himself and this strain was still growing in intensity. This one pleased him. At times like tonight, when things would go wrong, he would think of the Black Apple and its effects. It would make him smile. Early in the eighties he had consulted a chemical engineer at Stanford. The purpose was to create a virus so cunning that it would destroy the will for the body and soul to continue. The work was simple and was administered to a most willing subject. His lifestyle beckoned the lascivious to dance to the carnal beat. The world was sucker to this one and it consumed their consummations. Thorne watched as the afflicted withered and choked on their abandon. The fruits of their pleasures wrought poison seed and strangled whatever hope lurked within their meek mortal souls. They called it AIDs, the Black plague. He called it entertainment.

There were countless other events that spawned a glow in his veins. The grassy knoll. He was good with a rifle at one point in time, and the grassy knoll in Dallas was a perfect spot to exhibit his talents to the world. They still talk about it and he listens with a proud smile.

Fine the Pope was gone and he was one step closer to the grand plan, but now, he had to work on Graceson. He would be made to suffer. To hide from the world and destroy himself in the process. This man was weak. Like all men, he would fall to his knees and abandon the fight. Cowards they were, cowards. Not one had given him a battle worthy of note and Graceson did not have what it took to fight. Even if he did it would be quelled with counter attacks.

Thorne picked up the phone and spoke:

"Charon, the photograph you sent to the *Times* was an excellent choice. I want you to send another. This one will need work of the most professional caliber. I don't care who does it; you will assume responsibility for substandard results. It has to look so real that even the debunkers will not question it. This is a simple request I am sure you will indulge me. You have little time."

There was no argument on the other end and this was pleasing to Thorne as he thought of how long the librarian would last in the world of blood sport.

Two days...three tops.

He bet himself. The game was now heating up.

By the time the morning edition of the *Times* hit the street, both NYPD and the FBI were banging on the front door with little strength. The elevator was out of order and fifteen flights of stairs had to be tackled.

Ten armed men stood about the hall sweating profusely as the heat swallowed them and the exhaustion over took them.

There was no reply. Again. Harder!

"David Graceson. This is the FBI. Open the door."

A door opened next to David's and a young woman peeked through. One agent grabbed the door handle and swung it open.

"Don't get cute." He growled at her.

She ran back to her sofa and sat there awaiting instruction.

"Break it down." One of the agents's ordered the rest. Within seconds David's front door was in splinters and they carefully maneuvered inside not wanting to alter anything.

"I want this place turned inside out!" barked Gonsalvez. "This man is a prime suspect in three murders in the past forty eight hours, as well as the attempted assassination of Mr. Thorne. Dissect this place and give me something to talk to Jacobs about."

The room became a puzzle to put together. They split up into teams and each took a respective room in the apartment. By six o'clock in the morning nothing of great importance was located in the apartment. A picture of Graceson, an attractive young woman and Evan O'Connor, the dead man in the museum. A bible lay on the coffee table, closed but with tags sticking out marking pages. There was nothing indicating connection between him and any conspiring. The man was good. He did his work elsewhere, Gonsalvez thought; he never brought his work home with him.

They posted two armed officers at the door and the most of them left the apartment. Ten minutes later with the sirens screaming to clear a path, they came up to 42nd and 5th and were greeted by the curator of the library. On the steps the man was and scared. There were too many of them and too many weapons. He averted his eyes when they looked at him and he fumbled with the keys as he tried to place them in the lock. He dropped them twice, the third time an agent snatched the keys and opened the door himself. "Thank you sir." Gonsalvez was curt.

"As we discussed on the phone Mr. Forsyth, David Graceson is suspect in a number of high level murders. Any help you can give us would be greatly appreciated."

"Oh...I can't believe that young Mr. Graceson could be involved in anything like that. He's...he's such a nice man...he's quite intelligent...yes...yes...photographic memory...I think...yes ...yes. Nice young man. Murder, oh my gracious...no...not Mr. Graceson." Forsyth mumbled nervously as he showed the agents to the work area and to Mr. Graceson's locker.

"Thank you Mr. Forsyth. Please stay close by. We will need to ask you some questions once we are done here."

"Will...uh...we be able to open by...eleven o'clock?" Forsyth inquired.

"I highly doubt it, but we'll try to be out early." Gonsalvez promised and set out on the task of finding out more about Mr. Graceson.

His locker was the first target. With bolt cutters they cut the lock. With gloved hands they slowly opened the locker. It was an upright locker, tall enough to store a canoe paddle and above two shelves for storage of notes and books. It was an orderly environment. On the inside, 'Post-it' notes plastered the locker face. There were hundreds of notes pertaining to John and bible entries, Matthew and some verse numbers, Daniel, Revelations and more numbers. The man was obviously studying something in the Bible.

The name Nostradamus appeared many times on different pieces of paper. The names of Svedenborg and Edgar Casey were also present on a variety of chits. Hitler, Stalin, Hussein, Bin Ladin and several other names were scribbled on notes stuck to the locker door. One jumped out and grabbed his attention.

Gonsalvez delicately lifted one obstructing piece of paper and revealed the writing 'King.' and the rest was illegible.

"I'll be damned." He was ever so slightly amused until he caught a glimpse of another note. 'Pope assassinated' was scribed in clear print.

"Holy shit!" Gonsalvez hit the jackpot. "Rivers get over here. I want you to take all these notes and dust them for prints. Then I want to make sense of all this crap so I can understand what it means to this situation. Go."

Rivers carefully gathered all the notes in individual bags after he photographed the locker door.

Gonsalvez searched the locker meticulously. Several books were removed and placed gingerly on a table. A toothbrush, toothpaste, a sweater, the locker was emptied. Gonsalvez stared at the vacant locker and thought. He stared at the floor and noticed it was buckled. He twisted his head in query and squinted his eyes. The buckle in the floor suggested that something underneath was pushing up. He tapped on the base of the locker. It was hollow on the periphery and as he tapped towards the buckle there was something that stopped the hollow sound.

"Someone get me a crowbar NOW!" He hollered with a sense of urgency.

The tool was relayed to Gonsalvez and he pried the floor of the locker away. Underneath laid a newspaper. He pulled the paper aside and dropped the crowbar in amazement.

He was astonished at the buried treasure. An uzi lay at the bottom of Graceson's locker.

"Get this thing down to the lab yesterday!!" He yelled at his associates without removing his gaze from the weapon. "If this is what I think it is, we have our man."

He picked up the machine gun with a pen. Rivers was beside him with an evidence bag ready to rush the notes and the uzi to the lab for analysis.

Gonsalvez stood and looked about the library. He wondered what would possess a librarian to commit two such heinous crimes. What makes a man snap like that? He thought of the front page of the newspaper and how the weapon Graceson held in the picture matched the one here in his locker. How did he know Mackinnley and again what were the two of them doing in collaboration.

The easiest part of the job was over. The evidence was gathered. Motive would be determined upon retrieval of the suspects.

Graceson he could arrest with no problem. He wondered how he could slap the cuffs on his partner, his mentor, and his friend. Mackinnley. He could barely believe it.

The morning sun beat down unmercifully upon the city. At seven o'clock, it was so hot that the dew was incapable of holding on to the grass any longer. The air rippled off the pavement. Inside the motel room was a virtual inferno.

Elly slept on the queen size bed alone. Mackinnley on the chair and David found, what must have been, most uncomfortable part of the floor to rest his bones for the night. He awoke first, as his body spasmed him to move from the wretched location he chose to rest it. He stood up quietly as several joints in his spine cracked with complaint. He looked at Mackinnley asleep in the chair. He was a sight. Unshaven and in his undershirt looked like a husband banished from the bedroom. He shook his head and wondered how bad it had become if this was his only hope for salvation. A forlorn old fart with a gun and a badge.

He stretched his arms to the ceiling and twisted his back for relief. Four more joints cracked, including his neck. As he twisted his gaze fell upon Elly. She lay wrapped in a twisted tourniquet of sheets.

He ventured to the window and gazed outside. In the sanctuary of this decrepit motel room, he was safe for the time being. Once he crossed the threshold he would enter the world where bullets were out to find him. Out there his best friend was dead in some freezer awaiting condolence from friends and family. David felt horrible that he left his friend on the museum floor. The moment entered his mind and the event was relived. He shook with the remembrance of the gunshot blast. There by the window he cried silent tears of remorse.

It took him ten minutes to regain his composure and think about the day ahead. He wiped the tears from his face and tried to rid his mind of yesterday. Today would be far too chaotic without having that memory to take away precious moments of concentration.

Mackinnley stirred in his chair and awoke like a giant. He stretched and yawned and was about to moan when he noticed Elly still sleeping. His eyes searched the floor for David and caught him by the window instead.

David nodded salutations and put his finger to his mouth indicating quiet. Mackinnley respected the request and got up to the washroom. He met up with David outside the motel room after his morning ablutions were attended to.

"Mornin' Frank. Sleep well?"

Mackinnley leered at him and said nothing.

"Well Frank what's the plan?"

"I need a coffee before you say anything else." Mackinnley was like a bear coming out of hibernation. He scratched and sniffed, looking like he could tear apart anyone who crossed him. "I'll get Elly's keys and go grab something from a drive thru." Hoping that he could subdue the beast with the enticement of food, David sidestepped him and entered the room to retrieve the keys.

After picking up a greasy breakfast for five, he approached a deserted street and jumped out of the truck long enough to acquire a newspaper. He almost shit his pants when he unfolded the *Times* and saw it. Two pictures marred the front page. One was taken the instant Evan was struck by the bullet. His face was twisted in pain as his shoulders curled forward. The picture captured the anguish of murder at the precise second life was stolen. Thorne and Rosenstien stood in the foreground still in pose for the photo shoot.

The next picture was Mackinnley's prophesy to the letter. This photograph was from the Cerebral Vacation. A different angle from the previous days rendition. This one had David in the forefront and Mackinnley behind him. Evan was huddled on the floor, his face was completely obscured. The picture showed David sprawled out on the floor apparently talking to Mackinnley in an excited manner. In his right hand there was an uzi pointed towards the front of the club. If not for Mackinnley's prediction, the shock of the photo would have dropped David with a massive coronary. Still the picture was astonishingly real. It was his hand that held the weapon. He recognized his ring. There was no denying the appendage was his but there was denying that the incident occurred in space and time. Pictures don't lie, he remembered saying. They do now, he thought.

He jumped back into the truck and had to control the adrenalin that was surging through him. He drove with extra caution until he made it into the Knotty Wood Motel parking lot.

Mackinnley was still on the steps when the truck pulled up in front of him. David lunged out of the vehicle as if it were about to explode, and threw Mackinnley the paper.

"Coffee. Give me my coffee." The grizzly growled.

"Here's you fuckin' coffee. Now read!!" David was dangerously close to overstepping the limits of tolerance with the big man.

Mackinnley sipped his coffee and read the front page. He was only surprised by the timing of the first picture. The photographer must still be dancing. It was truly a Pulitzer Prize photo.

"Yeah. So." Mackinnley was nonchalant.

"What do you mean 'so'? Look at it. They put a fuckin' uzi in my hand, man. I'm being set up."

"Yeah. You're being set up pal, just like me, and if Evan were still alive, they would set him up too. I told you about this last night. It shouldn't be a surprise to you."

"It looks too god damned real Frank!"

"It's incredible work. Must have cost them a mint."

"I can't believe this. I just can't believe this." David walked to the back of the truck and then back to Mackinnley.

"Relax David. There's nothing you can do about the picture. What we can do is organize our strategy and forget about anything else. Eat your breakfast and you'll feel better." Mackinnley stuck his bear paw into the bag of food and pulled out breakfast.

David quietly entered the room and Elly was already finished in the shower. He tapped lightly on the door and it swung open.

"Good morning, Angel."

She pulled the door open and revealed her towel-clad body to his full view.

"Good morning." Her tone was as cheerful as the evening's events would allow. She approached him and hugged him tightly.

"Oh David. I feel so horrible." She stifled her tears.

"It's OK, Angel. We're together and we'll get through this together. It's you and I now, and I'll never leave you...ever. Understand?"

She nodded her head still buried in his chest.

"It's actually you and I and Frank. But I'm certain Frank's not going to be with us forever, you know what I mean?" He tried hard to make her smile.

She chuckled and pulled away from him to reveal a tiny smile.

"I love you, David Graceson." She wiped away a tear.

"I love you too, Miss Elly O'Connor. Now get your butt out here and have something to eat before Frank devours everything including the truck.

He hugged her again and left the washroom.

"David." She summoned.

He turned his head and saw her hike up the towel to reveal her right thigh. He stopped and tried to get a better look, but she closed the door as she let go of the towel.

"She's out to kill me too." He muttered to himself as he joined Mackinnley on the step.

David reached into the bag and grabbed a coffee and a sandwich. As he sipped his coffee he looked at Mackinnley.

"Well?"

"This is the plan. First of all, we have to get out of this hellhole. Neither of us is going to be any good if we can't get a decent night's sleep. They know what you and I look like so the only way we can get anything is through Elly. You got any cash?"

"Yeah, a couple of hundred."

"Good, we'll need it. We get Elly to get a room in a bigger place, downtown would be best, and they won't think we'll be there. You need some clothes, and we need to get a computer. Laptop will be fine. We can hook it up to a cellular and get what ever info Elly needs from there."

"What's for breakfast boys?" Elly sauntered out to join them. She was braless again and David shook his head in frustration. Mackinnley's eyes almost fell out of his head as he lost his train of thought.

"David couldn't you have found something a little more, edible?"

They both ignored her culinary critique.

"Elly, you're going shopping."

"David I can't go shopping, I have to attend to Evan."

"At this point in time you can't." Mackinnley interrupted. "If you head out to tend to Evan's business, I assure you that you will be followed. 'They' are undoubtedly counting on that and have several people waiting for you as we speak. I'm very sorry, Miss Elly, but that's impossible."

She looked at David with hope of over-ruling Mackinnley's decree.

"I'm sorry Elly. Frank knows the game that they're playing. I trust him."

"But David," she sobbed, "He's my brother." She broke down in tears.

David went to her and hugged her. "I know, Angel. He was my best friend and my brother, but we can't do anything for him now. We have to concentrate on keeping ourselves alive. If we end up dead these bastards will never be found and all this would mean nothing. Evan would have wanted us to find them."

She loved David, but at this moment, she didn't like him at all. Even with all the anger inside of denying her a last look at her big brother, she knew they both made sense.

"Alright boys, what do we need?"

They compiled a list of things to buy and do.

Just before checkout time, the manager wobbled his way down to their room. "Mr. Gabriel. You don't have any guests in there do ya?" He shouted from twenty feet away.

The three of them stood and watched the fat man struggle to find his way, feeling along the walls for direction.

"No, sir. No guests here." Mackinnley shouted back loudly.

"That's good." He replied, as he turned back, assured in the guest's honesty. "I'd hafta charge ya another twenty bucks, ya know."

They all looked at each other and laughed. It broke the tension. With the plan drawn up, Elly jumped into the Pathfinder and was off to gather the tools that would set them free.

Mackinnley and David sat on the steps and watched as their only link to the outside world drove off in search of ammunition.

-13-

The flight from DC to New York was quick and smooth. At LaGuardia, a car awaited Jacobs and brought him to the Hilton. The morning traffic was horrendous, and instigated more than its share of frustration. Tempers raged on the roads of New York, as motorists fought for every square inch of asphalt. The heat ignited passions and caused cabbies to invent new profanities to hurl.

In the middle of the city Jacobs wondered if it would be quicker to walk the distance. It could not possibly be any hotter outside than it was in the non-air-conditioned Fairmont. The sweat rolled off his temples and dripped off his chin. His shirt was pasted to his back and they were still at least half an hour away from the air-conditioned comfort of the hotel.

Beside him, he took note of the Pathfinder. The windows were all rolled up and he hated the sight that indicated trapped cool air. He dreamed of being inside it and seriously thought of commandeering it. It inched forward in the traffic, neck and neck with the Fairmont. For two miles and twenty minutes it rode shotgun with him and he stared at it all the way. The truck made its way ahead of Jacobs and he saw the plates. Government plates from DC. He would have jumped out and asked if the driver was named Ellen or Haley or what ever Fleming had told him his computer wizards name was, but the Pathfinder took off down a side street and vanished.

Forty minutes later they pulled into the drive of the Hilton. Drenched and disheveled, Jacobs grabbed his luggage and headed up to the conference room.

The room was stripped of all material dealing with the Pope's visit. All photos and route maps were gone and the room had regained some semblance of order. He spotted Gonsalvez by the far wall, on the phone, excitedly ranting. He approached him and Gonsalvez acknowledged him. He took a seat and waited.

"Mr. Jacobs, sir. Welcome to hell." Gonsalvez was honest.

"Gonsalvez, this situation is getting worse by the minute. If we don't find some answers and some faces to blame, I assure you hell is what we will catch. Tell me you have something that will make this sweat I'm in worth something."

"This is the story. We received a photograph this morning from the *Times*...no, wait I have to go further back. Last night... wait..." Gonsalvez had a hard time with the relation of the sequence of events. The day before, Sunday, King Kahid was assassinated in the Cerebral Vacation. He and ten or so others were murdered by a barrage of gunfire from a group of men in an old Buick. Inside the club we discover the place is wired with everything you could possibly dream of for surveillance. Cameras, microphones. We also find a party room in the back, hidden from public access. It turns out they have over fifteen million dollars worth of illicit drugs in the freezer. Mackinnley discovered that. I had called him and he came flying over there when I told him some serious stuff is going on. He flies down there like a bat out of hell. Now, he's never told me he was there before. Then that night we get a copy of a photograph. It's sent anonymously here to the Hilton. I open it up and there is Mackinnley with a gun in his paws, pointing up to the front of the club. Well it aint over yet.

"We go searching for him and he's gone. Vanished. Then we go back to the Vacation the next day, yesterday, and find more juicy stuff. That's when I called you. You called me just after the boys had found a relay box. We figured that it took all the fiber optic leads and sent them out to somewhere. I got orders to leave and I'm gone ten minutes when the place gets bombed to shit. Some reports say it was a SAM but we aren't certain. Witnesses state they saw a dark Fairmont with government plate's speed away. It sounds like one of ours. There is a shit load of them downstairs. We think of Mackinnley again.

"Then the Pope gets shot. Broad daylight in front of the Palace. We get one eyewitness, a one David Graceson. Says he saw the guy that shot the Pope but can't remember his face. Said it was a huge guy, maybe 280, 300 pounds. We let him go.

"This gets better, last night there is an assassination attempt on Mr. Thorne at the Metropolitan. Ahmad Mohammed Radjatsingham is the trigger man but he messes up and kills this young guy, uh...O'Connor...something like that. Anyway, the guy beside him turns out to be Graceson. The witness to the Popes murder. All hell breaks loose in the museum and Graceson's gone. Turns out these two are buddies, Graceson and O'Connor, but Graceson splits once the bullets fly.

"If that's not enough, we get another picture taken from the Vacation, with Graceson on the floor beside Mackinnley with a god damn uzi in his hands. Then, in his apartment we find nothing much, a picture, Graceson, O'Connor and some cutey. Nothing else. We head off to where this Graceson guy works, the library on 42nd and 5th. We crack open his locker and what do we find? Lots. The boys are still working on the notes we found on the inside of the locker. Hundreds of them. Quotes from the bible, Nostradamus, Revelations and really weird stuff. But the topper is I find an uzi in the bottom of his locker, under the flooring. The lab says it was the weapon used to kill the King. Ballistics proved it. We know that Mackinnley and Graceson are in it together but where they are is anyone's guess." Gonsalvez was excited but winded.

"The photos?"

"The lab tells me they are both real, untouched originals."

"What wc do now is plaster their faces all over the press and television, offer rewards and lock them in the city. If we can isolate them in city we have a better chance than if the get out. Pull whatever information you can on Graceson. Check INTERPOL and NSA and see if those pricks in the CIA have anything on him. Tell them it's national security! I don't give a shit. Just get me something. I want this guy."

Gonsalvez began tending to the director's wishes before he had finished his last syllable.

Jacobs grabbed his gear and headed off to a corner desk and snatched up the phone. He dialed and waited.

"Let me speak to Fleming. It's Jacobs and it's damn important."

"I don't give a good god damned if it *is* his quiet hour. Bang the shit out of the door 'til he gets his miserable ass out of his chair and answers. I want to talk to him now!!" He was bellowing into the phone. "Don't you dare put me on hold, I want to hear you pound on his door. Do you hear me??"

He stared across the room and waited to hear the pummeling. It came softly at first and then with the determination he commanded. There was an apologetic tone by the secretary to Fleming and then she came on the line to connect the two. Her voice was shaky and was on the threshold of tears. Jacobs did not thank her, he just grunted.

"Fleming, Jacobs. Tell me, and I'm sorry to interrupt your 'quiet time', what is that computer wizards name?"

"Why? Cause I want it now!" Don't mess with me Jeff or I'll hold you for obstruction."

"Elly O'Connor. Good." The name rang a bell of familiarity. "Does she have family up here in New York?"

"She does? Good. A brother perhaps?"

"She does? His name? Do you know his name?"

"Evan O'Connor. Great! One more thing, what does she drive?"

"A Japanese four by four? Really? Get me the license, I'll wait."

"Do it damn it. I swear I'll follow through."

He scribbled down a number and hung up on Fleming without so much as thanking him. He unfolded the soaking wet paper from his shirt pocket. Through the smudged ink he looked at the two numbers and slammed his fist on the desk. "God damned shit!!!" He was angry with himself that he didn't commandeer the Pathfinder. Now with this update from Gonsalvez she might have been able to help locate Graceson. Hell she might even be in on the deal.

"Gonsalvez!" He yelled across the room.

Gonsalvez had just hung up the phone and was about to dial out. "Yes sir."

"Put an APB out on a '93 Pathfinder, black on black. Government plates U,S,5,7,3,6,3. Elly O'Connor is the driver. I want her here."

Again Gonsalvez was on the phone relaying the wishes of his commander.

Jacobs was obsessed. Still in his soaking clothes he stared out the window and thought of Mackinnley and Graceson. He would find them and bring them to their knees. He enjoyed the thought of breaking Mackinnley and finally nailing the man for every injustice the world had not solved. This would be his recompense for the years of screw-ups and embarrassments. Divine justice was about to make his day.

In the busy downtown precinct, she sat on the farthest spot on the bench. With the hookers and social degenerates around the booking room, she thought it best, for sanitary reasons foremost, that she sit as far as humanely possible.

The police were crude and rough. They handled each delinquent in the same manner. There was no respect given to the criminals and she thought it fitting. She liked the police. They were there for people like her who lived in fear of those perverts.

The desk sergeant called her name and she was sent to a desk in the middle of the office. A young police officer took her statement after a kind and warm greeting.

"Miss White is it?" He smiled a comforting smile.

"Yes sir, that is correct."

"Tell me Miss White, what is it we can help you with?"

"It was Sunday afternoon, about two thirty. I was coming from afternoon church service when I was about to cross the street at 53rd and 3rd. As I was about to step onto the street to cross, an old Buick, I think that's what it was, came to a screeching halt in front of me. The light was green for me and I was in the right. But these animals that were in the car started screaming at me."

"You'd like to file an assault charge would you?" the policeman asked her.

"Well I don't know. You see I would. Well I should. People can't go around calling other people obscene names like that."

"Like what Miss White?"

The young lady became flustered. Her face turned crimson.

"It's important Miss White if you want to file a complaint."

The officer was compassionate and tolerant. He handled her with caring hands and with patience.

She started to tremble and tears welled up in her eyes. "They were animals," she whimpered. "There were four of them. East Indian or something like that." Her tears were consistent now. "They screamed at me and called me a...they called me a...a whore." The word set off a flood of tears.

If not for the intense display of emotion, the officer would have laughed. The young woman before him was serious though.

She continued. "That was not all. They called me a slut and bitch and...and...a F..., I can't say that word, something sucker. I'm sorry sir, please don't make me say those words." She pleaded with the officer.

"It's not true any, of it. How can people do those kind of things? Why do they do those kinds of things? They hurt other people. Don't they know that? Do they enjoy hurting other people? Do they?" She wept into her handkerchief.

The officer was dumbfounded. "Did you get a look at any of them Miss White?"

"Yes, I got a good look at two of them. The ones in the back seat. One of them had a gun and that's what really scared me." She shook with the recall. "It was a huge car. A Buick I'm quite certain. Red. An older one." Her voice came in gasps as she tried to regain composure.

"I'm sure I could identify them in a mug shot book but it's not necessary. One of the men was in the paper yesterday. That, that..." She fought hard to find the proper adjective, "That brute who killed that young man."

"Radjatsingham?" The policeman sat upright in his chair and became more attentive.

"Yes sir. That was him I'm most certain. That was one of them. He's the one who called me the worst names."

"Sunday afternoon at 53rd and 3rd you saw an old red Buick with four East Indian men? Did they turn onto 53rd?" He prayed she'd say yes.

"Yes sir, they did. West."

He almost jumped out of his chair. "Wait right here Miss White." He ran to the captain's office and could be seen in an emotional display as he related the story to his commanding officer.

Both men returned to the desk and continued a different line of questions.

"Miss White, this is Captain Phillips. Are you most certain that it was the man in the newspaper that offended you on Sunday?"

"Yes sir."

"Miss White, it would be a great service to this department and to the country if you would file a statement with the officer here in regards to the occurrence on Sunday. Would you be so kind?"

The captain was a very obese man who spoke with kindness.

"If you think it will help. I didn't think that you would be able to arrest them or anything, I just remember the papers saying that a number of people including a King got killed at the club around the corner from where I was and maybe that event can help you."

"It most certainly can help us Miss White. It most certainly can."

The Knotty Wood Motel was a deserted place. Far enough from the road to appear deserted and close enough to obscurity to remain invisible. In the morning light David stared at the street off in the distance. The road lead west. Out of the city. Away from the problems and craziness that enveloped his life now.

He was a simple man, of simple honest truths. He believed in good and evil and the principles of karma. There was heaven and hell and the difference was the voice of conscience. Some had it and some didn't. Those who did not have it; suffered the indignities of corruption, crime and punishment. There were many in society who was entrapped in the web of evil. It was New York after all, where else could they live.

David thought of all the evil that had presented itself to him in the past forty-eight hours. Far, far too much untimely death was surrounding him. Was he cursed? He contemplated the thought of being hexed. The King? The Pope? Evan?. All were horrible deaths, and he was there when they all occurred. Was he the catalyst for the evil? Was he the cause of his best friend's demise?

Sitting beside Mackinnley, he turned and looked at the large man. He was a good person, David conceded. The surly nature of the man was the callous formed from years of exposure to vulgarity. The vile acts that he must have been exposed to had covered him in armor impervious to emotion. He was tough and abrasive and had the sentiment of a cement mixer. Beyond the uncouth nature of the beast, lay a warm and caring heart; he could see it when he saw him look at Elly. The man was indeed a bear, but at times he was a teddy bear. David thanked the Lord that he was on his side.

Mackinnley drank a second orange juice after devouring the third bacon and egg sandwich. David watched in fascination as the FBI agent was concentrating on his feast. David kept his hands clear of him in fear that they may be caught up in the eating machine and lost forever.

"Frank? What are we going to do? I mean what the hell is going on?"

Mackinnley chomped down on the last morsels of breakfast. With food still in his mouth, he looked at David and waited for his chewing to make way for his speech.

"David my friend, let's take a look at this whole thing. You are, as I see it, you are the angel of death."

"Thanks Frank. Like I need to hear that kind of shit!"

"Relax David, I'm only being objective. Don't take it personally. You were around when the King got killed. When the Pope got killed and when Evan was killed. Taking into consideration that the universe is tied together and everything is correlated, then there must be a link between all these events. Let's think about it. First the King. What's the connection?"

David looked at Mackinnley like a moron. "What connection? I was in the bar when he got shot. That's the only connection. The only connection I can see is that gorilla that walked into my apartment is the same guy who pulled the trigger on the Pope and he worked as security for Thorne."

"We're jumping ahead of ourselves, but if that's where you want to start, fine. We now have to find out if he's on staff with Thorne. We have to get a list from the museum to find out his name and we'll take it from there. Next. You feel that you were the target at the Metropolitan? Correct?"

"After seeing that huge guy there, yeah I think it was me they were after. I went to the police after the Pope was killed. They asked me the standard questions I guess and I gave them a description of the big guy. Wait! If what you said about the authorities being on the bad guys side is true then they know exactly who I am."

"My friend, I've told you a hundred times that you're screwed. For the hundred and first time you have no friends but Elly and me. That's it pal. You have been locked out of the socially acceptable realm and have become a criminal. As such, you are being hunted as one and if you don't clear your name fast I can bet my pecker you'll be dead by the end of the week."

"Frank, you are just a bucket of sunshine, aren't you? I wish that you would stop telling me how bad things are and start telling me how good things could get. How are we going to get cleared man?"

Desperation echoed in David's voice. People around him had a nasty habit of getting killed. He worried about Elly and even Mackinnley. There was no way that he could handle one more killing. He looked out into the parking lot and felt better once he saw Elly's Pathfinder bounce into view. She caught the curb and the back end jumped with controlled excitement. As she pulled into the parking spot she rolled down the window.

"Ho Ho Ho!! It's Santa Claus." Obviously the shopping had allowed her an escape from the reality that engulfed them all. She jumped out of the truck and made her way to the back.

"I got digs at the Holiday Inn. I checked into a far corner room just by the fire exit. It's perfect for you fugitives. David I just got you a couple of pairs of jeans, some shirts and a pair of Nike's. I took a guess at your sizes, Mr. Frank. There are some Bermuda shorts and some polo shirts as well as a pair of deck shoes, size eleven. I took a guess, was I close?"

"Size ten and a half. Damn close. Thanks, Miss Elly."

"Did you get the electronics Elly?"

"Yes, David I got everything on the list, even those damn walkie-talkies. I never thought they were so damn expensive. They cost me a hundred bucks. I put it all on plastic.

"We had better get a move on then. Let's change into civilized clothes and be off. We've got a lot of things we have to get started on, like saving our asses."

"I'm with you." David grabbed the bag of clothes and ran into the motel room to change. Mackinnley followed and three minutes later they emerged looking quite dapper.

"You guys look very inconspicuous. They fit OK?"

"Everything fits great Miss Elly. Even the shoes. Thanks again."

"OK, OK, forget the fashion show. Let's get a move on."

David ushered them into the truck and they were on the move to the Holiday Inn. He smiled at the irony of the name but knew it would be anything but.

-14-

"One damned chaotic situation after another. Can't one thing proceed as the plan dictates! The slightest little insect should not cause such tumultuous difficulty. He is a measly librarian! If he was a spy or a Federal Agent I could understand a slight problem, but this situation is abhorrent. The salaries that I pay out are more than sufficient. The work I assign is simple for the professions you are in. As far as the equipment I supply you with, there is no reason that a simple extermination should cause me such grief and you such difficulty."

Thorne was livid. In the comfort of his own abode, the entire staff of the sixth floor, less one guard, sat at his mercy. The den was silent as they awaited the great one to cast his wrath upon them. Twelve of them sat in the room as Thorne, at his desk, scrutinized their faces.

"You were supposed to be the best, chosen years ago when you worked for me in Intelligence. But you have all become complacent." His gaze fell about each of them and each one could not hold their eyes to his for long. They bowed in humility and in fear.

"I have planned this event for many years now. The events in your history books have been written about my works. The whole of five decades hinge on the elimination of Mr. Graceson. The complexity of that may be lost in its simplicity. My life has been dictated. Destiny awaits my ascent to the presidency for yet another term. Many lives have paved the way to this point and you are all pivotal to the outcome. If you cannot find Graceson and bring him to me then I'll have failed the world in promise. It is simple."

He rose from his desk and they all shook with apprehension. "It is as simple as..." His sentence hung in the air until the sound waves were obscured by his footsteps. He stopped behind Jamison of security and pulled the revolver out of the man's holster. He cocked the weapon and put it to the base of the man's skull. "...this." Thorne squeezed the trigger and Jamison's frontal lobe was spattered across the table and onto three others sitting opposite him. They cowered from the blast, as Jamison's skull spilled forth all his life's essence. They attempted to wipe the blood and brain matter off themselves until Thorne pointed the gun at the middle one.

"Cease." His thunderous command was met with confused looks from all three. "You will wear Jamison as a mark. If Graceson is not found and brought to me by tomorrow at this time, consider your existence terminated."

Thorne walked about them and did not look at any of them. "You were all so very good at one time. All of you came from the same schooling. The finest the government could have trained. You protected my position for years and you have all served me well from the White House years. But I can and will part company with you should my desires not be met with absolute conviction."

He returned to the desk and summoned Charon.

"I have an interview with Mr. Larry King this evening. Carefully choose the security for the journey and make sure that the Jamison mess is cleaned up and he is disposed of accordingly."

Charon gave Thorne no excuse to part his hair as he did Jamison's. He tapped five of the men present and they all grabbed a part of the 'example' and hauled his remains out of the room.

Thorne turned his back on the remaining few and waved his hand in the air to indicate dismissal. Quietly they emptied the room as they all passed the bloodied table where fresh tissue still lay.

The room was empty and Thorne contemplated the evening's interview. He hated Larry King but the people loved him. Many would watch tonight and be impressed by his astuteness. He would mould Larry into a pedestal and be showered by the praises of the masses.

The picture that came over the wire was identical to the one found in Graceson's apartment. The woman, age 25, five foot two, 100 pounds, green eyes, was Elly O'Connor. No priors, no arrests, no traffic violations. No wonder Gonsalvez thought she was beautiful. She was stunning even in her DMV photo. The picture was forwarded to the central police computer and sent throughout the city on an all points bulletin.

There was nothing to do now but wait to see if anyone would respond. He stared at the phone almost expecting it to ring with reaction to the communiqué. Instead one of his associates brought him a note from NYPD.

Gonsalvez read the letter and smiled.

"This helps, but at this time I'm not sure how. If this is real then we have a larger problem than what we first thought." He thought aloud.

"What was that sir?" The rookie had strained to hear Gonsalvez but failed to pick anything out.

"Nothing. Nothing at all. Where is Jacobs?"

"He's down in the lounge sir. He wanted a breather."

"Fine. I need a breather as well. I'll go and join him."

Two minutes later Gonsalvez awaited his beer at the bar with Jacobs. "This just came over the wire sir." He handed him the copy of the police report. "It sure does open a whole new perspective."

"It does do that Gonsalvez." The director shook his head in disgust. "But I'll tell you one thing, it doesn't surprise me. The report does, but the subject matter doesn't. I've known Mackinnley for far too many years. He's been a blemish on the Bureau's record for all those years. It does not surprise me that he is mixed up with this type. Mackinnley must have worked the inside of the club with Graceson and Radjatsingham must have worked it from the outside. It was a perfectly efficient job. Personally I never thought that Mackinnley would be so careless as to do a job like this on his own. He must have got a fortune for it. How he linked up with Radjatsingham is beyond me."

"I can't believe that Mackinnley would be in company with him." Gonsalvez tried hard to salvage any remaining shred of his friend's name.

"How long have we been after Radjatsingham? Ten, twelve years? How do you suppose you stay ahead of the FBI if you don't have an inside edge? I'll bet you a years salary that if we go upstairs and take a peek at Mackinnley's bank account, we'll see some form of lucrative payment in there."

"No way. Not in his own account. I'll bet you whatever you want. There is no way that he'd be stupid enough to put it in his own account."

"If not his own, I bet it's in Switzerland or Gibraltar. But I assure you that there is money somewhere." Jacobs spoke with conviction. His hatred for Mackinnley was stronger with each passing moment.

"Let's go upstairs and see what we find. Shall we?" Jacobs extended his hand in the direction of the door.

"Sure."

They each stood in silence as the elevator whirred to the conference room level. Neither one spoke. Even when the rookie tickled the keys of the computer and requested the banking information, they were silent.

In DC, there was nothing in Mackinnley's account. Twenty-three hundred dollars in total. They searched the Swiss institutions and found his name. The grid appeared and denied them access to the records beyond the lockout. The rookie punched in a series of codes to distinguish the request as being from the United States Federal Bureau of Investigations. The computer screen paused, as if thinking of a reason why the FBI would like information. Then flashed to life. The Name Mackinnley, Francis was typed in and the monitor spewed a great list of transactions. Deposits of six digits and greater were chronicled for the last ten years. Present balance 9,450,000 dollars US.

Gonsalvez almost fell on the floor. He grabbed the chair behind him the moment his knees went weak. "Nine and a half MILLION?" The sheer magnitude of the amount could convict Mackinnley on conspiracy to commit just about anything. "Nine mill! Holy shit! Nine million, I just can't believe this." Gonsalvez was in shock. "He was my partner for three years and I never would have guessed that the man was sitting on a stash of that much cash. The guy lived like an average Joe."

"Keep the year's salary, Gonsalvez." The director was content just in proving to Gonsalvez that his ex-partner was indeed on the take in a big way.

"So, sir..." Gonsalvez tried to make sense out of the total picture. “Mackinnley, Graceson and Radjatsingham were hired to kill King Kahid for one million. That deposit there, made yesterday would probably be payment. Then would Graceson, Mackinnley and Radjatsingham also be involved with the Pope?"

"I believe they would. Graceson said he witnessed some guy pull the trigger. I figure he sent the NYPD and our boys running down the wrong street with that description of the large guy. He had a head injury, reports say. Bullshit I say. The man is probably an operative for some organization. Reports say he was calm and cooperative in the precinct. Gave full cooperation and also accepted a ride to his real address. Christ, that's so damn smooth. I would never have suspected anything elusive about that. They probably had Radjatsingham in some window and with all the people looking at the Pope, who would look up at some window? The job was smooth and perfect."

"Jesus, sir. No disrespect intended, but do you think that those three had something to do with the disappearance of Mr. Hoffa?" The outlandish views of the director could only draw sarcasm from Gonsalvez.

"Watch it, Gonsalvez. I'm giving you very plausible reasons. I'll even put money on the fact that they were involved with the attempt on Thorne. Mackinnley caught enough shit from Thorne personally when he was in charge. Radjatsingham was the triggerman. Graceson is a member of the Metropolitan who could have easily attained an invitation to the gala through someone."

"We did find an invite in his apartment. There was no stamp on the envelope." Gonsalvez was losing assurance in his argument.

"There you go Gonsalvez. Radjatsingham got in there early, waited for the right moment and 'boom!' good-bye Mr. Soon-to-be President. This time it was not perfect. They lost their triggerman. So what. With the money that sponsors them, they can find another six tomorrow."

Gonsalvez was mortified. In his wildest dreams he could not have come up with that scenario. It was absurd and ludicrous, even laughable, but above all it made perfect sense. At that precise moment, he lost all faith in Mackinnley. He just then became the criminal that Gonsalvez tried so hard to believe he wasn't. With renewed conviction, Gonsalvez hopped the fence and viewed Mackinnley as the enemy. He was a now partner with Jacobs.

"Punch up Graceson and Elly O'Connor's name on that computer. Chances are they're in the same bank. Lets see if their combined wealth can wipe out the national debt.

The rookie clamored on the keys and Gonsalvez walked away with mixed feelings. He was amazed at the director's prediction and disgusted that together Elly and David had over twenty five million in their accounts.

What disturbed him the most was that Elly was involved. Not that she was beautiful and he wished for an opportunity to meet her, but that she was with the State Department. She was in the research department and on the payroll of some very wealthy individuals. It could only spell trouble and treason.

He checked the wire for any response of her whereabouts. There was nothing.

He checked the computer screen one more time and then went up to his room, dreaming of how one could possibly spend nine million dollars in one lifetime.

From his desktop computer he watched the transmissions from the Hilton. Hundreds of thousands were spent on satellites and bugging equipment. Surveillance was their specialty. They probably had no clue that for the past twenty-four hours every move they made was under intense scrutiny.

From across the street in the well-seasoned office building, the main body of surveillance was situated. All phone lines were tapped and whatever the computer links, they, too were tapped. Whatever the boys in the Hilton did in the conference room, it was duly noted. Whatever they punched on their computers came through on theirs.

The head of organization was in his makeshift room at the time the bank figures came flashing on the screen. The young computer operator thought them bizarre. He jumped over to another computer terminal and hammered at the keys. His clearance was granted and information was retrieved from Gibraltar and Anguilla. He printed four pages of material and ran to the leader of operations.

The young man tapped lightly on the office door. There was no answer. He twisted the doorknob but it reminded him why there was no reply. The man wanted privacy. He should have remembered 'quiet time'. But this was New York and not DC. Did the ritual still apply in other states? It must for the door remained closed and the lock remained silent. He turned away and wondered what he would do if the place burned down during 'quiet time'.

The computer screen flashed again as someone across the street requested more information from Switzerland. Again the access codes allowed admission. One of the longest names the young mad had seen sprawled across the screen. Ahmed Mohammed Radjatsingham. Within seconds it responded *'not found.* The name was scrambled in order and still *'not found'* was announced. A.M. Rajat, Mohamed Raj, A.R. Mohammed was typed and instantaneously the transactions of several years chased the cursor across each line on the screen. Three pages later all the findings were gathered and ready to present the boss once he finished whatever he did during his time.

All was quiet in the office. Remarkably twenty-four hours ago it was a vacant floor. The recession had cleaned out whatever business occupied it and it was ideal for their work. Desks and tables and a wide variety of surveillance equipment filled the middle of the office. The main offices were converted into sleeping quarters and there were showers in three of them. It was perfect for a stakeout.

Since the call from the director of the FBI, the State Department had started to move their equipment into the building across the street. The New York branch had everything set up by the time Fleming presented his aromatic person into the suite. From the underground parking everything made its way up unbeknownst to the Federal boys across the way. Phone lines were spliced and satellite feeds were tapped. The giant satellite ear was set up to monitor all vocal conversations within the conference room. All their stations were monitored since set up.

The unlocking of the largest office door announced the formal end to 'quiet time'. Fleming emerged from the room and ambled toward the windows. They were mirrored and the monitored had no idea they were being watched. He studied the movements about the conference room and took mental notes. The tone there, by visual standards, was tense. They awaited something. A young Hispanic man exited the room. Another man stood with his hands on his hips around another computer.

"Jacobs." He mumbled to himself. "You've done it now, you bastard. I'll teach you to mess with my people." He spoke to the window and each breath steamed it up. "Call me up and demand information on the countries foremost computer expert. Then call me up to ask me personal matters. You bastard. I know you far too well, I'll nail your ass to the floor and force-feed you humble pie. You did this once before, remember Jacobs. I do. He was a good man Jacobs; he had lots more time to live. You and your god damned attitude. I won't let it happen again. Not with Elly. My hunch was right, you snake, and you're trying to implicate her like you did Michaels. That shipment of cocaine from Panama, the Cartel and Noriagua." Fleming cursed the opposing building." I couldn't convince anyone about that, but I'm damn glad I'm here now. You miserable schmuck. I know you'll get yours."

The phone rang in the distance. Fleming wondered whether it was his or from across the street. His secretary answered the call.

"Oh hello, Miss O'Connor. I'm so sorry to hear about your brother. My deepest sympathies."

"Thank you, Karen. Listen is Mr. Fleming available?"

"Just one moment and I'll connect you."

Fleming watched as the phone call made its way to where he was standing. He picked it up in his normal nervous way.

"Hello, Fleming here."

"Hello Mr. Fleming."

"Elly! How are things in New York?" He winked at Karen.

"They aren't so great. My brother was killed yesterday."

"I read about it this morning in the Post. Elly I'm truly sorry. Is there anything I can do?"

"Thank you, but no. I'm OK. I'm in a bit of a state right now and I don't have much time. What I would like are the security access codes for Central CPU, Bank Swiss, Gibraltar and Anguilla and our clearance for federal files, I should have them in Rolodex on my desk if you don't mind."

"I don't mind at all Elly. Can you hold?" He put her on hold and barked at Karen to call DC and get the numbers that Elly required. Within moments she passed him the numbers and he reconnected the line.

"Elly what are you doing up there in New York and you need these codes? You win a lottery or something?"

"It's such a long story Mr. Fleming that I don't even know where to begin."

"Just be careful Elly. We're all behind you down here in the nations capital. Here are the codes." He passed the three security codes to her and wished her well. He hung up the phone and was certain that she would be fine. He would make sure of it.

His makeshift office staff covered her plastic trail. The Holiday Inn was wiped off record. Her cell phone was wide open for use without the treat of tagging. The purchases of clothing, shoes, walkie-talkies and computer equipment were history..They never existed as far as anyone was concerned, no matter what type of equipment they had to track her.

There was no way that Jacobs was going to get a hold of her, nor was anyone else. Fleming knew there were others. Finding out just who they were was going to take some work.

The room was spacious and well appointed. On the top floor of the Holiday Inn, David somehow felt more secure. It was probably just an illusion. The suite was not an illusion, though. The suite had two rooms with, most importantly comfortable beds, one with a king-size and the other with two twins. It was perfect. Trust Elly to get the precise order filled. They had come up the service elevator and made their way past any looks from the total strangers that inhabited the hotel. Anyone could be one of them.

David flopped on the couch and tried to relax. He turned on the television and kicked back for the time being. CNN was already on and the he saw Thorne. “Christ! Every time I turn on the TV, I see this guy's face. What's the deal here?"

He looked at Mackinnley and didn't really expect an answer.

"Maybe he is the one hunting you, bud. You did kick the hell out of him the day I met you in the bar, remember?"

"Oh sure Frank. The ex-president of the United States is after me because of what I said in a bar?" David laughed off Mackinnley's excuse and watched the news.

The Metropolitan was the setting for the broadcast. Thorne ranted and raved about the state of the country and its increasing crime rate. He spoke about his condolences to the young man's family as he looked over the shoulder at what must have been Evan's dead body.

David looked about the suite and deduced that Elly was in either the washroom or her room and well out of earshot of the broadcast. He felt better that she was not reminded.

The anchor dictated the events at the Met and of a terrorist, Ahmed Mohammed Radjatsingham, who killed the young Evan O'Connor just prior to being killed by security for Mr. Thorne.

"Hey, Frank!"

"Yeah?"

"CNN says that security was Thorne's in the Met last night."

"Maybe we're on to something. We should set this laptop up and try to fish out some information. We still don't know whether Thorne hired the security or they are all on his payroll. I'll tell you one thing though, David. If we find out that those guys are Thorne's private army, it may not be too far off to think that Thorne is after you." Mackinnley knew exactly how to make a bad situation worse.

"Give me a break Frank. Thorne? The Republican candidate? The last president is trying to kill me? Frank, what the hell for?"

"Who knows David? But you fall in with good company. He would have had the Pope killed as well, if our intuitions are right."

David stared off well past the television into space. The thought of the ex-president and the ex-CIA director being after his soul shook him with fear. The man was powerful, wealthy and could easily have targeted him for termination. But why?

"Frank. You're messing with my head."

"Relax, David." Mackinnley chuckled. "I highly doubt that he would ruin his political career over a measly librarian."

"Measly. Frank you're such an..." His insult was cut short by the mention of his name on the news program.

"...is being sought in connection with two slayings in the New York area."

David froze in mid sentence.

"The FBI has a state wide search for Graceson and his accomplice, Francis 'Frank' Mackinnley, an FBI agent as well. The two are suspected for the murders of King Kahid and the Pope. Both murders occurred within forty-eight hours of each other. The two are also suspected of affiliations with Ahmed Mohammed Radjatsingham, a mercenary who has been sought by authorities world- wide for suspected terrorist activities. Radjatsingham was killed last night at New York's Metropolitan Museum at a gala event marking the opening of the James Elliot Thorne wing of the museum. Graceson was present at the dinner and suspected of hiring Radjatsingham for the Lincoln-style assassination of Mr. Thorne. The would-be target, Mr. Thorne, escaped harm but an Evan O'Connor, was caught in the crossfire and pronounced dead on the scene.

"An FBI spokesperson described the two as cunning and ruthless. They are armed and dangerous and should anyone see these two, to contact the number on your screen now. The authorities are also seeking an Elly O'Connor for questioning in the case."

The television screen was covered with pictures from the front of the *Times*. They looked so real, being on the news, that David felt faint. Both Mackinnley and David were captivated by the newscast when Elly walked into the room.

"Guys? What's up?"

"Elly you're wanted for questioning in the case of Graceson and Mackinnley versus the United States of America."

"What do you mean 'questioning'?"

"It means that they suspect you of involvement in the cases we're suspected of." Mackinnley offered his bureau logistics. "The bureau is putting it in a subtle, yet effective way that you are an integral player in this plot."

"Mr. Frank. I have no idea what the hell is going on about anything. My brother is dead and now they are suspecting me of killing him or anyone else? This is crazy!!"

"It *is* crazy. It's a messed up situation that has catapulted us into a strange and hellish world. Our only hope is to find a convincing enough case against someone or some organization, so that we can toss it to the authorities and they will get off our tail. The only way to do that is to get to work now. The longer it takes us the more congested with hunters the streets will become and we'll never be able to move from here. Miss Elly, it's time to do your stuff."

Elly grimaced. She looked at David who arose to meet her. He hugged her and kissed her forehead.

"It's alright, angel. We're going to beat this beast to death. That's the only crime we will have committed. They both walked over to the desk where the computer was set up. Elly's cellular phone was hooked up to the laptop and everything was ready to roll. She looked at Mackinnley and wondered where she was supposed to start.

"Well?"

Mackinnley reached into his shirt pocket and withdrew a piece of paper. "The first thing we have to do is find out who owns the Cerebral Vacation. Everything starts there so that's where we should start. Kick that thing to tell you who pays the bills there, Miss Elly"

Elly thought for a moment and then began furiously clicking the keyboard. She linked up with the mainframe in DC, punched in her clearance codes and from there started her search for the Cerebral Vacation. After five minutes of searching, she had come to a never-ending circle of companies that owned each other and in turn the Cerebral Vacation. Scillo's work on 'Eshers staircase' confused her yet made her suspect tampering.

Her puzzled look drew David's attention.

"What gives Elly?"

"Someone's trying to cover the roots of this place. Eight different companies own each other with the eighth company owning the first, all owning the club. It's very strange but it looks legitimate. Still you can't tell who really owns it."

"Someone's got to own the place!" Mackinnley barked.

"Sure someone has to. But whoever does doesn't want anyone else to know they do. Let me see." She thought for another moment and started on the keyboard again. "Damn!"

"What now?"

"I tried to check with the utility companies but they are all billed to the club name and address of the club. I'll check their supply shipments. Let's look at the liquor shipments." Her work took minutes and again she ended up nowhere. "Damn!!!"

"What?"

She didn't answer. Her typing became an incessant hammering on the keyboard, punctuated by the occasional cursing. Her work was all consuming and David and Mackinnley left her in her computer state. Obsessed and absorbed, she was in another world.

On the balcony the two stood looking down at the city. Somewhere down there CNN was scouring the pavement for hints of their whereabouts, hot on the heels of the FBI and Mackinnley's compadres, as well as the other heathens who put them in this situation.

"I could really use a drink."

"I could use a bourbon and Blue. You?"

"A bottle of scotch. Lets call room service."

"Hell of an idea."

Mackinnley walked passed Elly and rubbed her back. "How goes it?"

"Mmmmm. I got a...mmmmmm"

"Sounds good. Want something? We're ordering room service."

"Diet Coke."

He picked up the phone and ordered a bottle of scotch, a twelve of Labatt's Blue and a six-pack of Diet Coke. By the time room service hit the door, Elly was ready to throw the computer off the balcony.

"Shit! I can't find any holes in this place to get into. It's sealed up tighter than a drum." She was angry with herself more than the situation. "I don't know where to go with this thing."

"Take a break, hon'. Have a drink."

She reached out without looking and grabbed a can of beer. She pulled the tab and drank a mouthful.

"Mmmm! This is nice! What is this?"

"It's a Canadian beer. Labatt Blue."

"Canadian? And you can get it here?

"Yeah, you can even get it at some clubs."

"You can get this in clubs? It says it's made in Canada, Toronto, and Montreal. They must import it."

"They do. That's why it costs more. In the Cerebral Vacation they charged almost five bucks for a bottle."

Elly took another sip of her beer and thought about the cost of imported beer. Imported beer? The mention spurred a thought in her mind. She whirled around to face the computer and struck the keys with subtle hands. She grabbed the can of beer and read the side. Posted on the label was the address for the head office in Toronto. Her fingers gained momentum and by the time her thought had manifested into a rational pattern she was flying on the keypad.

"Elly? What ya doin'?"

"Hang on, David I'm almost done..."

A list came across the screen. Elly searched the screen and moments later she squealed with delight.

"Yes!! I got it!"

"Got what?" Mackinnley entered from the balcony and grabbed his bottle.

"If the Cerebral Vacation imports Blue from Canada, then the good folks at the Labatt Breweries would have records indicating shipments to the club. So I found it. Here, look. The address of the Cerebral Vacation is on 53rd street. The addresses on the invoices are to the Cerebral but the billing is to an address on the same street but a different address. Where is 152 East 53rd?"

"I think it's just across the street from the club."

"Across the street? Is there any club there?"

"Not that I know of."

"There must be an office there. It's Suite 6000."

Mackinnley perked at the thought. "An office? Who owns it Elly?"

"I don't know. It's marked down as Haidey's Holding Company Limited. I'll have to check the incorporation records." She hit the computer again with a barrage of fingertip assaults.

"Jesus Christ! What the hell is going on with these people?"

"What Elly? What's the matter?"

"The system is down at the registrar's office. How the hell is the damn country supposed to run if the damn systems crash all the time? Damn!!"

"Relax, Miss Elly. We'll just have to go down there ourselves and find out who's responsible for the 15 million dollars worth of dope in the club's back fridge."

"Who's going where?"

"We are going to, what is it again? 152 East 53rd street, suite 6000. We'll find out who is behind the cameras at the Cerebral Vacation."

"Are you out of your mind Frank? We have no experience in these matters. We have no idea what to do and '*we*' are ill equipped to handle something like this." David's fear made him ramble.

Mackinnley hated when people rambled. He was about to slap David across the head and remind him that people were out to kill him. He chose to wait out the verbal dread. "David." His voice took on the tone of a priest.

"You have to understand that if we do not fight this thing, it will destroy us. I'm talking physically and emotionally and spiritually. I've seen people break and it's not a sight you want to see. We, and I mean '*We*' have to take charge and turn this monster around. We go down there, all of us, and try and get some answers. I don't know what's down there, but it has to be more than we can get from this computer, no offence Miss Elly."

Elly looked at David with concern.

"I don't know, Frank. It seems kind of dangerous. What with them having all that surveillance stuff in the club and hiring Radjatsingham to kill me. I think that this is just too dangerous." He shook his head with disapproval and that infuriated Mackinnley.

"David let me spell it out for you. Every second we waste sitting on our asses; we get further away from any chance of succeeding. People are indeed trying to kill you, and to be dead honest my friend, if '*We*' don't do something about it, they are going to kill you and me and Elly anyway. Like the man says, you can pay me now or you can pay me later. Your choice, David. You can die now or you can die later. Personally, I'd like to take the chance and maybe beat the odds while we still have some in our favor."

David took Mackinnley's blasting very poorly. Before the woman he loved he became a six year old chastised for his lack of self- assurance.

"Be a man David. Reach down and pull that strength that is deep inside you out to fight. You want to stay alive? Maybe get married to this lovely lady here? Maybe have kids one day, man I don't blame you, but if you hide in this cocoon you will shrivel up and die in a matter of weeks. Get your ass up and we'll talk about it on the way. We're going to walk. Lets go!"

He gathered the two of them up and ushered them out the door.

The street was as crowded as the confines of the pavement would allow. It did not allow for talk but did allow for anonymity. They got lost in the tide of people and fifteen minutes later were washed up several blocks away from the corporate monument.

-15-

The afternoon air was stifling. It bore down on the lungs and lured sweat from every pore in the body. It was no wonder that most people on the streets were scantily clad. Only the anal retentive bankers kept their jackets and ties on.

The trio walked east on 49th street. The one-way street allowed for viewing of oncoming traffic and no vehicular surprises. Mackinnley walked on the curbside of the pavement. His eyes darted in every direction for signs of trouble. He was a professional at spotting surprises and he didn't want to single out any right now.

He was nervous. In his entire life he was never scared. He was an FBI agent. Wherever there was trouble there were at least ten other agents with him. He would be armed and pumped and ready for whatever danger lurked behind whichever closed door. This was different. He did not know who the enemy was, he did not have expert back up, he was poorly armed and he had two embryonic accomplices to drag around. It could not be more discouraging.

They stopped outside St. Patrick's Cathedral and grabbed a spot under the shade of an old oak tree. Their destination was four blocks over and four up and the ominous pressure of the unknown could be felt from there.

They discussed the plan and although David and Elly were frightened they understood their commands as set down by Mackinnley. They were ready to attack the Haidey's Holding Co. Ltd. Office and come what may.

Elly arose from the grass with help from David. They walked north on 5th Ave again facing traffic, but Elly stopped outside the doors to the Cathedral. She looked at the inscrolled doors and started to cry. David walked back to her and put his arm around her.

"It's alright Elly...come on."

"It's not alright, David. Evan is dead and I can't do a damn thing for his funeral. I can't go see him for a last time I can't do a single thing. I feel so horrible, David. I feel so horrible."

She wept into his shoulder. There was no use in rushing this state, it was understood that haste was imperative, yet without Elly in form it was hopeless.

"Elly. Let's go into the church and rest a bit. We can send a prayer out to Evan and maybe you'll feel better, OK?"

"Could we David? I would like that." Her words were punctuated with sniffles, but her eyes lit up when he offered the rest.

They walked up the stairs separately. First Elly, then Mackinnley and then David. By the time David had entered the church Elly was already at the altar kneeling in prayer. Mackinnley stayed in the back row. The last seat on the far right offered an excellent vantage point of the entrance doors and the entire cathedral.

David sauntered over to the far side of the basilica. He sat on the end pew and watched as an elderly woman exited the confessional. The door remained open and he gazed at the darkness within. It was inviting. It was secluded and safe and he wanted to crawl into it forever. To be sheltered from the world until all this madness he was enveloped in, subsided and his normal life could recommence.

Before he realized what he was doing, he had closed the confessional door behind him. The closet sized shrift was dark and hot. The seat was wet from the sweat of the old lady and the air smelled of her body odor.

The voice whispered from the other side of the grill.

"What is your confession?"

David stared at the obscured face and tried hard to remember how the ritual transpired.

"Bless me father..." He fought hard to remember the fastidious rites that were drilled into him as a child. "It has been far too long since my last confession but I am not here to confess."

"Then what brings you here, my son?" The priest was subtly annoyed yet his voice contained it well.

"I don't really know, father. I am in trouble. Very large trouble and the reasons for it are unknown to me. People are being killed all around me and now I truly believe that I am to be the next target."

"People get killed everyday, my child. This is not your fault. This is the work of Lucifer. He has engaged many to do his work. Unfortunately his armies are weak of faith and substance. He employs them and gives them what they believe to be worth. Do not blame yourself for the manifestations of the Devil, know who you are and who Christ is and in understanding the relation between you two. All that Satan does will be irrelevant in the end."

David stared at the grill. The priest must have been listening to the next window and answering that confessional. His speech was completely out of text. "But father. In literal terms people are being killed, shot. Murdered beside me. I feel like I'm the angel of death!" David's voice rose in pitch and volume.

"Well! What do you want me to do? Tell you that ten Hail Mary's will make a worthy recompense for this? No, I won't. Either you are good and you are a victim of circumstance or you are evil and in that case there is nothing either I or the church can do to help you."

"I didn't come for help, your eminence. I came for peace. I came because I am being hunted by an unholy presence that will not let me rest. Here in the church I came to mourn a friend whom I cannot pay my respects to because the authorities believe that I have killed him. They have accused me of two murders including the Pope's and I am innocent of them all. I saw the man who killed the Pope and I know his employer. Yet I cannot even approach the police because they would never believe me, nor would they believe my theory about the man."

The priest remained silent. He was engrossed in the sadness of the Pope's murder. Long moments passed before he continued with the conversation.

"My son. This church is the house of Jesus Christ, our Savior, His Father the Lord, and the Holy Spirit. You are safe here and loved. If you cannot bring yourself to the authorities because of the apparent implications then maybe we can help you. If you are indeed innocent then I am most certain that safeguarding can be arranged for you."

David was caught now. He had opened his mouth and perhaps out of fear, explained to a perfect stranger in not so many words, that he was the man the NYPD and the FBI were searching for.

"Father that would be wonderful. I would very much like to accept your offer but we have some work to do to confirm that our suspicions are correct and substantial."

"I understand my son. But please remember this though. The Lord is your salvation. He will help you if you heart accepts him and believes in the wonder of His love. You have come here today, for whatever reasons and I believe that you are a good man. A man of truth and belief. Although 'too many years' without confession is inexcusable, I trust that you are a child of the Lord and thus have the guarding of the Church and of Him. He will watch over you and give you the miracles that you require."

"Thank you, father. One more thing: please say a prayer for my friend who died in the museum yesterday. He was a good man, a regular here in this church and loved coming here. His name is..."

The door of the confessional had swung open and caught David's retina's wide open. He was momentarily blinded. The massive hand grabbed him and pulled him out of the seat.

"We have to go now." Mackinnley spoke with authority.

"Thank you for your time father. I will remember your words and please remember mine." David's voice was diminishing in volume as he walked down the side isle.

The priest opened the door of his booth and watched as the three walked hurriedly towards the doors of the cathedral. He was concerned for them. He had recognized the large man from the front page of the *Times*, and the younger man's face came into view just as they exited the building. Both were the men sought for the recent murders. So the news said. From David's time in the confessional, Father Peter did not know whether to believed him, as opposed to the media.

As the light flooded St. Patrick's Cathedral, Father Peter stood within it. He kept the door open long enough for the vehement heat to became unbearable. Still he watched them leave and vanish into the distance. He watched them and thought of what to do.

The authorities sought the two men. Whether they were guilty or not was not his place to judge. He closed the door and made his way to the office to report the incident to the proper authorities.

He prayed that he was doing the right thing.

All three had slipped into the corporate monument unhassled. The lower four floors of the building were vacant because of the blast from across the street. The receiving bays were still open for the remaining floors and through those doors they entered the stairwell. Mackinnley and Elly waited for David as he salvaged a necessary piece of equipment. He caught up with them carrying a two foot pipe he retrieved from a dumpster.

"So far so good. I'll go first. I'll be waiting on the seventh floor landing. Elly you come up next. David, you'll be right on her heels and then wait on the fifth floor landing. Got it?"

Both responded affirmative.

"Miss Elly, I can't tell you how real you have to make this. You have to believe it to make them believe it. I'm sorry but you have to think about your brother lying there on the museum floor. Think of him in the morgue right now waiting for someone to claim him." His intent was to get her emotional. It worked remarkably.

"Mr. Frank. I could have done it without that reminder. It wasn't a nice thing to do." She cried hard and fast. The tears streamed from her reddening eyes and she cursed him for the reminder.

Mackinnley felt bad for instigating the pain but felt great about the performance that was about to transpire. He took the stairs two by two and was out of sight.

The halting of footsteps indicated his arrival at his station. Both Elly and David ascended the staircase until the fifth level when he handed her the pipe and kissed her.

"Good luck, angel."

She wiped her tears away in vain and only reddened her eyes more. She smiled a futile grin and climbed one more flight to the sixth. There she looked up and saw nothing. She looked down and saw David's head peering up from between the banister-rails. She stared at the door and took a big breath. She put the pipe behind her on the floor and proceeded to pound on the door with intensity.

The pounding was consistent and she continued until her hands hurt. She cried harder and harder and the anger of Evan's murder forced her to trounce her emotions into the door.

After thirty seconds of hammering, the lock gave and the door was thrown open.

The swing of the door almost caught Elly on the shoulder. She stepped back and saw the large well-dressed man with a machine gun at the ready.

She dropped to the floor and started to cry. "No, please! Not again. Oh God, no. Not you too. Oh God have mercy. Please don't you hurt me too. Oh oouu..ouu!!" Her performance was exquisite.

The large man lost his sense of suspicion and dropped his guard. "I won't hurt you lady. It's OK. Are you alright?" He was as gallant as he could be with an uzi in his hand. He dropped the gun and the strap around his shoulder caught it. "Let me help you up."

Elly turned to look at him. More to get her sights than to inspect his chivalrous manner. "Oh thank you." She sobbed. She extended her left hand to him and with her right she grabbed the pipe.

The sound of the pipe scraping along the floor was noted too late by the ear that received the blow. She caught him full swing on the side of the head and he dropped like a sack of wet cement.

Elly was frightened and wondered whether she had hit him hard enough. Both Mackinnley and David ran to the landing and got there at the same time.

"Nice job Miss Elly. Very nice. He'll be out for a day or so." Mackinnley inspected the man. From the sight of blood trickling from his ear, he knew he was dead. He felt for a pulse and found none. "Don't worry, you didn't kill him." He lied straight-faced.

The sound of footsteps coming up the staircase forced them into the sixth floor office even before they could even get organized.

Inside the hall way Mackinnley stripped the dead man of his weapon. He kept it and tossed David his Berretta after he took the safety off.

"You know how to use one of these?"

"Point and shoot?"

"That's all you need to know."

"You stay here, Miss Elly. If you hear gunfire, get your pretty little self out of here and just keep on running. Under- stood?"

She nodded.

Mackinnley took the lead down the hallway and David followed. At each doorway Mackinnley stuck his face halfway around the corners and searched for life.

David felt like he was in a movie. With each step his fear engulfed him but was tamed with the thought of the gun in his hand. By the time they had reached the main office space, he had the courage of a well-seasoned soldier.

The office appeared clear. Still, both of them searched for any indication that someone was there until both came up empty.

"It's clean, Miss Elly. You can come out now."

Elly came out of the hallway like a scared kitten. They had gone over the entire office space and found nothing, which made her wonder whether the others would be back soon.

"We don't have much time Miss Elly so get to it. There are your instruments, Dissect this place." Mackinnley pointed at the computer and smiled at her. "I'm really sorry about doing that thing downstairs. I really didn't mean to hurt you. I just..."

"It's OK Mr. Frank. I know why you did it. There is no reason to apologize."

"I'm still sorry for hurting you, nonetheless."

She nodded at Mackinnley and dove into the records of Haidey's Holding Co. Ltd. She was lost in her computer state once again as David and Mackinnley ripped apart the sixth floor office in search of anything.

The main bank of monitors was lifeless, eight in all. On the panel before each of them were dials indicating cameras. Each screen monitored eight cameras. To the left of the monitors were ten different reel-to-reel recorders. They too had dials indicating specific microphone locations. The map on the wall behind the command post was a detailed floor plan of the Cerebral Vacation.

"Do you believe all this? The place was tapped, just like you said." David stood in awe at the discovery of surveillance equipment.

"This is where the pictures for the *Times* came from. The bastards set me up from across the street." Mackinnley was delighted and angry at once.

The drawers of each desk were pillaged and upon opening the largest of the desks Mackinnley found a folder marked "Graceson".

"David come here." He called as he opened the file.

"Jesus. Will you look at that?"

"That's very nice work."

"A little too damn real, I think."

David held the two pictures in each of his hands. One was of him on the floor of the club. It was identical to the picture in his left hand but without the uzi in his possession.

"I can't believe this. They bastardized this thing here!"

"Look at this." Mackinnley tossed him the original photo of the *Times'* homage to him and twenty others of the incident. There were pictures of them at the bar, on the floor, covering themselves from the shelling. There were even pictures of them fleeing the scene. They had covered every movement they had made since the trio had entered the bar.

They were not alone, though. The filing cabinet behind the desk had countless other pictures of clientele. Pictures of famous senators and dignitaries that David recognized.

There were even pictures of the back room. Mackinnley rifled through one of the twenty separate files of photos. They were marked with time and date encoded on the film. There were no names on these pictures. They weren't needed. Mackinnley recognized more than seventy percent of the people in them. Politicians and dignitaries, Kings and Queens, businessmen and judges. The back room photos were insurance. The participants were engaged in a variety of illicit acts. The sexual exploits that entrapped the many number of judges alone were enough to have their names banished from public office. Drugs were in the forefront of involvement. Many of the clientele were photographed with their noses deep into rails of cocaine. Crack pipes were abundant and the occasional syringe use was caught on film.

"This is unbelievable. Whoever is in charge here could have gone on forever with this blackmail material. Everybody in these pictures is so damn important it's not funny. I'm surprised that the president isn't in any of these. David, toss me a briefcase from over there. I've got to have these." Mackinnley eyed one photo of three lanky blonds engaged in a manage-beaucoup with a youngish easterner. It could only be the Swiss Stewardess Slurp.

David ran to the corner of the office and grabbed two briefcases, and tossed them both to Mackinnley who immediately opened one and emptied its contents. There were several files that spilled to the floor.

"What the hell are you doing Frank? We don't need pictures. We need information."

"Insurance, my friend. You can never have too much insurance."

"Guys!! I think you should take a look at this." Elly's voice was pressing. "This is gonna knock you on your butts."

The men ran to her side.

"Take a look at this. These are the files of the Haidey's Holding Co. Ltd. Their records are well kept. Meticulously handled. The assets are few but the wealth of this place is phenomenal. They have over five hundred million scattered all over the world in different banks. The hard assets, this office, which they own flat out and the... get ready for this, the Cerebral Vacation. You think that's wild? There are top-secret government files that have the location of every nuclear warhead the country owns. They even have, what appears to be the damn launch codes."

"Holy mother of God!" Mackinnley had to sit.

"There's more." Elly continued. "I was scanning through files and I across one titled 'Candy'. What do you think is in this sweet little gem? Shipment records dating back to '88 from Columbia, Thailand, Panama, Hong Kong."

"What's the deal?"

"The deal is they have dates and shipment sizes of cocaine, heroin, opium, marijuana it's all here in black and white. My guess is that this place is locked up tighter than a drum and no one gets in here that's not invited. These records are too dangerous to be placed on file. What are these people thinking?"

"Maybe they are untouchable."

"How can you be untouchable?" Elly was confused.

"Great insurance." He tossed Elly the photo of Supreme Court Judge Elenson with a face smeared with cocaine and two blond lovelies faces down in his naked lap.

"Jesus! That's insurance!"

"You got the account numbers of these banks?"

"Yes"

"Good. Now find out some names to go with the place. Check out security clearance files. They have to have some major shit happening there."

Elly ransacked the directory and within moments was into the employee files. Thirty names in all were on file. She pulled up one name and the screen changed to display a photograph and vitals on that employee. She went through every name and printed off a copy of each statistic sheet. The second last name was Anthony Terrace. As the screen presented the mans face, David peered at it with determination.

"That's the guy, Frank! That's the guy from my apartment, the guy at the museum and the same damn guy who killed the Pope. That's him!"

"You're certain?"

"Frank, I tell you It's him. I'm betting my life on it."

The computer spilled out very little on him. Height, weight, eye color, date of birth. Average stat's nothing worthy of note. His thumbprint was on file for reasons unbeknownst to Elly.

"Why the print?"

"Some of the locks in the place must be print identification. Very sophisticated stuff."

"Look, we don't have much time. Have you found out who owns this place?"

"I'm working on it. Don't rush me." She was frantically trying for results and she didn't need anyone telling her about haste. There was a man with a concussion, she thought, about to wake up any moment and squash them like bugs. She thwarted her way into the accounting files, personnel files. Files that listed companies and individuals and 'donations'. Elly chuckled at the word on the screen. Donations seldom run into the million-dollar amount. The names were familiar. Old money names; some politicians, judges, actors, many foreign names and foreign addresses. Then the name she was waiting to find came out in the next file she opened.

The James Elliot Thorne Re-election Fund.

"BINGO!"

"What'd you find?"

"Mr. Thorne owns this place. The ex-president of the United States of America himself."

"How do you figure?"

"First the fund. At least ten million is sitting in this account. Maybe it's his accountants place right? So I check into incorporation papers and there are few here in the computer, but here in the office files, are the have-to-sign to get anything papers that have the man's name and signature as president and co-owner.

"Are you certain about this, Miss Elly? If you are and we can get this out with us then I think we may have found a way out of this nightmare."

"I've copied as much as I can onto paper by printer and I've pinched a fair number of discs. I can't find anything on Radjatsingham yet but I imagine it's in here somewhere. Have you got what you need, or enough of it?"

"We've got the pictures, video's. A briefcase full of files we can make sense of once we get back to the hotel. Lets go then."

"Wait." Mackinnley grabbed Elly by the arm. "Miss Elly. Would you be so kind as to send out a fax to your office from here."

"Why, Mr. Frank?"

"This will verify that we were here. Should our validity be questioned, then we have a proper time and place."

"Fine." She sent out the top piece of paper on the pile. The personal file on Anthony Terrace.

Once the transmission was complete, they all grabbed their respective loot and made their way to the back stairwell. Mackinnley checked on the guard for Elly's sake.

"He'll be fine. Hell of a headache awaits him when he gets up, but otherwise he's fine."

Elly felt much better that the man was still alive. Mackinnley spared her the truth. They had enough things to worry about without adding a real murder to their resume.

-16-

Not only were they weighted down by the imminent fear of death; they were also burdened by their booty. The sixth floor office provided them four briefcases of information. Documents, videotape, photographs and computer discs. They walked hastily enough to seem in a hurry but not that fast as to indicate an escape. Their walk took them west across 54th, against the one-way streets again. At the Avenue of the Americas they headed south and past the Hilton at Rockefeller Center. Mackinnley realized his location just a mite too late.

"Where the Christ have you brought us?" His tone made Elly nervous.

"We're heading back to the hotel. You said take one-way streets that face oncoming traffic. Here we are facing traffic heading back to the hotel. What's the problem?" David whispered loud enough for Mackinnley to hear him.

"I'll tell you what's wrong, pal. This is where the FBI is stationed. Here in the Hilton. Should I remind you that we're walking just outside the lion's den? These guys are now the bad guys, after us, the good guys."

"Shit, Frank. You should have told me. How the hell am I supposed to know where they are? Let's just keep moving and we'll pass it in a minute."

The minute was a long journey for Mackinnley. All he needed was to see one of his associates and all hell would break loose. They passed the Hilton uneventfully and were in the sanctity of the Holiday Inn within fifteen minutes of leaving Haidey's offices.

The entire floor was a chaotically organized array of papers and photographs. Every picture was already dated and timed so David was assigned to place them chronologically. If he could recognize anyone, their names were to be placed on the photo as well.

Mackinnley gave the game plan the fuel and he got Elly digging into the bounty of computer discs while he checked the documents. They spent hours searching and filing and digging up whatever they could.

"Why don't you take a break?" Mackinnley could be a saint when he wanted to be.

"Jesus, thank-you." David got up off the floor and sat on the couch. His reflexes reached for the remote and he sat and watched the news. The program broke for a commercial and David took the opportunity to grab a beer. "Anyone for a drink?"

Both his partners were too busy to respond.

"Fine. I'll drink alone."

From the far end of the room he heard an advertisement for Larry King Tonight, where the night's guest would be Mr. James Elliot Thorne.

"Will you check this out? The son of a bitch who is hunting for us is going to spare time out from chasing to appear on Larry King. How do you like that?"

"So?"

"Oh Mackinnley, you're such a sympathetic ol' fart aren't you?"

"Hey! Don't call me old!"

"Sorry." David replied. "You fart."

"What's the problem? The guy had a rough couple of days after having a couple of people killed and he relaxes by hitting the campaign trail and lying to the public like politicians are trained to do from birth."

"I'd like to give him a piece of my mind." David thought about his comment. "Hey, I *can* give him a piece of my mind. King takes callers on his show. I should call him up and throw some of this information in his face on live television."

"Excellent idea. Now you want to get back to work so we can have something to throw at him?"

David left the beer on the counter and dove back into the pile of photos. He needed ammunition and some that could hit the man where he could feel it as bad as they had.

The lights in the Washington studio of the Larry King show were intense. Even after all those years, they still made Larry uncomfortable. In his shirt and suspenders he always sweats, because of the heat, not because of the powerful positions most of his guests held. As far as he was concerned, they were people with a story and history that needed to be told.

He was a professional who believed in the freedom of speech and his right was never challenged. Some thought him obnoxious, egocentric and arrogant. Pompous was the most common adjective. He loved it and adored the choice praise.

Tonight his guest was the ex-president. Under the bright lights James Elliot Thorne sat comfortably. He didn't sweat, didn't fidget, and didn't seem at all uncomfortable. On the contrary, King wondered if he had bathed in anti-perspirant.

The interview was uneventful. There was no punctuated dialogue between the two. Thorne would not persist and King did not have the desire to ignite the passion that he knew Thorne possessed. Thorne spoke of his campaign. The '04 election was the biggest one, as far as he was concerned and, "would be fought hard and with diligence."

"There is no possible way that the people of this exemplary country will allow their future to be ravaged by the irresponsible attitudes of the present administration. I am a citizen of this fine country of ours and I find the moral fiber is chaffing me like a hair shirt. We have come to a point in time when we must say 'enough is enough'. We should banish the policies that are weak and entrust ones that make us strong. We, the people of the United States of America, should become stronger than them. My message is not to take up arms, but to embrace a more impassioned belief in supremacy in both spirit and body. We were once the nation that others emulated. They dreamed of us and wanted to be us, today they look at us and laugh at the decay that has ensued as a result of our debauchery."

"In the coming years, I have great plans for our country. I will resurrect the desires of our forefathers and theirs before them. The dream will become reality under a more hard-lined, disciplined leadership. My opponent is a good man, if you like good men. Good guys end up last, isn't that what they say? We cannot afford to have a 'nice guy' president who is going to end up last on the world's political stage. There is still hope for us."

"Strength and power, drive and diligence and a never-ending pursuit of the dream. This is the force behind the Thorne campaign. We shall overcome the blasphemy that has entrapped the soul of the public and changed its course so long ago. I will personally redirect the spirit, and the soul will follow willingly, to a better world that we will create here on our soil."

"Mr. Thorne, we would like to take some calls if you are ready."

"I would be delighted, Larry." Thorne's smile was wearing thin. He checked his watch to see how much of this monkey show he had to contend with.

"Hello, Gabe from New York. You're on the air."

"Good evening, Larry. Good evening, Mr. Thorne. First of all let me express my great adoration for you, Mr. Thorne. I think that in recent history we have never had a president with the moral strength and patriotism that you, sir, possess. You are the definitive American and I am proud to know you are running for office again. You are by far the best if not the only, choice to lead this country into the darkness that the future holds for us, holding a torch to that blackness and show us the way."

"Thank you sir. You sound like a learned man. You are very astute and more people should listen to what you have to say. Then, come election time, I should be put in my proper place."

Thorne's pompousness overcame him and he was lightheaded with the praise. Awaiting more adulation, Thorne sat higher in his chair, beaming, hungry for more exalting, he smiled.

The praise was cut short. At Thorne's height of self-indulgence, the hammer came down with a vengeance.

"Do you know of the Cerebral Vacation Mr. Thorne? Do you know Ahmed Mohammed Radjatsingham? How about Anthony Terrace? And how about Andre Charon?"

"Who is this?"

"Someone who knows things, Mr. Thorne. You didn't answer my questions Mr. Thorne. You obviously know who the Pope is. How about Evan O'Connor?"

"Who the hell is this?"

"A very astute individual, Mr. Thorne. One that more people should listen too, remember?"

"Larry, this is ludicrous." Thorne spoke with authority.

"Mr. Thorne. The questions await answer." Larry wanted to see where this would go.

"Well, Mr. Thorne, can you tell the listening public about the Haidey's Holding Co. Ltd.?"

"Whoever you are, you have no right to slander me here like this on television."

"I have all the right in the world, Mr. Thorne. Do you know why, Mr. Thorne? Because I got away from your web."

"My web? Yours is the only web sir and you are tangled in the confusion of your own delusions. You are a minuscule fly."

"I may be a fly Mr. Thorne, but you are about to be swatted."

"Larry I've had quite enough of this call. Can we move on?" Thorne's request came across as an order.

"Mr. Thorne with all due respect, if you want to run from this call the public may formulate their own opinions." Larry watched the face of his guest turn angry. There may be a story about to break on the King show or there could be fireworks, either way this is what he lived for.

"Funny you should mention running, Mr. King." The caller's voice increased in tempo and tenacity. "I've been running for two days now because of Mr. Thorne."

"Because of me!! This is preposterous!"

"I thought the same thing, Mr. Thorne until Tuesday's *New York Times* came out. You want to talk about slander, Mr. Thorne? I'll tell you about libel."

Thorne was furious. He stood up and yelled into the camera lens. "Graceson, if that's you, you miserable creature, you are a criminal. The papers know it, the authorities know it, and you know it. You are trying to twist this whole thing around and drag my name through the mud. Well, I'll tell you one thing, I will not stoop to such a lame ploy to denigrate my name. Once the authorities find you and I'm sure they will soon, I will personally add at least five more charges to the list.

"New York does not have the death penalty, but by the time your court case is done, there may be amendments to that law and your sentence will be just."

"Listen to me, Thorne, you power-hungry manipulator. You can answer the questions here on television, or you can answer them in front of a grand jury. Your affiliation with the Haidey's Holding Co. alone will have you in maximum security for life. Oh, something else Thorne. I know about your ties with Radjatsingham. He was an employee of yours, wasn't he? Do you deny any affiliation with the Haidey's Holding Co. Ltd?"

"Damn right. I deny anything that you say right now you worm."

"Deny this, you hypocrite. Deny that Anthony Terrace is one of your employees. Deny it! You, miserable tyrant!"

"I deny it!!"

"You Deny it? Mr. Thorne the documents I have here are from a very reliable source on East 53rd. Ring any bells? Maybe six of them? These documents tell me you are lying.

"Who says they are my records, you bastard?"

"Mr. Thorne. We all know politicians lie, but don't tell me shit doesn't stink when we all know it does. You Mr. Thorne are finished. I will personally see to it."

"Graceson trust me..."

"Trust you?" David interrupted.

"Trust me, Graceson, you have nowhere to run and no one will believe you, if and when you ever get there. You are dealing with the wrong person. You will be made to pay in the dearest form. I would not be so boisterous in your commentary Mr. Graceson, people get hurt that way."

"That couldn't be a threat could it Mr. Thorne? Because you can't threaten me. You already tried to have me killed. By a professional hit man at that. I'm tired of running Jim-Bo. You killed my best friend, now I will make sure that you are definitely put in your proper place, way before Election Day."

"Mr. Graceson, your proper place awaits you where the flames of damnation will torment your soul for eternity."

"I'll see you there Jimmy. I'll see you there."

The phone line disconnected and everyone in the studio stood in complete silence and stared at the stage. The guest was rattled. In all the years they had seen him in the public eye, he was never fazed once. Today he was non-pulsed.

"Larry with all due respect, I cannot believe you let that call go on. There are far too many lunatics out there who use the media to manipulate. Let me assure the public that I have no idea about anything the last caller implied. Mr. Graceson is a criminal at large and wanted for the murders of King Kahid and the Pope. His intent, this evening was to discredit me by implicating me in his plot. He will be caught and made to pay for his crimes. All of them."

Thorne was vexed. He became flushed and humbled, two emotions that were new to him. Behind the cellophane smile his mind raced. How the hell did Graceson get all the information? Just the mention of Terrace almost made him shudder. He could not know that name without having been on the sixth floor at some point in time.

During the next commercial break, Thorne bolted from his chair, grabbed Charon and made his way to a phone. The punctuated conversation was short and had Charon nervous.

Back in the hot seat again Thorne took two more phone calls from people who hinted at David's line of questioning. By the time the show ended, Thorne was infuriated and stormed off the set without so much as a 'Thank you' to the host.

Thorne was a blur all the way to New York and the sixth floor offices on East 53rd.

-17-

Gonsalvez awoke from a well-deserved nap. Even an hour rest was enough to rejuvenate the cells. From his bed he hit the remote and scanned through the channels. With cable and satellite, he whipped through 40 channels before he caught Thorne reveling in some praise on the Larry King show.

The man was pompous and arrogant, and there on King's show some yahoo was inflating his ego far past demigod. The praise, though was short-lived as the caller, started in on Thorne like a starving wolf. The questions came hard and fast. Incriminating questions. Questions that far exceeded the limits of social etiquette. Questions that had relevance to Gonsalvez' case.

He listened intently and scrambled for a pen. He wrote the questions down as fast as he could. Then the name came. Gonsalvez stopped writing when Thorne cursed Graceson.

"Graceson?" He exclaimed with surprise.

The questions now took on a different light. Mackinnley was with him, he could tell by the detective like interrogation.

"Where the hell did they get all this?" He asked himself aloud as his pen was a blur of writing and he tried to capture as many questions as he could. Some names escaped him. Haidey's Holding Co. Ltd. along with the name Anthony Terrace was salvaged from Graceson's avalanche of interrogation.

The call ended with Thorne extremely agitated. After his address to the camera, it was highly likely that he was involved in something. Whether Graceson had hit upon something was not certain but he hoped that he could stumble onto the same track.

Gonsalvez hopped out of bed and ran down the stairs to the conference room. He burst through the doors and scared the hell out of six agents who were still working there.

"Someone pull up everything you can on the Haidey's Holding Co.

Ltd. They are based somewhere. Find it. Then tell me who owns it. Also, someone get me everything you can on an Anthony Terrace."

Gonsalvez was on the phone to DC within seconds. "This is special agent Gonsalvez of the FBI. I need transcripts and a video copy of tonight's Larry King broadcast here in New York as soon as possible. We will have an agent there at your door in twenty minutes. Give him your full cooperation. I thank you and your country thanks you."

He hung up the phone and immediately called Jacobs' room. He summoned the director to meet in the conference room. By the time Jacobs met up with Gonsalvez, the computers were printing out the information on Haidey's. Jacobs caught Gonsalvez by the printer.

"Gonsalvez, this important?"

"I think it might be sir. Tonight on the Larry King show, a person believed to be Graceson called up and gave Thorne a major shit kicking on the air. He blasted him with all sorts of questions implying that Thorne was involved in the killing of the Pope and King Kahid. Graceson, who I believe is consorting with Mackinnley, also made reference to Thorne's involvement with Radjatsingham. Say's he's been on Thorne's staff. I don't think either Graceson or Mackinnley could bluff something like this if it wasn't fact and I don't think that Thorne would have gotten so upset if there was not some validity to the matter. You should have seen him sir, he was damn near rabid."

Jacobs sat in silence and listened to Gonsalvez. He said nothing for the longest time. Then he gazed over to his colleague with a look of puzzlement.

"Gonsalvez, I don't buy it." He spoke with his face grimaced in skepticism.

"How in God's name could Graceson and Mackinnley get info on Thorne when we don't even know where the man lives? If we can't find his God damned address, how the hell is Graceson or Mackinnley going to find out his personal business? It's a farce and I don't buy it."

Gonsalvez stared at the director. His hunch was solid. It had all the markings of a plausible scenario, but still the director was right. Mackinnley had trained him and he knew he did not possess the expertise to find the info. Graceson was a librarian. But the girl. Maybe she found something.

"Sir what about the girl? Elly O'Connor?"

"What about her?"

"Sir?" An agent beckoned from the computer screen.

Gonsalvez and Jacobs spun around.

"You might want to see this."

The Haidey's Holding Co. Ltd. washed over the screen with its vitals. Like a heart monitor it revealed the life force behind the name. Incorporated December '88. President and co-owner Jimmy E. Thorne.

Address 152 East 53rd Street. Assets were few, their office space and the Cerebral Vacation.

"I...think we have a problem here." Gonsalvez spoke with constrained excitement.

Jacobs eyed the screen with minimum emotion. "I don't buy it."

"What don't you buy? These are government records sir? With all due respect, what's the deal with you?"

"Mr. Gonsalvez!" Jacobs became transformed into a different person. "You are supposed to be a professional investigator with the Federal Bureau of Investigation. Your behavior and your judgment are either being clouded by your friendship with Mackinnley or have completely taken leave of you. I should also mention that you are coming dangerously close to gross insubordination and dismissal. It seems to me that I have to retrain you, special agent Gonsalvez. Who is in with Graceson and Mackinnley? Who works for the State Department and can even alter your birth certificate if SHE wanted to? Who did you just imply might have found a link between Thorne and Radjatsingham? Come on Gonsalvez; give your head a serious shake. You truly believe the ex-president of the United States; the ex-director of the CIA and probably the next president is involved with the most wanted man in the world? Radjatsingham? Are you out of your bloody mind? Either you get your head on straight young man or I'll have to enforce an extended vacation."

"But sir." Gonsalvez tried hard for salvation.

"Don't 'but sir' me Gonsalvez. Don't dick around with this. O'Connor planted all this information in the computers and they are trying to push the blame on a very respectable citizen. We have a plan to find Graceson, Mackinnley and O'Connor and bring them in. Alive is best, dead if you have to. Understand me, special agent Gonsalvez?"

Humbly, Gonsalvez conceded to the threats of the director. He hung his head and surrendered, "Yes sir."

The information on Anthony Terrace rattled the printer to life. The director read the name and he picked up the print sheet as he passed. Without looking at the rest of the printout he tore the transmission in pieces and walked out with it.

At the door he turned and spoke to all the agents in the room.

"No more time will be wasted on this Thorne theory. Anyone caught wasting bureau time pursuing that line of investigation, will be thrown out of the bureau and brought up on charges of treason. I'm dead serious about this."

The door slammed behind him, sucking all the air out of the room and leaving Gonsalvez in an emotional and professional void.

With nowhere to go in New York, Fleming was even more compelled to stay in the office and work. Something was awry with the situation across the street. Just what it was eluded him. The State Department handled many affairs involving the FBI. It was unorthodox but not so unusual. The bureau had seemed to be untouchable in the days of Hoover but today they were scrutinized by the State Department. As far as Fleming was aware, many painstaking steps were taken to keep this branch of the state department quiet. It was their sole purpose, and with the integrity of the government at stake it was determined that the State Department would assume the responsibility. This was the fifth time his team was called out to 'spy' on the federal boys, and every time they blew the corrupt agents out of the water. As far as the agents knew, it was a bust gone badly. Fleming didn't care how it looked. Whether they came across as the mob, or psycho-killers didn't matter. As long as the unscrupulous got eliminated.

The '*Eye*' as they were referred to, started up almost four years ago. The group was selected after careful scrutiny and intensive study. Fleming would have liked to take more on board but the larger the team, the greater chance of self-destruction.

Elly was to be inducted after her vacation, to complete the research division. The call from Jacobs put him on edge and his suspicions were correct. The director was out to bury his computer wizard and by God there would be a battle for her soul. The president offered little resistance when the topic was brought up. Fleming had 'carte blanche' as long as the mission was kept in its confidential and non-existent status.

Fleming stared at the Hilton. Within the conference room he could see Jacobs musing in his chair. As the young Hispanic was drawn deeper into the room, Jacobs followed him.

"Sir." The voice from the computer desk summoned.

"This is what they are looking at."

The screen had already revealed to them the statistics on Haidey's Holding Co. Ltd. This was to be inspected later. Now the monitor spread a face across the screen. He was Anthony Terrace.

"Who the hell is this guy?"

The cursor raced across the screen and Terrace's vitals followed. Male. Caucasian. Six foot seven. 298 pounds. Thirty-eight years of age. Ex-CIA. Ex-Secret Service. Ex-Navy Seal. Status: Deceased, July '89.

"So they got some dead giant. I don't understand this."

The fax machine behind him beeped for his attention. He turned and watched as the paper rolled and hid the transmission as if too shy to jump out. He grabbed it reluctantly as the second facsimile rolled into view.

"Jumpin' Jiminy!" He was shocked.

The second transmission was almost pulled out of the fax machine before it could print the information requested. It read: *'Mr. Fleming. This transmission just came over the wire about four hours ago. It came through on Elly's fax in her office and seeing that you are looking out for her up there, I thought it might be of some importance. It was sent from an office up there, on East 53rd street. The address is on the top right. Hope it can be of some help.'*

Fleming reeled his head around towards the Hilton's conference room in time to see Jacobs ripping paper and raving to the staff.

His gaze raced to the screen of the computer before him. The photographs were identical. "Print it now!"

The printer was far to slow for his liking. Finally it surrendered the information. He grabbed the printers offering and read it carefully. The facsimile was a contradiction. He was older in the facsimile. The transmission could not have put five years on the man's face. His record on the fax stated 'presently employed'. The printer said he was 'deceased'.

"What the...what the hell is going on? What are they talking about over there? Make some sense of all this for me Richards"

The young man at the hearing station printed out the last five minutes worth of conversation from the Hilton.

Fleming read with determination. His eyes perked when he read about Graceson and Larry King. He laughed aloud when he got to the part about Elly's ability to alter birth certificates.

"I'll be damned." Fleming was most impressed. "That little minx was in the offices of the Haidey's Holding Co. Karen did you know that Elly is already into espionage? "

He finished reading the transcripts and his excitement was lost. Jacobs was not impressed with the line of thought the young Hispanic Gonsalvez had going. His threat only made Fleming wonder about the director's loyalties.

"I need a transcript of this conversation that Graceson had with Thorne. Karen call up CNN and have them fax the Graceson segment. Have them fax it to the office in DC and then have them relay it here. I want it in five minutes."

Fleming stared at the two separate bio sheets on Anthony Terrace. They introduced a new little wrinkle into the plan. There was a connection with him and with Thorne. Terrace was dead for five years yet Thorne and Haidey's had him on staff at present. Something didn't fit right and as if there was any doubt in his mind about Elly, the 'Graceson, Mackinnley and O'Connor' story was starting to look quite interesting.

The flight from Washington was intolerable. It was the fastest form of travel and yet it took eons to reach the Big Apple. The limousine had picked the entourage up at the airport and escorted them with haste to the 53rd street office.

From the receiving docks they entered the building. Four guards had corralled some of the workers who had been there all day and had already attained detailed descriptions of everyone who had come in. The guards stayed downstairs and were thankful they did not have to be in the office when Thorne would behold the sight of the inviolable asylum.

The lobby of the building was empty at that time of night and the sound of the ten men walking echoed throughout the concourse. Upon entering the sixth floor office Thorne was paralyzed with anger. The view that presented itself was intolerable. Filing cabinets were wide open and emptied. Computer discs were missing from their cases, all of them. His sacred office was violated by the insolent bandits. There were papers strewn all over the place and every drawer in the offices was left gaping open.

Every muscle contracted in his body. Breathing became shallow and rapid as his blood pressure skyrocketed. His hands became fists and the guard beside him took the first blow in the face. The force was so great that his mandible splintered and several teeth dropped to the floor.

"Where the fuck is security?" Thorne screamed in a possessed manner. Almost in convulsions, his mannerisms lost all semblance of being human.

"Jorgenssen!!" The demonic call cut the air like sirens.

The large man appeared from the back hallway. His head was hung, as reprimand was imminent. "Sir?" His voice was far too feeble for such a large man.

"You have failed me. Give me your gun." Thorne reached out as the revolver was surrendered to him.

"Any excuse?"

Jorgensen was silent.

"Very well." Thorne pointed the gun to the mans forehead and pulled the trigger. The man dropped after the shot. The crack of his skull, on the marble floor caused Charon's stomach to flip.

"Where the fuck is Denison? He had the simple responsibility of guarding this place. Bring me Denison now!!!" The president of the Haidey's Holding Co. Ltd. was far past the point of sensibility. His reasoning became focused solely on retribution. The body of the guard was dragged from the back hallway to the dismay of Thorne. "Damn!!!!" He shot the carcass twice and spit on it.

"You and you." He pointed to two other guards. They came reluctantly to him. "Where were you when all this was happening?"

"We were at your home, Mr. Thorne, sir. For the meeting."

"This is my home you pathetic scrot's. They violated my temple and all shall pay. You." He pointed the gun and took off half the guard's head with the shot. "And you. Come here."

The man checked the distance to the door and thought of how fast he could draw his own weapon.

"Come here *NOW*." Thorne was seething.

The man approached and the barrel of the pistol was placed deep in the socket of his left eye until the screams were intolerable. The trigger was eased back as the sensation of tension built against his fingertip. The scream was silenced after the bullet pierced the guard's cranium.

"Dump them. All of them. Now! And get me those guys from the loading docks. Bring them to the main lobby. Move on it or you will all join your *ex*-associates"

The stampede to the door could have been likened to the running of the bulls. No one was going to stay with the man to endure yet another one of his tantrums.

The three men awaited Thorne's arrival in the concourse. Five guards stood by them far enough away to avoid another spree.

"You! How many of them?"

"Ah...three. Two men and a woman. One guy was big, solid, about fifty, maybe. The other guy was slim, thirty, thirty-five. The chick is a babe. Twenty two, shapely, blonde, loaded, nice legs."

"Did they come in with anything?"

"No. Nothin'."

"Did they leave with anything?"

"Yeah...Briefcases. Four of them. Yeah four."

"Anything else?"

They all shook their heads.

"Thank you gentlemen." Thorne pardoned them and he hopped in the elevator to the sixth floor. Charon stood at the door as his master entered.

"What now sir?"

"Now we don't dick around any longer. I have a campaign to run. I have far too many people to influence and sway. The time will pass and if the outcome is not the desired one..." He stared at Charon for a short second and let his sentence trail off.

"Graceson had a big mouth. I use the past tense because we shall, after tomorrow, know him as exterminated. Mackinnley, that bastard. Kill him violently and slowly. Cut him up with a circular saw. But I want the woman. Bring her to me. That whore will pay the master. She buggered my office. She stole my files and opened my soul. I will crucify that bitch and teach her violation."

Charon sat with Thorne as he discussed the plans. Tomorrow would not end with any one of those thieves alive.

-18-

The morning sun pierced the room with light. Mackinnley wanted the drapes open. The drapes remained open. The previous night's attack on Larry King's guest proved to be the start of brighter things.

Thorne was their man. He had to be. David thought over the preceding week and with the newfound information, Thorne was the culprit. The Cerebral Vacation was where David started his intoxicated rambling. The first day of summer allowed him too many liberties and his ranting must have been well noticed and recorded. He remembered the accusations, the government scandals and the way they misled the public. Most of his accusations were based on Thorne's time in office. If he was not president when all of David's allegations were observed, then he was behind the scenes. An integral player. Iran was planned. He remembered saying that. Maybe it was. Maybe he planned the attack on the president when he was vice-president. Maybe the man on the grassy knoll in Dallas was he. He had access. He was CIA then, must have been awfully high up in there be awarded with such a secretive duty. He did indeed have status because in just a few short years he became the director of that body.

It was all becoming clearer. If there were a possibility that it was all true then it would explain why the man wanted him dead. It was ludicrous, though. People talk all the time about theories and ideas about government issues and events. David tried to free himself of the thought that was enveloping him.

He sat up in bed and looked in the mirror. His morning face looked back at him. He looked hard at the reflection and knew why he was the target. The Cerebral Vacation.

"Frank. Frank! Wake up. I got it!" He was excited yet terrified and although he did not like the answer he came up with it was an answer nonetheless.

"WHAT!" Mackinnley shot up in bed. "This better be God damned important Graceson, to get me up at....NINE THIRTY! In the bloody morning!"

"Jesus, Frank. Time to lay off the coffee a little, don't you think? Look it's important. Get your shit together and meet me in the living room."

By the time Mackinnley made his way into the main room of the suite, David had already ordered continental breakfast for five. On the coffee table he had several sheets of paper and a couple of pens. A stack of stolen files from the sixth floor office was also on the corner of the table.

"Frank, coffee's on its way, hang on pal, you're gonna make it."

Mackinnley eyed David with disdain.

"This is the way it is Frank. I figure that James Elliot Thorne is involved in too many things to be allowed to walk the streets, let alone run for office."

"Talk to me and try to make it sound sensible." Mackinnley had no urge to listen to the amateur detective's theory. He wanted either his sleep or his coffee, not a nine-thirty meeting.

"Thorne had all opportunity to be involved in: *A.* The Iran contra, right? *B.* The Iran hostage crisis, right? *C.* The assassination attempt on his presidential leader back in the late eighties, correct? *D.* He was in the CIA when Kennedy was picked off in Dallas, wasn't he? *E.* He has the upper echelon of the American and international world caught on film and video performing in illicit activities. *F.* He has Anthony Terrace on staff there on 53rd street. *G.* His club contained illegal drugs didn't it? "

"Yeah. All that stuff is possible. He was around when all that stuff came down, I guess, but tons of other people were also around David. You want to nail Thorne with every crime committed in the past three decades?"

"No I don't. I just want you to realize that he could have. This is the stuff that I was blabbing about in the Cerebral. If the place is his and is all wired up with cameras and microphones, then the guys up there on the sixth floor could hear and see me, right?"

"Yeah, right. Go on."

"So the guys up there pass on the information to Thorne that some yahoo in the bar is hitting on a lot of raw nerves, stuff that nobody in their right mind would profess in public or even consider thinking. I'm a history fanatic, Frank. I retain information like a sponge. Who would know better about American history than a librarian with a photographic memory? So Thorne's running for office. If this stuff gets out and verified, hell even if it's not verified, what are his chances of sitting in the president's chair? Pretty damn slim if you ask me. So he tried to shut me up. He sends over the walking condo, Terrace, over to my apartment to check and see if I've got anything tangible on my theory, which at that time I didn't even know was a theory, and he comes up empty. I've already got the phone call telling me to 'shut up'. They must have sent another guy over to check my place out because I spotted a footprint in my carpet. That's beside the point.

"Then Sunday we all end up in the Cerebral to grab a beer. That's when we run across you. You remember what was on the tube when we were there, Frank? It was some documentary on Thorne. Can you remember what I was saying about him?"

Mackinnley was waking up quickly now. "Something about Vietnam and him floating in the ocean in Korea, something like that."

"That's exactly what I was saying. You know you can't find a book anywhere that will tell you all that information. You have to piece it together like a million piece puzzle. I got lucky and fell upon it one year when I was doing my dissertation.

"So we're in the club, we're having our drinks, everything is groovy and we are being taped and photographed and bugged and then it seems that Thorne gets pissed off at me that I revealed more incriminating stuff in public. He sends out Radjatsingham to dust me and shut me up forever. But the fuckin' guy misses and messes up the bar, kills a King, gets the FBI into the club and the party room is not a secret any more.

"You and I get framed for the killing of the king and we get life with no idea what we've done wrong."

Mackinnley sat back in the chair and eyed David. His head whirled and the theory was becoming more and more concrete. The timing was right, the opportunities were there and history made him open his eyes a little wider to see the whole picture. His first impressions of David were bang on. He was intellectual without being pretentious and although this scenario was preposterous, it might be true.

"So let me see. Radjatsingham misses you in the bar and Thorne figures that he can get you to the Metropolitan and get you killed off by Radjatsingham. I figure he's going to dust Radjatsingham after he kills you because he knows far too much anyway. He misses you, kills Evan and makes it all look like an assassination attempt on him. It's bloody brilliant."

"Sure makes him look good and me look like the criminal. Thorne is unbelievable. I can't believe that he pushed all this shit on me."

"David. Librarians are not known for their strength. He figured that you would probably be an easy mark."

"What I can't figure out is what the Pope has to do with all this. The King was probably an accident and most certainly the reason Radjatsingham was killed."

"I can't figure it out either but I'll tell you one thing, I like the sound of all this. It makes a lot of sense, although it's way too huge to comprehend at first. You're telling me that for one reason or another, Thorne has been involved in executions, terrorism, arms trades and high level crime for three decades and has some plan for all this?"

"Plan? Maybe, but he doesn't really need a plan! He's probably making a fortune on those pictures alone, never mind the rest of history. You figure that everyone one of those people in those pictures is hooked for life to Thorne. I counted at least two hundred high profile individuals last night in those photos. Some of them, man, will blow you away. Here take a look at this one." David fumbled through a couple of piles of photos. He was careful not to upset the order he had worked so hard to create.

Mackinnley watched David yet saw the life of James Elliot Thorne unfold in a different light. David was remarkably astute and definitely would have made a great agent.

The knock at the door signaled room service. It startled them both as paranoia was now a way of life.

"Yes. Who is it?"

"Room service."

Mackinnley stood up and reached for the uzi. He approached the door with caution.

"Who?"

"Room service, sir."

Mackinnley looked at the door as if he could see through it.

"I've just come out of the shower and I've got nothing on. Leave the stuff on the floor. How much do I owe you?"

"Fifteen dollars sir."

Mackinnley unfolded a twenty and slid it under the door.

"Keep the change. Thanks!"

He waited until the carpet muffled footsteps faded towards the elevator. He then quickly retrieved the tray from the hall way and shoveled half the breakfast down his throat before he got to where David was sitting.

David watched in fascination as Mackinnley almost inhaled the food. "Frank, you're unbelievable. You almost look like this guy in the picture."

He handed Mackinnley the photo. "This guy's got more cocaine all over his face than in all of the west side. He's got those straws sticking out of his nose and he looks like he's having a grand old time. Check out the chick. She's got coke; it sure looks like cocaine, all over her naked body and the guy's snorting it with his whole face. Can you believe it? I don't recognize the guy though."

Mackinnley looked at the picture and immediately choked on his food. He bolted upright and twisted the picture toward the light for better viewing.

"Holy shit!!"

"Frank! What is it?"

"It's Jacobs!!"

"Who the hell is Jacobs? You know this guy?"

"Know him? I work for him! He's the director of the FBI!!"

"Get outta here. You're pulling my chain. The director of the FBI? You're a riot."

"This is Harold D. Jacobs!" Mackinnley was in a trance like condition.

"Frank. You're serious aren't you?"

"I'm a detective, David. I think I can recognize my boss in a goddamned picture, don't you think? This is he for sure!"

Mackinnley walked about the hotel room holding the picture and muttering incoherently. He paced about the room for five minutes as David watched him parade to and fro.

"What are you gonna do?"

"Shit! I don't know. This picture alone is worth millions, more like billions. If Jacobs is in with Thorne then there is no chance that I will live. Jacobs will have every agent in the world out looking for me, with even more conviction if they know that we have these pictures. Maybe all these partiers know about their pictures. They must, that's why Thorne can operate that party palace with such secrecy. Nobody dare open their mouth with these dangling in Thorne's hands. Let me see the rest of those pictures."

"Careful with them. I worked too damn hard getting them all in chronological order, for you to mess them all up now."

"I'll be careful."

"I'll get Elly. I'm surprised she slept through all your racket." David ambled down the hall towards the master suite.

He tapped on the door of her room. There was no reply. He turned the knob and slowly pushed the door open. The curtains were drawn and there was little light in the room.

"Elly," he whispered. There was nothing but silence. This scared him.

"ELLY!" He called her name hoping for a reply from somewhere in the massive room. He ran to the en suite bathroom and she was not there.

"ELLY!!" He ran screaming her name from the bedroom and almost lost his footing as he rounded the corner to the living room.

"Where is she?" Mackinnley was nervous.

"I don't know. She's not in her room. Where the hell can she be?"

"Do you suppose she went out to get some breakfast or something?"

"I don't know. You think she'd leave a note somewhere or something to let us know where she was." David's voice crackled with concern.

"Did you look for one before you shit your pants?"

"Well...no...I didn't." It was a great idea and one that David acted upon. The entire suite was searched and there was no note found. David became ill. The bile could tasted in his throat and he fought to keep it in its place. He walked to the washroom to wash his face and perhaps vomit. As the water splashed his face he looked up and there it was on the mirror.

"Frank!! I found it!"

The note was short and simple. '*I love you. I love my brother. Gone to say good-bye.*'

"Shit!!"

Mackinnley rounded the corner and caught David cursing.

"She went to the funeral, didn't she?"

"Yeah. How did you know?"

"I'm a detective, David. I know people."

"I don't like this at all Frank. I don't like it one bit."

"What do you want to do?"

"Go get her. Make sure she's OK. What do you mean?"

"David let's sit down. We'll talk about it."

They made their way into the living room again and they sat on the couch.

"We are in some serious shit here David. Everybody and their dog is after us and personally, I have no idea what they look like. Theoretically it could be anyone. Elly did an emotional thing, like women do sometimes, and all we can do is hope that she will be all right. If she is in trouble out there, chances are there won't be a damn thing we can do about it. All we can do is pray that she makes it back here."

"Frank, shouldn't we go out to make sure she's fine?"

"If we head out those doors, pal I can almost assure you we're going to be in deeper shit. It's easier to get lost in a crowd when you're one person. Two or three is a completely different story."

Mackinnley was a marvel at making sense. The situation called for a mental approach not an emotional one. David was illogical and his heart told him to run to her. Regardless of bullets or bombs or death, he wanted to be with her to protect her as best as the Berretta Mackinnley gave him could. But he walked to the window, his head was spinning.

He looked down into the busy street and tried to envision her coming towards the hotel.

She would be back.

The grounds were meticulously maintained. The lawns were just recently cut and the scent of fresh cut grass hung heavy in the sweltering morning air.

The sermon had been a lengthy one. The newspaper said that service would be at nine and burial at ten. Elly stood in the shadows of a grove and awaited the arrival of her brother. She felt scared and alone and the delay in the arrival of the procession only added to her unease. There in the shadows she wept and between each wiping of her tears, she searched the grounds for any suspicious looking people. Every one looked suspicious in a graveyard, she thought. It was stupid of her to come, she knew it but she could not bare the thought of not being at her brother's funeral. It was enough that she could not be at the church for the service. There in the shade of the old oak trees, a hundred feet from the family plot, she would await a glimpse of Evan's casket.

Slowly the train of mourners arrived and meandered toward the plot. Father Peter delivered a most beautiful sermon from what Elly could hear. The congregation stood about the burial site as most of them wept. Their sorrow for the deceased was as overwhelming as the heat. At least ten people of the gathering fought off heat stroke and sought shelter in the nearby shade.

From behind the trees, Elly watched the service. She saw her mother weeping intensely. Her father, nearing seventy, stood by her and attempted the strong role. He tried to maintain his composure but shook with grief. At least a hundred friends and family graced the burial site. The roadway was an endless ribbon of cars, lead by five black Lincolns.

At ten thirty the casket was lowered into the ground. Both mother and father lost all control and broke down in a flood of emotional disarray. Elly wished she could be there to hold her parents. To share their sorrow and her own. It was improper not to be by her parents, but the situation disallowed her even to be a hundred feet away, let alone graveside.

As the whirring of the burial machine stopped, Elly fell to the ground and prayed for her brother, for her family and for her forgiveness. By the time she looked up the entire assembly had left the site. All that remained was Father Peter.

Elly thought it strange that he alone remained. Her curiosity pulled her from the shadows towards the grave. Her emotions had overridden her thoughts of safety and she neglected to search the setting for anything out of the ordinary.

Her pace was slow and deliberate. Her sights remained focused on the grave and Father Peter. As she drew nearer, the mumblings of the priest grew more defined.

"...And bless this young man, oh Lord. He was a good man, a man of simple truths, and a holy man. His friend is sorry beyond comprehension. His family is lost in the confusion of this senseless killing. Watch over him, oh Lord. Let him accompany you in the glory of Heaven and rejoice with the angels of salvation. He left this world far too early and did not reap in the splendors of life.

"All of us will miss him my Lord. Please take care of him and those that loved him."

"Thank you Father Peter." Elly had approached the kneeling priest unbeknownst to him. She had startled him and he jumped at her arrival.

"Elly! Where have you been?"

"Father, the story is far too long for the time I have here. Did he look peaceful?"

"He looked very peaceful, my child."

"Oh Father Peter, I feel so horrible for not being able to attend. People are after me and the man I love. They are the same people who killed Evan and that is why I did not attend. Father, you must tell my parents this. You must let them know that I tried to be here for the service. You must Father, you must tell them that I am not a selfish person. It's just that losing two children would be worse than one." She wept with the added weight of guilt.

"My child." He hugged her. "I will tell them. I have read about your situation. I don't believe that you are involved. I will do my best to help you."

"You have done enough." The husky voice startled both Elly and the priest.

"Who are you? What do you want?" Father Peter was as gallant as his profession would allow.

"Shut your God damned yap." The other man barked and clubbed The priest with a blackjack.

Elly was paralyzed with fear. There was no air in her lungs to scream and her worst fears were becoming reality.

The men flanked her and carried her to the waiting Lincoln. Elly went limp. In complete shock, she was carried without struggle. Her senses took leave of her and she passed out before reaching the vehicle.

-19-

"I don't know, sir. It all happened so damn fast that before we even had a chance to get out of the damn car, they knocked out the priest and grabbed her. She didn't fight or scream. Nothing."

"Where are you now, damn it?" Fleming was more concerned than afraid. His men were experts. They would follow unobserved and find out where she was headed.

"They left St. John's Cemetery and are heading north on Woodhaven Boulevard. We're coming up to Long Island Expressway and they're heading...hang on...west, they're heading west."

"Stay on them like hemorrhoids. If you lose her, we're all up the creek. I'll get another car out for back up. Just stay on the radio until you find out where they are headed."

"Yes sir."

Fleming was beside himself. There was no indication from across the street of any attempt to nab the girl. Not a word was uttered in reference to her. If the federal boys had her, something would have undoubtedly been said. Across the street the office moved at the same speed as they had for the past twenty-four hours: slowly.

"Who the hell has got her?" His question evoked images of the Haidey's Holding Co. Ltd. She must have been in the office to fax out the personnel records of Anthony Terrace. The incorporation papers named Jimmy E. Thorne as one of the owners and as president of the company. Jimmy E. Thorne? There was no way that was a co-incidence. That bastard Thorne was indeed in on this thing somehow. The trio had scaled security in his office, pillaged whatever information they could carry out, called Thorne on Larry King, and now Thorne wanted it all back in a trade off for Elly.

"Where the Christ are you now?"

"They just headed off 495 and are heading north on the Queens Expressway, I think that's 278 sir. So far there is no indication that they know they're being tailed."

"Keep it that way. I want a report every thirty seconds. Got it?"

"Yes sir. We won't lose her."

Fleming slammed a fist down onto the desk. How the hell could she be so damn stupid! Alone! She went alone to the funeral with FBI and NYPD combing the streets trying to find her, and neither Graceson nor Mackinnley were even remotely around. How could she have done this? Fleming was starting to panic. His star player was in the Lincoln and his game plan was on the verge of disintegration. She had tons of information on far too many people and her knowledge had cost her, her freedom. He had to get it back.

"Sir we are still in pursuit heading west on Central Parkway, they are an easy tail sir."

"Don't get too damn cocky. Stay back and make sure you see her get out of the car when they stop."

"Yes sir. Sir they're getting off the highway now and heading west on Astoria. We'll keep you posted of any changes."

Mackinnley or David would not let her take off for the funeral alone. She must have left without their knowing. Fleming looked at the phone and picked it up. He dialed the phone number posted on the wall and the phone rang and rang and rang.

"Hello?" The voice was apprehensive yet controlled.

"David this is Jeffer--"

There was no need to explain his position in Washington. Graceson had already hung up. He dialed again. This time things were different. After twenty rings and a pardon from the hotel operator the phone engaged. This time a deep authoritative voice answered.

"Mackinnley? Frank Mackinnley? There is no need to panic. We are on your side."

"Bullshit. The only people one my side, are the ones that I put there. Not some...what the hell are you?"

"State Department, Mr. Mackinnley."

"State my ass. State doesn't get involved in domestics nice try pal." The phone came down hard and Fleming was left hanging.

"Just great." He had to get in touch with David and Mackinnley. They had all the roots of the allegations David spewed out on King's show and Thorne would want them in exchange for Elly. But Elly wouldn't tell him about the Holiday Inn. She would die first before she told of her man's whereabouts. Of that he was certain.

"Sir. We've just left the main road about a mile off. We turned off Central Parkway and headed east on Astoria. We're here on this monstrous road for about a mile and we haven't seen them for a while. We'll crawl slowly up there and we'll check it out ourselves. The road is absolutely the worst I've ever seen."

"Stay on them"

"We've got them cov-" The transmission went dead after the sound of shattering glass.

"Hello!"

Nothing.

"Martins? Burton?"

Nothing.

"Jesus Christ. Hello??!! Anyone.?" Fleming was staring at the microphone as if it would become a screen and he could see what had transpired.

"Answer me, Damn it! Answer me!!!!"

There was nothing but white noise coming across the speaker. One minute later the radio went completely dead.

The office had gone completely silent. They all stared at their superior and awaited an answer from him, them, and the situation. All he had to offer was a blank look of shock.

"We lost them." He dropped the radio and sat in a chair.

"They're gone and Elly's gone." Fleming was limp in the chair. His entire project hinged on protecting Elly and nailing Jacobs and so far he was failing miserably. The Jacobs thing could go to hell. He wanted Elly back.

He grabbed the phone and called the Holiday Inn one more time.

"Elly!!" Graceson was obviously alarmed at Elly's prolonged absence.

"They've got --" He was cut off. The line went dead before he could explain to Graceson that she had been abducted.

"Damn!!

There was an ominous feeling of discovery within the suite at the Holiday Inn. David was scared as hell and Mackinnley, although not noticeably so, was alarmed.

"Who was it?"

"I don't know Frank. A man, older. Might be the same guy who talked to you earlier."

"Who the hell knows we're here."

"Christ Frank. The only person that knows we're here is Elly. Either they have found us or..." He swallowed hard as if not to have to say the words, "Or they've found her."

Mackinnley gawked at David. Even though he knew he had a stupefied look on his face, he could not wipe it off to appear confident. His face was pale.

"Well! Tell me something Frank. You're FBI for Christ's sake! What the hell is happening?"

Mackinnley's profession only allowed for the worst-case scenarios to be drawn up. He was perplexed by the knowledge of the phone caller. This played on his mind. Why did he call?

"David, I think first of all, that the phone call must be someone who is helping us. How, I don't know. But look at it this way. If it was Thorne or his posse you think they would call us? No damn way. They'd come busting through the door with swat team tactics and pump enough holes in us to make us look like Swiss cheese. These people would not give us a warning. He said he was on our side to me. What'd he say to you?"

"I don't know. Something like 'they got' and then I hung up. I was expecting Elly and then some guy's voice comes over the line, I got scared it was the 'condo man'."

"They got?" Mackinnley walked over to the window and inspected the street below from the lofty perch. "Hhmmm."

"What the hell is this 'Hhmm' business? Talk to me Frank! Where the hell is Elly?"

From his window perspective Mackinnley answered David in a very somber tone.

"Thorne has her." He did not move to see David's response. He knew David knew it. The actual words were finally spoken though, to cement the assumption.

David hung his head as his heart was torn from his chest. His head clamored with the drums of anger and fire raced through his veins. He shook with a vengeance that only an endangered love could bring out.

"Where the fuck is the bastard Frank? Let me find him and rip his head off myself. What if he harms her, Frank? What if he touches her? Jesus Frank, we gotta go get her and save her before... before he...before he kills her Frank. We gotta find her now!"

Mackinnley had long since felt the emotion of heartfelt loss, the anguished despair of selfless suffering. He felt for David, probably because he had grown fond of Elly. He pictured her as what his daughter would have looked like, should he ever had gotten married.

"Alright David, this is what we are going to do. We have most of the files of the Haidey's Holding Co. Ltd. right here at our disposal. We have very little time and a lot of hunting to do. Somewhere in all these files, there has to be a link between Thorne's house and the office on 53rd. We have to find that piece of information before we can even think about setting foot outside this hotel. It can be anything. Letters, bills, receipts for purchases anything that has another address on it. I figure it's got to be out in the burbs some place. You know this town, look for something in a secluded place or real fancy and exclusive. I know that the government has no idea where he lives now. His pension cheques have piled up for years uncashed. He's in selective hiding and we have to find him David. There is no other alternative."

David meticulously went over the material in the briefcase closest to him. Page by page he combed each line for an address that might reveal the whereabouts of Thorne's castle and Elly's dungeon.

Mackinnley walked over to the desk and unplugged the cellular from the computer. He punched in the seven digits and awaited the connection.

"Good morning, New York Hilton, Janice speaking, how may we be of service?" The voice was far too pleasant for the situation.

"Mr. Gonsalvez' room please. Enigo Gonsalvez please."

"Just one moment please."

This might have been the wrong approach. It may have been the right one; Mackinnley had no clue which way to go now. Time was a sparse commodity and it was depleting exponentially. Calling into the den was a risky venture but he vowed he would only speak to his friend and partner. Chances are they could not trace the line. Coming from the hotel switchboard and originating from the cellular, he could be anywhere in New York State, let alone the city. The phone in Gonzalez's room rang only once and was answered.

"Gonsalvez here."

"Gons. Listen I don't have much time."

"Mac? Is that you?"

"Yeah it's me. Shut up and listen to me. Neither Graceson or myself or for that matter Elly O'Connor, are guilty of any one of the charges you guys have us up on."

"Mac where the hell are you?"

"Never mind. I need your help. I have enough information to indict a certain individual with at least two hundred counts of extortion. This individual is also responsible for the murder of the Pope and Evan O'Connor."

"Come on Mac. What can you possibly have to prove it?"

"I have a shit load my friend but for now I need one thing from you. Do you have Elly O'Connor in your custody?"

"Mac?"

"Just answer me. Does the bureau have Elly O'Connor?"

"No."

"Are you sure?"

"Yeah I'm sure. Mac what the hell kind of game are you playing?"

"This is no game, my friend. Look, I'm dead serious about this. There is some major shit going down and I happen to be right smack dab in the middle of it. It's not a nice place to be and personally, I'd rather be at home watching a ball game, but I can't. There are at least two organizations out after my ass and a third one is chewing on my butt as well. You are the only one that I can trust."

"Trust me with what Mac?"

"I need to find an address for James Elliot Thorne's house or cottage or farm, some kind of shack that he calls home."

"Sorry pal. I can't help you. We checked it out earlier. We've got nothing."

"Nothing at all?"

"Jack shit."

"Damn. Then do this. Check out the White house records for purchases made in the year that Thorne was in office. Maybe he picked up a little shack on the side at the public's expense I don't know."

"Mac, I'd love to help you but I have specific orders to forget about Graceson's theory and concentrate on finding you three and bringing you in. Jacobs wants you all either dead or alive."

"Fuck Jacobs. That bastard is in on this whole ordeal. I've got dirt on him so juicy that you'd shit your pants if you saw it. Listen to me pal, don't trust Jacobs. He's as dirty as they come. He's probably out to crucify me, isn't he?"

"You can say that. He's already got the lumber."

"I knew it! Gons believe me. This thing is huge. Keep your ear to the ground and be careful. Find that information and call me at this number when you've got something. 555 7898. Got it?"

"Mackinnley are you out of your tree? I'll trace this and find you."

"Good luck pal. It's a cellular. Get busy and call me back as soon as possible."

Mackinnley disconnected the line. He looked over at David in the other room and observed his diligent efforts at stage one of rescue operations. He walked over to the room and started in on the papers.

Two hours and every sheet of paper later, they came up empty handed. The computer files offered no clue to the location of Thorne's hideout.

"Nothing Frank." David was exasperated. A look of terror had replaced the one of worry from an hour ago.

"There's only one thing we can do. I have a call into a friend of mine in the bureau. Don't worry, he's clean and I can trust him with my life. He's looking into where Thorne might be hiding Elly. I'm not a hundred percent sure that he's got her but I can't think of anyone else who would do it. Gonsalvez says that the bureau doesn't have her and I can only imagine that after the call to Larry King Thorne's got a hard on for you so bad, it's taking all the blood from his brain."

"So what do we do?"

"What we do is take this thing right to the top. I'll call back Gonsalvez; he'd been my partner in the bureau for years now. I'll tell him I'm coming in. I approach him secretly and hope that all goes well. I tell him our findings and show our evidence and maybe then we can kick-start the authorities into action."

"Are you completely deranged? I tell you that you won't be able to set one foot into the Hilton. They are just dying to find a fall guy for all this and you think that Jacobs, a member of the elite Cerebral Vacation party, is not aware of this picture? He's the director of the FBI Frank. There is no way on God's green earth that you are going to live if he ever finds you within a block of other federal agents."

"So he doesn't have to know. I trust Gonsalvez. He'll keep his mouth shut, I can bet on it."

"I don't know Frank. It's awfully risky."

"It's a risk we are going to have to take. After we get Gonsalvez into this thing then we can move faster. He can grab several men and from there we can use the bureau as a shield. We'll call the game plan and Gonsalvez will follow them through. It's perfect."

"Then what?" David was more than a little weary. His head was not on straight from the emotional beating he had taken. He was lost and alone and the last thing he needed was to loose Mackinnley to the authorities. He did not want to go mono a mono with the beast.

"Then..." Mackinnley contemplated what would come next. His next step would depend on the one before it and so on. There was too much room for variables and spontaneous errors to think too far in advance. "Then we could head off to...where was that service for Evan?"

"St. Patrick's."

"That the church we were in yesterday?"

"Yeah. Why are we going there?"

"We're going to talk to the priest there. Maybe he saw something that might help us. A license, anything, who knows?"

"I don't know, Frank."

"Jesus, David. How the hell do you think things get done? You sit on your ass and hope that the skies will open and grant you what you desire? The things in life are to be hunted my friend. They are game and you are to set your will and put it into action. You have to take chances. The bigger the risk, the bigger the gain. If you plant your butt in the sand sooner or later the tide will come in and drown you. Make a decision, plan it out and go for it. You don't and you become a wishy-washy, meek, kicked around puppet for people to toss around like a toy. Get yourself some of that self-esteem and confidence that your educated mind reflects. Your brains are strong David, get your guts and heart into it and lets beat this fucker."

David was embarrassed. Mackinnley was right. If chances were never taken, opportunity was lost forever. He thought of Elly and all the opportunities he had had to love her.

"Damn it, Frank. Let's do it"

"That's my man. First I'll go and talk with Gonsalvez. I should be back in about an hour. Then we head out."

"Shouldn't I come with you? For cover or something?"

"I'll be fine. There is nothing to worry about David. Plus I don't want to have to worry about covering anything. In an hour pal."

Mackinnley ambled out of the hotel room and down the stairs. Armed with an uzi, a cell phone and, he hoped, an attentive angel.

-20-

She had given up trying to scream fifteen minutes into the abduction. She had been bound, gagged and any effort she made to move was greeted with a rifle butt to her ribs. Her eyes were filled with terror as the Lincoln moved stealthily along the road out of the downtown core. From the floor of the vehicle she knew nothing of the route they were taking. Even if she could see more than their trouser legs, panic would not allow her to remember the path they took.

They said nothing at all to her. They were mean, heartless men with the look of precision killers. Occasionally one would look down at her. His eyes traced over every inch of her frame. She felt her skin crawl where his gaze fell and she wanted to vomit when he licked his lips and stuck out his tongue and flicked it in the direction of her legs. The other looked down and whispered to his colleague. They both laughed and took the rifle barrel and drew her skirt up above her thigh. The barrel was cold as it wormed its way up to her panties. She twisted her body to avoid the perverted intrusion, but was met with a revolver to the temples.

"You want to live, pussy?" The voice rasped.

She stared into his eyes and felt her pulse pound her temples. Even if it meant her life, she would not hold still and allow these animals to violate her at will.

She writhed in anger and defiance until the rifle bearer pushed hard on the weapon and it dug deep into her upper thigh. It was close enough that another move by either party could lodge it into her sex.

She stopped her fight abruptly and stared at the two with panic in her gaze. They looked at each other and smiled. One reached down to grab her, just as the Lincoln hit an enormous pothole. Then it hit another and yet another until every second was filled with the cars violent response to an unkempt roadway.

"I hate this fuckin' road." The one cursed as he was jostled in his seat. The sentiment was echoed by all in the car as they all convulsed with the jarring of the roads condition.

The sudden onset of rough terrain caught the kidnappers off guard and the rifle was tossed from its grip and fell behind Elly. She was tousled about the floor of the car and many times her hands came in contact with the weapon. On one occasion she actually had it in her grip. The restrictions on her hands prevented her from actually aiming it and taking at least one of the bastards down.

They wouldn't kill her. She knew it. They were taking her to Thorne. He may kill her but these two brutes wouldn't. To waste one of them would only spare the world of just one less parasite.

After ten minutes of violent rocking and listing, the road leveled off onto a somewhat smoother surface. The humming of the tires and the subtle little bounce was reminiscent of cobblestone roads.

The Lincoln came to a stop and the two men slowly exited the vehicle and cursed a mean streak as if they had a long-standing grudge with the condition of the road. The larger of the two reached down and grabbed her by the shoulder and sat her up. His hand slipped forward inside her blouse and roughly grabbed her breast.

She twisted violently and brought up her bound legs and kicked him square in the crotch. He screamed in agony and hit the pavement writhing in pain.

The other thug laughed sadistically at his partner's agony and reached to sit Elly up.

"Don't fret lady. I'm in no mood to talk soprano. Just get out of the car." He bent down and to the side of her legs to untie the ropes that bound her. She was a prisoner now, in the driveway. There was no place to run. No escape. She could scream and curse and nobody could remotely care. He untied her legs and she thrashed them about once the ropes came off. One of her kicks caught him on the chin and sent him reeling.

"You god damned bitch!" He came at her with purpose and conviction. "I'll teach you, you fuckin whore."

Elly braced herself for him. His charge passed her flailing legs and his fist connected with her cheekbone. It was not hard enough to break anything but her spirit and her insolent attitude. She wept with the blow and succumbed to the brutish manner to which he removed her from the back seat.

He dragged her towards the house, sidestepping his wounded co-hart on the drive. She walked with him as best she could so as not to incur further assaults. Once inside the front doors of the lavish home, she was thrown to the floor of the foyer and left there. No one followed her in and no one awaited her.

Alone she lay on the floor, hands bound behind her back, a gag in her mouth and tears streaming from her eyes. For fifteen minutes she lay there waiting for something, hoping nothing.

The air was heavy in the house. It carried with it the scent of age. Musty thick air, that was furnace-like. The heat was unbearable. She lay there sweating in the still vestibule listening for any sounds of approach.

She neither wept now nor screamed. She took on the still of the room and just breathed in short shallow breaths. For three hours.

The phone rang again, and he grabbed it and expected someone else.

"Gonsalvez."

"Gons, it's me again."

"OK. What's up, Dillinger?"

"I hope the endings different. Listen Gons, the way I see this, Graceson and I can't do this thing alone. We need your help. I trust you, Gons and I know you won't screw us up."

"What do you want from me Mac, other than digging up old White house files?"

"I'm coming in."

Gonsalvez froze in his seat. He stared off out the window and thought of the notion as one of extreme stupidity or classic genius.

"What have you got up your sleeve?"

"I've got something to show you that will definitely prove to you that something is amiss in the bureau. I can't tell you about it on the phone, you have to see it to believe it. I can't come to the Hilton 'cause the place is crawling with our associates. I'll meet you at a little place about eleven blocks south called Straps. I'll be there in fifteen minutes. Gonsalvez, don't let me down pal."

"Mac. This had better be good my friend because the minute I walk out the door of this hotel, not only is my job on the line, but my freedom is as well. Sure as shit and taxes man, if anyone sees the two of us together my ass is grass and the lawn boy's going to chew the damn thing off."

"Toro, Toro, Toro baby."

"You're a howl, Mackinnley. This thing is supposed to scare the shit out of you. Instead you're making damn jokes about it?"

"Gons, listen to me you stupid prick. I'm scared out of my wits. I have half the city out after my ass. Half of them are the bad guys and the other half are the good guys who think I'm the bad guy. I'm damn scared to walk out of this place but I have to, pal. I gotta clear my name and get my life back before it gets slapped into prison or worse yet, a box six feet under. I'll meet you in fifteen minutes OK?

"Mac!"

"OK Gons?"

"OK Mac. Fifteen minutes. Straps about eleven blocks south. You trust me. I'll be there."

"Thanks pal. I owe you real big."

Gonsalvez held the phone after Mackinnley had hung up. The clicking of the disconnecting line was very distinct, but odd. Gonsalvez thought of his phone at home and at the office and recalled the disconnecting line to be one definite click and then dial tone. This was different; one two then three clicks before the tone came on.

He hung the phone up gingerly and concentrated hard on the clicks. Was he paranoid? Was Mackinnley's admission of evidence playing havoc on his imagination? Was he frightened of the association of a suspected assassin? Was he just more than a little leery of his ex-partner's suspected connections and Swiss bank account? A few moments of trepidation passed and then it had occurred to him. The call had come in from the hotel switchboard. From there the call was re routed up to his room. The number of distinct clicking sounds would be indicative of the severance of each of those lines. He breathed finally and thought of possible line tracing and tapping on his phone fled his mind as rapidly as it had consumed him.

He grabbed his jacket and his gun and headed out to the club eleven blocks south, hoping that his partner and friend were not on the other side, like all the records had indicated.

"I knew it! Damn it I knew it. I could have bet my dick on it. You don't get to where I am without thinking way ahead of the game."

Jacobs was elated. The rookie at his side was perplexed and knew of only the task he was ordered to perform. He didn't like this job. It was sleazy and low and he hated it. Agents spying on agents. He wondered if he was being spied on in his own home, in his bedroom or his bathroom. This was by far the worst assignment he was ever placed on and he hoped that it would not be a permanent one.

Jacobs slapped the young man on the back and commended him on a job well done. He then walked briskly to a far corner desk in the conference room and dialed the phone. The line connected and the ringing started and lasted for three minutes before the desired party acknowledged the call.

"We have Mackinnley, sir." Jacobs' voice was nervous.

"Do you have him there?"

"No sir, not yet, sir. But we will in twenty minutes Sir."

"You take it for granted that this man will obviously fall into whatever pit you have laid out for him do you? Let me remind you how much I hate being disappointed Harold. If I were you I would have called after I had him in my grasp." The voice was calm, yet assertive; like a lion's purr.

"But, sir. There is a great amount of certainty involved here. There is no inkling of suspicion by either party. I had taken it upon myself to monitor Gonsalvez' phone in his room. It was inevitable that Mackinnley would try and contact his old partner. They will meet in fifteen minutes and I should have him in custody shortly after that."

"Very impressive, Harold. The librarian, Graceson, is he going to be in the package?"

"I'm not sure, sir. There was no indication of either he, or the girl being in on the meeting."

"The girl is not a problem. I have her here."

"You do?"

"Do not ever doubt my word Harold. Ever! Do you understand?"

"Y-yes S-Sir. I u-understand."

"Very good. Bring me Mackinnley. Alive, dead, it does not matter to me. The job will be done with the precision of surgery. Personally I would prefer him exterminated there on the street like a common criminal. You will indulge me Harold. I will have two of my men at your disposal. They are there in the lobby of the Hilton. Take them with you and use them at your discretion. As long as they are effective in the 'elimination' I will be very happy. Give them badges, they like that sort of thing, humor them. Just eliminate Mackinnley in a very definite and audacious fashion."

"With him out of the picture and with the girl as bait, we will be able to find Graceson. He will come to me willingly, the bleeding hearted speck. There will be retribution in every beat of his heart as it spurts out his life's blood to wash away my suffering. Again, do not disappoint me Harold. I would hate to have to expose you to the elements of the establishment."

"I will not let you down, sir."

"No, you will not."

Jacobs dropped the phone ever so softly as if not to offend listening end. He looked about the conference room and slowly made way down to the lobby.

Upon entering the lobby two men stood abruptly and grabbed Jacobs' attention. They did not have to stand. Jacobs recognized the one man. He was massive with huge arms and expansive chest that were hardly contained in the well-cut Italian suit.

Jacobs walked past them and into the main washroom. They both followed at an inconspicuous distance and pace.

In the washroom, Jacobs surveyed the area and found the place empty. He stood before the two men and looked up at them both.

"Very simple. Mackinnley is to be eliminated. Thorne's words, not mine. Do not disappoint the man or me. He'll be in a bar down the street called Straps in a few minutes and there he will die. Just *him*, understood? Not the entire club, just him, Mackinnley. I can justify his death." Jacobs spoke slower to the monumental man as if muscle had accumulated in his ears and sense was a foreign commodity to him.

They both nodded acknowledgement and altogether left the

washroom en-route to creating Mackinnley's chalk circle.

Sleep was hard to resist. It hung on her eyelids like the weight of the world and closed them regardless how hard she tried to fight it. Exhaustion had overcome her and she lay on the marble floor and took on its stiffness through osmosis.

She had not heard it but more so sensed the presence of something looming above her. She was reluctant to open her eyes and witness the beginning of the end of her life. For a short minute she kept her eyes closed and prayed it was just a lifelike nightmare she was enveloped in and not reality.

"Welcome, Miss O'Connor. It is indeed a pleasure to finally meet you."

Elly opened her eyes. They fell upon the frame of James Elliot Thorne. It was no surprise to her that his house would be her final stop on the kidnapping program.

"I must apologize for the condition that my employees have left you in. Allow me, please, to make you more comfortable.

His voice was hypnotic. Low in volume and tone, very bass like. It was gentle in an eerie manner but it made her skin crawl. She had heard him speak on thousands of occasions but never while she was a bound and gagged prisoner. She fought hard to escape his touch as he attempted to undo her bonds.

"Miss O'Connor. I assure you, you will be most comfortable once I untie you."

She persisted with her squirming until Thorne got increasingly frustrated and more forceful. His strength was remarkable for such a slight man and he easily overpowered her and undid the ropes and the gag.

"There now. Your room awaits you, Miss O'Connor. This way."

Elly watched him carefully. As he made his way to the grand staircase she looked towards the door.

"I would recommend against that thought, Miss O'Connor." Thorne spoke without even turning to witness her actions.

"There are two men just outside that will indeed escort you back into the house with great haste and less tact than you would desire. Please, spare yourself the indignity of injury and come to your room. You are a guest of mine now. Allow me to treat you as an honored one." He pointed towards the stairs with an open palm.

She had no other option. She would be dead any way that she looked at it and this game of Thorne's was obviously to keep her alive until he acquired both David and Mackinnley. She followed him, hesitantly, up the stairs to one of the guest rooms.

Thorne opened one of the doors at the top of the landing and offered Elly entrance inside. She slithered along the wall, maintaining as much distance between them as possible, and entered the room.

"I do hope you are comfortable here Miss O'Connor. Lunch will be served in one hour, I will send for you then." He closed the door behind him and did not lock it. This worried Elly even more. If there were no lock on the door then there would be no escape from the house at all. Security must be on the outside.

She stood with her back to the door and scrutinized the room. It would have been a dream room on any other occasion. It was a large, well maintained space. The decor was lavish. Renaissance paintings hung on three of the four walls. Covering the fourth wall was a tapestry that must have been at least three hundred years old, Turk Oman by the look of it. The curtains were drawn as if to make it clear that the morning sun was not invited to shed light on the room, or the situation. Against the far wall, under the tapestry was the bed. It was antique. A four-poster with canopy. Henry The Eighth or Charles the Tenth like in its majestic splendor. It drew the eye to its grandeur. It was large enough to accommodate six adults comfortably and laid out with impeccably embroidered linen.

She was drawn to it, compelled to inspect the quality of the workmanship. She held one of the bedposts as she rounded the chaise. She wandered towards the closet and gently turned the doorknob. With a subtle click the door opened and within the expansive depth hung one dress, and a pair of shoes beneath it.

The dress was enchanting. It reminded her of Cinderella in its elegance. She twisted it about to view its entirety and the note on the hanger came into view.

'*I hope you like it, Miss O'Connor. It is indeed for you.*'

Elly jumped back and felt the anger of manipulation yank on her spirit. The dress was a treasure, literally. It must have been an original 16th century piece and probably priceless. She ached to try it on but still fought hard to evade the temptation that beckoned. She stared at it for half an hour. All the time thinking of her situation. Thinking of Evan and of David and Mr. Frank. Thinking that they would save her and pull her out of this nightmare that had transpired and swallowed her up whole. For her part, the name of the game was to survive long enough to give them a chance. She had to play along despite how difficult that may be. If Thorne put her name on the dress then she would wear it.

Trying the gown on would not concede her fight. It would not even be a signal that Thorne was in control of her. But he would think that it was. Besides, if Thorne were to kill her, this would be the dress to die in, she thought to herself as she unzipped her skirt and it fell to the floor.

It fit remarkably well. It was like it was made for her. And the shoes! Another perfect fit. This uneased Elly for a very short moment until she saw herself in the mirror. At that point everything but the reflection was washed from her mind. Even her brothers' death was forgotten as the vision of herself induced a hypnotic trance. She had pulled her hair back and looked ravishing.

The knock on the door went unheard. It was knocked upon again, louder this time. On the third knock, all diplomacy and manners were discarded and the pummeling on the door brought Elly out of her trance and closer to the reality of confinement.

"Yes." Her voice was soft and timid.

"Lunch is being served, M'lady."

"Thank-you, but I'm not too hungry right now."

"Mr. Thorne expects your presence in the garden room immediately. Voluntarily or otherwise."

Elly looked at the door and thought of 'otherwise'.

"I'll be right there."

"I shall wait for you, M'lady."

The title 'M'lady' added to the love of the dress. She felt splendid and majestic and exalted. It was a dream of sorts with a nightmare soundtrack and direction. But for now there was the dress and lunch. She could definitely survive both.

-21-

The Manhattan streets swelled with the increasing familiarity of overbearing waves. Amongst the throngs of people, Manson could walk and not be recognized. There was not enough space to even focus on the person next to you let alone familiarize yourself with them.

Within the tide of swelling humanity, Mackinnley bobbed his way to the blues joint that David informed him of. There was uncertainty in his mind. Gonsalvez was his friend and they had been partners for years. There was a bond of mutual survival between them that only those in the policing trade could understand. They covered each other at the expense of their own lives. There was no doubting that Gonsalvez wouldn't let him down. Not now, when the darkest hour of Mackinnley's existence was before him. When the clouds of chaos had inundated the sky and the tears of suffering were sure to flood his soul. Gonsalvez was a good man and would help him now.

There was still a feeling of hesitancy, of uncertainty. The disquieting feeling of visibility played on his mind and made his walking pace hasty. He would bump into people and apologize face down.

"Where the hell is that damn club?" He muttered to himself as he stole selective glances at the surrounding buildings. Finally, before him on the opposite side of the street, the simple placard indicated his destination.

He stopped on the curbside and judged the traffic. It was steady and without any rhythm one could follow. Taxis speckled the roadway weaving in and out of the flow of traffic with the consistency of an epileptic seizure. Mackinnley set one foot forward and then retreated his step to the sanctuary of the sidewalk. Five times he attempted to cross to no avail. His sixth time got him across one lane of traffic, with four more to go.

His gaze was on the oncoming traffic. He lunged and made it to the safety of the middle of the road.

Alone and in the open like he was, Mackinnley feared being

discovered more than being picked off by some lunatic in a cab. There was no cover here and he was stuck in an ocean of moving vehicles. For almost ten minutes he attempted a crossing and was about to chance the move when he saw it approaching.

Again it could have been his imagination. It could have been any one of a thousand of them but something about it told him it might be the same one. The curb lane allowed the movement of the Lincoln to be slower than the inside traffic lanes. What with deliveries and cabs and cyclists, the Lincoln was almost at a standstill for as much time as it was moving. The driver's window was down halfway and he was obviously trying to find something. Mackinnley thought more along the lines of someone; him.

He had to get out of the middle of the goddamned road. They were the ones looking for David and him. They were the ones that had Elly and he was certain to get picked off standing in the busy street like a sitting duck. Still he watched the Lincoln as it puttered past Straps and the driver was still scoping the street for whatever he was indeed looking for. He looked to the passenger and then over to the opposite side of the street.

Mackinnley watched as the driver signaled somewhere beyond Mackinnley's shoulder. He spun around and was about to run back to the safety of the sidewalk he originated from, when a cabby refused him access via horn. The traffic was still moving and Mackinnley had forgotten where he was. He turned his head back towards the Lincoln's position and it was gone. He spun around quickly and noticed it a block further down with the driver's arms still wagging out the window pointing up then down the street.

"Sweet Jesus, thank you!!" He looked up at the sky and raised his hands in praise. "I owe you one."

The traffic seemed to ease up enough so that a crossing could be made without becoming an ornament on some cab's hood. Precious few steps brought him to the refuge of Straps and he made his way to the back of the club into an ill-lit booth. He sat for only a minute before his confidante joined him.

"Mac. I'm here." Gonsalvez spoke softly from behind the booth as not to startle the big man.

"Gons. Jesus. Am I glad to see you."

"I wish I could say the same to you compadre, but I can't. I shouldn't be here Mac. I'm obstructing justice, interfering with a federal investigation. Christ I could get twenty years for this."

"I know Gons, I know. But I'm still damn glad to see you."

"Tell me Mac, what's the deal here? What have you got that's so damn hot you're risking everybody's everything to see me here."

"Shit! If I told you everything that has been going on you'd shit a bus sideways. First of all, do you believe me when I tell you both David and I are innocent of any of the killings?"

"Mac? What is this?"

"Do you?!"

Gonsalvez thought about it for a moment. He looked deep into the eyes of his partner and knew that behind the brutish, self-assured exterior the man was scared as hell. If there had been any doubt that he had about Mackinnley, that look on his face wiped it all away.

"Yes Frank. I believe you."

"Good. Now I can start. The three of us, through some eloquent computer hacking, mainly Elly's doing, discovered who owns the Cerebral Vacation."

"Haidey's Holding Co. Ltd."

"You watched Larry King didn't you?" Mackinnley implied that his partner couldn't have found it alone.

"Yeah so what?" Gonsalvez conceded.

"Regardless, we find an address and head out to the offices and pillage the damn place for everything that they have. Discs, videos, files, pictures. You know that party room in the back of the club? It was wired too, cameras, videos the whole deal. Every-thing that went on there was captured on film. We must have at least five hundred pictures back at the Holiday Inn."

"You staying at the Holiday Inn?"

"Yeah. Nice room. 1454. David's up there now waiting for us. Any way the photos are something to see. There are so many hotshot lawyers, businessmen; Gons there were judges, Supreme Court judges in these pictures, sitting in piles of cocaine. Congressmen, Senators, actors, the King that was killed, he's there, in some orgy on that stage. But I tell you nothing beats the one David found this morning."

Mackinnley opened up his jacket and from his vantage point Gonsalvez saw the uzi.

"What the Christ are you carrying Mac? Is that a damned uzi? Are you out of your mind walking around downtown Manhattan with a damned uzi?"

"Keep your pants on Gonsalvez. David has got my Berretta."

"What?!! You gave a civilian your gun? You've lost it. I can't believe you gave a civilian your service weapon. I can't believe it. Tell me it's not loaded."

"For fuck sake, Gons, yeah I gave him my gun, yeah it's loaded and I tell you something else, the situation we're in dictates that the poor bastard may in fact have to fire it. So relax about that and look at this."

Mackinnley pulled out the envelope and placed it on the table.

"Gons, once you see what's in this envelope it's going to change the way you see a lot of things. The world is going to look a lot different than it does now. There is something in there that will make you doubt yourself and maybe your entire existence, I don't know but it sure as hell not going to be easy to take. It'll open your eyes and make you wonder about a lot of things."

Gonsalvez slid the envelope towards him and opened it. He was about to take out the picture when Mackinnley jumped in his seat.

"Gons. Tell me you didn't set me up." There was dread in his voice.

"What Mac? No I didn't." Instinctively he looked up at the main body of the joint. A large man flanked by two others walked toward the rear of the club and were approaching their table.

"That's Anthony Terrace." Mackinnley professed.

"So what's he doing with Jacobs?"

"Jacobs?! Jesus Christ. If you didn't tell them they must have tapped the fuckin' line in your room!"

Gonsalvez immediately thought of the clicking on his line.

Mackinnley stood and brandished the uzi from its cover. Gonsalvez stared in disbelief as the large man raised his arm and was already armed.

"Check out the picture Gons." Mackinnley beseeched his friend before he freed the safety on the weapon. That movement was the one that cost Mackinnley dear microseconds allowing Terrace to mark Mackinnley's chest and head with three bullet holes.

The sparse crowd in Straps dove to the floor for cover But Gonsalvez remained in his seated position as Mackinnley's body was thrust backwards until it hit the wall and then flopped onto the table.

Gonsalvez was speechless.

"FBI. Got any ID?" Terrace flashed a badge and stuck his smoking gun in Gonsalvez' chest.

"It's OK. I'll take it from here agent." Jacobs moved to the seat opposite Gonsalvez.

"You OK Gonsalvez?"

"Yeah." The shock of death, his partners' death, mixed in with the confusion of the situation, prevented him from communicating.

"Gonsalvez, I know he was your partner and your friend, but he was a murderer. You see this uzi? Does it look familiar? It should. It was the same type that you found in Graceson's locker, the same type that killed the King. God only knows whom else they were going to kill next. Maybe me, maybe you, maybe the president of the United States!" There was coolness in Jacob's voice. A certainty that emanated reassurance. Yet in his eyes there was a sense of urgency. There were questions waiting to be asked. Serious questions but for now the director spoke as a commander.

"Look Gonsalvez, why don't you head up to your room in the Hilton and I'll be up in about an hour or so and we'll talk about all this. Try and remember what he said to you. It's important for your sake. I take it you were in the process of arresting him were you not?"

"Sir?" Gonsalvez was even more confused.

"If you were not arresting Mackinnley then I would have to take this as defying a direct order, obstruction of justice you know. The stuff that would land your ass in jail. So I am most certain that I will have a report on my desk in an hour or so pertaining to your arrest. Correct?"

There was definite purpose in Jacob's verbal assault and implied threat. Gonsalvez wanted to slide out the picture. To see what Mackinnley had died for, what he was on the edge of losing his job and freedom for. He would have grabbed it from under Mackinnley if Jacobs had turned his head, for a second even, but he never did. He watched as Gonsalvez walked past the table and out the door of the club and onto the busy street.

"You damn windbag, Mackinnley. You couldn't just give me the damn picture. You had to give me a damn lecture about life changes. You fat headed bastard, your damn life just changed didn't it." He walked aimlessly cursing his dead friends character and fighting off the tears that big boys don't cry. He walked for half an hour until he found a bench, sat down and wept.

His tears were torrential and they washed a trail of sorrow down his cheeks. He looked up into the sky and prayed that God would take care of him and bless his soul.

The derelict was quiet in his approach and sat next to Gonsalvez.

"When the night is its darkest and all that remain are but vanishing shadows of the day, The Lord looks down and wipes the slate clean. Ready for you to start your next day cleansed of yesterday's sorrow. There is a sign. Look for it my friend. It is there in the distance and it heralds the word of the Lord."

With his head still buried in his hands, Gonsalvez looked up to see the bum depart. He looked up towards the horizon as if there was hope in the advice of the derelict and was amazed at the vision.

He stood up as if having seen an angel. He wiped the tears from his face and regained his composure. Straightened out his clothes and walked across the street and into the lobby of the Holiday Inn.

Time was obstinate, each second refusing to surrender to the next. He was there, caught in that moment in time that hung in space. Even though Mackinnley was only gone half an hour, David had been beaten by those hands of time and it showed in his eyes.

He cursed the fact that the suite had no walk out balcony. He pressed his face to the window and tried to see the street below. The angle was all wrong and nothing was visible but the thickness of the pane.

"Come on Frank." He walked back to the pile of pictures on the coffee table. "You were supposed to call me Frank, remember? Just after you meet with Gonsalvez." David started to pace the floor in the suite. Back to the window where he would tilt his head to aid his vision onto the street. "Damn you Frank. Call me you dick!"

Back to the pictures again. He plopped himself down on the couch and feathered his hands over the pile of photographs. "I can't believe this." He picked up a picture off the table and studied it. The subject matter was perverse. All the photos were warped in some sense of the word. He peered at this one in particular. The cocaine theme was quite prevalent in most of the stills but this one had lots, all over the place. The man was in his mid to late fifties, thin and drawn. Clean cut, though and very professional. Upon his shoulders were the slender, lithe legs of a woman. Her face was not visible from the camera's angle, but from her shoulders down, her nudity suggested wicked abandon. The man's face was plastered with a smile induced by the alluring woman's sex in his face. It, and his face were both were caked with the white powdery dusting of what could only be coke.

"This is nuts. How in hell's name can you find a place like this to party and not get caught doing it." He shook his head and thought of the goings on at the party room in the Cerebral Vacation. "I guess if you're the president of the United States they allow you a few avenues for debaucherus escape."

He tossed the picture on the pile and sat back in the couch. The knock on the door came softly and that worried David. Frank had the key so why would he knock? He approached the door with caution, and was shocked when his hand reached out to the doorknob. The knocking became more rapid and stronger as the visitor expressed more urgency with each added announcement on the door.

As if mesmerized by the beating of primal drums David twisted the knob and allowed the hallway occupant into the suite. Without even looking to see who it was, David moved toward the couch and sat down. The door was closed and the visitor entered the suite and addressed the young man.

"David?"

David nodded without looking up towards the speaker.

"You alright, pal?"

He nodded again, this time looking toward the man. He saw him reach into his jacket and the moment had come that David anticipated. The handgun would come into view and end his life there in the hotel.

"I'm Enigo Gonsalvez." His identification was pulled from his jacket pocket, "FBI. I was Mackinnley's partner."

One word was trapped in David's ears, 'was'

"You Frank's partner?"

"Yes, for years now."

"Did you kill him?"

"No David. It was some gorilla. Mac called him Terrace."

"Anthony Terrace. Frank is in good company."

"The director was with him. They tapped my line in the hotel and set Mac up for targeting."

David sat motionless on the couch and stared at the pictures on the table.

"Frank told me of the director, Jacobs is it?"

"Yes, Jacobs. What did he say David?"

"Not much. He had a hard time trying to find the right words." David tossed him the picture from the top of the pile.

Gonsalvez caught the picture mid flight. His eyes scanned the picture and immediately recognized the man.

"Holy shit!! It's Jacobs!!"

"That's exactly what Frank said. Word for word."

"This is at the Cerebral Vacation. The back room."

"It's one hell of a back room."

"Mac told me. Judges, senators, governors, kings and the sort."

"They are all here, for the times of your life."

"This is why Jacobs killed him."

"No. That's why Thorne had Jacobs kill him. Thorne's behind the Cerebral Vacation. He owns it."

"Mac told me you guys busted in and 'borrowed all this stuff." He pointed to the scattered mess of pictures and papers about the room.

David was still in a daze. The stranger in the suite could easily be one of Thorne's men teasing him, playing cat and mouse. He could easily take his life just as David suspected that Mackinnley's life was erased. He awaited the click of the safety to come off the intruders' gun and the nightmare to end. He waited a long while and wondered why it was taking this Gonsalvez fellow so long.

He looked up at Gonsalvez who was still engrossed by the photograph. "You going to kill me?" He asked sheepishly.

Gonsalvez stared down at the young man and felt the fear.

"No David, I'm not going to kill you. I need your help. Mackinnley was a dear friend of mine, the only family I had, not to mention my partner. His case is my case and together we'll solve this thing and bring the whole damn house down."

"We have to find Elly, Gonsalvez." David looked up and pleaded before the agent with his eyes. "Thorne has her and we have to get her before he...before he...he..."

"It's OK David we'll find her. We'll find her and we'll get him and make him pay. Don't you worry, pal. We're on the case now."

"We were going to head off to the church and talk to the priest who buried Evan. Frank said that he might have a lead or something that could help us find Elly. What do you think? Did you find out any info on property?" David threw this last bit of information in as a test. He had overheard Frank talk of properties purchased by the White House.

"I found nothing. I was checking anything that the White House purchased during Thorne's years, but Mac called me and it was cut short."

David heard the words he wanted to hear. Gonsalvez was clean.

"Well we don't have much time. If they tapped your line they could easily know we are here. I'll gather up this stuff, evidence you know, and then we should split."

"Fine with me." Gonsalvez added.

David reached over to the table and grabbed the Berretta, two extra clips, checked the cartridge and took off the safety.

"What the hell..."

"Don't worry. Frank told me how to use it. Point and shoot."

Gonsalvez shook his head and then thought that it might be best in this situation that he have some backup.

They crammed two briefcases full with most of the sixth floors loot and shuffled out the door and headed to the church where the holy man who had promised assistance awaited.

David prayed the man would be true to his word. If you can't trust a man of God...then he thought of some Tele- Evangelists and shivered.

-22-

From the far desk in the conference room, he took the call. The ring almost went by unobserved. His full concentration was on the bloodstained envelope, as he stared at it before him on the desk. The phone wailed for attention. This time it knocked him out of his trance and he snatched it from its cradle.

"What!!?" He was disturbed and agitated.

"I've found him."

"Where?"

"Holiday Inn, Royal Plaza. He wandered a round for a spell and then made his way into the hotel. He took the elevator up to either the twelfth, fourteenth or fifteenth floor, I'm not quite sure but he's in there."

"Stay on him. I'll have Terrace meet you there and you can cover the stairs and the elevators. In fact I'll get five other men out here and we'll nail him. Hopefully he's with Graceson and the problem will be solved."

The call was terminated and Jacobs barked out orders to four other agents. He gave them explicit instructions to bring in Gonsalvez for questioning. He excused them and immediately called Terrace in his room. He was briefed and told to be on standby to accompany Charon once their location was verified.

The silence of the room was annoying. It hummed in his ears like a void and it was thundering on his mind. Who else had seen this picture? He thought it was for his eyes only having had destroyed the original one sent to him three years ago. It was the biggest skeleton in his closet and the shackle about his legs.

He picked up the envelope and stared at his likeness. He shook his head at the remembrance of the night. It was the first night in he ever went to New York and the Cerebral Vacation. He had been looking for a place to drink and perchance get lucky. The bar he found. It was trendy without being plastic. high profile clientele, lawyers, CEO's, corporate junkies. The parking lot would probably be full of Mercedes', Jag's and the occasional Ferrari. It all came back now.

The woman he was looking for found him. She was a sexy, sultry sensual siren. He loved the way she smelled and it charged him with sexual energy. She came to him within three minutes of entering the establishment. He thought it strange, at the time that he could get a woman before he could get a drink at this club. She wanted him. It was her sole purpose in life and he felt it. She was urgent with her movements, impatient with his response time. She pressed herself against him and her legs straddled his thigh. He could still remember her words, 'I want you deep inside me now. Any how, take my soul.'

He was slow to respond and she grabbed him forcefully and dragged him down the stairs. At the bottom of the stairs she pulled him past a sentry who smiled at them both.

He spoke into a headset and awaited a command of sorts. With a nod and push of a VCR remote like control, the right wall slid to the side to allow them entrance.

An escalator awaited to take them down. Their descent was quick and they had arrived in the spot where she thought it suitable to be taken. She peeled off her dress and dropped to her knees. She fumbled with his trousers and was pushed aside by his hands.

He was dumbfounded by the palatial ballroom. It was an exquisitely decorated party room fit for kings and queens. And in the midst of the orgy of decadence he saw more that ten faces that he recognized. The two Supreme Court judges came to him and welcomed him to the fraternity of the party. Along with them came the 'host'.

He was welcomed and had the rules of the party room explained to him. The consequences were severe for defying the sanctuary. Just the mere entrance to the room inducted him into the ranks. There was no turning back.

He remembered the spectacle that carried on around him. The party was one of wicked abandon, and irreverent of the laws that governed the outside world.

True pleasure said the host. All that you want of anything. If they didn't have it they would get it. To fulfill your pleasure is the clubs duty.

The drinks were passed around. A tray of cocaine was brought, and a straw was presented to him. He grabbed it and looked at the judges before him. They too were with straw in hand awaiting their new member to christen the tray. He bent and snorted a generous rail into each nostril. The games had begun.

For hours he enjoyed the freedom of legislated laws. He was in paradise. He frolicked and flaunted everything that was denied him in the outside world. His conscience was wickedly free and he had complete disregard for anything that his position stood for. He found the siren that led him into temptation and continued with the program she had started with at the bottom of the escalator. She was elated to see him and the games continued well into the night.

The photograph he held was a hard copy of the baptism into the ranks. The club's insurance, so to speak, that secrecy would be upheld. Jacobs was afraid of the picture. He had a greater fear of the ramifications of snitching. He knew that everyone to whom he was related would be killed most brutally should he breath a word of the existence of the club to anyone.

Now the librarian had all the pictures from the offices and God only knew what else he had taken. He was only a stones throw from becoming public.

He had to get hold of Graceson and Gonsalvez before they caused all the New York socialites to fall from grace.

Fleming had been on the phone ever since Jacobs had called Thorne. The fever was peaking and time was running short.

"Yes sir we have a direct violation of at least three federal laws and request permission to initiate proceedings."

Fleming nodded and thanked the voice on the other end.

"Its all set." He spoke urgently and without any hint of nervousness. "This calls for all of us to spring into action. I have called the president and we have the authority to move in. Two others, Smithers and Wright, and myself will head across the street to get Jacobs. The rest of you will take three cars and head out to the Holiday Inn to cover Graceson and Gonsalvez. They will have all the evidence that we need to indict all these bastards. We have work to do and not enough time to do it. Keep your radios on at all times and we will report when events warrant."

The room split up into its preordained factions and they all left the room in a blur. Fleming stood by the window and watched the activity across the street in the Hilton's conference room.

He was still there. His back against the window looking at something in his hands, a file, a photo. Jacobs had been a suspected risk for many years. Fleming had been detailed by the president himself to keep an eye on him. His actions were for the most part on the level, but more times than would be acceptable, Jacobs' overlooking of important facts and suspects had led lead the government to become suspicious of his affiliations. He had covered up certain details on a number of very high profile cases and resulting in them being dismissed from the courts. Eight cases in all had been mishandled. None of them could be pinpointed to Jacobs' involvement, but Fleming knew it was he. And now he had evidence linking him with the abduction of Elly O'Connor. He also had the location of Thorne's home in Astoria. The phone call was traced and the address was found. This could all come down just in time or just seconds too late.

Fleming grabbed his wool jacket and with the two agents headed out across the street to arrest Jacobs. He prayed that the other agents would get to Graceson and Gonsalvez before Jacobs' goons could do the same to them as they had done to Mackinnley in broad daylight.

The table was set in the garden amongst the varying shades of red flowers. The expansive yard seemed to go on forever and there he stood awaiting her: the Thorne in the garden.

"Welcome, Miss O'Connor. I see you have acknowledged my wishes. The dress looks beautiful on you."

She looked down at the dress and tried to smile demurely. She managed a thank you. In the light of the afternoon sun, in the real world, she hated herself for even trying the dress on. There was something about it, about him. A strange compelling power that he possessed over her. Here, before her, stood the man that had her brother killed and she was about to have lunch with him. She felt like vomiting. Deep within her though, she was losing hold of herself. Being drawn into a realm where he was her master. She felt her strength slip away and become more at ease with his mellifluous voice, with his charm. She looked up to him and he smiled at her, as if adoring a little child. She smiled at him apprehensively and was seated.

There in the garden, amongst the oxblood flowers, she abandoned herself to the powers of James Elliot Thorne. They ate their lunch in the splendor of the garden and talked as if they were old friends. Whatever semblance of anger, or hatred she had for the man was dissolving with every word that he spoke. He became more and more charming as the afternoon wore on. At one point in time she almost reached out to touch him. To feel his hand and know the man that held her captive, both in body and now in soul. She had abandoned herself to the extraordinary allure of her host. Whatever he wanted was to be her gift to him.

She had forgotten her brother's death. David was not even a memory at this point. The world consisted of her and of Thorne and the garden. She still felt a little uneasy. She almost shook uncontrollably. Was it fear? Residual memory of the wrong that he had done her? Was it anticipation, excitement of the things to come? She contemplated the latter and wondered about her abilities to please this man. She gazed into his eyes and was drawn deeper into his soul. She was helpless in his gaze and she became weak with arousal.

"James? May I see the rest of the house?" She was dreamy in her lilt.

"Certainly my dear. Whatever your heart desires. Come let me show you my humble abode." He stood, pulled her chair and helped her up. Arm in arm they entered the house as they tour began.

She marveled at the art that graced the entire house. Millions of dollars of paintings and sculptures adorned the mansion and with every step she became more mesmerized with the man's taste and charm. He chatted with her about each of the painting's history and how it was acquired, how long it had been in the family but never once mentioning the cost.

It was like a museum, very spacious and tastefully appointed. The tour took them to the second level of the house. The study housed thousands of books. The office was lavish, rich in colors and materials. The entire house was nothing compared to the master bedroom.

Upon entering she was taken back by the opulence. The room was massive in size and effect. The ceiling was at least twenty feet high and supported a huge intricately designed chandelier. A Persian rug covered most of the floor and the furnishings were antiques spanning hundreds of years. The bed was expansive. She was drawn towards it. She reached the bed and held the bedpost. It was large and quite phallic. Her hands wrapped around it and she brought the side of her face to it as she looked back to him. Her smile was naughty in its nature and she cooed.

"Do you sleep here?"

"I do."

"Have you had many guests?" She was brazen in her suggestion and the words shocked her. Two hours ago she could have spit on the man and now, in his bedroom, her words invited a different exchange of body fluids.

"Very few my sweet. I am very selective with my quarry."

"Not too selective, I hope." She tipped her head back and eyed him over her shoulder.

"Extremely selective."

He stood in the doorway and did not move towards her. She felt unworthy of him and her disappointment showed in her eyes.

"Come, little one let me show you the rest of the house."

She skipped back to his side as if obedience would make her more deserving of his attentions.

The survey brought them to the basement where a large hallway led them away from the stairwell. The first door they approached lead to the wine cellar. The room was the size of a baseball infield and was stocked with thousands of vintages. The next two rooms were storage for a wide variety of art pieces that Thorne had chosen not to display. She saw a number of Dali's and Raphael's, a Picasso, all in storage there. She was very impressed.

"Come."

She jumped at his command.

"There is one more room that I must show you."

"This is wonderful. It's a shame that this tour could not go on longer. You have a fascinating home, James."

"Thank you my sweet. Behold."

He opened the door of the last room on the tour. It was an ominous space. Even with the lights on it seemed dim. She had a difficult time focusing on the structures within, but he took her hand and led her into the heart of the room. He pulled her close and she let him. Her breasts heaved within the confines of the dress and her heart raced with anticipation. She wished for a kiss. Just one kiss and it would quench her desire for now. There was no kiss and the expectation of one made her shiver with wanting.

"You are a most beautiful woman Miss O'Connor." He brushed the hair from her face, back over her ear. "There is a purity to you that I have not seen in many, many years. We all need a purity to cleanse our soul. I have lost that purity. Many years ago. Wars and politics scrub that veneer away and leave one bitter and angry. But you are an angel, brilliant in aura and soul, untainted from the cutting realities of the world. The innocence will end for you one day. You will wake one morning and find that the world has betrayed you and all that you thought was virtuous and sacred are but a facade of transparent illusions. You will be hurt and your beliefs will be desecrated and you will be angry. You will pray to your God and the answers will come too slow to be heeded in time. You have a right to be angry with Him. I am truly angry with Him and I despise his messengers and his writings. The words of peasants, sold to other peasants who were angry with Him in the first place for making them peasants. The word is a lie. We are truth."

"We create truths every day. Even our lies are truths and we believe them as others do. Your integrity stands like a flag bearer. You will be an easy mark and die and someone else will pick up the flag and walk on until they die for the sake of a belief. Believe in the truth. Your truth. My truth. My sheer presence is truth by nature. The reality of mankind and his downfall is not believing in my truths. Do you believe in me?"

She was intoxicated with his sermon. "Yes, I believe."

"Do you truly and is this a truth?"

"Yes, a truth." She agreed only for the sake of worthiness. Any thing to be touched to be held to be taken by this master of her soul.

"Turn around." He gently twisted her around. "Place your hands behind you." She eagerly responded to his command.

From his pocket he pulled out a handkerchief and rolled it into a blindfold. He placed it carefully over her head and covered her eyes.

"Relax, my sweet. The moment you anticipate draws near."

A slight fear encapsulated her but his voice soothed the apprehension. If she resisted, she would never be worthy, so she allowed him his eccentricity for the sake of her reward.

He led her forward ten steps and turned her around.

"Truth, my dear, is the essence of reality. The reality lies within your soul. I will extract your truths and you will be free from the monstrosities of your meager existence."

He lifted one of her arms and´tied it to a beam. There was no struggle from Elly. Her other arm was brought up and bound.

"Take me." She whispered in a voice dripping with abandon.

He looked at her there and chuckled.

"Soon my sweet thing. Soon."

He watched her for a while, hanging on the cross, and left the room for her to contemplate the truth and reality of James Elliot Thorne.

David had given up hope. In the safety of the hotel room he still felt vulnerable. This man, Gonsalvez, seemed kind and genuine but still in the back of David's mind he wondered whether he had killed Mackinnley, abducted Elly and was now about to kill him.

He watched Gonsalvez as he checked the hallway. If he was on the other side, he would most likely would have been dead already. This was the reality of the situation. All the evidence and the best opportunity were present for this Gonsalvez fellow to execute him there, but he hadn't. David was still alive and they were off to find Elly. The agent's offerings were trustworthy based on those facts alone.

Gonsalvez signaled David and they were out the door and down the hall. They slipped into the stairwell and walked down six flights of stairs before entering the corridor. They stood before the service elevator and in the secluded shipping bay Gonsalvez reiterated the plan.

"This is the way I see it, David. They are after you and just about now they figure I'm not back at the Hilton and thus Mac must have told me something. They're out after my ass too. We have to be covert in our movements. The church is, what, five blocks from here? Whatever, we'll walk up two back one, and so on. We have to lose anyone who may be tailing us. Once we get into the church I will wait outside the office. If the priest sees two people, especially a strange face, he may get worried and think your in trouble and call the authorities. You go talk to the priest alone. You talked to him before, you said and he was sympathetic. If you believe it then I believe it. Talk to him about the funeral. Ask him if he saw anything out of the ordinary. Ask him about suspicious people or even a license plate. At this point we could use anything. If you need me I'll be just outside the office doors. Got it?"

"Yes, Mr. Gonsalvez."

"David, call me Gons. It's a hell of a lot easier."

"Got it, Gons."

The elevator presented itself and they got in. They took the ride to the sub-basement and checked the hall before they exited. The coast was clear and they made their way to an emergency exit. Gonsalvez cut the line for the alarm and they left the hotel unscathed.

Half an hour later they were walking up the stairs to the church. St.

Patrick's awaited them with open doors and they quickened their pace to find shelter from the revealing light of day.

The cathedral was empty. Not a soul inhabited the pews and there was no activity at the altar. This made David uneasy.

"Aren't these places supposed to have some old Italian or Hispanic ladies dressed in black crying and praying at the front at all times of the day?"

Gonsalvez looked at David disdainfully. "You watch too much television, pal." He shook his head and wondered how a supposed intellectual could possibly contemplate such a notion. He looked about the church and noticed a man moving behind the altar.

"Is that him David?"

David twisted his head to catch Gonsalvez' cue. "Yeah, that's him. I'm on my way." He looked over to Gonsalvez with nervousness in his eyes. "Cover me." He mocked the police lingo.

"You're covered. Move."

David moved with cat-like care amongst the pews. As he approached the office of the priest he heard voices coming from inside.

"No, I'm fine. Thank you for asking."

The nature of the conversation indicated to David that he was on the telephone and not with company. He would wait until the conversation ended before announcing his presence.

Gonsalvez approached David from behind and tapped him on the shoulder. Caught completely off guard, David jumped and yelped, thinking it was one of the enemies.

"Are you out your damn mind, Gons!!? You scared the hell out of me. Don't ever do that kind of shit again.!!"

"Sorry David, really. But please watch your mouth though, you're in church now and you don't want to offend the Big Guy when we need all the help he can give us."

David, still shaken by the scare, crossed himself.

"What's going on?" Gonsalvez asked.

"He's on the phone. I'll give him a moment then knock."

"Hello! Is somebody there?" The voice of the priest came through the door.

"Wish me luck, Gons." David whispered and entered the room concealing Gonsalvez' presence behind him.

"Good afternoon, Father," said David politely.

The priest looked at him and could vaguely remember the young man. After a few moments the priest's face lit up with in recognition.

"Good afternoon, my son. You are the young man who came and saw me in confession the other day. You are Evan O'Connor's friend." The priest held the side of his head and grimaced in pain. "It is an awful shame."

"What father, what is?"

The priest looked up at David and searched his eyes for truth.

"Evan's death, for one and that poor young girl, Evan's sister. Elly I think it is."

"Yes it is Elly. What do you know about her?"

The priest looked at David curiously. He was originally under the impression that David was in association with Elly. But he did not know what had happened to her. Something wasn't right.

"Who are you to Elly?" The priest asked with suspicion.

"I'm her friend,...a...a boy friend. It doesn't matter. Tell me what you remember." David was losing patience.

"I can remember very little."

"Tell me what you can remember."

The old man felt threatened. David had become just a mite too overbearing in his tone and urgency. He stood now, overlooking the seated priest and seemed to almost demand answers to his questions.

"What happened?"

"She came to me after the service." The clergyman was nervous now and visibly shaking. "She thanked me for the kind words and then two large men came and thanked me."

"Thanked you? For what?"

"I don't know. They said I'd done enough and then one hit me on the side of the head and that's all I can remember. When I woke up I was still at the site and everyone was gone."

David was frantic. "Two men, what did they look like?"

"I can't remember."

"Remember! Damn it. Think hard. Big, small, thin, fat, bald, something, anything??!"

The emotions mounted on either side of the pastor's desk. David was dangerously close to rage and the priest was afraid. On two occasions the priest spotted the large caliber pistol in David's jacket. This added to the mounting fear in his soul.

Trying to think quickly, the priest told David. "I can't remember much of the event, but there was a young man from the church who helped during the burial of your friend."

"Where is he?" David demanded.

"He's here in the church. If you will allow me I will summon him." The priest looked up with nervousness. He was lying straight faced to the young, armed, angry man. It was a sin but one that could be forgiven under the circumstances. The young man was demanding help. Did he want to know if any one knew anything about the abduction? Was he searching for witnesses to eliminate? The priest rose from his chair.

"Go find him and bring him here father. Now." David's insolence grew with every second. He watched as the priest left the room via the back door, in search of the 'young man'.

Outside the office the priest looked back towards the closed door. The man he left inside was changed from the one he had met days earlier. He was coarse and discourteous. This type of behavior suggested a brazen disrespect for the church and society making the young man in the office a potential criminal. The media must have been correct in their judgment of him. The priest walked towards another office and picked up the phone. He dialed operator assistance and asked for the FBI. He had spoken to them before about the young man and now he was afraid and needed their help. The number was given and he dialed it. The receiving end transferred his number to the Hilton where the case was being worked on. After several rings the phone was answered and the priest explained the story to the man they said was in charge.

"Hello, FBI, Jacobs."

"Hello. I don't know whether you are the people I should be talking to but I am the priest at St. Patrick's Cathedral and in my office right now I have a young man I am certain you are looking for. He is the one from the newspaper that was working with that FBI agent who killed the king." The priest was nervous and kept looking to see if the young man in the office would venture out and finds him on the phone turning him in.

"Graceson!?" The voice was excited and intense.

"Yes, that's him. He's here now asking all sorts of questions about Elly O'Connor's abduction. He says he's her friend and then he says he's her boy friend. I don't know if I believe him. I think he may have been involved in that whole thing and he's trying to find out if I know anything. I'm afraid here."

"Keep him there father and I will have someone out there in a matter of minutes. Remain calm and just listen to what he has to say. Minutes, father. We'll have someone there in minutes."

"Thank you sir, Mr. Jacobs, thank you."

He hung up the phone and nervously re-entered the office where David was pacing.

"Well? Where is he?"

"He is just finishing up some things and he will be here shortly."

"Good, good. Very good." David fidgeted and squirmed as the time passed agonizingly slowly. He eyed the priest.

The priest eyed David and they entered into a battle of wits. Who would break down first? Both were nervous. Both seemed scared. Yet the priest had seen the weapon and regretted that he had not told the FBI man that Graceson was armed.

The knock on the back door of the office startled them both.

"Come in please." Beckoned the priest.

The door opened slowly and for a moment nobody entered the room.

"Come in. It's OK." The priest spoke serenely.

David pictured the young church helper to be in his early twenties and quite meek. Once the door opened completely the vision that came to his eyes was the exact opposite. There, filling the doorframe was a mountain of a man with an expansive chest and massive arms.

"FBI! Don't even think about moving Graceson."

David froze. Anthony Terrace had presented himself under the guise of a federal agent and was before him now. David almost lost control of all his bodily functions and the pounding of his heart was like a jackhammer in his chest.

"Mr. Graceson, you are under arrest for the murder of King Kahid and his Eminence, the Pope. Stay where you are and don't move." The behemoth spoke slowly and without the New Jersey drawl that he had spoke with at his apartment a few days ago.

David sat upright in the chair and remembered Mackinnley's advice about the Berretta, 'point and shoot'. The safety was off and he was trying to remember which way the handle was pointing in his jacket.

David stared at the monstrous man and then to the priest.

"You set me up you bastard. I came to you for help, you said you would help but instead you set me up. This man is not FBI; he is the man who killed your Pope. He is a mercenary. He kills for a living!" David wondered where the hell Gonsalvez was during this heated exchange.

"Graceson shut your hole. You will soon die for your actions. And seeing that we are in a church, would you like to die on the alter like a lamb? Hey Graceson? Like a sacrificial lamb?"

Terrace thought the remark to be hugely funny. He laughed at his own joke and the more he laughed the funnier it appeared to him.

David looked at the priest with disgust. He looked at Terrace in his fit of laughter and thought that the moment was right. He reached into his jacket and pulled out Mackinnley's Berretta and in slow motion he saw Terrace notice the pistol and reach for his own. By the time Terrace had a grip on his weapon David fired off the first round, which caught Terrace in the center of the chest.

The look on Terrace's face was one of shock. His weapon was still not out of the holster when the second shot caught him just under his chin followed by a third, which took the left side of his scalp off. Terrace swayed and tottered before crashing to the floor like a timbered mighty oak. He didn't move again.

David stood from his chair, and with the gun still smoking, he looked to the priest. Before he could say anything Gonsalvez grabbed him by the shoulder and David whirled around and pointed the gun at him.

"Jesus David, what the hell are you doing?"

"Gons! Shit I told you not to do that again. Are you nuts?"

"Am I nuts? Are you? What have you done here?"

"Gons this guy was going to kill me!

Gonsalvez looked down at the mass on the floor. With his foot he turned the face towards him. "Terrace?"

"Yeah, Anthony Terrace. Muscle for Thorne. This is the guy who popped the Pope."

"The guy who killed Mac." Added Gonsalvez.

. David looked at the priest who was well past disturbed at this point.

"Who'd ya call?" barked David now, completely disrespectful.

"FBI." The priest obviously feared for his life.

"Who'd ya talk to?"

"The man they said that was in charge. A Mr. Jacobs."

"I knew it." Gonsalvez shook his head, "The bastard is in deep with Thorne. Listen, David, this guy wouldn't have come down here alone. I bet there's a guy outside in a car waiting to take this piece of shit back to wherever they came from. I also bet that the guy in the car knows where Thorne's place is and that's where Elly is being kept."

"I say we check it out." David was pumped. He had just killed a professional hit man. What could he be afraid of now? The guy in the car, if there was one out there, could not be more of a threat than Terrace. He was ready. He checked the clip and they moved out.

Before leaving the room David threw a glance over to the priest. "Father, the divinity of Christ was never meant to be housed. You stole from the church of Christ the concept of religion. You herd the people in, fill them with a notion and ask them for money. You lied to me. You lied to the populace. Truth is in the heart, Mister. And it is there one finds the only true church."

He closed the door and headed out to join Gonsalvez at the end of the hall.

"There it is, David. Black Lincoln. Engine running. It's them."

"What's the plan?"

"I'll take the back seat and cover any one there. This will draw the driver's attention should no one be in the back. Once I open the door you take the drivers side, open the door and point the gun to his head. If he moves shoot him. Don't kill him, maim him. I suspect that they sent only two monkeys over to take you out. Suspecting that you were unarmed why send in two men to get a librarian. You ready?"

"All set, partner?"

"Let's do it."

The plan was executed flawlessly. Gonsalvez took the rear door, opened it and found it empty. The driver, Charon, turned to witness Gonsalvez ducking below view. As Charon turned to get a better scope on the intruder, Mackinnley's trusty Berretta was on his temple.

"Don't even breath you bastard." David had become Bronson in a matter of minutes.

Gonsalvez jumped in the back seat and brought his gun up to the other temple.

"I don't suppose you could give us a lift?"

Charon was in shock. Graceson was supposed to be dead. He heard the shots. He even chuckled when he had heard them. He could smell the powder from Graceson's weapon. He tried to look at the young man face to face. As he turned his head both David and Gonsalvez pushed their guns deeper into each respective temple.

Gonsalvez searched Charon for any form of weapon. He took everything from the man. Watch, rings, belt, two pistols and a knife. With David watching over him and knowing that he had killed Terrace, Charon was afraid of his response to any sudden movement.

"Where is Thorne?" Gonsalvez asked

There was no reply from Charon.

"Where is the girl?"

Again there was no reply.

"Where is the girl you son of a bitch!?" David took over the interrogation.

Charon kept his face forward and chuckled, but said nothing.

David took his gun from Charon's temple and whipped it down to his crotch. He felt the fleshy target and pushed the barrel down hard.

"Talk to me you fuck or I'll take them off one by one."

"Bullshit!"

"Bullshit this." David retorted with a squeeze of the trigger. Charon screamed as the muffled blast of the Berretta took off one of his most treasured appendages.

"You can enjoy life with one ball and I got at least five more bullets in here you semi-dickless fuck. Now tell me! Where is she?"

Charon wept like a child. "Astoria, just off of Hell's Gate."

"Take us there now." David demanded as he jumped in the back seat. His hot pistol was placed in the nook on the back of Charon's skull. The drive started.

"Don't mess this up, prick. You take us there and you will live. If you have to report in, report in. Get us to Thorne's place, to where the girl is, and you can go free. Or go to a hospital. Understood?"

Charon grimaced in pain as his hand went to comfort his ailing gonad. He drove the Lincoln carefully amongst the traffic, his hand clutching his parts as if it were a shifter, while his foot spasmed for the first part of the trip.

He neither spoke nor moved, just whimpered with the remorse of a man's fate worse than death.

-23-

The lobby of the Hilton was crowded with a wide variety of people. Tourists for the most part. Cameras hung about their necks. At the cashier's desk many were seen concealing valuables in money belts. There was no need to approach the front desk; Fleming and his men knew where they had to go. They boarded an elevator and headed up to the conference room level.

The ride was swift and silent. Even with all the tourists on board there was no conversation on the elevator. The muted bell announced their floor and they stepped off only to witness Jacobs entering the far elevator.

"There he is, sir!" Smithers proclaimed just a tad too loud.

Jacobs turned and saw the two men and Fleming run towards his elevator. He pushed the 'close door' button hard and prayed that it would catch quickly. It did just two steps ahead of the pursuers. As the doors glided shut Jacobs heart started to race. The photo he thought, Mackinnley had shown the photo. He must have. What the hell was Fleming doing in New York looking for him, if he hadn't seen the photo?

"Shit!" He cursed aloud in the elevator and almost jumped to make the descent faster. "Come on, come ON! MOVE you bastard!"

The doors opened in the basement and he ran to one of the cars that were approaching just as the next elevator signaled its arrival. The doors opened and Fleming and another man ran out, heads twisting to find him.

The approaching car was an FBI vehicle. Jacobs stopped it and demanded the agent exit. He almost threw the man out as he commandeered the Ford Fairmount and fled from the scene, tires spinning as best they could in a Fairmont.

"Jacobs!!" Fleming screamed at the fleeing automobile.

The car screamed out of the parking level in response.

"Damn!"

"Our man is on street level with the car, sir."

"Let's move it! With any luck he'll be stuck in traffic and we'll nail the bastard."

They ran up the parking ramp into the light of the afternoon sun. The heat was stifling and the exhaust only added to the discomfort. Wright was within steps of the ramp as his colleagues jumped into the car and the driver stepped on it.

"I've got a visual on him, sir. Grey Fairmont. It's about eight cars up. I've got him."

"Stay on him like glue. I've got you now, Jacobs." Fleming was on the trail and he salivated knowing that justice would come down like a clap of thunder. Judgment day had indeed been marked on his calendar and Jacobs had a date with destiny.

The radio crackled to life. "Sir, we had a call just minutes ago from the Hilton."

"What was it?"

"A call made to Jacobs, sir. The voice said he was the priest at St. Patrick's Cathedral. Said a young man fitting Graceson's description was there. Jacobs told the priest he would send someone over. Then he called to a room in the hotel and sent over a man named Terrace. Isn't that the name that came across on the fax, Thorne's employee?"

"Yes that's him. Jacobs didn't want Graceson arrested, he wanted him killed. He killed Mackinnley, too no doubt. Anything else?"

"Yes sir. Police report four shots fired at St. Patrick's Cathedral two minutes ago."

"Are our people there yet?"

"Just got there now sir."

"Anyone on over there? Jones!! Williams!! Is any one awake over there!!?"

"Just barely sir." The voice came sputtering over the radio.

"We just arrived sir. One dead here."

"Is it Graceson?"

"No sir. A hell of a lot bigger than Graceson. Looks like Anthony Terrace. That's what the priest says Graceson called him. Priest says that Graceson plugged him."

"Graceson!!?" Fleming was both shocked and impressed.

"Sir the priest is a mess here. He says that Terrace showed up as FBI. A badge. The works. He wasn't on the bureau was he?"

"Never."

"Didn't think so. The priest is doing Hail Mary's and he's freaking out over here thinking that he got a federal agent killed."

"Don't worry about him. We don't have time. All three of your vehicles should be en route to Astoria. Thorne's place is there and I figure that's where the party is going to be. Jacobs is on his way there now no doubt. Graceson and Gonsalvez are probably doing the same. The rest of us, as they say, are in hot pursuit. Move it."

"Yes sir."

Fleming could see Jacobs' vehicle up ahead in traffic. There was still a sense of urgency in the director's driving. He was suspicious of a tail. From six cars back, Fleming watched as Jacobs weaved in and out, cutting into side streets before reappearing. He covered the same stretch of road three times before moving on. Twenty minutes later and they were still in the same city block as where they had started.

"This is making me dizzy. I think we should just shoot him and get this thing over with." Fleming was not amused with Jacobs' ill attempt at losing a tail. He must have believed that he did because his driving became more relaxed and consistent. Fleming's car kept a respectable distance as they followed the director east on 57th onto the Queensboro Bridge and then north on the way to Astoria.

The three vehicles from the state department roared down the freeway oblivious to the limits of acceleration. As they drove to reach the Astoria residence, the leading cars raced ahead. The third car got left behind at a slow down approaching an accident site. The congestion was considerable and the agent driving was infuriated. He swore up and down that precious time was being wasted.

In the midst of his ranting he looked to his right and saw the young man in the rear of the Lincoln beside him. He looked twice before the window was rolled up and the vision was lost. "Did anyone else see that guy?" The driver, Flikas asked urgently.

"What guy, Pappy?" Came the reply from the rear seat.

The agent in the passenger seat acknowledged the response.

"That sure as hell looked like Graceson, at least like the pictures I've seen of him. It looked exactly like him as a matter of fact."

"Be real cool now. Call this into Fleming without them seeing what's going on in here."

The passenger grabbed the radio and held it in his lap out of view from the nearby Lincoln.

"Mary, Come in Mary. We have a situation here." His voice was calm and his facial expressions were casual. He turned towards the driver and faked a conversation with him.

"Go ahead. What have you got?" Fleming was irritated.

"We've got Graceson in a black Lincoln right beside us sir. We're stuck in traffic on the Queensboro Bridge just above Franklin Roosevelt Drive. What do you want us to do sir?"

"Are you sure it's Graceson?"

"Pretty sure, sir, in fact we're positive." The agent feigned laughter after turning off the radio switch and smacked the driver on the shoulder as if just hearing a joke.

"Don't do anything. Just follow them. Is Gonsalvez with him?"

"I don't know sir. The windows are tinted and we can't see inside. Graceson's in the back seat and we can't tell how many others are in the vehicle."

"Just follow them. Where are Dyson and Mactavish?"

"Both vehicles made it past this god damned accident site before the police and ambulance got here. The road is choked up tight."

"Whatever you do, don't lose them. They have all the evidence that we need to put a lot of people away. Just don't lose them."

"Yes sir, we won't. Over!"

The traffic did not move for half an hour. The heat built up and tempers became overheated on the blacktop of the bridge. Several idiots parked themselves on their respective horns in an attempt to get people moving or to let off steam. Either way, it got people moving out of their cars and in the direction of the source of the added aggravation.

There were several fights that broke out on the roadway and the police that were busy with the accident let the brawling continue. Several others jumped out of their cars and joined in on the miniature riot that was transpiring on the bridge.

The police could no longer ignore the degree of violence that was transpiring as it was only escalating in intensity. For the two cops that were there it was too large an ordeal. One of them ran to his cruiser and picked up the radio. His frenzied hand actions indicated that he was fearing the situation was getting out of control.

A tire iron was hurled from somewhere away from the carnage and cracked the windshield of the state department vehicle. The cop had seen the flight and, after gauging the trajectory, ran towards it.

As the officer approached the affected vehicle two shots went off in rapid succession and he dove for cover at the drivers side door.

"Jesus I hate this fucking job!!" The officer was definitely affected by the heat and the circumstance. "You folks OK?"

The driver leaned out the window with his badge dangling in the face of the officer.

"Flikas. State Department. We're OK in here and sure as hell once you clear this crap every one else in this jam will be OK too. Listen to me and listen to me good. I want you to call for backup. At least three other well armed vehicles. And I want you to be ready just north of here."

"Fuck you, pal. I'm busy enough here I don't need some starch shirt to tell me what to do!"

"Listen to me you insignificant little fuck, I work for the president of the United States of America. When I talk to you, he's talking to you. As we speak now you are obstructing a federal investigation and I personally don't think that twenty years in a state pen would be a nice place for a police officer do you?"

The question was understood as rhetorical yet the officer on the ground responded with a shake of his head.

"You will call. Get your ass back to your cruiser and you will give the plate number of the Lincoln beside me and the plate number of this vehicle. With me?"

Still on the ground, the officer nodded.

"Good. The Lincoln and its cargo are not to be harmed in any way."

"Who's in it?" The curiosity of the officer forced him up as he tried to steal a glimpse.

Flikas caught his head and pushed him back onto the pavement.

"It's the president himself. This is an unscheduled outing and if anyone knew that he was in a traffic jam we could have unprecedented chaos here. Just clear the road, have backup waiting at 21st and Astoria. Spread them out so as not to look too suspicious and monitor radio channel eight as well."

"Where's the Secret Service?" inquired the officer.

It was a damn good question. "One car is in the accident and the third is way the hell back there somewhere." He waved his hand to the rear of the car. "Just do as I requested and the President will thank you personally."

The cop raised himself to an upright position and made his way back to the cruiser.

Flikas saw him pick up the radio and in an emphatic display of emotion he relayed a lengthy message to dispatch. He looked towards Flikas' car and nodded ever so slightly.

The timing was perfect. Three tow trucks came on the scene and the flow of traffic was crawling back to the pace that it was intended to go. The Lincoln eased into gear and as soon as it made it past the scene of the accident the throttle was opened and it was in motion again.

In pursuit was Flikas, but not too close. The others were probably in Astoria by now. The only excitement that was now available was getting Graceson and Gonsalvez. Each one intact.

She could see nothing with the blindfold on tight and her hands became numb in the knots that bound her. She was now the reenactment of the crucifixion, hung up to die for the sins of her kind. She had liberated a knife from the lunch table, a sharp one, but within the confines of her cleavage it was impossible to reach now, nor was it possible to reach at any time during the tour.

The man must have believed her dreamy, obedient attitude. She tried to seduce him, to make him weak, to make him forget the plan he had so dearly worked on. But he had not taken the bait. He would not kill her yet and she banked on it. In the meantime she would emphatically proclaim him master and ruler of her soul and body and he could have whatever he so desired. She would tease him and make it harder than ever.

He was waiting for something. For David, most likely, and the reassurance that the pictures were intact. She remembered the pictures, and with the blindfold on, focusing on them was easier than she thought. They were disgusting displays of carnality. The excess, the disrespect for each respective individual, the vulgarity of the un-ruled. And many of those people photographed were even recognizable to her. Mackinnley had called it an insurance policy. That's what Thorne wanted from David and Mackinnley and until they or the pictures were found she would remain alive.

She was alive. She could feel the intensity of her heartbeat as she sensed his presence draw near. This time, as opposed to the two other times he had come in to check on her, he came very close to her. Close enough for her to feel the intense heat that came off of him. She had to slip back into character. Her performance had to be flawless or the curtain would come down on this one-woman show.

"James?" She whispered seductively. "Is that you, my lord?"

There was silence in response. Yet the presence moved from one side of her, to the other. She twisted her head to follow the aura the man exuded.

"Have I not been a worthy servant? Take me oh master, take me and show me your wisdom. Let me feel the truth of your grace and power. I have lived a shallow life without knowing the true virility of strength through spirit. Take me Master and fulfill the void within my soul. Take me I beseech thee." She bit at her lower lip as if the tease was reversed.

He moved closer to her and brought the back of his hand to her face. It connected hard and fast and it shocked her. She whimpered ever so softly and then turned towards him.

"To become worthy I must be punished. Please Sir. Another."

The next attack was laced with anger and it reeled her head as his forehand connected with the other side of her face.

"Oooh" She moaned. "Another oh master, another."

Again the hand made contact with her face. It had not the force and impact as either of the first two assaults.

"Thank you Sir. Thank you. Another."

The hand came to her face but softly this time. It caressed the cheek of the twice-hit side and trailed down to the front of the dress. Over the décolletage and down the side of her body.

She purred with anticipation and pushed her body toward his hand.

"Please, master, please. I am your subject and slave, your pleasure. Have me all."

His kiss came hard and she tried not to vomit as his tongue probed deep into her mouth. His hands came up behind her and drove her pelvis into his own. She could feel the hardness of his erection as it pressed into her belly and she fought hard the impulse to pull away. Instead she reciprocated the gyration and brought a leg up and around his as if to draw him closer to herself.

He pulled away from the kiss as saliva still strung them together. His hands cradled her face and she could feel him gazing at her face.

"You are a whore of soul."

"I am your whore."

"You will please me whore."

"Forever, master."

His hand left her face as he grabbed the dress and pulled it upwards.

"Master?"

"Whore."

"Master, let me indulge you with my pleasures. I may not be worthy without lesson but I beg you the opportunity."

His hand froze in position and again his gaze could be felt through the blindfold.

"Very well." His words were wispy and strained. "But you will indulge my wishes and leave the blindfold on. Your hands will be your eyes and your soul will be your guide. Please me whore. I command thee to please me."

He untied the ropes from her wrists and her arms fell with the weight of surrender upon his shoulders. She hated to do it but she kissed him with fervor. Her hands raced through his hair and she drew him into her kiss. Her tongue swirled about his and enticed it into her mouth where she sucked it hard in promise.

'It's only an act', Elly thought to herself. It was not real. It was not truth. It was a bad dream and this was the only path back to her reality. Her world. To David.

She opened her eyes and felt his eyes staring at her. Was he searching her soul for his ordained 'truth'? Was he not enjoying her ministrations? She would turn up the heat and make this man beg.

Her hands left his face and made their way to his back, where her nails dug into him hard. Bingo! His moans told her he was losing himself to her. She had gained some control.

She clawed her nails down to his trousers and towards the hardness that he had advertised earlier. Her hand reluctantly made it to the area just to the left of his treasures when the gunshot went off. Outside.

He pushed her away as there were two more shots fired and an explosion.

"What the f..." He stared out towards the window in the direction of the roadway. He looked down at Elly who had landed on the floor with his push. "Get up whore. Now!!"

He grabbed her and haphazardly tied her back to the beam. "I will come again, whore. Be still." He ran up the passageway and up the stairs to retrieve the ringing bell.

The phone. Saved by Ma Bell, she thought as she tested the strength of his haphazard knots. A smile grew on her lips as she realized that they were far too lose to restrain anything. She slipped her wrists from the knots and dug deep into her cleavage to retrieve the knife that she would use to cut off his balls.

-24-

Progress on the road was still slow enough to have Jacobs not notice his tail. Fleming's vehicle passed the three-stationed police cruisers en route to Astoria. Flikas had informed him of the 'back up' and Fleming was still a little uneasy about bringing outside help in. But the secrecy of the operation was still intact and help could always be used if it was indeed needed.

"Come in, Mary?" The radio called for attention.

"Go ahead."

"Sir, Lamb Three, we are about a hundred feet from the entrance to the subjects address. Unmarked street but we figure this is the one. Lamb Two is just behind us another hundred. We lost Flikas...uh Lamb One back on the Queensboro Bridge and we haven't seen any one else go in or out."

"Excellent. We are on the rabbit's tail and he should be in your sights in about two minutes. We will drop back and you take over spotting. Standard issue vehicle, gray."

"Roger, Mary."

Smithers eased off the gas and allowed Jacobs' vehicle to stretch out the distance between them. Fleming sat back in his seat and contemplated the reasoning behind Jacobs' heading to Thorne's house. His face became contorted with question.

"What the hell is Jacobs doing?" he thought aloud.

"Pardon sir?"

Fleming adjusted himself in his seat. "If you were being sought by the authorities, would you drive to your ringleader's house?"

"That's simple enough. No!"

"Of course you wouldn't. So why is Jacobs?"

Both Smithers and Wright thought about it.

"Maybe..." offered Wright, "... Jacobs has dirt on Thorne that he thinks may provide him some type of protection."

"I doubt it. If anything, Thorne has dirt on Jacobs. Still, why run to Thorne? It doesn't make sense. Do you suppose it's a trap?"

"A trap? You mean an ambush?" Smithers further questioned.

"Yes, exactly! An ambush. Martins and Burton were headed up this way after the funeral. They entered Astoria and headed up a miserable road, remember? We lost contact with them and haven't heard from them since. I really don't think they went out for donuts this long. Maybe Jacobs knows that there are sharpshooters out there and he's trying to lead us down the garden path, so to speak."

"I don't know sir. That sounds pretty wild."

"Smithers, personally, I don't particularly care what you think about it. That's the way I'm going to play it."

He grabbed the radio. "Attention Little Lambs, this is Mary, access down the road is denied. I repeat access down the subject's road is denied. Is that clear Lamb One?"

"Clear sir."

"Lamb Two?"

"Roger Mary"

"Lamb Three?"

There was no response.

"Come in Lamb Three!!"

The lack of reply told Fleming that he had been right.

"Come in Lamb Three, damn it!"

"Sorry Mary..." The party acknowledged communication. " We are already in pursuit of the rabbit. We sighted him running up the road, and what a road. This thing is a monster. I've never been on any thing so wicked in my life. Mary we have rabbit in our sights, seventy five yards up..."

"Get the hell off his tail now!!! Do you understand me now! It's a trap! Hit the brakes and get your asses out of there immediately!!"

"Trap? There is no trap here."

The gunfire forced him to hit the brakes and realize that the commander was indeed correct with his intuition. He watched in horror as the side window of Jacobs' vehicle fragmented from sniper fire. The car bounced its way forward with increasing velocity while trying to avoid further fire. Jacobs' Fairmont spasmed with each pothole it hit. Another shot was fired from the left side of the car and another came from the front splintering the windshield and jolting Jacobs head backward. The final shot must have pierced the gas tank of the Fairmont and the director of the FBI went up in flames as a giant fireball.

"Jesus Christ! Did you see that? Did you see that?"

"What the hell is going on over there?" Fleming was consumed with question, doubt, anger and worry for the agents that were not answering their command.

"Lamb Three come in damn it!!"

After thirty seconds of silence the radio crackled to life.

"Lamb Three here. Mary, rabbit's dead."

"Dead?"

"Three hunters and a barbecue. Fifty yards up from our camp. We lost verbal with you cause we dropped the radio high tailing our butts out of the vicinity. Confirm. The road is a trap, Mary."

Fleming stared up at the ball of smoke in the sky and thanked the all-mighty presence that he would not have to inform two more women that they were widows. The agents had escaped and Jacobs was brought to his demise by the affiliations he had held.

As Fleming and the others pulled to the side of the road, the long black Lincoln casually rolled past them at a legally defined speed. Fleming quickly turned to face the front and read the plates. They were identical to the ones Flikas had relayed to him earlier.

"It's Graceson and company boys."

Smithers was confused. Was he to follow them? Pull them over?

"What shall I do, sir?"

"Pray. Graceson doesn't know who we are. If we pull him over he could pop us all off. He's armed, remember? He's scared and the combination of the two makes him a loose cannon."

"So then what?"

Fleming was lost. "Pray boys. Pray that they make it past the snipers."

A minute had not passed before two police cruisers fled past them on the side of the road, with sirens screaming for a clearing in the road. They were seconds ahead of two fire trucks and an ambulance. Fleming watched in dread as the emergency vehicles sped to the sight of the explosion.

"Come in Mary. Come in!"

"Mary here." Fleming took the handset.

"Lamb Three sir. Black Lincoln pulling up the roadway sir."

Fleming was in a tither. He couldn't stop them. Their imminent doom was sealed if they made it up the road much further. He thought hard.

"Mary! Oh Mary, we have a major situation here."

"I know, Lamb Three. Emergency vehicles. Are they pulling into the road way?"

"Affirmative sir!"

Fleming's eyes widened. "Follow the rescue teams in." He barked into the radio.

"Repeat, sir."

"I said follow them in. I don't think that they will fire on the police. They might, but I can't see them trying to put down the entire NYPD. If they fire on the front car the rear car will call for as much back up as is deemed necessary to quell the sharpshooters. That means SWAT teams."

He was inspired by this. "How close is Fort Schuyler from here?"

"Fifteen minutes from here sir. Two by chopper."

"Damn! This is beautiful. Call them and tell them to send two birds up here armed and at the ready. I want them up here in minutes. Priority one. Tell them it's authorized by the president and give them our clearance codes. This is going to be absolutely beautiful."

Fleming slapped Smithers on the shoulder just as Flikas pulled up beside them.

"What the hell is going on here? You guys having a coffee break?"

"Flikas, we're going to a barbecue, you want to come? We are serving up 'presidential seal'. Follow us."

Both cars were put into high gear and they drove toward the smoky beacon on the road to hell.

"Somebody better give me a damn good reason for all this!" Thorne was incensed and he lashed out on the phone.

"Sir, we tried to take him out but the bastard kept on going."

"*Who* you insolent insect? Tell me who the hell was it was that you desecrated the sanctity of my home for!!?" The reprimand came in a voice that made Thorne hoarse. Color rose in his face and every vein above the neckline protruded and was dangerously close to exploding. "Talk to me, you bastard, Who was it?"

The voice on the other end did not reply immediately.

"Who the fuck was it!!??"

The man on the other end was obviously contemplating his retreat, from the situation, from Thorne and the wrath that was undoubtedly about to follow.

"Jacobs, Sir." It was a meek voice. Timid with the admission of guilt and very much afraid.

Thorne was somewhat relieved for a short second. Jacobs had outlived his usefulness and his extraction from the picture was not a bad thing at all.

"Any one else with him?"

"Sir he was unannounced and the orders were to..."

"I made the damn orders you moron." Thorne interrupted. "Answer the damn question. Was there any one with him?"

The man was reluctant to share the news. Thorne's attitude had swung to the passive side. Bad news was not needed now.

"Well?"

"There was another car following sir. It was outside the two mile quadrant and so we left it alone."

"You did what?" The blood pressure increased again and his voice escalated to frightening volume. "Jacobs was being followed and you let whoever follow him go? Are you incapable of any rational judgment you intellectual midget? What kind of car was it?"

"Very federal, sir. Looked like FBI. We didn't get a scope on it because it was outside the quadrant."

Thorne thought hard. Jacobs had sent out Terrace to get Graceson. Maybe, just maybe it was Terrace in the following car. The cars were not identifiable. Terrace must have feared being a target like Jacobs was, and he turned back. This thought quelled his anger.

"Sir."

"What now?"

"I have car two coming up the roadway. It's Charon's, sir."

"Very good. Don't shoot him. Let him in. Clean up the mess and thank the powers that be that I haven't already come down there and ripped off that useless mass on your shoulders."

He hung up the phone and walked to the window. For the first time since the explosion, he saw the smoke rising. Seconds later the sound of emergency vehicles could be heard approaching dangerously close to his sanctuary.

"No!"

The phone rang again.

He snatched up the phone, "Tell me something good, scum!"

Quickly the sniper responded. "There are five emergency vehicles sir. They have stopped at Jacobs car. They don't seem to be interested in anything else but the car."

"Are any of them heading towards my home?"

"Negative, Sir. They seem to be searching the area, though."

Thorne pictured the scene. The burnt out car with the charred body roasting within. Crispy black with at least one bullet hole in him. They were not capable of finding the bullet wounds at the sight, but they would be able to find his marksmen. There were ten in all on the ridge above the roadway. He thought of them and the absence of security about the house.

"I want all of you to make your way to towards the house. Cover the front from well-positioned vantage points. Use that CIA training that you have all so meticulously learned and I have so dearly paid for. Charon will be arriving shortly and we will convince the authorities, should they approach the house, that we have no knowledge of the events. Jacobs was an old friend from the Whitehouse years. He came to visit, but met with ill fate. I can show them a picture of his past antics and they will think up their own reasons for his demise. Come to the house now."

The situation was growing increasingly tense. He was not accustomed to the feeling of pressure and the fact that an insignificant librarian induced it, only added to his frustration. His castle was crumbling in the wave of invasion. The erosion started with the minuscule name drop from Graceson. He had started to talk in the Vacation. His words were truth. Truth that could destroy the opportunity for leadership. The leadership race was pivotal for his pre-ordained destiny. The victory in '04 was not to be spoiled by the ranting of a loudmouth. Graceson hit too many raw nerves, and though Charon had beseeched him to let sleeping dogs lie, he started the hunt regardless. He should have listened to him then. Now his judgment had placed him in the precarious position of the hunted.

He thought of Graceson and how he had eluded all of the attempts on his life. How in hell's name could this petty mind evade the wrath that he had cast upon him? He must have had help from above. He looked up to the heavens and screamed. "You bastard!! I'll find him! I'll find him and kill him like the other. I'll find him and I will tear out his intestine and hang him by it. You bastard!!!"

Thorne had reached his apex fury. He reeled about the room and screamed with anger. The closest object to him took flight, as he hurled the self-portrait bust of Michelangelo across the room.

"So this is what it has come to. There is still a fragment of hope in salvaging the situation," he ranted to himself.

He left the study with his mind a flurry of thought. This situation was not as bad as he had initially perceived it to be. The gunfire, the call from the sniper and the sirens pushed him over the edge. The woman's promise of pleasure had made him weak and he had lost composure. Now things would be mended.

"Whore!" He screamed. "I'm coming for you whore and I will take from you your pleasures, bitch! I'll rip out your pleasures and that will please me."

He ran down the steps to the basement and to the fourth door .As he swung the door open he noticed she was gone.

He looked about the room. She was not there. He cursed her escape aloud.

"You pathetic little wench! Do you think you can play games with me? I cheat, bitch! I will cheat you out of your soul once I find you. And find you I will. You have very little time to live and you spend the last minutes of your life in hiding. How appropriate." He talked to her as he searched.

"You and the rest of the planet spend their days hiding from the likes of me and mine. We are the strong and we will survive whatever the likes of you will throw at us. At me."

The search of the basement revealed no sign of her. He climbed the stairs and heard movement above him on the bedroom level of the home. He took the stairs two by two and started the search for her again on higher ground. As the probe for her location intensified, the Lincoln could be heard pulling into the roundabout in front of the house. He looked out the window and could not believe the vision that was before him.

Graceson exited the Lincoln from the rear door. He opened the driver's door and from there he hauled out a wounded Charon who clutched his bloodstained groin with both hands. Graceson had a gun to his head and from the other side of the vehicle another man emerged.

"What the fuck?!" Thorne squirmed to avoid being seen from the window. "Where the hell is Terrace? What has happened to Charon? What the hell is happening to everything destiny has laid out for me?"

More sirens shrilled closer and closer towards the house.

"Shit!" He peeked around the frame of the window.

He grabbed the telephone and called the marksman.

"Yes Sir?"

"Where the hell are you now? This second?"

"I'm a mile and a half from the house Sir?"

"Do you have any one closer?"

"Yes, Sir. There is the entire D-Squad about a quarter mile from the house by now."

"Charon is in the front drive and so is Graceson and some other clown. Radio D-Squad and tell them to take aim for all of them but Charon. Do it now!"

Thorne ran back to the window and watched as the trio walked toward the front doors. They approached the steps when the barrage of gunshots rained down on them.

Thorne watched as Charon convulsed from rifle-fire. Graceson had fallen and his body lay on the landing just out of Thorne's vision. Behind them both, the third body lay in an ever-increasing puddle of blood. Nobody moved from what Thorne could see and he smiled at the notion that the whole fiasco was over.

"Yes!!" The man smiled gleefully as he looked up to the sky.

"I beat you again. Maybe next time you pussy."

The sirens had drowned out the sound of the shots and David had no idea what had happened. He had stumbled on the step leading up to Thorne's house and the next thing he knew Charon was beside him with half his cranial vault exposed to the outside world.

"Holy shit!" His cursing was but a whisper.

"Gons! Gons? Gonsalvez are you alright?" He twisted his head back from the sprawled out position he was in on the landing and saw his new partner lying on the ground with blood oozing out of a gun shot wound in his back.

"Christ no!!" David cursed the almighty for the theft of his comrade's life. He looked up to the heavens and beseeched the powers that were.

"What do you want from me, man? What are you putting me

through? I'm trying my damnedest here and all you're doing to help is having everyone near me die! Is that what I'm supposed to do, control the fucking population here? I need some help pal. Not killing everyone that can aid the situation, I need *LIVE* help!" He looked at the two bodies. They lay lifeless in the afternoon sunlight. He was truly alone now.

Not more than three feet away from his sprawled out position was the door to Thorne's lair. He prayed that the snipers were rejoicing in their successful assignment and were no longer watching them. He would play dead for another thirty seconds and then he would make the dash to the interior of the house. Anything would be better than waiting for the mercenaries to come and inspect their fallen game.

He looked back at Gonsalvez and thanked him silently. It was then that David remembered the briefcases. They were in the Lincoln, or were they? He could not remember taking them from the church. In all the excitement he had left the most crucial bit of evidence they had to link Thorne with everything, in the possession of the snitch. "Shit! I'm screwed." He dropped his head to the flooring and the impact stung his senses. It was self-punishment. The evidence, he rationalized, was not the issue now. Elly was. She was in there and so was Thorne. He had been outside playing possum for long enough.

He looked back slowly and surveyed the surroundings for movement. He saw nothing and his feet took flight. His hand grabbed the doorknob well before his body reached the doorway. He swung the door open and dove across the threshold. In mid flight he scoped the foyer and prayed that the lobby was not full of assassins armed with uzi's. He hit the floor and rolled with Mackinnley's trusty Berretta pointing out there into space, anywhere that they may be. He saw enough movies to know how to hold a gun in this situation. He took from Clint and Chuck and Arnold's teachings and wielded the weapon knowingly.

There was no one in the foyer. There was nothing in the foyer other than a large stone wheel. From his cover at the base of the wheel, David squatted on his haunches and checked out the house through the center space in the wheel. The house was massive. He could be anywhere. This was Thorne's territory and he knew every nook and cranny in it. David only knew there was a stone wheel in the lobby, a maniac in the structure and his angel was being held somewhere within.

The intercom engaged and a voice came through the box in the wall. David wheeled around with his gun pointed at the source of the voice.

"Mr. Graceson, welcome to my home."

David felt naked there in the lobby with nothing to shield himself with. He sprang from the cover of the wheel and ran into the receiving room. He had seen a door that lead from that room to another. He ended up with his back to a doorframe and Charon's gun cut into his butt. It too was loaded and was an emergency weapon.

David chose to ignore the taunting of Thorne.

"Graceson. You infantile little mite. What in the name of hell do you suppose you are up to?"

David turned swiftly to the monitor beside him with gun aimed. The sound quality was frighteningly clear, almost as if the man was actually beside him. The chill that engulfed him almost contracted his bladder. He looked at the monitor and cursed the man under his breath. He would not allow the man to get under his skin any more than he already had. He would find Thorne and put a bullet under his.

"Graceson, you are extremely rude and your impudence is but a reflection of your anxiety."

"Go to hell, Thorne!!" David relayed his message without the aid of the intercom. His voice carried better than he had hoped for.

"Go to hell?" Thorne chuckled through the voice box. "I've been Mr. Graceson. I've been there and I like it. Soon Mr. Graceson you will be there. You are in my home now. Closer to hell than you could possibly dream of. You are within a sliver away from the place you call hell. I will make it hell just for you."

David ran from the receiving room into the large dining room. It was at least fifty feet long with a thirty-foot table in the center. He scrambled to the side furthest from the door, and slid safely under cover.

"You're running Mr. Graceson. This is good. Do you feel your heart beat? Listen to it. It will be the last time you hear it for eternity. Does it call out to your beloved Mr. Graceson? Does it call for the woman with the hypnotic eyes and virtuous soul? Have you had her Mr. Graceson? Have you had the pleasures of her flesh? Have you taken her soul and lifted it to the gods of surrender and taken her breath from her lungs so as she could not even speak? Well Mr. Graceson. Have you had the pleasures that I have had with her?"

David froze there on the floor. Every muscle in his body locked up. Like a catapult drawn tight he was ready for release. He ran to the intercom in the dining room and cut off Thorne's next verbal assault.

"You listen damn close to me, you miserable excuse for a man. You will not make it out of this house in one piece. I will rip your body limb from limb and I will dance on your fuckin' bones. If you so much as even think about touching that woman I will make sure that you suffer for the rest of eternity! If you have touched her, my actions will be far more severe.

"Why Mr. Graceson. You speak!"

"Damn right, asshole!"

"And so eloquently, I might add."

"Fuck you!"

"A linguist." Thorne chortled.

"Where is she Thorne?"

"She was in my bed at one point. Then on my face screaming at the loving of a real man, you inadequate eunuch."

"I guess she's a far cry from Terrace's ass, Thorne."

"Oh Mr. Graceson I am truly hurt by your assault. Hurry and end my life here where I stand so I might not have to endure this flogging you impart."

David ran to the door of the dining room and came upon the expansive kitchen.

"Mr. Graceson this visit is growing quite tedious. What do you want from me?"

David ran to the intercom in the kitchen and pressed the button.

"I want your lungs on a plate, in tiny little pieces." He whispered into the grill.

"If you are able to fight me and kill me, this fortress and its treasures will be yours Mr. Graceson. But if I prevail against you then I assure you the young woman will be my slave forever. But you are not even a worthy opponent. You come to me here armed with a pittance of intellect and inadequate weapons. You have no luck here Mr. Graceson. I will give your flesh to the birds of the sky and the beasts of the field. You have not the faith nor the courage to kill me Mr. Graceson."

"David!"

It was Elly's voice. She was alive!

"Elly?"

There was no reply from within the room.

Again the intercom called out his name in a sweet melodic tone.

"David?"

He ran to the monitor and punched the call button. "Elly is that you? Are you alright?"

"She's better than alright Mr. Graceson. She is marvelous."

With that last comment Thorne turned off the monitor and all that was left was silence.

-25-

Fleming positioned his men just behind the rescue teams at the site of Jacobs' charred Fairmont. They made it up the road without event except that one of his kidney stone's turned into powder, with the jarring his body had taken coming up the path.

The rescue teams had all made it without incident and that gave Fleming a little more confidence in his call. He and the eight other State Department agents reassembled apprehensively in the middle of the road and spoke with the police officers present. Fleming kept his eyes peeled on the hillside.

"Anything?"

"Nothing, Sir. We covered most of the immediate vicinity and didn't find a sign of anyone."

"That should make me feel better but it doesn't." He looked around the area. "Where the hell are those damn choppers?" He looked toward the sky and cursed the army birds.

"They are on assignment, Sir. They guaranteed me they would be here in fifteen to twenty minutes."

"Fifteen to twenty! Christ! It might all be over by then," he said, "and too damn late!" Fleming grew more agitated as the events transpired. His hands were tied and there was nothing he could do without jeopardizing the welfare of the girl.

"Too late for what?" The curiosity of the cop was piqued by the presence of the State Department agents and the mention of army helicopters.

Fleming eyed the cop. He studied the face hard and looked for trust. Reluctantly, he surrendered enough information about the case to drop the officer's mouth into gaping amazement.

Fleming left the cop in shock and walked up past Jacobs' barbecued body, and could see the house off in the distance.

"This is huge!" said the cop. "Maybe we should get the SWAT

teams in here."

Fleming burned his eyes into the cop. "This situation is one of intense national security and an extremely dangerous one. We can't handle this one with John Wayne shoot 'em up heroics." He moved away from the cop and checked out the hillside for snipers

. The cop tagged along with Fleming. "How many do you suppose are watching the road?"

"All of them." Fleming looked at the cop wise-ass like. "We found nothing on the hillside, which leads me to believe they have been moved towards the house. Thorne is there and he still has the girl hostage."

"Hostage? Thorne? Thorne has somebody hostage?" The cop became increasingly incredulous.

"We have him cold on kidnapping, forcible confinement, conspiracy to commit murder, murder and at least fifty other indictable offenses."

"You've got all that on Thorne?" The cop was delirious with the magnitude of the collar.

"And more," added Fleming. "What we want is the girl alive. I don't want to go busting in there if there is the slightest chance that he'll harm her. Have any of your men headed up the road yet?" He addressed the officer.

"No, sir. No need to."

"Good. If he sees us heading up there he may get nervous. We have enough evidence on him, whether he knows it or not, to make him more than a little twitchy. The last thing we need is for him to get spooked and pull a Waco thing up there."

"So Sir. What are we going to do?" Flikas inquired.

Fleming looked at the house in the distance. "I don't have a clue. If we charge up the road like the damn cavalry, he might smoke everyone in the house. If we only had those damn choppers here then we could get a better understanding of the lay out and where his men are. Maybe, if we just stay here, they might have a better chance of him sparing them, I don't know. I just don't know. We need more time than the situation is allowing us."

"Should we call in for reinforcements, sir?" Smithers tried not to push the issue to far.

Fleming heard the question but chose not to answer it. He was engrossed by the complexity of the situation. Thorne could have two hundred men around his house and along the periphery. There could be missiles, rockets, land mines, and trip wires. The place could be virtually impregnable. Going in might be possible. Coming out alive was another story.

"Sir. Sir! We can't just sit around. What do we do?"

"We sit around and wait."

"Wait? Wait for what?"

Fleming stared towards the house and waited for the right answer.

The Thorne mansion was indeed beautiful. But it was a hellhole of hospitality. She roamed the upper level stealthily. She had removed her shoes and they were a memory down in the basement. She did not want him hearing her. She kept her ears honed to the sound of Thorne's movements and only that.

David was in the house. Whether he had a hope against the monster was not to be thought of now. What she tried to think of was how to help him help her.

Thorne had turned off the intercom from the master control. She tried to tell David that she was all right and that the things Thorne had said were all lies.

The man was evil. Pure evil. They would beat him, for good always prevailed over evil in the end. Then she thought about babies dying and why and then she thought of God, if there was one, and how good He was and He still allowed babies to die and then it came back to her that maybe good did not always win over evil. She realized she was playing psychological games with herself and losing. It was discouraging her and she tried to shake the thought from her mind. If the Christian belief of God could not help her for the moment she would rely on her belief in Karma. What goes around comes around. With Thorne it would come around his neck and hang him from the tallest tree. This was the picture that comforted her mind. She could conquer any situation now, mentally at least.

She had made it out of the basement undetected, and in her search for sanctuary she came to find the closet in the study upstairs by accident. She had run to it after Thorne cut the power to the intercom in the study.

There was ample room in the closet. It allowed her room to move, to stand and to sit. She would wait there for him. With two knives and a cleaver she had a damn good chance of cutting off some part of his anatomy.

She had stumbled into the study upon hearing David's voice through the intercom. After she was cut off she saw the desk and the name on the sheet of paper. It almost caused her to lose control of the situation and break down like a little girl. The form read, 'A.R. Mohammed. Bank Swiss. Amount deposited three million dollars US.' She knew the name. It was jumbled but it belonged to the man who killed her brother in the museum.

She sat in the closet with the bank note in her pocket and the cleaver clutched tightly with both hands. She went to shift her weight when she heard the steps. They approached the door. Her heart picked up its pace and surged too much oxygen to her brain. She could hear the blood as it rifled through her temples and it almost drowning out the sound of the footsteps. She wondered whether to spring out of the closet and hack him into tiny pieces or to wait until he opened the door. She was paralyzed with fear and the messages that were sent from her mind, restrained her muscles from reacting to the signal of movement. She was literally petrified.

The steps outside the door were slow and deliberate, calculated but with definite purpose. Was it David? Was it Thorne? She could not tell and the thought of jumping out and hacking the wrong man by mistake only added to her inability to even draw the cleaver into striking position.

The footsteps drew closer to the closet door and halted. They did not move for the longest time. She had to remind herself to breathe, but quietly. The steps outside the door were so close that they could likely hear her breaths. They came shallow and fast regardless how she tried to control them.

Then the voice came. It startled her and with her heart beating at machine gun tempo, she could not tell whose voice it was.

"You will die today."

The footsteps moved with definite purpose. Leather shoes. David wore running shoes. It was Thorne outside the closet door.

"Thorne, where is the girl?" The voice was remarkably clear.

The response was slow in coming.

"Thorne, you miserable excrement! Where is the girl?"

"Mr. Graceson, are you still here?"

"Damn straight, Thorne. Tell me where she is and I might let you live."

"She's dead, Mr. Graceson. I had her pleasures and I killed her myself. Do you believe me?"

From his tone she would have believed him and that enraged her. Within the confines of the closet she pictured Thorne's position in the study. She knew where the intercom was. It was but ten steps from the closet. She could jump out and chop him into tiny pieces with all the strength that rage could promote. The man was foul. He cheated and his games were wicked. She worried whether David believed his comment. There was too long a pause before David responded. This frightened her. Maybe he did believe Thorne. Maybe he would declare himself defeated and run with his own life intact. David had never been placed in such a situation before, and she wondered what affect it would have on him. She tried to picture him there in the house somewhere. Hand on the call button of the intercom and head hung in sadness. Had the desire to overcome Thorne been washed from his soul by the tears of sorrow? She waited and prayed for his response.

"You bastard. I believe."

Her heart dropped.

"I believe that you lie!"

'Yes!' she exclaimed under her breath. David had not taken the bait.

"I'm coming after you Thorne!"

"Come to me Mr. Graceson. I will enjoy killing you. I shall then call the police and they will see your bloodied carcass and that of your accomplices and they will ask me if I am alright and if I'd like a coffee and they will be glad that I am indeed alright. Then I will get telegrams from the social elite sending me best wishes and hoping that I was not traumatized by the event."

"Mr. Graceson, even if you win here you lose. The police will take you to prison where you will spend the rest of your life with a non-functioning anal sphincter. You can't win even if you stop this 'knight in shining armor' routine now. You will be a prison slut by the end of the week I assure you."

"Thorne, I have four briefcases full of enough information on your antics that I am sure you will be slammed into Vaseline alley 'til the day you die. Don't fuck with me Thorne. You have nowhere to run."

Elly was elated with her man's conviction. Thorne was in the hot seat now and her reflexes took command causing her to jump in her place. A hanger above her head was hit, it rattled and signaled her location. She realized it the instant Thorne did. She froze and prayed.

"I'm coming for you, Thorne. Give me the girl and we will let you be."

The man did not answer David and this was her indication to arm herself. Yet, in the darkness of the study closet, she had momentarily forgotten where the door was. She did not hear the footsteps and so she reached for the doorknob. As she grasped it she could feel it turning from the outside. She released her grip and stood back with the cleaver poised above her head ready for the downward stroke that would split his cranium.

The door did not open. There was no sound. Thorne's presence was undetectable. Where had he gone? For the longest time she held the cleaver above here head. Her arms became tired with the anticipation of strike. They became heavy but she kept them aloft.

Two minutes shy of eternity passed and she had not heard a thing from outside the door. She twisted her head to hear the slightest movement but she heard nothing, so she dropped her arms from above her head. The instant her arms reached her sides the closet door flew open and Thorne stepped in with a large caliber revolver and brought it directly in contact with her forehead. She was unable to move or scream. Breathing was the only function she had left and it was becoming labored.

"Miss O'Connor, you disappointed me."

He quickly moved the gun from her forehead to her lips. He pried the metal past her teeth and buried the muzzle deep in her mouth.

"Hungry?"

He pushed the barrel further down her throat as she choked on the metal taste of the weapon. She dropped the cleaver. The long bread knife was noticed by him and kicked away.

He teased her hair and ran his fingers through it. He grabbed a handful and pulled her head towards him. "Bitch. You didn't answer my question. Iron is the only thing on the menu." He smiled at the image of her. Her tears came streaming down her face and the gun had pushed her tongue too far to the side to scream for David.

He grabbed a better hold of her hair and dragged her from the closet with the revolver still warming in her mouth.

"Come, my little harlot, we have guests we must entertain."

His hand tightened about the locks of hair and he pulled her towards the back stairwell, which led to the kitchen.

She gagged on the barrel and her hands dared not move above her neckline. There was no indication what might set the man, or the gun off. She followed his lead and she reached for her chest. She could still feel it. Buried deep within her dress she felt the knife from the lunch table.

The silence of the roadside was violated once again. He could hear them but had no reason to think much of them. There must have been a severe accident somewhere to call upon so many emergency vehicles.

Fleming walked back to the group of agents and was becoming more concerned with the proximity of the sirens.

"Those things getting closer?"

"Yes, sir." Flikas walked down the road a bit and his face exhibited shock.

"Don't tell me." Fleming was taken back.

Flikas didn't tell him. He nodded.

"Shit! Who the hell did this? Who called?" He stared directly at the cop he had spoken to earlier and wished that manslaughter was not a criminal offence.

"Are you out of your fucking mind? Here I am telling you that I don't want to upset the man inside the house and you send me, how many more incompetents? This is just great!" Fleming was beyond upset. He threw up his arms as if to surrender the thought of getting anyone out of the house alive.

"I thought the situation required back up." The cop shrugged his shoulders and was surprised that Fleming did not appreciate the gesture.

"Listen to me you moronic gumshoe. This is a federal matter, you understand? Federal jurisdiction. Fuck with me and you will be charged with treason. Look in your book under treason and tell me what you find, asshole. When those cars get here you tell them to stay in their vehicles or I will personally shoot them. I'm not screwing around. I'm dead serious."

Fleming was pointing his finger into the chest of the ever-shrinking cop.

"Sir?"

"What the hell is it now Smithers?"

"Fort Schyer sir. Choppers are on their way. ETA five minutes. Any instructions?"

"I've got many, give me the line." Fleming grabbed the radio and spoke with the commanding officer. After giving his clearance Fleming relayed to the army what his wishes were. There was to be a sweep reconnaissance flight over the area. Heat monitors were to be used to calculate the number of individuals on the hillside. Their positions were to be tracked and plotted and reported back to him. Guns were to be on the ready but no shots were to be fired until the command came from him.

Fleming's commands were met with eagerness and consideration and he wondered why the police didn't work with that type of efficiency.

"Sir, more bad news."

"What?"

"We have media, sir."

"Jesus. The first amendment. I hate that thing. Keep them back there. Tell them that the entire area is a crime scene and that if they interfere with anything within a quarter mile they will do hard time. Grab a couple of these NYPD yahoos and get some crowd control in effect before it's too late."

The situation was going from bad to worse to ugly. The panic started to set in when he saw cameramen running through the woods towards the house. "Stop them!!" He screamed at the two police officers. They took flight after them.

"This is going to end up being a god damned circus. We'll have the media up in the hills along with snipers and if we want to take the bastards down with gunfire I'll have to be certain they don't drop any civilians. I don't believe this." He shook his head in disgust. He looked over to the cop he had blasted. "Come here."

"Yes, sir!" The man was eager to compensate for his over zealousness.

"Get all those men you so generously invited and get them spread out every fifteen feet - perpendicular to the road. Nobody is to pass them and they have authorization to fire upon violators of that rule. Do you understand?"

"Yes, sir!" He ran off in the direction of his colleagues to extend Fleming's orders. Most of them were reluctant but soon enough they were spreading out and securing the perimeter.

Fleming smiled, not at the cop's formation in the woods but the sound that he was waiting to hear for fifteen minutes now. The choppers were closing in on the area and their blades sliced the air with the promise of action.

He had just come out of a bedroom when he saw them descending the back stairs. From his angle he could only see Thorne grabbing her by the back of the head and lead her downstairs. David stayed where he was. He thought of the lay out of the house. From his memory he drew out the floor plan as best as he could. Those stairs would lead into the kitchen he surmised.

Elly was alive, thank God for that. Now he had to be cool and level headed. One mistake and it was a completely different game. At the foot of the stairs David sat and thought of his next steps. These were the most crucial of his life, and hers. His feet took off before his brain knew where they were headed. Before he realized it, he was in the receiving room and on his way into the dining room.

"This is good. I know where I'm going; I've been here before. The kitchen is right up there and I can get a bean on them there." He spoke softly to himself as if to let him know he was not alone.

He approached the intercom in the receiving room.

"Thorne." He whispered as not to alert the man to his whereabouts. "And now, the end is near."

"Yours, Mr. Graceson. Your end." Thorne did not use the intercom. He yelled into the air and let the emptiness of the house carry his words.

David slithered into the dining room on the floor. The marks from his running shoe slide earlier showed him he was safe. Thorne's voice came from the kitchen. This he was sure of. But what the hell was he still doing in there? He moved across the floor in true military crawl and reached the entrance to the kitchen. From the floor he could see nothing. As he got to his haunches he could hear them, her. It was a muffled cry, a grunt and then silence. David rose from his squat and eye balled the kitchen. Very little of his face was visible from around the doorframe. He saw them, by the other door to the kitchen. Where that door led, David had no clue but from the floor plan that he made up that door could lead to the front of the house just to the side of the staircase and into the foyer. He would have to stop Thorne from leaving the house. If he got out the front doors, the guys who killed Gonsalvez and the driver of the Lincoln would most definitely take her down and he would be alone in the house with no way out.

His heart raced to damn fast for his liking. It was a reminder that he could beat him. With every beat of his heart he thought of Elly and how once all this was over he would take her and make love to her for a long, long time. This bastard Thorne would not take this away from either of them.

David looked away from the kitchen long enough to check his clip. The Berretta was running low, but with one other clip in his pocket and Charon's gun poking his left butt cheek, he had enough firepower to bring down this criminal. He looked back into the kitchen and they were gone.

"Shit." The panic came back to David's eyes. Now where to go? He checked the dining room and thought it too far if they did not head out to the front of the house. He decided to give chase through the kitchen and come what may after that. With gun poised in classic 'cover me' position David entered the kitchen. If he was going to die, it would be trying to free the woman he loved and not as a coward. The kitchen yielded no clue on their whereabouts and as he approached the door where he last saw them, the guns firing outside the door knocked him onto the floor in reflex.

The firing was reminiscent of the Cerebral Vacation the day the King was killed. But this time the firing lasted a lot longer. The sound was accompanied by a strange sound, a helicopter, he presumed. The firing continued and was matched by additional fire until all of space was filled with the sound of gunfire.

For a minute solid there was no gap in the firing and there may never had been one, if the explosion had not rocked the foundation of the house. From where he stood, David could just see the front window of the receiving room but he could most definitely hear the glass as it imploded into the house.

"You bastards!!" Thorne screamed towards the front of the house. "What have you done to my garden?!!"

He was in the foyer. David ran to the door and saw him just approaching the stone wheel in the vestibule. He drew his weapon into position and would have fired if the second explosion had not thrown him to the floor.

-26-

All hell was breaking loose. No sooner did the long awaited choppers arrive, when the chaos began. Fleming received the initial reports. Ten armed men confirmed within a half-mile radius of the house. It was not as bad as the hundred that he first imagined.

Fleming had ordered the choppers to be on the ready. When the first shot was fired from the hillside Fleming did not wait for their request, he ordered them to return fire. That's when the carnage began. Within a minute the hillside was ablaze with gunfire. Shots from the ground, shots from the air.

As the battle heated up, all Fleming's men and twenty men from NYPD took off up the road towards the house. They made it halfway up when one of the choppers got hit in a crucial spot and exploded in mid air. The eruption was immense, as all the artillery went up with the craft.

Fleming's makeshift platoon had made it to the clearing just before the house. The barrage of gunfire was relentless and overwhelming and caused Fleming and his men to run for cover. The remaining chopper hovered above and proudly signaled the all clear. Just then came a shot from the ground. From the front of the house the sniper had taken aim at the fuselage of the helicopter and detonation was instantaneous. The sniper fired a few more rounds into the burning, diving mass of flames just for good measure.

Fleming could see the man. He stood to the left of the house and he laughed aloud at the spectacle before him. The man's laughter ended in a maelstrom of bullets.

Fleming was confused. Who had fired the shots? Twice more the body thrashed with ballistic ecstasy before it hit the floor. Fleming scoped the area and came upon the source of the Samaritan shooter. The young Hispanic on the drive was now trying to get up with no luck at all. He clung to the bumper of the Lincoln and kept fighting to stand, until he fell down and did not move.

Fleming thanked the 'boy scout' silently and then slowly and methodically, the platoon split up and made tracks toward the house. The worst of the plan was just starting and Fleming prayed that the two explosions did not set off the rage of the man inside the mansion.

The second detonation was cataclysmic in proportion to the first. Whether it was the proximity to the house or whether the device was larger, David didn't know. All he knew was that the entire face of the house was strewn in the front hall. He summoned up all his nerve and checked around the corner. They were still there, at the base of the stone wheel, cowering from the debris that continued to rain down all around them.

He checked his weapon one last time. Mackinnley's trusty Berretta had served him well and he hoped that the tradition would continue here and now. He peeked around the corner and saw for the first time the barrel of Thorne's gun in Elly's mouth.

"Just marvelous. If I kill this guy, he's going to tighten up and take her head off. Think, David think!" He jumped out from around the corner and called to him.

"Thorne! You bastard. Let her go now!"

He stood there poised as if at target practice, and took slow and deliberate steps toward his target. Thorne was considerably slighter then Terrace and he wondered whether it was sheer surface space that helped him drop the walking condo.

"Mr. Graceson. Welcome to our little party. A blast isn't it?"

"I'll blast your fucking head off, prick. Let Elly go."

"I'm afraid I can't do that, Mr. Graceson."

"I'm afraid I can't let you live, Thorne."

"Then, Mr. Graceson we are at an impasse."

"Impasse this Thorne." David was practiced in the point and shoot operating instructions of the Berretta. He squeezed the trigger and the bullet grazed Thorne's shoulder. "Pretty damn close wouldn't you say Mr. Thorne?"

Thorne flinched with the superficial wound but was stunned that the librarian actually took the shot.

"Mr. Graceson. Should your minuscule mind and vigilant attitude stop and consider that if I die, so does your lovely?"

"You're going to kill her anyway, Thorne. Who are you trying to kid? The only way anything will be done here is if you and one of us die. Any other combination is a waste of newspaper space."

"You think that I will die here with either one of you?"

"I certainly do."

Thorne smiled, then chuckled and then exploded into thunderous laughter.

"Who the hell do you think you are Thorne?"

"Who the hell am I? I am Hell, Mr. Graceson. I have been brought from the flames of damnation to make sure that your pitiful little planet does not see the next millennium. Armageddon, Mr. Graceson. Are you familiar with the phrase? I am its escort. The Pope was the first of many signs foretold. I fulfilled that prophesy myself. There will be more and I will lead them from the pages of seers to the stunning truth of reality."

"You're out of your mind."

"No Mr. Graceson, I'm not out of my mind. I am above all that. I have been ordained. Cast out of your pious heaven at the beginning of time to lead the weak and make them strong with a belief that there is a purpose far greater then the one ordained by your lamentable God. It was my destiny. This pathetic species had not one shred of dignity or pride. It was I who induced the spirit of mankind. Man was piteous, weak and I had made him strong. Fight for what you want and the cost is secondary, tertiary even. Any means will justify the end. And you, all of you, ignorant of who I am, think you will banish my existence? You are beyond fools.

They have written for thousands of years of me. They have foretold and I am the prophecy. I am the beast-master some of you have feared and others have revered. I will lead you into temptation and not deliver you from evil. For I am Evil. I am pure and refined and your meager existence is but a finite aspect in a scheme so engrossing that your infinitesimal minds could never even begin to comprehend the purpose.

I have been here forever. My abode is my legacy of conquest. You are all impotent in spirit and easily prevailed upon. You will be manipulated by the simplest notions and do my work without so much as a second thought.

All will be as told. In your glory-bound bibles. You have read of the Evil. Nostradamus has told you of all that is written in my journal. The books are identical. Your only hope is faith and today my work has abolished whatever shred you have. It is only a matter of time until the evil will surface and eat up your children and leave them heartless to rip out your souls.

You will bleed the hope of fools. Your tears of salvation will go unheeded and your neglect of compassion will be because of me. I have swallowed your souls and I spit out compassion. It is a weakness. You will die and be mine, to please the master with the conviction of a whore and you will moan with the molestation of your spirit, only to beg for the raping again."

David stood dumbfounded by the magnitude of belief Thorne held in his sermon. He was dead serious.

"So I am to believe that you are..."

"The word you so eloquently use Mr. Graceson is the 'Anti- Christ'"

David didn't know whether to laugh or cry for the man.

"History was but a strategic exercise in plan and effect. One action brings upon a series of reactions. It was conceived thousands of years ago, Mr. Graceson that the chosen year would be the end of your God's lease on the world. It belongs to me after that. I have worked hard all this life to pave the road that will lead me to the most powerful position in the world. Come Election Day 2004I shall take command of my true destiny and destroy the life that you have come to know."

"Then you leave me no choice, Thorne."

Elly was dumbfounded by his speech and her senses had become drawn into the nightmare Thorne portrayed. If not for David's words she would have been sucked into the vacuum of Thorne's vision. The knife was retrieved just after the initial explosion and now was the time. She took David's cue and pulled her head violently away from the gun at the same time her arm brought the knife across and planted it in his chest. His eyes widened in shock at the attack. She scrambled from his grasp as he reached to pull the weapon from his right lung. He yanked the knife from his chest and started to cough up blood. Breathing became increasingly difficult.

"You bitch!" He scrambled after her as David fired off three rounds, all of which missed Thorne and hit the stand of the stone wheel. Thorne had grabbed her leg and she kicked him twice before he lost his grip on her as she ran for cover in the adjacent room.

"I will take both of you with me to become the damned." He cursed them and focused his attention on David.

David fired off as many rounds as the Berretta contained. He reloaded and shot the entire clip. His intentions were better honed then his aim, for all he managed to repeatedly hit was the stand of the sculpture behind his target. When he was all out of shells Thorne sat up and took aim at him.

"Say your worthless prayers now, Mr. Graceson."

David's gun was empty. He looked at Thorne and tossed the gun onto the floor between them.

"Go ahead, Thorne kill me. Here shoot me in the heart and get it over with." David stuck his hands behind his back and pushed out his chest like a prized rooster. "Right here Thorne, go ahead."

"Oh, Mr. Graceson. I will enjoy this so." Thorne laughed.

David loved it when they laughed. He reached into his belt and pulled out Charon's weapon and squeezed the trigger. The sound caught Thorne by surprise and the kickback knocked the gun out of his own hands and threw him on his ass.

From the floor David looked towards Thorne. He had grazed him again. "Damn!"

"Mr. Graceson." Thorne coughed and grabbed at his side. The .44 had caught him just under the ribs and gone clear through him and lodged in the now bullet eroded base of the stone wheel.

"You...will die here." Blood sputtered from his lips as he spoke and he fell backwards. He landed on the floor and his back hit the stand.

"Damn you, Thorne."

"Thank you, Graceson. Don't mind if I do." He tried to get up but fell back twice.

By this time Elly had found refuge by the door of the receiving room and she prayed that the cavalry would come charging into the house and save them.

Without a weapon David had no method to kill the man. Thorne had the weapon, the loaded weapon. David watched the man falter and fall back once more.

David looked to the sky and pleaded with God that this was the time to take this psychotic man off the face of the Earth.

"This is not my destiny, Graceson." He coughed. "I shall not parish here without my purpose being fulfilled." He shifted his weight and attempted once again to stand. He fell back against the stand and the stone wheel rocked in its place.

"Keep a place for me in hell, Graceson." Thorne pointed the gun at David and went to take the shot just as the stand gave up supporting the stone wheel. Thorne looked up towards the ceiling as the crumbling structure came crashing down on his skull.

She ran to him. Her savior, her lover, her man. "Oh David!" She wept with the tears of sorrow and joy. She was alive, though and so was David.

He hugged her with all the strength he could. The only stable object in his mad, spinning world was in his arms and he held her until his shaking stopped.

Neither spoke. The events of the last week had finally come to an end and there was relief in their embrace. David closed his eyes and thought of everything that had transpired. He thought of Evan, of Mackinnley and of Gonsalvez. But most of all he thought about Thorne. The man was satanic in his convictions. His speech evoked memories of Revelations and certain episodes in Nostradamus' predictions. There could have been a lot of truth in Thorne's words. Many things that Thorne represented were in direct similarity with the predictions foretold. He was as evil as the books had predicted. Wicked in action and belief. The party room was his playpen, he thought, where he would lead others into temptation and then keep them there at his beck and call. They were indeed the lost ones, lost in the debauchery of excess. But there was no way that Thorne could be the Anti-Christ. It was all fiction. Wasn't it? They thought that Hitler was the Anti-Christ. They thought Charles was the Anti-Christ. Thorne? He may have thought he was the one. His history led him to believe that he indeed was the ordained King of the Underworld. Thorne could have convinced himself that he was. This scared the hell out of David and he shook as he held Elly.

"David, it's over. It's OK." Her words were soothing yet they still did not take away the thought that terrorized his mind. If Thorne thought for real that he was the true Anti-Christ, putting himself in the president's position in the year of the foretold Apocalypse, may have given him the opportunity to hit the switch and destroy the planet and all it's peoples.

"Oh God, thank you." He praised the powers that be and held his angel closer.

They held each other until the multitude of men charged into the house. The first five men were in suits with guns drawn and it caught both of them completely off guard.

David thought the war was over. Thorne was dead and the nightmare should have ended; yet the armed men panicked him. He went scrambling for the .44. These were Thorne's men seeking revenge, he thought. Protecting Elly was his only concern now.

"Mr. Fleming?" Elly's voice was not one of fear but more of surprise.

David knew of too many people who were involved with Thorne through the Cerebral Vacation's party room. He couldn't trust this Fleming fellow. Not just yet. He grabbed Charon's cannon and pointed it at the man with the woolen jacket Elly called Fleming.

"Who the hell are you?" David pointed the gun directly at Fleming.

"Mr. Graceson. Please relax. We're not here to harm you. My name is Jefferson Fleming. I'm with the State Department. I'm Elly's employer." Fleming spoke slowly and peacefully so as not to further excite David. "We are in charge of a special operation task force of the American Government which over sees wrong doing in the FBI. We have been on this case since Jacobs got to New York. We are not after you and we are not here to arrest you."

"How do I know that? How do I know that you are not part of this whole God damned circus and that you aren't some way involved with Thorne? Huh? Tell me? Too many damn people are up Thorne's ass, How do I know that you aren't?"

Fleming looked at David hard. The questions were solid and if he had not seen the pictures in the briefcase Flikas had retrieved from the church, he would not have understood David's apprehension.

"You forgot the briefcases David. We picked them up from the church. We tapped Jacobs phones at the Hilton and knew he sent out men to kill you. We got there too late but not too late to pick up the cases with all the pictures and files."

David was still wary. The briefcases were the key to nailing Thorne. "So you have the briefcases?"

"We have the briefcases and also enough evidence to find that you are innocent of any crimes. You killed Thorne here in self defense, Jacobs is dead, Terrace is dead and the story is over."

"Over?" David said wide-eyed.

"Are you sure that someone won't come after us later on?" Elly was concerned for the future.

"Who? There is no one left. Haidey's Holding Company is out of business. Permanently."

Both Elly and David looked at each other and believed the promise. There was nothing they could do to rid the memories of the last week, but Fleming's words gave them some comfort.

"David!"

The raspy voice came from the back of the crowd that had gathered in the foyer.

"Graceson!"

The crowd had parted and a bedraggled Gonsalvez made his way towards the embracing couple.

"Gons!!" David was overjoyed to see that one person he met during this ordeal was not dead. "Jesus, am I glad to see you. I thought you were dead. Are you gonna be alright?"

"Yeah, yeah I'll be fine. You?"

"I don't know?" He looked at Elly and smiled at her loving eyes. "Yeah," he added. "We'll be fine."

He motioned for Gonsalvez to come closer.

"Is this for real? The State Department and all?" David eyed the crowd behind the federale. He could trust Gonsalvez, the rest of them he was uneasy with.

"It's for real pal. They are the good guys"

David hugged his angel again and he kissed her long.

"Uh..." Gonsalvez coughed as a precursor to his interruption.

"Uh, David."

The two stopped their display.

"Yeah, Gons?"

"Look if there is anything that the bureau can do for you two, please don't hesitate. We can get you anything. You feel unsafe and scared as hell, we can get you new lives if you want?"

"Gons, we're going to have a new life, together, and I think that it'll be just fine."

"Oh, Mr. Gonsalvez." Elly interjected. "There is one thing that perhaps the bureau could give us."

"You name it."

"I think that we could both use a vacation. Some place far and away from all this madness."

"Where to? Name it and you're there. It's that simple."

"I was thinking Switzerland."

"It's as good as done." He winked at her.

"Thank you Mr. Gonsalvez." She elbowed David.

"Oh yeah, thanks Gons." David looked strangely at Elly as they were escorted out of the house. They had never spoke of Switzerland. He never even dreamed of Switzerland. This puzzled him. He leaned over to her and whispered. "Switzerland? Why Switzerland?"

She eyed him and a huge smile came to her lips. She brought those lips to his ear and whispered.

"Thorne banked on twenty five million reasons why we would like Switzerland."

**

ABOUT THE AUTHOR

Van lives in Toronto with his wife and two children. This is his first novel with promise of more to come. He has written several stories and screenplays spanning the genre spectrum.

Printed in the United States
20252LVS00004B/199-252

GOLIATH

Set in New York after a devastating earthquak[illegible] rown into a world where the walls have ears. And if the [illegible] man rules supreme, he will be dead before the week is o[illegible] angle with him is Elly O'Connor, a beautiful friend fro[illegible] puter genius with the State Department. Together they [illegible] d of intrigue and suspense that involves ruthless assassina[illegible] and psychotic self-delusions of Biblical proportions. All [illegible] o the highest office in the land.

They race against seemingly sure failure u[illegible] most powerful organizations in the world, while coming f[illegible] ving forces behind the human spirit. One that is staging a remarkable comeback. That of pure evil.

"An exhilarating read...unpredictable plot twists, truly believable characters and a writing style that grips you to the end. Pornaras makes sure that you won't put it down. I loved it."

~ Angie Stein RVHS Toronto ~

"GOLIATH reads as a 95 mile an hour thrill ride. Buckle up and hang on as the streets of Manhattan become a battleground of biblical proportions. Hell has a face and it is James Elliot Thorne. Evil personified and brought to life with Pornaras' descriptive talents. Not for the faint of heart, Goliath is as intense as it is graphic. Sure to be a hit."

~ David Bruce, Producer ~

"Gripping, intense and thought provoking. Goodfellas meets the White House in a brilliant explosion of graphic script. Prophetic as it is insightful. It hits just a little to close to home."

~ A Goodfella ~

Contact Van Pornaras
WePublishBooks@Earthlink.net
Order at www.books1234.com

FICTION/Suspense FIC030000

ISBN 1-929841-06-X
51995
9 781929 841066
$19.95 USA $28.95 CANADA